COBRA
TRAITOR

BAEN BOOKS by TIMOTHY ZAHN

Blackcollar: The Judas Solution

Blackcollar
(contains *The Blackcollar* and
Blackcollar: The Backlash Mission)

The Cobra Trilogy
(contains *Cobra, Cobra Strike,* and *Cobra Bargain*)

THE COBRA WAR TRILOGY
Cobra Alliance
Cobra Guardian
Cobra Gamble

THE COBRA REBELLION
Cobra Slave
Cobra Outlaw
Cobra Traitor

MANTICORE ASCENDANT
A Call to Duty (with David Weber)
A Call to Arms (with David Weber & Thomas Pope)
A Call to Vengeance (with David Weber & Thomas Pope)*

*forthcoming

To purchase these titles in e-book format,
please go to www.baen.com

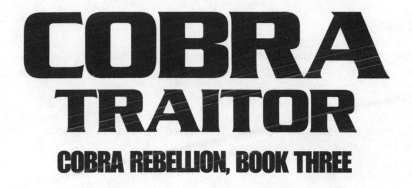

COBRA
TRAITOR
COBRA REBELLION, BOOK THREE

TIMOTHY ZAHN

COBRA TRAITOR

This is a work of fiction. All the characters and events portrayed in this book are fictional, and any resemblance to real people or incidents is purely coincidental.

Copyright © 2018 by Timothy Zahn

A Baen Books Original

Baen Publishing Enterprises
P.O. Box 1403
Riverdale, NY 10471
www.baen.com

ISBN: 978-1-4814-8280-6

Cover art by Dave Seeley

First printing, January 2018

Distributed by Simon & Schuster
1230 Avenue of the Americas
New York, NY 10020

Library of Congress Cataloging-in-Publication Data

Names: Zahn, Timothy, author.
Title: Cobra traitor / Timothy Zahn.
Description: Riverdale, NY : Baen, [2018] | Series: Cobra Rebellion ; Book
    Three
Identifiers: LCCN 2017042951 | ISBN 9781481482806 (paperback)
Subjects: LCSH: Science fiction. | BISAC: FICTION / Science Fiction /
    Military. | FICTION / Science Fiction / Space Opera. | FICTION / Science
    Fiction / General.
Classification: LCC PS3576.A33 C5696 2018 | DDC 813/.54--dc23 LC record avail-
able at https://lccn.loc.gov/2017042951

10   9   8   7   6   5   4   3   2   1

Pages by Joy Freeman (www.pagesbyjoy.com)
Printed in the United States of America

COBRA
TRAITOR

CHAPTER ONE

Martial law. Martial law. Martial law.

The words echoed through Lorne Moreau Broom's mind, running a counterpoint rhythm with the soft hiss of tires on the pavement beneath their car. *Martial law. Martial law. Martial law.*

"How you doing back there?" Badger Werle asked from the front passenger seat.

Lorne tightened his fingers around the armrest. How was he *doing*?

His father Paul, all but kidnapped by Colonel Milorad Reivaro of the Dominion of Man Marines and taken to one of the Dominion War Cruisers orbiting their silent threat over his world. His mother Jin, vanished somewhere in the Dominion-controlled province of DeVegas, her whereabouts and fate unknown. His sister Jody, somewhere on the hell world of Caelian with only the Cobra friends she'd made there standing between her and violent death. His brother Merrick, taken by the Trofts in the waning days of their invasion of Qasama, vanished without leaving a hint of his whereabouts. Lorne himself on the run, a wanted fugitive.

And his entire world placed under martial law by the same Colonel Reivaro who had started this whole mess.

How did Badj *think* he was doing?

"I'm okay," he said.

Seated behind the wheel, Dillon de Portola made a decidedly rude noise. "Liar," he said flatly. "I can see you, you know. You look like you're ready to start eating through the side of the car."

1

Lorne focused on the center mirror, keying on his optical enhancements to boost the faint starlight. Sure enough, de Portola had shifted the mirror's angle to focus on Lorne instead of the traffic behind them. "Whatever happened to keeping your eyes on the road?" he growled.

"It's not what's behind us that concerns me," de Portola said. "It's what's ahead. And *that* I can see just fine."

"I suppose," Lorne said. Twitching his opticals up another notch, he focused his attention out the side window.

He frowned. Fighting fatigue and immersed in his own dark thoughts, he'd paid only token attention to the landscape around him for the past hour or so, relying on whatever plan Werle and de Portola had cooked up to get them safely into Capitalia. Now, as he studied the trees and hills rolling past, he realized to his chagrin that he had no idea where the hell they were. "So where exactly are we going?"

"What, you don't recognize the area?" Werle asked innocently.

Lorne checked his nanocomputer's compass. De Portola had told him they would be taking the road that ran south of Capitalia, and they were now heading northeast. Assuming they'd already passed the Old Town sector on the eastern edge, and were somewhere on the southern edge of the city proper while he'd been brooding, that should mean they were heading through the Alice Lane district of Capitalia's satellite towns.

But none of the surrounding terrain looked like what he remembered of the district. "Not a clue," he admitted. "We *are* still going to Capitalia, aren't we?"

"Of course," Werle said. "You remember a guy named Emile Chun-Wei?"

Lorne frowned. "I don't think so."

"Well, you should," de Portola said. "He tried to stop you from sneaking Governor Treakness out of Capitalia the first day of the Troft invasion."

Lorne winced as the memory came back. Emile was a Capitalia Cobra who had ordered Lorne to follow Governor-General Chintawa's stand-down order and turn Treakness over to the invaders. The discussion had been short and unpleasant, and it had ended with Lorne dropping the other man with a stunner blast. "Right. *That* Emile."

"That Emile, indeed," Werle said. "Anyway, we got in touch with

him before we broke you out of Reivaro's clutches, and he's going
to meet us at the Indus Entertainment Center." He raised his eyebrows. "Along with another old friend of yours. Aaron Koshevski."

Lorne nodded heavily. He could see now where this was going.
"The drainage system."

"It got you out from under the Trofts' noses," de Portola
reminded him. "I doubt the Dominion will be looking for us
down there any more than they did."

"Probably not," Lorne said. "You sure you can trust them?"

"I think so," Werle said. "Koshevski proved himself before, and
he still seems grateful for what you did for his family. As for
Emile, after you got Treakness off Aventine he decided to ignore
Chintawa's order and spent the rest of the invasion organizing a
civilian resistance group in Capitalia."

"The whole time, huh?"

"Okay, so the Trofts weren't here all that long," Werle conceded.
"But he didn't know how long a stretch he was letting himself
in for at the time."

"And he caught a fair amount of heat for doing it," de Portola
said. "Dreysler pulled his seniority and would probably have
kicked him out completely if he'd been able to figure out a way
to do that."

Lorne sighed. "Fine," said. "Let's give it a try."

It was a good idea, of course. Certainly better than trying to
bluff or blast their way through whatever checkpoints Reivaro's
Marines had set up around the central and governmental sections of the city.

Still, those drainage conduits were an absolute pain to get
through.

De Portola brought the car to a halt beside one of the entertainment center's service entrances. The door had a large padlock
on the hasp, but it turned out to be just there for show. As Lorne
and the other two Cobras walked toward it, the door swung
open, and a pair of familiar men stood framed in the opening.

"Hello, Broom," Koshevski said, giving a short, abbreviated
nod. "Good to see you."

"And you, Koshevski," Lorne said, nodding in return. He shifted
his eyes to Emile Chun-Wei and nodded again. "Emile."

"Broom," Emile said, his voice rather flat. "Good to see you alive."

A neutral, maybe even slightly backhanded greeting. Pretty much what Lorne had expected. "You, too," he said. "Let's all stay that way."

Emile grunted. "No argument here. You ready?"

"Ready," de Portola said. "You got us a route?"

"I've got you a great route," Koshevski said, beckoning to an access cover a meter behind him. "If one of you gentlemen would oblige, we can get this show on the road."

The trip through the underground conduits seemed faster this time around. One factor was probably psychological: the second time through something usually seemed easier than the first. The other factor was that this time Lorne wasn't dragging three squabbling civilians along with him.

Still, by the time Koshevski announced that they'd reached their destination he was more than ready to get out into the open air again.

Their exit was unexpectedly delayed, though—unexpected to Lorne, anyway—by the fact that the access cover seemed to have been welded to the opening. The shaft-mounted ladder looked old and was dangerously corroded, so instead de Portola hopped up onto the palms of Werle's upstretched arms. Balancing there like they were part of an acrobatic show, he used his fingertip lasers to carefully slice through the welds, beveling the cut so that the cover wouldn't fall on them. He finished and eased the cover a few centimeters upward, listened for a few seconds, then moved it sideways off onto the ground.

And Lorne found himself looking up, not at the starry Aventinian sky, but at a slab of metal fifty centimeters above the opening.

The underside of a vehicle, presumably, since most of these access shafts were on the streets. But even granted that Lorne didn't spend much time looking at the undersides of vehicles, this one looked odd. The usual maze of pipes, struts, and attachment points was missing, replaced by what looked to be a smooth, unbroken sheet of metal. A protective seal, maybe, or possibly armor plating.

And then he got it.

He looked at Emile. *You're joking*, he mouthed silently.

The other Cobra shrugged. *They're sure as hell not going to look for you here*, he mouthed back.

De Portola had pulled himself high enough to put his eyes

just above ground level and was doing a slow three-sixty. He finished his sweep and pulled himself the rest of the way out of the hole, disappearing into the gap between the pavement and the Dominion vehicle. Werle jumped upward, caught the edge of the opening, and followed.

Lorne looked at Emile. Emile responded by politely gesturing Lorne toward the shaft.

So Emile was apparently going to stay down here. Fleetingly, Lorne wondered just how much of the other Cobra's purported activity during the Troft invasion had been real, and how much had been after-the-fact embellishment.

He stepped beneath the hole, bent his knees, and jumped.

The presence of the armored vehicle above them had led to the conclusion that Koshevski had brought them inside a commandeered parking structure. That turned out to be correct. From Lorne's new vantage point he could see the wheels of other vehicles, lined up in neat rows to either side of him, with more lined up across the interior driveway. Werle and de Portola had already moved out from under their vehicle, and Lorne could see their feet as they slipped silently around the garage, checking it out more thoroughly.

And then, through the soft, diffuse rumble of background noises, he heard a new set of footsteps approaching.

He notched up his auditory enhancers. The footsteps were brisk and rhythmic, with no indication that the owner was trying to be stealthy. Werle and de Portola had stopped, and from the angles of their ankles Lorne could tell they were crouched down out of sight between the cars. The footsteps were getting closer, and Lorne turned his head back and forth, trying to pinpoint their location through the echoes bouncing off the walls and other cars.

He had tentatively concluded the newcomer was coming from his left when a movement caught his eye: Werle's hand dropping into view under the row of cars and beckoning. Hoping fervently that the Cobra knew what he was doing, Lorne pulled his way out of the shaft, slid out from under the vehicle, and rose into a crouch. Curling his hands into fingertip-laser position, he eased his head up for a look.

To find that their visitor was none other than Governor-General Chintawa.

And he looked terrible.

The man had never looked all that good, in Lorne's private and

completely nonpartisan opinion. For years there'd been rumors
that his health was on the decline, but he'd never let whatever was
going on behind the scenes keep him from his appointed duties.

But in the fifteen days since Lorne had last seen him, Chintawa
had gone seriously downhill. His face was pale, the skin of his
cheeks and throat sagging. There were large bags under his eyes,
the eyes themselves seemed dull and lifeless, and Lorne would
swear that his hair had gone a little grayer.

But there was the same hard set to his jaw that he'd always had
in times of political warfare, a grimness that warned there was still
fire inside the crumbling body. As Lorne rose from concealment,
he wondered briefly whether that fire was for him or against him.

Chintawa stopped short as Lorne came in view. "You," he bit
out, "are an absolute and utter pain in the butt."

Lorne sighed. So much for Chintawa's fire being for him.

"That's not fair, sir," Werle said, rising out of his own hiding
place behind Chintawa. "Broom didn't start any of this."

"That's debatable," Chintawa said, his gaze hard on Lorne.
"Regardless of who started what, he's certainly not doing anything
to lower the tension level."

"Neither are they," de Portola said, also standing up.

Chintawa's lip twisted. "No, they're not," he said. "Fine. I'm
here. What do you want?"

Lorne shot a frown at Werle. What did *he* want? He wasn't
the one who'd set up this meeting.

But Werle just made a little gesture toward Chintawa. Apparently, they were all laboring under the same misconception.

"Come on, come on," Chintawa growled. "We're burning day-
light, and the next shift of Dominion goons could be coming at
any time to get their cars. Your uncle said you wanted to talk.
So talk."

Lorne felt the tightness in his stomach ease a little. So it was
Great-Uncle Corwin who'd set this up?

That was good. In fact, it was more than just good. After a
lifetime in politics, former Aventinian Governor Corwin Moreau
knew as much about the Dome's inner workings as anyone on
Aventine. More than that, his years of service had gained him
an assortment of contacts and—hopefully—a few unredeemed
favors to go along with them.

And the fact that he was having quiet chats with Chintawa

also implied he'd made it back safely from Smith's Forge after his clandestine meeting with Kicker Pierce.

So Uncle Corwin had sent him here to talk? Good. Because he had one or two things he very much wanted to say.

"Talk is good," he said to Chintawa. "Talk is also cheap. Are you ready to do more than just talk and listen? Because if you're not, I have better things to do with my time."

"I'm sure you do," Chintawa said. "But before we get all high and mighty, let's remember some recent history. *I'm* the one who's been sitting here under the Dominion's guns trying to keep a lid on this whole thing. *I'm* the one who talked Commodore Santores into easing Colonel Reivaro down from a Code One martial law order on DeVegas to a Code Three, which at least allows civilians some liberty in their day-to-day activities. And *I'm* the one who tried his damnedest to keep your father out of their hands."

"Let's drop the campaign mode, shall we?" de Portola suggested. "No one's voting today."

"Not to mention that all three of those particular laurel leaves have wilted," Werle added.

"And whose fault is that?" Chintawa demanded, jabbing a finger toward Lorne. "If he hadn't insisted on tearing through Archway like a deranged hornet—"

"After Reivaro murdered three Cobras?" Werle shot back. "What did you want him to do? Invite the man to Sunday tea?"

"I *wanted* him to stand out of the way and let the politicians deal with policy," Chintawa said bitterly. "If he had, maybe we could have confined the trouble to DeVegas instead of forcing Captain Lij Tulu to put the whole planet under martial law."

"Which kind?" Lorne asked.

Chintawa blinked at him. "What?"

"Which kind of martial law?" Lorne asked. "Code One or Code Three?"

For a pair of heartbeats Chintawa just stared at him. "It's a Code Three for everyone," he said at last. "Civilians are largely unaffected, except for the nine o'clock curfew." He breathed out a tired-sounding sigh. "You're not going to ease off, are you? You're going to move this insane war of yours to Capitalia."

"The Cobras didn't start this, Governor-General," Lorne reminded him. "But we didn't bow down when the Trofts invaded our world, and we're not going to do it now, either."

"At least *some* of us didn't," de Portola said. "The question is whether Capitalia will be with us this time, or whether they'll—how did you put it? Stand out of the way and leave policy to the politicians?"

Chintawa looked back and forth between them, his gaze finally settling back on Lorne. "I kept the city safe, you know," he said. "We had just thirty deaths during the whole occupation, and all of those were people who ignored the Troft order to stay indoors and were killed by spine leopards. DeVegas province, with barely a third of our population, lost nearly three hundred."

"We also had twenty-two confirmed Troft kills," Werle said. "How about you? Any of the Capitalia invaders trip and stub their precious little toes? Face it, Governor-General—you'd still be getting your morning orders from the Trofts if it hadn't been for us."

"And the Qasamans," Lorne murmured.

Werle shot him a glance. "And the Qasamans," he echoed, a little grudgingly. "The point is that you and Capitalia came out of the last invasion looking pretty pathetic. You've got a chance to redeem yourselves. Are you going to take it?"

Chintawa sighed again. "You have no idea the position I'm in," he said heavily. "Not just with Lij Tulu and Reivaro, but with my own government. There's still a significant faction that opposes even having Cobras inside Capitalia, let alone letting them do anything against the Dominion forces. If open warfare erupts on the street, they *will* move to isolate and paralyze me."

"So don't give any orders," Lorne said. "No orders to resist the Dominion; no orders to stand down. Let each Cobra decide for himself what he wants to do. They can hardly blame you for that."

"They can blame me for anything they choose," Chintawa said bitterly. "But the point is already moot. Lij Tulu has ordered all of Capitalia's Cobras to be fitted with those loyalty collars. Once they're in place, they'll have no choice but to stand down."

"Yes, we know about the collars," Lorne said. "They did the same thing to the DeVegas Cobras."

"So you see the problem—"

"*All* of them," Lorne interrupted. "Including Badj and Dill here."

"Because—" Chintawa broke off, his eyes narrowing. He looked at de Portola, then at Werle . . .

And when he turned back to Lorne there was a sudden hint of fire in his eyes. "You got them off," he murmured.

"Yes, we did," Lorne said. "And we can do the same for the Capitalia Cobras."

"Assuming they're not just looking for an excuse to sit on their hands," Werle said pointedly.

"They aren't," Chintawa said firmly. "Some of them aren't, anyway." He took a deep breath. "All right. You're going to need freedom of movement. That means keeping the martial law level at Code Three as long as possible so that there's a populace out there for you to mix with."

"We also need to get into the city's personnel records," Lorne said. "I had a disguise in Archway, but because my new face wasn't in any of the databases they were able to nail me. We need to wipe out everyone's records so that they don't know who's who."

"Won't work," Chintawa said, shaking his head. "From what my people said, Santores has already had all the records uploaded to his ships. Erasing the records here won't do anything."

"So we need to get into *their* computers?" de Portola asked.

Chintawa snorted. "Yes, and there's not a chance in the Worlds we can do that. Certainly not from down here."

"Maybe all we need to do is block their transmissions," Werle suggested. "Reivaro's Marines can't have their whole computer system downloaded into their brains or eyeballs or whatever. They have to be calling up facial recognition programs on a real-time basis."

"And they can't be getting it all from the ships," de Portola pointed out. "Their orbits would put them in Aventine's shadow too much of the time. Do we know if they deployed any monitor satellites? They could be relaying signals through those."

"Santores hasn't said anything about satellites," Chintawa said. "I can check. You'd still have the same problem of getting to them."

"Not necessarily," de Portola said. "We can't run the *Dewdrop* against a Dominion war cruiser, but we might be able to sneak it up to a relay satellite or two."

"Especially since Reivaro's all hot to wrap his damn armor plate on the thing," Werle said, sounding cautiously intrigued. "Somebody will need to take it out for a test drive. See if the balance and thrust and whatnot all still works."

"Like they'd let any of us near the ship," Lorne pointed out. "Which brings us back to the original question."

"Let me work on it," Chintawa said. "In the meantime, you'd better get going. And don't tell me how you got in—I don't want to know." And to Lorne's mild surprise, he actually forced a small smile. "Good luck, Broom. Try not to get yourself killed. Or anyone else."

He turned and strode back the way he'd come. De Portola signaled Lorne to wait; and only when the governor-general had disappeared from sight around a curve did the other two Cobras head toward the hidden access hole, beckoning Lorne to join them.

Two minutes later, they were all back in the drainage conduit and the cover was once again welded in place.

"Well?" Emile asked.

"He's going to help," Lorne said.

"Even better, it sounds like you're all going to get to choose whether to fight or sit on the sidelines," Werle added.

"Good enough," Emile said. "Better than I'd hoped, really. Ready to go?"

"Sure," Lorne said. "Where are we going?"

"Someplace where you can lay low for a few days," Emile said. "Collect intel, see what kind of support you can get among the rest of the Cobras." He gave a little snort. "See what Chintawa comes up with in the freedom-of-movement department."

"We're not really going to depend on *him*, are we?" de Portola asked.

"No, no, you're perfectly free to come up with something brilliant yourselves," Emile said. "But that's *you*, not *us*. I'm back on duty in two hours, and it's a little early to be throwing away my cover. I'll keep my ears open and try to get whatever I hear back to you."

"What if they give you one of their dog collars?" Werle asked.

"Then I'll have to try a little harder, won't I?" Emile gestured to Koshevski. "Come on. Let's get out of here."

"Well, that's it," Corwin Moreau said, his tone that of a tired but proud father. "What do you think?"

Jasmine "Jin" Moreau Broom fingered the two curved strips of ceramic her uncle had handed her. Each strip was about five centimeters wide and three millimeters thick, with the edges curved slightly outward from the main arc in a sort of flattened saddlepoint shape. Placed end to end, the two pieces formed a circle about fifteen centimeters across. "And they work?" she asked, looking up at him. The odd echoes from the basement walls and low ceiling somehow made the whole thing feel even more cloak-and-dagger than it already did. "They really work?"

"They really work," Corwin assured her. "Don't let the thinness of the material fool you—remember that the whole point of this hobby was to come up with a more bio-friendly ceramic bone laminate for future Cobras. This stuff is *very* tough."

"And there's probably not a lot of explosive in the Dominion's loyalty collars anyway," she agreed, feeling her stomach tighten. The Qasamans had used explosive collars on the members of the first Cobra Worlds expedition to that world, including Jin's own father and her other uncle. She remembered thinking after the expedition returned what an utterly barbaric tactic that was.

She also remembered wondering when she first went to that world whether she and her teammates would face the same kind of intimidation if they were caught.

And now, the supposedly civilized Dominion of Man was using the same deadly and humiliating method to suppress resistance from the Aventinian Cobras.

But like the Qasamans before them, the Dominion had no idea who they were dealing with.

Cobras didn't take this sort of thing lying down. Neither did anyone else in the Cobra Worlds.

"From what I hear, there's hardly any at all," Corwin confirmed. "Just enough to ensure that the wearer is killed without making a mess of the surrounding landscape."

"Lovely," Jin said, shivering. "Probably don't want a Cobra grabbing the nearest Marine and decapitating two for the price of one."

"Possibly," Corwin said. "Or else Dominion Marines don't like cleaning blood stains any more than anyone else. Either way works for me. I just hope they don't tumble to our little trick and start packing in more bang."

"If they do, you can just make the shields thicker," Jin said, handing back the two sections.

"Though only up to the point where they're so thick they choke the wearer to death before the collar even has its chance," Corwin said. He picked up a mug from the table, started to take a drink, then set it down again. "I'm sorry—did you want some tea?" he asked, looking around as if trying to remember where the rest of the mugs were kept. "I can make you some tea if you'd like."

Jin felt the ever-present knot in her stomach tighten another couple of turns. She'd sneaked into Capitalia three days ago, but between dodging Dominion Marines and evading the city's own patrollers it had only been today that she'd found a way to get onto her uncle's estate without being caught.

Only to learn that the day before she'd hit town Corwin's wife Thena had packed her bags and moved out.

Even worse, she'd filed with the Dome for a restraining order against her husband.

In a world that seemed to have become a never-ending series of gut punches, that had been the worst one of all. It was also the most utterly unexpected. To all appearances, her aunt and uncle had had the perfect relationship, with all the interlaced threads of love, respect, humor, and commitment that should have made it rock-solid.

Now, it seemed that the outward appearance had been nothing more than a façade laminated onto a rotten core.

What made it worse, from Jin's perspective, was that the occasional fumbling and misty-eyed moments she'd observed in her uncle since she'd arrived made it clear that the separation was entirely Thena's idea.

"Nothing, thanks," she said, waving away the offer. "How hard is it to make these things?"

"Not too hard," he said, his mind visibly dragging itself back to the task at hand. "Let me get you some—no; you didn't want tea. All right. We'll start by mixing up a batch of the material and getting it into the molds. It needs an hour or so to set, and then we can fire up the kiln."

"You need to bake them?" Jin asked, frowning. Cobra ceramic laminae was injected directly onto the bone, where it did its final setting without any added heat. If Corwin had been working toward a replacement for the current material, this didn't seem like a promising direction to take.

"There are a couple of catalysts you can use instead," he said. "Unfortunately, I don't have any of them left, so we'll have to go with the kiln instead."

"Ah," Jin said. So at least he hadn't been blind to the obvious requirements of what he was trying to make. That would have been heart-breaking, especially after all the years he'd put into the hobby.

Distantly, she wondered if Corwin's work had been what had

driven the wedge between him and his wife. Perhaps it had become an obsession that Thena simply couldn't take anymore.

"I'm going to need more base and admix," Corwin continued, nodding toward the table by the wall. A portable kiln sat there, a heavy-looking cube about sixty centimeters on a side with a locking door in front. "Could you go upstairs and get them for me? They're the coffee and flour bags in the back of the pantry."

"The—? Oh. Right."

He smiled faintly, the first smile she'd seen from him since he first welcomed her into his house an hour ago. "Exactly," he said. "The Dominion could raid me at any time, and if they're determined enough they'll find the stuff. But there's no point in making it easy for them."

"Coffee and flour—right," Jin said, heading across the basement toward the stairs.

"And stay clear of the windows," Corwin called after her. "At last count there were a hundred forty Cobras in Capital province, and Lij Tulu has promised to scrape up enough loyalty collars for all of them. We need both of us working if we're going to stay ahead of them."

"Got it."

It was important work, of course, Jin knew as she headed up the stairs. But equally important was that this would give Corwin something less anguishing to focus on than his personal problems.

And maybe it would help Jin set aside hers, as well.

Her family had been torn apart, her husband and children taken or vanished, their locations and fates unknown. There was nothing she could do about any of it except see it through and hope and pray for their safety.

But maybe she *could* do something about Corwin and Thena. Not now, of course, but maybe later. Once this was all over, she would sit down with them—together if possible, separately if necessary—and find out what exactly had precipitated this tragedy. With love and perseverance, maybe she could help heal their rift.

And if the Dominion's clampdown on Aventine had caused or precipitated the split, she thought darkly, God help them. *All* of them, from Commodore Santores and Colonel Reivaro on down.

Because there *would* be a day of reckoning for their actions. A dark, and probably very bloody day. And it was coming soon.

Jin would make sure of that.

CHAPTER TWO

Merrick Moreau Broom had spent a lot of time in the Muninn forest over the past couple of weeks. More time than he liked. Way more time than was probably healthy for him.

And he was getting damn sick of it.

It had been bad enough when he was traveling with Anya Winghunter. She spoke the language without Merrick's potentially damning accent, and though she'd been away from her home world for the twelve years she'd been a Troft slave, at least she knew the people and the basics of the social norms they were trying to fit into. The fact that they'd never really had a chance to blend into the population wasn't her fault.

Only now Anya was gone, vanished somewhere unknown. Possibly with the parents she hadn't seen for half her life. Possibly without them.

Either way, she'd left Merrick to face the dangers of the forest alone. Or rather, with a new traveling companion.

Who happened to be a Troft. And not just any Troft, but an agent of the Kriel'laa'misar demesne, sent to Muninn to learn the details of the mind-control war drug the local Drim'hco'plai Trofts were creating to use in the Trofts' war against the Dominion.

The fact that the Drims had already promised to sell the weapon to the Kriels was an additional twist that made Merrick's head spin. The reason the Kriels had sent Kjoic here in the first place was to try to steal the drug, thereby avoiding any need to pay the Drims for it.

And Kjoic was deadly serious about his mission. He'd already killed an entire transport ship's worth of Drim crewers, plus another handful of Drim soldiers, in pursuit of that end. He was also clearly ready to kill again if and when it became necessary.

It was hardly the way allies were supposed to behave toward each other, in Merrick's view. But then, Trofts didn't see things the way humans did. From what Merrick had read in the history books, Troft demesne-lords were never so much allies than they were temporary partners of convenience. If and when one of them saw an advantage in abandoning his partners, he would take it.

And since Kjoic's current partner of convenience was Merrick himself...

There was a soft rustling from the top of the tree they were passing. Merrick craned his neck to look upward, keying in his infrareds. The bits of sky visible through the forest canopy were starting to lighten with the approaching dawn, but the masses of trees themselves were still dark. Up till now he'd been relying on Kjoic and whatever IR or light-amplification gear the Troft had to guide them through the night, unwilling to risk inadvertently revealing his own Cobra equipment by seeing better than a normal human should.

But as it had a dozen times throughout their long trek, the presence of a possible predator trumped the need for absolute secrecy.

Some of the earlier encounters had carried potential danger. Fortunately, this time the animal crouching on the branch above them was small and alone and therefore probably not likely to be a problem.

Unlike Kjoic, the odd thought occurred to him, who was also small and alone, and was absolutely, positively dangerous. By any measure, it was a terrible position for Merrick to be in.

But he still had a hole card. Kjoic knew his human partner-of-convenience was also an agent, though working for another demesne. What he *didn't* know was that Merrick was a Cobra.

"It does not appear dangerous," Kjoic murmured.

"What, the animal up there?" Merrick asked. "Good to hear. Are you ready to tell me where exactly we're going?"

"Soon," Kjoic assured him. "The remaining distance, it is not great."

"Mm," Merrick said, a shiver running up his back. Kjoic had

taken a long and winding path through the forest over the past few hours, though whether the route had been designed to confuse Merrick or lose enemy pursuit Merrick didn't know.

If it was the former, it hadn't worked nearly as well as Kjoic probably thought. The nanocomputer snugged in beneath Merrick's brain had a built-in compass, and Merrick had been carefully monitoring their progress. And if there really wasn't much farther to go, Kjoic could have only one destination in mind: the village of Svipall, and the warehouse-type building where the Drim Trofts were creating and testing their new war drug.

"We're heading to the test facility, aren't we?" he asked, just to see what Kjoic would say. If the Troft lied, that would be a strong indication that their temporary alliance was already coming to an end.

"Not to the facility, but to a spot nearby," Kjoic said. "With hope, it will prove a place where we can observe without being observed ourselves."

"Ah," Merrick said. "I take it that when you say *observe* you're not expecting us to take any direct action?"

"Not at the present time," Kjoic confirmed. "Shortly after your departure from the home of Alexis Tucker Woolmaster with the older female, I observed your female—Anya Winghunter—and the older male gather six bags of unknown content and depart into the forest. After the Drim soldiers arrived, I concluded that the humans had deliberately allowed you to be discovered and captured."

Merrick felt his lip twist. He'd been mulling at that same theory for the past couple of hours.

It was impossible for him to believe Anya would do such a thing to him, certainly not willingly. But her father, Ludolf Treetapper, was something else entirely. The man was cold, calculating, and had been fighting the Trofts for the past decade and more. Or so he claimed. "Not sure what that gains them."

"My theory, it is that they expected you to escape," Kjoic said. "They also expected you to leave destruction and confusion behind."

"Ah," Merrick murmured. That possibility hadn't occurred to him. But it was a logical enough theory, especially given what he knew about Ludolf. Even if Ludolf didn't know Merrick was a Cobra, he'd had enough hints from Anya about Merrick's hidden skills to suspect he could break free of the Drims. "And if I left enough confusion, they might be able to slip inside the Drim facility."

"That thought, it is mine as well," Kjoic said. "I am hoping we will observe whether that was their plan."

"And whether it worked?"

"That is also my hope."

"And if it didn't?"

The radiator membranes on Kjoic's upper arms fluttered. "Possibilities, there are two of them. They may not have attempted entry. If that is true, we will need to search for them elsewhere."

"Or we can just let them go and hope they stay out of our way."

"We will judge their usefulness before we choose our path," Kjoic said. "The other possibility is that they did attempt entry and were captured."

"In which case, there's a good chance they're undergoing the treatment right now."

"Yes."

Merrick scowled. Ludolf might have betrayed him, but that didn't mean he could just stand by and let the Trofts turn the man's brain inside out. That went double if he'd dragged his daughter in on this insane scheme with him. "What if we can't get them out?"

"I do not expect we can," Kjoic said. "Instead, we will watch for a time and see if they emerge."

"And?"

"My assumption, it is that if they are conditioned, they will have instructions to locate and kill us."

Merrick snorted. "Wonderful."

"Not wonderful," Kjoic said. "But useful. It will tell us how much time is required for the conditioning. If we additionally allow them to confront us, we will also learn the depth of the conditioning and the combat strength of those to whom it is given."

Again, very logical. Also incredibly cold-blooded. Kjoic and Ludolf were definitely made for each other. "What if they're stronger than you expect?"

Another flutter of Kjoic's radiator membranes. "If or when it becomes necessary, we shall kill them."

Merrick had guessed that would be the Troft's answer. Even so, the casualness of the death sentence sent another chill through him. "Wouldn't it be better to keep them alive? It might give us a chance to see what it takes to break the conditioning."

"That datum is of little interest to me," Kjoic said. "Such a truth would be useful only to you."

"And you're thinking I may already be dead by then?"

"As I have said, it may not come to death between us," Kjoic said calmly. "Still, if you are the victor, you may consider that path."

"I'll keep that in mind," Merrick said. "But let me suggest that such a truth *is* of interest to you. If the drug's effects are easy to defeat, the technique won't be worth much in your war against the Dominion."

"Even a limited effectiveness will be of use," Kjoic said, his membranes fluttering thoughtfully. "But your point is well thought. I will consider it further."

Which was probably the best Merrick was going to get, at least for now. "Good enough," he said. "Do you have any thoughts on how we watch the facility without being spotted ourselves?"

"From there." Kjoic stopped and pointed upward. "Your ability to climb trees, you have already demonstrated it on the journey to Svipall."

"We were all pretty inspired at the time," Merrick said, wincing at the memory as he peered upward. They'd run into a jormungand, one of the huge and damn-near unkillable snakes that lived in the forest. Merrick had gotten them out of that one, but he couldn't rely on his same trick working again if another of the beasts came slithering past.

All the more reason to watch the Drim facility from off the ground, in fact. And Kjoic was right: one of the taller trees, if properly chosen, should indeed provide a decent view.

Of course, sight-lines went both directions. No matter how much of himself he hid behind the trunk there would be a certain amount of visual leakage. And if he was spotted, the only quick way back to ground level would reveal who and what he was.

Not to mention that if Kjoic was planning a getaway or a betrayal, putting Merrick up a tree would be the perfect time to pull off either.

"Any of the trees here should provide an acceptable view," Kjoic said, waving a hand around them. "You may choose and adjust as you wish."

"While you stay down here?"

"For the present time. When you tire or need sleep, I will take your place."

"Fair enough," Merrick said. A meaningless offer, of course, if Kjoic planned to unleash some mischief in the next couple of hours.

With an effort, he chased the thought away. The situation hadn't changed: he and Kjoic both wanted a closer look at the Drims' war drug, and neither could realistically manage that on his own. Until they got inside the lab, their alliance was probably solid. "Any tree in particular you had in mind?"

"As I said, it is your choice," Kjoic said. "You must first take this."

He reached into his left ear and pulled out a small, tapered object. "Human ears, this may be too small to fit them," he said, holding it out toward Merrick. "You must find a way to make it work with your anatomy."

Cautiously, Merrick took the device. It was small and lightweight, about the size of his thumbnail at its widest. The business end was indeed too narrow to fit into his ear canal without falling out. "What does it do?"

"It warns of approaching vehicles," Kjoic said. "Aircraft and groundcraft alike. The volume, it increases as the vehicle nears. The tone, it changes with the vehicle's direction. If it is in your left ear, the highest pitch indicates that you are facing the vector of approach."

"Sounds handy."

"It has been a key factor to the safety of our current journey," Kjoic said. "There were many aircraft in the sky this night. Knowing their locations, I could lead us away from their search pattern."

Which explained all the meandering they'd done since leaving Alexis's house. Merrick thought about pointing out that Kjoic could have told him about this sooner, decided such a comment wouldn't really add anything to the conversation. Besides, it wasn't like Merrick wasn't keeping a secret or two himself. "How does it work?"

"It detects the emissions of the driving power sources," Kjoic said. "It is . . . I do not recall the word. It does not send emissions of its own."

"Passive?" Merrick suggested.

"Yes—passive," Kjoic said. "That is the word. A passive sensor, it is one."

"Good," Merrick said. Active sensors typically had longer

ranges, but they could often be detected by some other kind of sensor. The designers of his Cobra optical and audio enhancements had kept those devices strictly passive for precisely that reason. "You're right, it doesn't fit my ear. But I'll make it work. I assume the plan right now is to just observe?"

"The plan, that is it," Kjoic confirmed. "If you see any humans come from the building, watch and note all details. Entrance procedures into the outer door, they would also be useful."

"Got it," Merrick said. In the past few minutes the sky above the forest had lightened considerably, and he could now make out the individual tree limbs without using his opticals. "If you need me...hmm. Actually, I guess you'd better *not* need me."

"Communication, it will be difficult," Kjoic agreed. He peered at the ground around them, then reached down and picked up a pair of small objects that looked like spiral-shaped pine cones. "If you are in danger, or see danger approaching, drop one of these to the base of the tree."

"Good idea," Merrick said, taking the cones. "But with one slight alteration." Carefully, he broke off a dozen seeds on one spiral arm of each of the cones. "We don't want you getting confused if a random cone happens to fall on its own," he said, holding up the modified cones for Kjoic's inspection.

The Troft's radiator membranes fluttered. "Well thought," he said. "I will stand ready if you need me. You have your weapon?"

"Right here," Merrick said, patting small of his back where he'd tucked the laser pistol Kjoic had given him before they started their all-night hike. He didn't need the weapon, of course, and wasn't particularly thrilled at having to lug the thing around.

But it was a symbol of Kjoic's trust, and something a normal human would certainly not have turned down.

"Good," Kjoic said. "Be careful, and watch well."

The tree was easy to climb, with well-spaced limbs and convenient gaps in the foliage where he needed it. Three minutes after leaving the ground, he found a spot where he could see the Drim warehouse through the leaves.

It was decidedly anticlimactic. There were two entrances: a regular, human- or Troft-sized door, and a larger one scaled for medium-sized vehicles. In his mad escape earlier that night he'd only seen the smaller door, but there had been two on the village side of the building and it only made sense for that arrangement to be duplicated here. Both doors were closed, and there were four armed and armored Trofts standing guard in front of each.

Inside the village, just visible past the edge of the warehouse's roof, he could see that a new fence had been erected between a pair of houses near the village's outer fence. He couldn't tell where else the fence went, or whether the house nearest the building was completely enclosed, but it was possible the Trofts had decided to switch the pre-combat work on their human test subjects to that house instead of keeping everything inside the warehouse. Given the way Merrick had torn a path through the lab and work areas, it would make sense for the Trofts to rethink their setup.

Of course, if that *was* what they'd done, it would make stealing a sample of the drug that much simpler. Something he and Kjoic would need to keep in mind.

Though the Trofts would surely have thought of that, too. Merrick couldn't see if the inner fence was patrolled, but the outer approach certainly was. He couldn't remember whether or not there'd been any guards on the exit doors when he broke out of the building, but under the circumstances it wasn't surprising the Drims had thrown on an extra layer of security. In fact, if Merrick had been in charge he would probably have added a roving perimeter patrol and a combat vehicle or two to the mix.

What was painfully clear was that if Ludolf and Anya had gone inside, they weren't coming out anytime soon.

In the meantime, there was nothing to do but watch and wait. Every security system, Merrick's commanders on Qasama had told him, had a weakness. It was a tactician's job to find that weakness and a way to exploit it.

Just above Merrick, on the far side of the trunk, was a pair of limbs that would serve as a seat. He got himself settled as best he could, wedged the laser Kjoic had given him into a notch in the bark where it would be handy but not digging into his kidney, and settled in to watch.

Seated across from Jody Moreau Broom at one end of the *Squire*'s long mess table, Smitty lowered his fork and eyed the man beside Jody. "Kemp, you know I hold you in the highest esteem, both as a fellow Cobra and a friend," he said. "But I think I speak for all of us—"

"That as a cook, I suck swamp water?" Kemp interrupted, an edge of challenge in his voice.

"I *was* just going to say you were terrible," Smitty said. "But sucking swamp water also covers it."

Jody looked down at her own plate. Smitty had a point, she had to admit. The thin slab of meat was dry and stringy, some of the vegetables were dry while others were mushy, and the dinner roll was far more chewy than bread had any business being. Worse even than the texture was the blandness of the taste.

Though in Kemp's defense, he didn't have a lot to work with. They'd had plenty of experience with the Dominion courier ship's disappointing larder on the five-day trip from Caelian to Qasama, and Jody had hoped to load some fresh food supplies before they continued on their journey. But the mad scramble off Qasama hadn't given them enough time, which had put them back on Dominion rations.

Smitty's comment had been in jest, Jody knew. Unfortunately, Kemp wasn't in the mood. "Well, I'm just so very *damn* sorry about that," he growled. "If you think you can do better, you're welcome to give it a shot."

"That wasn't a criticism," Rashida Vil said quickly, reaching a hand across the table and almost but not quite touching Kemp's arm. "We know you're doing the best you can with what you've been given."

"Or course it was a criticism," Kemp bit out, ignoring Rashida's hovering hand and glaring at Smitty. "If you were serving this slop, *I'd* be grousing about it, too."

"Kemp," Jody murmured.

Kemp shifted his eyes to her, and she saw his face stiffen and then soften as he made the supreme effort to throttle back his anger. "In fact, I already am," he said in a more civilized tone. "I'm just doing it—you know. Quietly. To myself."

"Sorry," Smitty apologized. "I was just trying to lighten the mood."

"Was the mood doing that badly?" Kemp asked. "I guess I missed that."

"You've been slaving over a hot microcooker all day," Jody reminded him.

"Well, for a whole half hour at a time, anyway," Kemp said. "What's the problem?"

"No problem," Smitty said. "At least, nothing that needs to be addressed right away."

"Well, we're not exactly enjoying scintillating table conversation," Kemp pointed out. "Might as well serve a side dish of trouble."

Smitty and Rashida looked at each other. "Okay," Smitty said, turning back to Kemp. "We're currently twelve days from the system Jody pulled from that crashed shuttle on Qasama. We're wondering what happens once we get there."

"We find Merrick," Jody said.

"Right." Smitty paused. "How?"

"We are speaking of an entire world," Rashida reminded her gently. "Possibly with great cities. Certainly with great tracts of land. It will be like finding—" she looked at Smitty again. "What was the phrase?"

"A tick in a tick factory," Smitty supplied. "And if he's in a Troft prison, you can multiply the complexity by about twenty."

Jody took a deep breath. Down deep, she'd known this conversation was coming. Also down deep, she didn't have a clue. "The short answer is that I don't know," she said. "I'm taking this one step at a time. To be perfectly honest, I never expected us to get even this far." She shrugged helplessly. "All I can do is hope that we'll figure something out by the time we get there."

The other three exchanged looks. "Okay," Smitty said. "I guess there really isn't much else we can do at this stage. Not until we find out what exactly we're flying into." He twitched a small smile. "Which won't stop us from worrying, of course."

"At least it'll give you something to do," Kemp said. "Last time I dropped by the CoNCH, it looked even more boring than the kitchen."

"CoNCH," a quiet voice came from somewhere to Jody's left.

She twisted her head around, peripherally aware that the others were doing the same. There was a man standing in the open doorway. A young man, maybe her age, a bit shorter than Kemp, with dark brown eyes, a skullcap fuzz of brown hair, and an equally fuzzy several-day growth of beard.

And he was wearing a Dominion Marine combat tunic.

CHAPTER THREE

Jody felt her mouth go dry. There had been two Marines still aboard when the combined force of Cobras and Qasaman Djinni captured the courier ship back on Caelian. One of the Marines, the one who'd barricaded himself inside the portside gunbay, had emerged during the voyage to Qasama, ostensibly to negotiate, in actuality to provide a diversion so his compatriot in the other gunbay could remotely fiddle with the *Squire*'s helm settings. The gambit had failed, on all levels, and the Marine had been taken off the ship by Shahni Moffren Omnathi and his men when they landed on Qasama.

The other Marine had given them no further trouble, remaining silent and invisible for the rest of the trip. Somehow, Jody had assumed that the Qasamans had managed to extract him during the time she'd been in Isis getting her Cobra enhancements, or at least sometime before she and her companions headed off-world again.

Clearly, she'd been wrong.

And that false assumption had now cost her everything. The parrot gun lasers built into the tunic's epaulets were every bit as deadly and accurate as the Cobras' own weaponry. With Kemp's and Smitty's legs all but trapped under the table, and their lasers pointed in the wrong direction, there was no way they could bring a counterattack to bear. Not in time.

But that didn't mean they wouldn't try.

Beside her, Kemp made a small throat-clearing sound. Jody keyed up her new audio enhancers—

"Split and hit," Kemp murmured softly. "On three."

A chill rippled through Jody's core. The split-and-hit was a technique to deal with a predator who'd managed to get within point-blank range. The Cobras who were the predator's target would leap to the sides, both firing at the animal; if there was a third Cobra in the group, he would stay motionless and fire from the middle. The idea was that the movement would distract the predator long enough for one of the Cobras to score a killing shot.

But there was no possibility of any such distraction here. The Marine had undoubtedly already target-locked all four of them, and would be waiting for just such a maneuver. The first move by any of them would be death for all of them.

"What do you mean?" Rashida asked calmly.

The question was so unexpected—especially given that Rashida seldom started conversations—that for a second Jody's fears and nervous anticipation sputtered to a frozen halt. From what she could see out of the corners of her eyes, Kemp and Smitty were similarly puzzled.

"It called CoNCH, not *the* CoNCH," the Marine said calmly. He seemed as untouched by the three Cobras' sudden tension as—

As untouched as Rashida, actually, now that Jody fully focused her attention on the Qasaman woman. Was she seeing something the rest of them weren't?

"Yes, we know," Rashida said. "We are somewhat more casual about these things than you are. If you don't plan to kill us, you had better say so at once, before there is unpleasantness."

And then, belatedly, Jody got it. The Marine had caught them completely unawares. If he'd wanted to kill them, he could have done it without any of them even knowing what had happened.

But he hadn't. And not only hadn't he opened fire, but he'd started a calm, civilized conversation. Or at least a grammar lesson.

Rashida had spotted that right away. Distantly, Jody wondered why she herself hadn't.

"Let's do this in order, shall we?" the Marine suggested, his eyes flicking to each of the others. "First, I want you to acknowledge that if I wanted you dead, you'd already be dead. Do you so acknowledge?"

"What are you, the ship's lawyer?" Smitty growled.

"Do you so acknowledge?" the Marine repeated.

Jody looked at Smitty. Smitty's eyes were on Kemp, and Jody sensed the Cobra beside her give a microscopic shrug. "Okay, fine," Smitty said, looking back at the Marine. "You win. We're dead. Now what?"

"Now," the Marine said, "I want to make a deal."

"Sorry," Smitty said. "We don't negotiate under duress."

"I didn't think you would," the Marine said.

And to Jody's surprise, he reached up to his throat, turned his back to them, and shucked off his tunic. Holding it out at arm's length, he set it down onto the deck—it was rigid enough to mostly continue standing straight up—and turned back around. "There," he said. "We all feel safer now?"

"Well, *we* do," Smitty said. He had his hands up now, fingertip lasers pointed at the Marine, his thumbs on the ring-finger nails in full-power firing position. "How about you?"

"It's all right, Smitty," Rashida said quietly, reaching out her hand and resting it lightly on his arm. "He came to talk, not to fight. Let us hear what he has to say."

"I'm not sure I want to listen," Smitty bit out.

"Oh, I think we can spare him a minute or two," Kemp said. His right arm was stretched out over Jody's plate, the laser in that hand also targeting the Marine. "Let's start with his name."

"I'm Marine Gunnery Sergeant Fitzgerald Plaine," the Marine said. His lip twitched. "I'd give you my service number, too, but I doubt you really care."

"You want to quit stalling?" Smitty growled. "We're busy here."

"Really?" Plaine's eyebrows rose a bit. "A minute ago all you were doing was being bored. No matter. The point is that I know who you are, and what you're doing. And I'm here to offer my assistance."

"Why?" Smitty demanded suspiciously.

"Because he's hungry," Jody said. With the immediate threat gone, she'd finally been able to focus enough attention on Plaine's face to spot the telltale thinness of hunger.

"More thirsty than hungry," Plaine told her. "But, yes, both. Also, though you probably can't tell from there, I'm badly in need of a shower."

"Fair enough," Kemp said. "You can eat, and then Smitty and I will show you to your new quarters."

"If you want to lock me up, I can't stop you," Plaine said. "But I think I can be of more use as part of the squad."

"Part of the squad?" Smitty echoed. "Part of the *squad*? What part of *our prisoner* don't you get?"

"The part about you needing my help," Plaine said bluntly. "The part about flying an unfamiliar ship into enemy territory with no intel, no backup—" He looked Jody squarely in the eye. "And no plan."

"Eavesdropping out there for a while, were you?" Kemp asked.

"For a lot longer than you think." Plaine gestured in the direction of the starboard gunbay. "You and your allies figured out—well, eventually you figured it out—that the gunbays run secondary duty as emergency CoNCHs. It apparently never occurred to you that one of the obvious capabilities of such a center would be to obtain data and facilitate communication by remotely activating the ship's intercom system." He smiled faintly. "And I mean *all* of it."

Jody felt a creepy sensation crawl up her back. Did he mean he'd listened to *every* conversation they'd had aboard ship?

Maybe Kemp was thinking the same thing. "*All* of it?" he asked, an edge of warning in his tone.

Plaine shrugged slightly. "Well, everything for the past day or two, anyway," he amended. "Enough to get the gist of things." He shifted his eyes back to Jody. "Your brother is missing. You think you know where he might be. I understand that kind of concern. Dominion Marines also stand by the rule of no man left behind."

"You sound so enthusiastic," Smitty growled.

"In principle, I'm very enthusiastic," Plaine said. "In practice... frankly, Ms. Broom, my guess is that you're out of luck. From what I read of your recent tiff with the Trofts—"

"Our *tiff*?" Smitty cut him off.

"Well, it was hardly a war, was it?" Plaine countered. "Four planets and a few weeks of fighting? Hardly even qualifies as a tiff."

Smitty took a deep breath—

"Whatever," Jody cut him off. "Fine; but there's one thing your little spy ears didn't tell you. Shahni Omnathi told us the Qasamans have thoroughly searched the forest and cities and all the areas the Trofts traveled. They've already located the bodies of most of the missing Qasaman soldiers and civilians. My brother wasn't among them."

"Interesting," Plaine murmured thoughtfully. "You sure they didn't just tell you that to spare your feelings?"

"No," Jody said flatly. She looked at Rashida. "They wouldn't, would they?"

"They would not," Rashida confirmed. "The Shahni respects you too much to offer you such a small and ultimately futile lie."

Jody felt a small frown crease her head. That was a strange way to phrase that.

"Assume you're right," Plaine said. "It still seems strange that they would bother taking him prisoner. It's not like he could tell them anything useful."

"Maybe they wished to check out his Cobra gear," Rashida suggested.

Plaine shrugged. "Like I said: nothing useful."

Smitty raised his left hand. "Show of hands," he invited. "How many want to just drop this clown out an airlock?"

Plaine shook his head. "You don't want to do that."

"Oh, I'm pretty sure I do," Smitty growled.

"No, you really don't," Plaine said. "For starters, if you do you'll never get another decent meal aboard this ship."

"So Dominion Marines also double as gourmet chefs?" Smitty asked. "Yeah, I totally believe *that*."

"Actually, I haven't cooked since I joined the Service," Plaine said. "I just happen to know that you're supposed to put freeze-dried meals in the microcooker *before* you peel off the shrink-wrapping."

"Then how do you get the water in to rehydrate it?" Jody asked.

"You don't," Plaine said. "The appropriate liquids—*all* the liquids and juices, not just the straight aitch-two-oh—are drawn out into the wrapping during the process. They come back out of suspension during the reheating and cooking process and reinfuse the meal."

"Really," Kemp said. There was the sound of a chair sliding back. "Show us."

"Now?" Plaine asked, frowning. "I thought we were negotiating."

"We are," Kemp said. "We're negotiating your butt over to storage and whipping up some better food."

Plaine shrugged. "Whatever you want."

He strode forward, angling to his right to pass the table behind Smitty and Rashida. As he passed Smitty, the other Cobra quietly stood up and fell into step behind him. Jody winced as he went by; the man definitely needed a shower.

"Tunic," Kemp murmured in Jody's ear. "Take it, and fry it."

She nodded and pushed her own chair back, heading the opposite direction from everyone else.

The tunic Plaine had left in the doorway was surprisingly heavy, though considering all the weapons, defenses, and power supplies tucked inside, the weight might actually be a little light. She slung it over her arm for easier carrying and glanced over her shoulder. Plaine was at the food storage cabinet, with his view in her direction blocked by Kemp. Making sure not to bang the tunic against the door jamb, she slipped out into the corridor.

It would be easy enough to neutralize the tunic, she knew. Unfastened and off its owner as it was, it was completely inactive. A few well-placed fingertip laser shots across the epaulets, or even a good arcthrower blast to each of them, and the tunic would be nothing more than a decorative piece of clothing. It was what Kemp had ordered her to do, and it certainly made the most tactical sense.

And yet...

She didn't trust Plaine. Not a single solitary centimeter. He could talk all he wanted about not leaving anyone behind, but Jody was pretty sure a starving man would say whatever he had to in order to score himself a meal. He could easily just be biding his time, pretending to be passive, until he got the chance to make some kind of countermove against them. In fact, given the way the Cobras and Djinni had captured the *Squire*, a countermove was the most probable scenario.

And given how much better Plaine knew the ship than she or any of the others did, leaving *any* weapons where he could get his hands on them would be just begging for trouble. The rest of the tunics and spare weapons parts had been taken off the ship—Omnathi had made sure of that—and it only made sense to destroy this last weapon as well.

And yet...

Plaine was right about one thing: Jody and the others were way in over their heads. Even if all this was just an act, there could well come a point where his survival would be inexorably linked to theirs. If and when that happened, she assumed he would fight as hard as they did.

But only if he had something to fight with.

The whole interior of the *Squire* was riddled with small rooms and equipment access cubbies and crawlspaces. She found a pump room near CoNCH and stuffed the tunic inside. A few careful shots with her fingertip lasers to spot-weld the door closed, and Plaine wouldn't be getting inside without collecting some tools and making a lot of noise.

As an afterthought, she spot-welded two other nearby storage room doors, as well. Any of the Cobras could blast off the welds in a few seconds if they needed to get in, but Plaine would now have to guess which one held his tunic. If his powers of observation and deduction got him even that far.

She returned to find Plaine seated at the far end of the table, digging hungrily into a newly reconstituted meal. Smitty had taken up position behind him, while Kemp faced him from across the table. Rashida was still sitting where she'd been earlier, a thoughtful expression on her face as she gazed at the Marine.

And for the first time since leaving Caelian Jody's sense of smell was treated to the aroma of good food.

Kemp looked over at Jody as she walked in, his eyebrows raised in silent question. Jody gave a small nod and sat down across from Rashida.

If Plaine noticed her return, or if he even realized she'd been gone, he made no sign.

He finished his meal in silence and then nodded to the micro-cooker. "I presume you won't mind if I have seconds?" he asked. "I've been on very short rations the past few days."

"That was your own fault," Smitty pointed out. "You could have come out at any time."

"And been made a prisoner?"

"The Qasamans treat prisoners honorably," Kemp said. "You'd have gotten used to their cuisine."

"Perhaps," Plaine said. "But since I haven't had that opportunity—?"

Kemp rolled his eyes. "Yes, fine, you can have a second meal. But first we talk."

"About what?"

"You said you wanted to deal," Kemp said. "Let's hear the offer."

"The offer is for expertise," Plaine said. "Knowledge and skills that you don't have. You don't know this ship, for starters, certainly not as well as I do. You also don't know how its weapons function, or how to get the best speed out of it, or how to key in the pre-programmed battle maneuvers. I do."

"I thought Marines were soldiers," Smitty said. "Weapons grunts. What makes you think you can fly or fight this thing better than we can?"

"Because while I've been stuck in that gunbay I've been studying the manuals," Plaine said. "All right, granted, I can't straight-up fly it nearly as well as you can. I don't know how you got our pilot to teach you, or how you learned so quickly"—he threw Rashida a thoughtful look—"but it made for interesting listening. But I *do* know the gunbays backward and forward. I also know a lot more about fighting groups of Trofts than you do."

"And why would you want to help us?" Kemp asked. "As far as the Dominion is concerned, we're traitors. Or at least renegades."

"Three reasons," Plaine said. "One: as I said earlier, I understand and appreciate the concept of no one left behind. If Ms. Broom's brother *is* still alive, I'm ready to help get him out. Two: as also already stated, you stand a much better chance with my knowledge and combat skills added to yours. And three—" He hesitated. "If the worse-end scenario happens, there are systems and equipment aboard this ship that we'd rather not fall into Troft hands. I know which systems those are, and how to destroy them."

Jody felt a hard knot form in her stomach. "You're talking about a self-destruct?"

"*Localized* destruct," Plaine corrected her. "Nothing that would turn the *Squire* into a flaming fireball or anything. That's not how I want to go out, either." He considered. "Unless we were ramming a Troft warship at the time. In that case, I'd say we go for it."

"Great," Kemp said. "Let's keep that one tucked away in the do-not-open file, okay?"

"Sure," Plaine said. "Part of a soldier's job is to consider all the options."

"Consider it considered," Kemp said. "Go ahead and make your seconds. We'll be at the other end of the table if you need us."

"Take your time," Plaine said, standing up and heading for the food cabinet. "I'm certainly not going anywhere."

Kemp caught Smitty's eye and gave a sideways nod. Smitty gave Plaine's back a long, speculative look, and then the two Cobras headed back to where Rashida and Jody were sitting.

"Thoughts?" Kemp asked quietly when he and Smitty were standing behind the women. Both Cobras' eyes, Jody noted, were still on Plaine.

"I don't trust him," Smitty said flatly.

"I think that's pretty evident," Kemp said, a little dryly. "Jody? Rashida?"

"He may be playing a game," Rashida said. "However, I should point out that he didn't need to reveal himself to us. He could have slipped out at night for food and water when we were all asleep or in CoNCII."

"I suppose," Kemp conceded. "No, actually, that's a good point. I sure the hell didn't know he was still in there. He could pretty much have had the run of the ship at night."

"Wait a second," Jody said, frowning as an odd thought struck her. "Why *didn't* we know he was there?"

"Because we didn't think to ask and no one thought to tell us," Kemp said.

"Yes, but *why*?" Jody persisted. "Omnathi is usually right on top of things like this. It's not like he didn't know we were going to take the ship."

"I suppose even Omnathi slips up sometimes," Kemp said. "I'm guessing that between his negotiations with Captain Moreau and keeping an eye on the *Dorian*'s injured he probably told someone to get Plaine out of his hullmetal cocoon and assumed it had been done."

"How it happened is not of immediate importance," Rashida said. "We have the situation. We need to decide how to address it."

"You're right," Smitty growled. "But I guarantee you that Omnathi's going to hear about this when we get back." He waved a hand. "I already hate the guy, so I'm not the one to make any decisions. What do the rest of you want to do?"

"Well, obviously, he doesn't run around loose while we're asleep," Kemp said. "That means locking him up in the guest suite at night."

Jody wrinkled her nose. She'd been a similarly unwilling guest aboard the *Squire* for the better part of two days back on Caelian, quartered in a cabin whose lock had been reversed to convert it into a prison cell. Kemp had nicknamed it the guest suite after they'd used it to isolate the other gunbay Marine during the trip to Qasama. "We'll want to make sure the last occupant didn't do anything to the stuff in there that Plaine might use against us," she warned.

"Trust me," Kemp said. "I plan to go over it again *very* thoroughly."

"And when he's *not* locked in his room?" Smitty asked. "What do we do with him then?"

"I think I've got an idea," Kemp said. Even without looking Jody could sense in his voice that there was a wry smile on his face. "Come on. Let's go welcome our newest club member."

Jody and Rashida stood up, and together the four of them walked to the other end of the table. Plaine, already halfway through his second meal, looked up as they approached. "That was quick," he said. "I hope that means it's not the airlock."

"No, it's not the airlock," Kemp assured him, once again stopping directly across the table from him. "It's far worse. We're going to make you work."

Plaine's eyebrows went up. "Let me guess. I'm on KP?"

"What's KP?" Jody asked.

"Kitchen Patrol," Plaine said. "It's not exactly a new term."

"Well, it's one we haven't needed to bother with," Kemp said. "And no, you're not going to do the cooking. You're going to teach us how to run those gunbays."

The politely raised eyebrows went down again. "I'm not sure I can do that."

"I'm sure you can," Kemp said. "I'm also sure that you *will*."

"Oh?" The eyebrows went up again.

"Because you want to live through this just as much as we do," Kemp told him. "That means using this ship to the best of its abilities. Among other things that means having people who know what they're doing in both gunbays."

Plaine's lips compressed. But he gave a reluctant nod. "I suppose that makes sense," he conceded. "All right."

"And," Kemp continued, "you get locked into your cabin at night. Nothing personal."

Plaine smiled faintly. "Understood. If the situation was reversed, I'd do the same."

And as Jody looked at that faint, slightly condescending, vaguely knowing smile, she felt like an idiot.

Because her new Cobra opticals included infrared sensors that were sensitive enough to detect the small variances in heat from someone's facial blood flow. Variances that would indicate changing levels of nervousness or fear. Variances that might indicate whether the person was telling the truth, or lying through his teeth.

And she'd completely forgotten about them.

Silently cursing herself, she activated them. But as she'd already suspected, it was too late.

"Glad you understand," Kemp said. "Go ahead and finish eating, and then we can start the tour."

"We'll be in CoNCH if you need us," Smitty added.

Kemp gestured, and the four of them once again headed across the room. This time, they continued through the doorway and out into the corridor.

"Did you get anything?" Smitty asked quietly as they headed aft.

"Nothing definitive," Kemp said. "Plenty of emotional twitches, but that could just be a member of the high and mighty Dominion of Man having to submit to a bunch of unwashed wilderness types. Nothing I could positively state was a lie."

Jody caught Rashida's eye. "Our Cobra opticals can detect the changing heat from a person's blood flow," she explained. "Sometimes that lets us figure out if a person is lying."

Rashida nodded. "Yes, I had heard that. Perhaps we need to know him better."

"That's what I'm thinking," Kemp agreed. "But we've got twelve more days before we reach wherever. Whatever Plaine's cultural differences, we should have time to sort them out between now and then."

"And once we've got a baseline," Smitty said darkly, "maybe we can figure out what he's hiding behind that arrogant little smile." He gestured to Kemp. "You weren't really planning on all of us waiting for him in CoNCH, were you?"

"Of course not," Kemp assured him. "Off you go."

"Off I go," Smitty confirmed, coming to a halt. "I'll see you there in a bit."

"And if he wanders off somewhere else?" Jody asked.

"You might hear his last scream." Smitty shrugged. "Or," he added offhandedly, "you might not."

CHAPTER FOUR

Captain Barrington Moreau was in a shallow, restless sleep aboard the Dominion of Man War Cruiser *Dorian* when his aide, Lieutenant Cottros Meekan, awakened him with the bad news.

Meekan was waiting outside the shuttle bay when Barrington arrived. "They're saying it was some kind of undetected infection," the lieutenant said as he punched the hatch release. "They're still hoping they can still save the leg, but they're warning that it's going to be touch and go."

"Understood," Barrington said, his heart pounding as the two men hurried across the bay toward the shuttle Meekan had prepped for him. Seven days ago, Lieutenant Commander Eliser Kusari, *Dorian's* engineering officer, had been badly wounded in the *Dorian's* brief battle with the unidentified Troft warships at the flicker-net trap. Even as they escaped from the battle, Dr. Lancaster, the ship's chief medical officer, had warned Barrington that Kusari's leg would have to be amputated.

But Barrington had refused to allow the operation. The Cobra Worlds' records indicated that Qasama had incredibly advanced medical capabilities, and he'd gambled that he could get Kusari there in time to save his leg.

The gamble had worked. Against all odds—and the private expectations of most of Barrington's officers—Shahni Omnathi had agreed to take in their wounded. Not only had the Qasamans' medical magic saved Kusari's leg, but it had likewise brought all the rest of the *Dorian*'s severely wounded men back from the brink of death.

Only now, it appeared, some of Barrington's relief had been premature.

And it couldn't have happened in a worse way, and to a worse person. Though Kusari was quiet and generally nonconfrontative, he was nevertheless one of Barrington's strongest supporters among his officers. More than that, his patron in the Dome was an equally strong ally of Barrington's patron. Kusari's death would be a serious blow to Barrington's standing, especially in his ongoing clash with Tactical Officer Castenello. "Did they say what he wanted to talk to me about?" he asked Meekan.

"No," the aide said. "Just that he was calling for you."

Barrington hissed between his teeth. Normally, there wouldn't be a need for the captain to fly to the surface to talk to his engineering officer. Radios were everywhere, and with Dominion scrambling technology there was no chance the Qasamans could listen in on any ship-to-shore communications.

But in this case, Barrington wasn't worried about the Qasaman eavesdropping nearly as much as he was worried about his own officers getting an earful. Kusari had been quietly looking into ways to identify the Troft ships they'd fought at the flicker net, and he might have thought of something new that he hadn't yet had a chance to relay to his captain.

If so, it could be vital that Barrington get that information before anyone else. Especially Castenello.

The shuttle's pilot, copilot, and Barrington's five-man Marine guard were already strapped into their seats as Barrington climbed through the hatch. "Do you want me to go with you, sir?" Meekan asked.

"No, that's all right," Barrington said as he dropped into his seat and started strapping in. He was already making a suspiciously big deal about this by going down to Qasama personally. He had no intention of turning it into a parade that Castenello would be bound to notice. "I left a message with Commander Garret that he's to take my watch. Go to CoNCH and make sure he has everything he needs."

"Yes, sir." Meekan hesitated. "Good luck, sir."

It wasn't exactly the correct farewell for the situation, Barrington mused as the shuttle dropped away from the *Dorian* and headed groundward. But he understood what the younger man had been trying to say. Good luck dealing with the Qasamans. Good luck to Kusari.

And good luck to Barrington himself if Kusari didn't make it.

The Qasamans had a van waiting for them at the landing area that had been set up earlier to handle the Dominion medical shuttles. Three minutes after climbing out of the shuttle into the heavy and oddly aromatic Qasaman air, Barrington and the Marines were striding through the front door of the hospital.

A middle-aged woman in hospital garb was waiting for them. Her smock was rumpled, Barrington noticed, and there were deep stress lines in her face. "Follow me, please," she said, turning and striding quickly down the right-hand corridor.

"Has there been any change?" Barrington asked as he and the Marines followed.

"Commander Kusari is still alive," the woman said over her shoulder. "That's all I know. In here."

She led them through a door into a wide corridor with doors opening off both sides and a circular nurses' station in the middle of the corridor. There was a ring of monitors on each of the two central desks, and as the group passed the stations Barrington noted that one of the monitors showed an overhead view of an operating room. Grouped around the table were half a dozen white-robed people, working feverishly on their patient's leg.

Even with the patient's face half covered by the anesthetic mask it was clear that it was Kusari.

And he looked terrible.

Barrington felt his stomach tighten as they hurried past the station and the monitors. Even that quick glimpse had been enough to show the gauntness of Kusari's face and the tenseness in the shoulders of the surgeons working on him. Kusari was in serious trouble, and Barrington could only hope he would be in time to hear whatever the commander had to say.

"In here," their guide said, stopping beside a closed door with what seemed to be warning signs in Qasaman script. "Through the airlock is a changing room where you'll need to strip down and don sterilized clothing." Her eyes flicked to the Marines. "I'm afraid there's only room for one in there, but there are two other rooms. Shall I take your escort to them?"

"Yes, thank you," Barrington said. He turned and pointed to

two of the Marines. "You, and you—go with her. The rest of you stay here."

He turned back to find the woman had the door open, revealing a short passageway that ended in another door. "In there," she said, pointing. "Don't open that door until I close this one."

"Understood," Barrington said, stepping into the corridor. He reached the second door and glanced over his shoulder to confirm the woman had closed the first behind him. Then, bracing himself for the worst, he pushed open the second door and stepped through.

He got two steps before he stopped short, blinking in confusion.

It wasn't a changing room, at least not like any such facility he'd ever seen. This room was narrow and curved, with a single row of a dozen seats at the far end that faced a glass wall. Beyond the glass, sunk three meters below him, was an operating room, dark except for a few muted lights.

As near as he could tell, it was the same operating room he'd just seen on the monitor outside. Only now, it was deserted.

His first horrified thought was that he was too late. That Kusari had died on the table and been removed while Barrington was covering those last few meters to the changing room door.

And then, his brain caught up with him. Tearing his eyes away from the empty operating room, he focused on the space he was standing in.

Aside from Barrington himself, there was only a single occupant. He was seated in one of the center chairs, his back to Barrington, making no move or sound. Perhaps, Barrington thought through his frozen brain, he was waiting for his visitor to take the lead.

And now that Barrington finally had it figured out, he decided he might as well. Whatever was about to go down, he'd already lost the opening gambit. He might as well face the rest with some dignity. "Good morning, Your Excellency," he said. "Nicely played."

"Thank you," Shahni Omnathi said without turning around. "My sincere apologies for the deception. I needed to talk to you in private, and this seemed the only way to do so."

"And Commander Kusari?"

"Alive, perfectly well, and recovering nicely."

"You took a risk, you know," Barrington pointed out. "What if we'd tried to contact him before I came down? Or his Marine guards?"

"Oh, I'm quite sure you *did* call him, Captain," Omnathi said.

"You or your people. We'd taken the precaution of shielding his room from all transmissions. As to his guards, they'd already been informed he was being moved here to the hospital for further tests, which was I'm sure what they told your men."

"Clever," Barrington said. "What if I called my ship or my Marines right now?"

"This room is also shielded," Omnathi said calmly. "At any rate, there's no need for dramatics or concern. I merely wish that I be allowed to ask you a question, and that you give me an honest answer. After that, you and your Marines will be free to leave."

"What if you don't like the answer?"

"You'll still be free to leave." Omnathi half turned, presenting his profile to Barrington. "Come now, Captain. It's not like we haven't already made private agreements together. Surely a private conversation isn't so far out of line."

Barrington grimaced. Yes; the *Squire*, with Jody Moreau Broom and her friends aboard. Most likely headed to their deaths. "You could have just invited me," he pointed out, circling around the end of the row of seats and coming over to Omnathi.

"Would you have consented to come without your guards?"

Barrington sighed as he sat down beside the Qasaman. The Cobra Worlds records had indicated that Omnathi was extremely good at reading and manipulating people. He should have remembered that before he went charging off to the shuttle. "I'm here," he said. "Ask your question."

"Thank you." Omnathi gestured toward the empty operating room below them. "First, I want you to understand why I chose this place for our conversation."

"I assume because this is the room where you saved Commander Kusari's leg," Barrington said. "That *was* the record of that operation you had playing in the nurses' station, wasn't it?"

"It was," Omnathi confirmed. "And you're correct: I wanted to remind you of what we did here. Not just for Lieutenant Commander Kusari, but also many others of your crew."

"I'm not likely to forget," Barrington said, some of his anger fading away. He did indeed owe Omnathi and the rest of the Qasamans. And the Shahni was right; he *wouldn't* have come here without his guards.

That might not prove a good thing. For either of them. "What do you want to know?"

"You've been searching for us for a long time," Omnathi said. "That effort has cost a great deal of effort, as well as the lives of many people on Caelian, Dominion, and Cobra Worlds citizens alike." He paused. "Very simply: *why?*"

There were lies Barrington could tell, he knew. Easy lies. Believable lies.

The Dominion was looking for lost colonies. The Dominion was concerned about all human lives. The Dominion wanted to look at the damage the recent Troft attack had inflicted so that they could help.

They were lies Commodore Santores would have ordered him to tell, lies that would help defuse Castenello's inevitable list of charges at the next Enquiry Board that the tactical officer chose to call.

Lies that Barrington was weary of telling. To others, and especially to himself.

"The Dominion of Man is at war," he said. "We're fighting a consortium of Troft demesnes—we're still not sure how many are in the group."

"How are you doing in that effort?"

"When we left Dominion space about nine months ago, not too well," Barrington admitted. "Right now—" He shook his head. "No idea. At any rate, our mission was to get around the Troft Assemblage, contact the Cobra Worlds, if they still existed, and—" he braced himself. "Try to draw off some of the enemy."

"You mean lure them into an attack?"

Barrington nodded, his throat aching. "We were supposed to build a military presence on the Cobra Worlds," he said. "More realistically, the *appearance* of a military presence. Certainly neither our task force nor Aventine has the resources or infrastructure to create a genuine threat. But the planners at Asgard—that's where our military command is located—didn't think that would matter. Once the enemy noticed the build-up—and we fully expected the word to get back to them quickly—it was hoped they would withdraw forces from the battle front and bring them here."

"And we would be left to their mercies?"

"No, not entirely—" He broke off as the word suddenly penetrated. "You said *we?*"

"Of course, *we*," Omnathi said, his voice going dark. "It's perfectly obvious what Commodore Santores's new plan is. Instead of luring the Trofts to the Cobra Worlds, you intend to lure them to Qasama."

"I didn't—" Barrington broke off. *Tired of the lies.* "Yes," he confirmed. "For whatever it's worth, I don't like the plan. Any of it. I never liked it from the start. Neither did my patron back in the Dome."

"But you were desperate," Omnathi murmured. "You of the Dominion. And desperate people do whatever is necessary to survive."

Barrington looked sideways at him. He'd expected the Qasaman to react to the revelation with blazing fury or at least a cold, bitter rage. But there wasn't any such tone in the other's voice. "I don't expect you to understand," he said. "Our culture—"

"On the contrary—I understand all too well," Omnathi interrupted. "We faced that same decision during the Troft invasion. Many times." He shrugged. "Which doesn't mean we agree with your conclusion or your plan, of course."

"Of course," Barrington said. "As I said, I don't like it myself."

"But you have no alternative to offer?"

"No, I don't," Barrington said, frowning as a sudden thought struck him. Barrington himself certainly had no alternative plan... but sitting beside him was a man who was reputed to be the best strategist on Qasama. "But perhaps you do?"

Omnathi gave a little snort. "You give me far too much credit, Captain. The finest minds in your Dominion of Man have puzzled at this problem for months without an alternative. Yet you expect *me*, who has only now heard the true situation, to find a solution all the others have missed?"

"I don't give you any more credit than you deserve, Your Excellency," Barrington countered. "And to be perfectly honest, I don't know how much effort those fine minds on Asgard and in the Dome put into this plan. The Cobra Worlds have been half history and half myth for so long I doubt the planners even thought of the citizens as human beings anymore. If they didn't care to factor in the cost of colonist lives, the idea of luring a Troft force to their destruction may have looked good enough that they stopped right there with their planning."

"What about the lives of you and the others aboard your ships?" Omnathi countered "Don't *they* matter?"

"In a war, sacrifices have to be made," Barrington said. "And this isn't *quite* the straight-up suicide mission you're probably thinking. There's one more piece to the strategy that I hadn't mentioned: there's a second task force coming in behind us, and already on its way. Once the Trofts have launched their attack on us, the secondary force will suddenly appear behind them and catch them in a cross-fire. With luck, we'll destroy them completely. At the very least, there should be considerably fewer ships to rejoin their allies on the Dominion front."

"Perhaps," Omnathi murmured. "Though they would be fools to send so many ships to this battle that even their total loss would seriously diminish their efforts at the primary front."

"*If* the balance of power isn't already right on the edge," Barrington said. "It might be. And *if* they're thinking tactically, which they may not be at that point. There are indications they may be on the edge of desperation."

"An ironic statement, if I may point that out."

Barrington winced. "No argument there," he conceded. "But the number of ships lost or not lost may not matter. Troft alliances are notoriously fragile, and a solid defeat here might induce some of the members to withdraw and pursue a separate peace with the Dominion. At any rate, any uncertainty or chaos we can create in the Troft ranks is to our advantage."

"Even if it costs you your lives?"

Barrington felt his throat tighten. "We're the defenders of our worlds," he said. "If by our deaths we can secure peace and freedom for those worlds, that's our job. Yes, even if it costs us our lives."

For a moment the room was silent. Barrington gazed out at the empty operating room, wondering how many such rooms it would take to treat all the casualties if the Trofts took the bait.

Too many, he suspected. Far too many.

Beside him, Omnathi stirred. "I will consider the problem," he said. "Perhaps there is another way." He half turned toward Barrington. "My question is whether Commodore Santores would accept an alternative if it was offered to him."

The reflexive words—*of course!*—unexpectedly stuck in Barrington's throat. "I don't know," he admitted. "I personally would grab a better plan with both hands. But there are those who believe Asgard's plans and pronouncements come straight from God's mouth. They might require more convincing."

"Commodore Santores?"

"Not so much him," Barrington said, a small pang of guilt flickering through him. Dominion Fleet personnel weren't supposed to talk about their fellow officers this way. Particularly not to outsiders.

But with hundreds of thousands of civilian lives hanging over the chasm, propriety no longer seemed so important. And the more information Omnathi had, the better his chances of coming up with an alternative plan. "But Captain Lij Tulu is definitely one of them. So are a few of my officers."

Omnathi chuckled. "You might be amused, Captain, to know that throughout much of Qasama's history the words of the Shahni were also considered to be on a level with those from heaven. Our peoples—or our cultures at least—are not so different than you might imagine."

"Perhaps," Barrington said. "Though our military structure isn't necessarily an accurate reflection of the Dominion in general."

"Your overall culture isn't like that?"

Barrington ran the question over in his mind. The Dominion's strong centralized government; planetary and local governments whose job was largely to carry out the Dome's orders; people who accepted those orders without complaint...

"But of course, that's not really relevant to the problem at hand," Omnathi continued. "I appreciate your honesty, Captain. Though it's no less than I would expect from a member of the Moreau family. I will consider our joint problem, and search to my fullest ability for a solution." He gestured. "And now, your two Marine guards will have finished preparing themselves to join you in the operating room. You had best go and assure them that all is well."

"Before they start shooting," Barrington agreed, standing up. "Thank you, Your Excellency. I'll look forward to our next meeting."

"As will I," Omnathi said, remaining seated. "Farewell, Captain Moreau."

Barrington again circled the line of seats, wondering distantly if the Qasamans were really going to just let him and the Marines leave. He had, after all, just threatened their entire world with destruction. There were plenty of war theorists on Asgard who would agree that this was practically the definition of a justifiable preemptive strike.

He was still waiting for some kind of move against him when their shuttle settled back into its place in the *Dorian*'s hangar bay.

Meekan was waiting for him outside the main hatch. "We received a call from the Qasamans half an hour ago, sir," the lieutenant said as the two men headed for the elevator. "I understand Commander Kusari is all right now?"

"Yes, he's fine," Barrington said.

"Ah," Meekan said. "Did they tell you what the problem was?"

"It seems to have been a false alarm," Barrington said. Clearly, Meekan was hoping for more details.

Barrington wasn't about to give him any. Not yet. He would upload the bare bones of his visit into the data stream, but that was all. "Inform Commander Garrett that I'll be taking back the watch as soon as I reach CoNCH," he told Meekan.

"Yes, sir," Meekan said. "And I know he'll be anxious to see you. He hasn't put it on the data stream yet, but it looks like Ukuthi has left."

Barrington frowned, something cold running up his back. "Ukuthi's *gone*? Where? Why?"

"I don't know," Meekan said. "Garrett said a first-approximation on the vector wasn't very helpful—it didn't point to any known system. He was going to keep fine-tuning the data in hopes of having something more useful before he released it."

"Good," Barrington said grimly. "Thank you, Lieutenant. I'll go see how he's doing."

He headed to the elevator, a hard knot forming in his stomach. Ukuthi, a senior commander of the Balin'ekha'spmi demesne, had worked very hard to nurture this arrangement with the Dominion on behalf of his demesne-lord. Why would he suddenly leave now, especially without telling Barrington what was going on?

But the Troft was gone, and there was nothing Barrington could do about it. Which was just as well, given that he had a far more urgent matter to attend to.

He had no illusions that he was smarter than the strategists on Asgard. Maybe there *were* no other practical alternatives to the plan they'd come up with to siphon off some of the forces threatening to overwhelm the Dominion.

But he was damned if he was going to sacrifice the lives of fellow human beings—Cobra Worlds citizens *or* Qasamans—without at least taking a crack at it himself. And that meant pulling up and studying every detail of the task force's plan.

And if he or Omnathi *did* find some alternative...

Barrington scowled. He'd told Omnathi that Santores wasn't one of those who believed orders from Asgard carried divine weight. But that didn't mean the commodore would violate them without a *very* good reason. If he or the Qasaman came up with an alternative, it would be up to Barrington to sell it to both Santores and Lij Tulu.

But surely he could. After all, both of them were reasonable men.

CHAPTER FIVE

The time for talk was over. The time for action had arrived.

Or so Commodore Rubo Santores had told Paul Broom before he'd loaded Marines aboard six of the *Megalith*'s fighter-transports and launched them from orbit toward the Caelian capital of Stronghold.

Seated in the command chair that had been wedged just behind the pilot and copilot, Paul gazed through the curved canopy, wondering uneasily what exactly the action Santores had promised was going to consist of.

And wondering why a broken Cobra like Paul Broom was aboard.

Santores had been talking about negotiation and conciliation while his men helped Paul into the fighter and strapped him in. The words had been soothing, and had made it sound as if Paul was the key to persuading Governor Uy to renounce his government's decision to secede from the Dominion of Man and unite with Qasama.

But those soothing words had come before six fully armored Marines climbed into Paul's fighter behind him. The conciliation speech had come before Paul had seen the other five fighters being prepped and similarly loaded with Marines. And the negotiation talk had come before Santores had announced to the strike force that the time for talk was over.

So why exactly was Paul here?

Stronghold was a faintly glowing spot on the nighttime horizon when he finally found out. "Governor Uy, this is Commodore Santores," Santores's voice boomed from the flight-deck speaker. "I know you won't answer, because you're afraid we'll backtrack your transmissions and find out where you've gone to ground. But I know you can hear me. So listen closely, and consider this your final chance to end this before more blood is spilled.

"My troops are on their way. They're accompanied by enough firepower to level your town and turn every one of you to blackened cinders. I don't want to do that. But what you're doing is treason, and treason against the Dominion of Man will not be tolerated.

"I know you'll have your Cobras on hand to protect you. Consider their lives forfeit. You can ask Cobra Paul Broom what happens when your hundred-year-old technology comes up against battle-ready Dominion Marines."

Paul stared out at the rapidly approaching spot of light. Stronghold was a little dot of civilization, a refuge that had been built in defiance of everything the planet's hellish flora and fauna could throw against it, maintained by an underlying optimism that human beings could indeed live and thrive here.

And now, Santores was preparing to wipe out everything the people had fought and struggled and died for.

"You have one chance," Santores continued. "The same chance you've had since the beginning. Renounce this insane secession document, return to the Dominion fold, and nothing more will be said."

Paul clenched his teeth. No, nothing more would probably be said about the Caelians' attempt to secede. But that didn't mean Uy would be free and clear. There was still the matter of the *Squire*, Captain Lij Tulu's missing courier ship, and Paul had no doubt that Santores would pursue that question with as much vigor—and firepower—as he deemed necessary.

On one level, Paul could hardly blame him. He'd caught a glimpse of the long canoe-shaped hole in the *Algonquin*'s side when he was taken aboard several days ago, and he could see why Lij Tulu wanted the ship back.

The overall design made no sense to Paul. Why would anyone build a warship that lost a section of its outer hull every time one of its courier ships went for a spin? But apparently it was reasonable to *someone* in the Dominion, because all three of the war cruisers seemed to have that same design.

Lij Tulu would certainly want the *Squire* secured in place before he headed into any real trouble. Santores strongly suspected the Caelians of having made the ship disappear, and he wasn't going to let up until he got to the truth.

On a purely theoretical level, Paul was mostly with the commodore on this one, too. Making a ship that size disappear without a trace was a good trick, and he was rather curious to see how the Caelians had pulled it off.

"That offer ends when my fighters get within firing range of Stronghold," Santores continued, his voice chillingly calm. "Once we engage, your choices will be to die or to surrender unconditionally."

"Wait for it," the copilot murmured, just loudly enough for Paul to hear.

"And in case you're thinking about opening random fire on the fighters," Santores said, "be advised that one of them is carrying your friend, benefactor, and deliverer: Cobra Paul Broom."

The copilot half turned, offering Paul a mocking smile. "There you go, Broom. Time to find out how much they *really love* you."

"You might be surprised," Paul told him, a hard knot in his stomach. So that was it. No negotiations, no subtle but earnest attempt to barter Paul's high standing with Governor Uy and the rest of the Qasamans for some kind of reconciliation. Santores had decided Paul's best use was as a hostage and human shield.

"Surprised how?" the copilot asked. "How much they do? Or how much they don't?"

Paul smiled. He had no idea what kind of response the Caelians were planning. There was no way to know whether Paul's forced appearance in the battle zone had caught Uy by surprise, or whether he'd anticipated Santores's ploy.

But whichever it was, this was very likely going to be good. "Neither," he told the copilot. "You're just going to be surprised, that's all."

The copilot gave him an odd look, and turned back to his board without further comment.

Three minutes later—barely enough time for Uy to even get out of bed, Paul thought cynically, let alone surrender—the six fighters reached the city.

They did a quick pass first, weaving a complicated pattern barely a hundred meters above the town. The section of the outer wall that had been breached during the Troft invasion was largely repaired, Paul noted as they went by, though there was still a small gap covered by the improvised barrier the Caelians had thrown together in the last days of the war. The fighters finished their swoop and swung wide of the city, then came back around and settled into a circular formation over the entire wall, completely surrounding the town, with their noses and weapons pointed inward. "Broom, this is Strike Leader," a voice came from the speakers. "Where does Uy live?"

"I couldn't tell you," Paul said. In fact, the governor's residence was simply the top floor of the government building, a structure he was pretty sure Santores had already tagged. But the idea of a top official living in the same building where he worked apparently hadn't occurred to them, and Paul was in no hurry to enlighten them.

"Soldiers of the Dominion of Man," Uy's voice came from the speaker.

Paul tensed. Against Santores's prediction—and all tactical logic—the governor had indeed chosen to answer the commodore's demand.

"You have no right to be within Caelian airspace," Uy continued. "You are ordered to leave at once, or you will be considered an invasion and met by force."

"Got him," a different voice cut in. "Three-omicron, three-story building. Three men standing in the middle of the roof."

Frowning, Paul glanced at the grid overlay on the helm's tactical display, found the proper square, and craned his neck to look out the canopy at the indicated spot. In the faint starlight he could see there were indeed three figures standing motionlessly in the center of the roof. He keyed in his telescopics, and in the zoomed-in view he could see that the three were Governor Uy and two of his Cobras, Popescu and Tammling.

Abruptly, Paul caught his breath as a sudden realization slammed into him like a brick.

He keyed in his telescopics?

But he didn't *have* telescopics. Not anymore. Not since Lij Tulu's MindsEye brain sifter had fried his nanocomputer.

Yet there was the scene, floating right in front of his eyes: an enlarged view of Uy and the two Cobras calmly gazing back at the circle of Dominion fighters.

Had Paul's nanocomputer somehow rebooted or repaired itself?

Surreptitiously, he lifted his arm from the armrest. But no. The limb was as sluggish as ever, with his muscles forced to lift the extra weight of his bone laminae without the accustomed assistance from his servos. Whatever had happened to his nanocomputer, it wasn't a complete restoration.

But then, the optical sensors were implanted in the skin around his eyes. Probably there was simply a direct linkage between them and his brain's optical center that bypassed the computer completely.

Uy and the two Cobras were still just standing there, making no attempt to hide or run from the Dominion force. Were they the bait for some sort of trap? Were they waiting for assistance?

Were they waiting for Paul to make a move?

Because they had no way of knowing that Paul had lost his full capabilities. For all they knew, he was ready to spring into action at their signal.

Their signal.

Frowning, he lowered his gaze a bit. Tammling was doing something with his hands. Not an attack, or the preparation for an attack, but just rotating them slowly back and forth at his sides.

No, not *rotating*. *Waggling*.

He wanted Paul to waggle his fighter's wings, or in some other way indicate which of the craft he was in.

Paul smiled tightly. *That* one he could do.

The pilot was peering out the canopy, his hand gripping the control stick. Carefully, Paul lifted his leg, pulled his knee to his chest, and kicked between the two seats, slamming his heel into the back of the pilot's hand.

It wasn't a hard blow—the hand and stick were just barely within reach. But it was enough. The fighter dipped slightly forward on its grav lifts before the pilot was able to pull the stick back into position. Paul just hoped Tammling had spotted it.

Certainly everyone else had. "*Damn* it," Strike Leader's voice boomed from the speaker. "Broom, you *horking* son of a—Three, Four: move in!"

Two of the fighters leaped forward, driving across the silent city toward the figures on the rooftop. The copilot grabbed at Paul's leg, but Paul had already pulled it back behind the seats. "Pull something like that again and you're dead," the pilot snarled, rubbing the back of his hand where Paul had kicked it.

"Six, you go too," Strike Leader added. "At least we know they won't try to shoot *you* down."

"Copy," the pilot said. He shoved the stick forward, and the fighter shot inward over the city. "And don't think you're not going to be the first one out," he added over his shoulder to Paul. "They start shooting, you're the first one dead."

"I doubt they're going to kill anyone," Paul said.

One of the Marines behind Paul snorted. "You got *that* right."

The first two fighters were nearly to Uy's building now, both aircraft slowing as they neared the spot. One of them angled down toward the roof, apparently planning to land, while the other angled up into a high-cover position. "If your friends try to play this cute—" Paul's pilot said.

And without warning, a brilliant blue light flashed from somewhere to the left, turning the red glow from the higher fighter's grav lifts into an explosion of yellow flame. Paul had just enough time to see the fighter spin away from the rooftop, crabbing sideways in a barely controlled slide, before it disappeared from sight behind some of the other buildings. Before anyone could react, a second shot blasted into the underside of the lower fighter, dropping it with a spine-wrenching thud to the rooftop.

"There!" someone snapped as Paul's fighter swung toward the spot the shots had come from. Something was on the move: an aircar, rising from the forest beyond the hulk of the Troft ship that had been toppled in the war. The aircar turned away from the city, heading for the deep Caelian wilderness—

And exploded into yellow fire as multiple shots of laser fire blasted at it from the circle of Dominion fighters. "Got him!" Paul's pilot bit out.

"Three, Four—report," Strike Leader cut in.

"Four: we're on the street. No casualties, but this bird isn't flying again soon."

"Three: on the roof, ditto on casualties. Marines now heading to—what the *hell*?"

"Three?"

"They're gone," Three's pilot snarled. "Where the *hell* did they go?"

Paul looked back at the building. The crashed Number Three fighter was disgorging its cargo of Marines onto the roof.

Three's pilot was right. Uy and the two Cobras had vanished.

"Down or in are the only options," a brisk voice put in. "We'll check the roof for trap doors."

"Six, get in close," Strike Leader ordered. "Fly low cover. One, Two: grid search of the streets. Five, high cover over—"

He broke off as another blue flash lanced out from the forest, slicing across the underside of one of the other fighters as it moved inward into the city. The fighter twitched up and sideways as if trying reflexively to get out of the line of fire, then angled sideways and slid into its own controlled crash onto the Stronghold streets.

Apparently, the weapon *hadn't* been on the fleeing aircar the fighters had destroyed.

Strike Leader had come to that belated realization as well. "*Damn* it!" he swore viciously. "Five, take out that damn laser."

"On it." The fighter that had been rising to high-cover altitude swiveled around on its grav lifts and laid out a withering pattern of laser fire into the trees where the shots had come from. "Where the hell are they getting heavy weapons from, anyway?"

"Use your brain, and check the data stream," Strike Leader growled. "That Troft hulk down there? One of the heavy lasers is missing. Looks like they pulled it out and got it working."

Paul pursed his lips. That much he'd figured out with the Caelians' first shot.

Though it was certainly fitting. He and the other Cobras had had to face those lasers. It seemed only fair that the weapons be pressed into service on the Caelians' side.

The question he still hadn't figured out was how the Cobras were aiming them so precisely. They couldn't be using the original Troft targeting rangefinders—the Dominion fighters would surely have picked up those emissions and realized the fleeing aircar was a decoy.

"Not anymore they don't," Five's pilot said grimly. "There's nothing alive or functional anywhere in that half-hectare now."

"Unless they've got another one," someone else warned.

"They don't," Strike Leader said. "Check the data stream—the survey team scan shows all the other lasers still in place. Marine Three: any luck?"

"Got a trap door here, all right," another voice came on. "Welded shut, of course. We'll get out our—what the *hell*?"

"What?" Strike Leader snapped.

"Shotguns," the Marine said, sounding more incredulous than angry. "They're firing *shotguns* at us."

"Damage?"

"Of course not," the Marine said. "In fact . . . this isn't even shot. It's some kind of liquid. Berries or something."

"Acidic?"

"Doesn't seem like it. Definitely not hurting our armor. Don't know what this was in aid of."

Paul cleared his throat. "If I were you, Marine Three," he called toward the flight deck microphone, "I'd pull my men back inside the fighter. It's about to get very unpleasant out there."

"Why?" Strike Leader demanded.

"Check the data stream," Paul said. "Look under *roseberries.*"

And then, it was too late. The roseberry packets the Caelians had fired at the invaders had been burst by the auto-fire lasers in the Marines' epaulets, as had probably a fair percentage of the berries themselves. But momentum had carried the juice the rest of the way to splash onto the Marines' armor.

And now, drawn through the night by the aroma of the juice, swarms of mothlike fluffers were converging on the rooftop.

The first warning was a sputter of laser fire from one of the Marines as the first wave of fluffers came within his epaulet computer's defensive kill zone. The rest of the squad had just enough time to turn around—

And suddenly, the rooftop exploded into a dazzling light show as the Marines' lasers went into full attack mode against the incoming swarm.

It was, Paul knew, likely to be a long battle. Uy would have instructed his gunners to be more than generous with the rose-berry juice, and the planet itself had far more fluffers than anyone wanted or needed. He was rather surprised that the lasers were able to target something that small, but the defense screen system seemed to be serving the Marines well.

The fluffers themselves were not even remotely dangerous, of course. The big problem—and a crucial fact that the Marines probably didn't know—was that blasting all those fluffers into charred puddles would quickly attract the attention of split-tails, jigsaws, and other, far nastier birds. Assuming the lasers' power supplies held out, the Marines would soon be neck-deep in combat without the Cobras having to lift a finger. If their power *did* dry up, even the intruders' fancy armor was going to be in trouble.

And if Uy decided the situation was desperate enough for him to risk bringing a few screech tigers into Stronghold, the Marines were going to be in a fight for their lives.

For now, though, they were well up to the challenge. "Marine Three: crouch and brace," Strike Leader ordered. "We'll toss some concussion grenades at your position and see if we can clear out some of the clutter."

There was another flicker of blue light, this one coming as a muted reflection from the buildings near where the other fighter had gone down. Paul silently counted to five; and suddenly, that area also erupted with a light show as the fluffers found a second target. Apparently, that Marines squad had run into a second batch of roseberry juice.

There was a muffled double *crack*. Paul turned back to the rooftop in time to see the crouching Marines begin regaining their balance after the concussion blasts, their epaulet lasers momentarily gone quiet. Again Paul started a silent count, and this time he got to ten before the automatic defenses began blazing away again as the fluffers who'd been outside the grenade's blast range continued on in.

Or maybe something else had joined the party. The flying things being shredded by the Marines' lasers seemed bigger this time. Paul keyed his telescopics and zoomed in on the view.

He'd been right. Those weren't fluffers, but split-tails.

And with split-tails on the scene, jigsaws and rainbirds wouldn't be far behind. "Strike Leader, you may want to pull your people out," he called toward the mike. "The fauna's been mostly a nuisance up to now, but from here on it starts getting dangerous."

"We appreciate your concern," Strike Leader growled sarcastically. "But my men can handle anything this planet can dish out."

"I wasn't just thinking of your men," Paul countered. "There are other people in Stronghold, including women and children. You're drawing dangerous creatures into the city—"

"*We're* not drawing anything anywhere," Strike Leader cut him off. "It's Uy and his Cobras who are doing this. If you want it to stop—"

He broke off with a yelp as another blue flash of laser fire burned into the underside of his fighter. "Five, what the *hell*—?"

"New contact—twelve-delta," one of the pilots snapped. "South of the landing field."

"Shred it!" Strike Leader ordered. His fighter was going down, Paul saw, with the same marginally controlled fall as the two earlier aircraft. Whoever was handling the laser attacks was achieving some impressive pin-point accuracy, doing just enough damage to the grav lifts to kill the upward buoyancy without dropping the fighters like rocks into the city. Paul's fighter swiveled toward the landing field, and he saw multiple trails of fire arrow out from both of its flanks. The missiles spread out toward the landing field—

An instant later, the entire field exploded into flame, tearing up the ground, ripping up the vegetation, and roiling the air into a distorted mushroom cloud.

"Hope you've got some more friends on the ground," Paul's pilot snarled over his shoulder, grim satisfaction in his voice. "Because that's it for *that* bunch."

"I've got plenty of friends," Paul assured him, his heart pounding. He was pretty sure he knew what had just happened down there, but there was no way to know for sure. If he was wrong, he had indeed lost some friends. "I'd be more concerned right now about *their* friends. Don't forget, you thought this was over before."

"So they played it cute." The pilot was yawing the fighter's nose gently back and forth, probably doing a more thorough sweeping of the area with the aircraft's active sensors. "Doesn't matter. We've got the high ground, and we've got superior firepower."

"You're missing my point," Paul said. "According to your data stream, there was only one heavy Troft laser unaccounted for. Only now you know there were actually *two* of them. What makes you think there aren't three? Or four? Or five?"

"Because it doesn't matter how many they are," the copilot said. "We'll find them, we'll ash them, and we'll ash whoever's firing them. We're going to win, Broom. It's just a question of how many people die before Uy gives up."

"Hell," Strike Leader's voice came over the speaker. "Got more of the damn juice over here. No, wait—this time it's small fruit. Fruit in juice, about the size of oranges, catapulted or something onto the canopy."

Paul frowned. *Juice and small fruit?* He knew the roseberry trick—the Caelians had used it against the Trofts during the invasion.

But roseberries were tiny little things. What was with this escalation to orange-sized fruit? He wasn't even sure which type of fruit the Cobras were using.

Unless...

It was risky, but at this point risky was probably all that Uy had. And it would be just like him to try something like this. "Commodore Santores, pull your men and ships back," he called urgently. "Right now. All of them. Call them back."

He counted off three painful seconds of silence. "Explain," Santores said.

Paul took a deep breath. "Your people did a quick survey of Caelian," he said. "I'm guessing they concentrated their attention on the area around Stronghold. If so, I guarantee you missed some of the animals. Including some that can rip right through the canopy, grav lifts, intakes, and anything else on these aircraft that isn't solid hullmetal. If you don't want your men and fighters turned into bloody scrap, you need to get them out *right now*."

There was another pause, this one lasting five seconds. "Strike Leader, what's your OpSit?" Santores asked at last. "Can you get home?"

"Yes, sir, we can," Strike Leader said. "But there's no need to pull out. Whatever this planet thinks it's got—or whatever ghosts Broom's jumping at—we can handle it."

"I'm sure you can," Santores said. "But we've seen what this planet can do, and I'm not willing to risk good men and irreplaceable fighters. Full withdrawal. Now."

"Yes, sir," Strike Leader said between obviously clenched teeth. "Okay, Marines, you heard the Commodore. Withdraw to your fighters, and make damn sure you don't bring anything live in with you. Five and Six, you still at full power?"

"Yes, sir," Paul's pilot confirmed.

"Affirmative," Five's pilot added.

"We'll need a tow to altitude," Strike Leader said. "Five, you're on Two and Four. Six, you're on One and Three."

"You sure you don't want us on high cover instead?" Paul's pilot asked. "What if the bastards have another laser stashed somewhere?"

"They won't fire," Paul said. "You're leaving, and that's all they care about." He hesitated, but he couldn't resist. "Governor

Uy understands that the ultimate goal is to win the game, not destroy the pawns."

"Yeah, keep laughing, Broom," Strike Leader growled. "It'll make for a better-looking corpse. Five, Six—get towing."

Paul had wondered how exactly the fighters were going to attach the requested tow cables, as well as how long the procedure would take. The answers: quite easily, and very quickly. He watched through the canopy in fascination as Five hovered over one of the downed fighters, unreeled a cable from its underside, and locked the end into a self-centering connector about a third of the way back from the bow. The fighter's grav lifts brightened as it raised the crippled aircraft into the air, swiveled around, and dropped another cable to the other damaged fighter. This second cable snaked around the side of the first aircraft and continued on another five meters, leaving the three fighters in a hanging stack where no one's thrusters or grav lifts would interfere with anyone else's. Even as Paul's fighter made its own second connection, the first hanging stack headed for the sky.

It was a remarkable demonstration of power, even given that the limping fighters' grav lifts were providing at least part of the upward boost. Still, it was yet another sobering reminder of how much more advanced Dominion's equipment and weapons were compared to those of the Cobra Worlds.

A medtech and gurney were waiting just inside the hangar bay hatchway when the Marine at the rear of Paul's fighter popped the hatch and lowered the ramp. Beside the medic, to Paul's surprise, was Commodore Santores.

"I must say, Broom, your Governor Uy is nothing if not imaginative," the commodore commented as Paul trudged his slow and painful way toward them. The Marines from the other fighters were streaming past on both sides, most nodding briskly to the commodore as they passed him. None of them spared so much as a glance for Paul. "I've been studying the data stream since you headed back," Santores continued, "and I haven't been able to learn what exactly you were so worried about with that fruit barrage. Would you care to enlighten me?"

"I expect Governor Uy would prefer to keep that a surprise," Paul said as he eased himself onto the gurney. In theory, his muscles should be getting stronger as they adapted to handling his body's extra weight. In practice, though, the advanced anemia induced by his bone laminae put a severe limit on how much exertion he could manage before fatigue set in. "But I do want to thank you for not uselessly sacrificing your men."

"As well as sacrificing the Caelians in Stronghold?"

"That, too," Paul said. "I'm sure there's a better and more peaceful solution to all this than an all-out invasion."

"There's certainly a more useful way for us to spend our time," Santores agreed, falling into step beside Paul as the medic guided the gurney through the hatch into the corridor.

Paul frowned. There'd been something in the commodore's voice... "I presume you're talking about negotiation?"

"That may come later," Santores said. "While you were battling roseberries and repurposed Troft lasers we had a visitor: the *Iris*." He looked down at Paul. "One of the *Dorian*'s courier ships."

Paul felt his stomach tighten. *No. Oh, no.* "Qasama?"

"Exactly," Santores said with grim satisfaction. "Captain Moreau's located the system, and made initial contact with the locals. As soon as the *Iris* reaches us and has been refueled, we'll be leaving."

Paul nodded, determined not to let his true feelings show. After everything the Cobra Worlds had been through—after all he himself had been through—and now all of it for nothing. "Well, good luck to you," he said, keeping his tone civil. "Bear in mind that they won't be nearly as docile or as easy to conquer as Aventine was."

Santores shook his head. "Aventine hasn't been conquered, Cobra Broom." But his eyes drifted away from Paul's as he said it, and there were fresh tension lines in his cheeks.

"You don't seem convinced of that," Paul suggested.

The tension lines deepened. "There's been some trouble."

"I know," Paul bit out. "I was there."

"I mean more trouble." Santores looked at Paul, then looked away again. "In fact, I may send you back to Capitalia with the *Iris* to see if you can help mediate things."

"Because that worked so well here?"

"Touché," Santores conceded. "Though to be fair, I didn't really give you much of a chance with Uy."

"Nice of you to at least point that out. What makes you think Captain Lij Tulu will actually listen to anything I have to say?"

"I'm thinking more along the lines of the Aventinian Cobras listening to you." Santores pursed his lips. "More specifically, your wife and son."

Despite the seriousness of the situation, Paul had to smile at that one. "You *are* joking, I presume," he said. "If they're on any kind of war footing—"

"*This is not a war!*" Santores snapped. "This is insurgency containment. Nothing more."

Paul waited until they'd gone another two steps down the corridor. "Fine," he said. "If they're on any kind of *insurgency containment* footing, they'll know better than to accept any deal or negotiation that involves a hostage."

"You wouldn't be a hostage."

"Wouldn't I? Lij Tulu would just set me down in Capitalia and let me go? Free and clear and unmonitored?"

"I'd give him orders to that effect."

"And he'd be required to obey them?"

"Of course."

"Even if he decided the situation warranted action outside those orders?" Paul persisted. "Because if that's not legal then you're telling me that Colonel Reivaro had explicit orders permitting his men to open fire on Archway's Cobras even if they didn't fire first."

Santores threw him another glare. "Of course the commander on the scene has final authority," he growled reluctantly. "Just as a field officer always has responsibility for making sure his men are in the safest and most defensible position possible, consistent with their orders and mission."

"Right," Paul said. "In other words, once you leave for Qasama, Lij Tulu can do anything he damn well pleases."

They'd made it to the elevator before Santores spoke again. "If you go back to Aventine, you may be able to save the lives of your family," he said as they entered the car. "If you go to Qasama, they'll be on their own. I'll let you decide."

"How about we add a third option?" Paul suggested. "We *both* go back to Aventine, you fix whatever mess Lij Tulu has made, and then we both go to Qasama."

Santores shook his head. "I'm pushing my timing to the limit as it is. If we're going to get Qasama ready in time, we have to start right away."

"What are we getting them ready for?"

"The same thing we're getting Aventine ready for," Santores said. "A Troft incursion."

Paul felt his stomach tighten. "Thanks, but we've already done that."

"Not like this," Santores said grimly. "The last invasion was for conquest. This one will be for annihilation." He looked down at Paul. "And like it or not, we're the only ones who can keep that from happening. Keep that in mind when you think you want to fight against us."

CHAPTER SIX

"Easy, now," Corwin said from over Jin's shoulder. "Use the narrow probe—that one there. Work it between the neckband and the mold, just enough to break the air seal. Relax—you're not going to lose it."

Clenching her teeth, feeling sweat running down her face from the heat of the kiln on the table to her left, Jin got a grip on the probe and placed its tip where her uncle had indicated. Putting as much pressure on it as she dared, she pried a small gap into existence—

And with a soft *pop*, the neckband section came free.

Jin grabbed for it as it dropped toward the table. But Corwin was already in position and caught the precious piece of freshly glazed ceramic on a thick hot pad. "There you go," he said approvingly as he set the pad carefully on the side table along with the others. "Perfect."

"Semi-perfect, anyway," Jin said, wiping her sleeve across her forehead and keying in her telescopics for a closer look at her latest masterpiece. At the spot where she'd dug in the probe she could see a slight imperfection. "What about that notch?" she asked, pointing. "Is it going to be a problem?"

"Shouldn't," Corwin said. "It's not going to create a fracture line, if that's what you're worried about."

"You sure?" Jin asked. This neckband piece and its fitted mate were going to be all that stood between an Aventinian Cobra and instant death. If there was the slightest chance it would fail in that job, they should scrap it right now. At the very least, they should figure out a way to test it.

Corwin might have been reading her mind. "I'm positive," he said. "I've already tested a couple that were in worse shape than that one. That ceramic's tougher and more forgiving than you might think, at least once it's cooled and set."

Jin smiled lopsidedly. Reading her mind, or more likely had already run through all the thoughts and doubts himself. "Good to know," she said. "So we give the kiln a few minutes to get back to temp and start the next one? Or did you want to take a break?"

"The Cobras don't get a break," Corwin reminded her grimly. "What are we up to, twenty-four sections?"

"Right," Jin confirmed. "Plus however many you'd already made before I got here."

"That was twenty sections," Corwin said. "Making a grand total of twenty-two complete neckbands."

Jin suppressed a sigh. Twenty-two neckbands, for the hundred forty Cobras in the province, and the three thousand elsewhere on the planet. All of whom were being fitted with Dominion loyalty collars as fast as Reivaro could turn them out.

But she and Corwin could only work so fast. Besides, if Aventine's response to the Troft invasion was anything to go by, most of the Cobras would probably be content to just wear their collars and watch from the sidelines, anyway. It was only the handful who decided to fight back that she and Corwin had to worry about.

And even twenty-two Cobras—if they were the right Cobras— could do a lot of damage to Reivaro's calm.

She peered at the kiln's temp reading. It was ramping up nicely, and should be ready by the time she finished mixing up the next batch of ceramic. "If we can get six more finished today—" she began.

And broke off as a sharp three-tone came from the computer in the far corner of the basement. "Uh-oh," Corwin murmured, hurrying across the room toward the computer. Jin keyed in her telescopics again, focusing on the display.

One look at the formation of incoming Dominion aircars was all she needed. "They've found us," she snapped. "Come on—we've got to get everything under cover."

"No time," Corwin said, spinning on his heel and hurrying

back. "No use, anyway—even a toy-store infrared would pick up the kiln. Time to minimize our losses."

"What do you mean?" Jin asked, shaking her fingers to loosen them up for combat. "We're going to fight them, right?"

"And get us both killed?" he countered. He jogged past her and the table to the wall behind the kiln. "Not to mention wrecking my house?" He did something to the wall—

And without even a squeak a door-sized section of the wall swung open, revealing a person-sized hole in the concrete and dirt behind it.

"As I said—minimizing our losses," Corwin said. "Get in while I grab you some neckbands."

"But—" Jin said, staring at the hole. When in the Worlds had he had the time to make *that*? Surely it hadn't always been there. Had it?

"No *buts*," Corwin cut her off, grabbing a cloth bag from a nearby chair and stuffing in as many of the finished sections as he could fit in. "That's about as many as I could do alone," he added, peering briefly at the number of sections left on the table. "Don't want them getting suspicious in either direction. Come on, come on—they'll be deploying any minute."

"I can't leave you here alone," Jin protested as he returned and gave her a not-very-gentle push toward the hole.

"You have to," he insisted. "You know as much about making these things as I do. You can start again somewhere else. Besides, you're a Cobra, and I'm a retired politician. You're the best one to carry on the fight."

"But I can't just let them have you," Jin said even as she let him guide her into the hole.

"They won't hurt me," Corwin assured her. "I'm not dangerous, I don't know anything, and there's nothing else they can gain by ruining my day. There's no room in there for two, and I certainly can't hide while you stay here. It's *my* house—they're going to believe you're here and I'm not?"

Jin took a deep breath. She hated every bit of this, but he unfortunately had all the logic on his side. "What do I do?"

"First, cultivate your patience," Corwin said. "The kiln should be close enough and hot enough to mask your heat signature, at least until it cools down. Hopefully, they'll be long gone by the time that happens."

"Then what?"

"You take these and get out," Corwin said, reaching past her to shove the bag of neckband sections into a deep alcove carved into the dirt above and behind her head. "On the far side of the room, between the furnace and the cleaning machine, there's another hidden door—the catch is on the right, same kind as this one. Not enough time for us to go that way now, but you'll be able to take the tunnel into the storm drain system. Don't go anywhere you ever liked to go—they'll probably be watching everything. There's an eyehole in this door here—see it?"

"Yes," Jin said, leaning out for a closer look. The hole was barely a slit, but once the panel was closed in front of her she should have a view of everything from the kiln to the stairway in the middle of the basement and a little bit beyond it.

"Okay," Corwin said, getting a grip on the edge of the door. "Make sure it's clear before you come out." He forced a smile. "Good luck, Jin, and be safe."

The Marines were good, all right. There was no loud bashing in of doors or windows, no clumping thunder of heavy feet overhead, no faint and distant shouted commands or warnings or threats. Corwin had barely made it around to the other side of the table and resumed mixing the ceramic when a trio of armored and helmeted men suddenly appeared on the stairway, their eyes sweeping the room. "Don't move!" one of them barked, the words coming faintly to Jin through the door. "Hands where we can see them!"

Corwin froze. "Which one?" he called back.

"Which one what?" the Marine demanded as they continued the rest of the way down the stairs. The first Marine headed straight toward Corwin, while the other two circled back behind the stairway, checking out the part of the basement back there. All three had laser pistols belted to their sides, Jin noted. Odd that they still bothered lugging the weapons around, given that practically everyone on Aventine surely knew about their epaulets by now.

"Which one do you want me to do?" Corwin said. "I can't freeze and lift up my hands at the same time."

"Yeah, you're real funny," the Marine growled. "Hands behind your back. *Now.*"

"Whatever you want," Corwin said, setting down his spoon

and putting his hands behind his back. "I don't suppose you have a warrant or anything."

"Martial law, Governor," a new voice came from the stairway. "Remember? We don't need warrants."

And as Jin's stomach tightened at the bitter memories associated with that voice, Colonel Reivaro walked down the stairs into view.

"Is that you, Colonel?" Corwin called, his lip twitching as the Marine fastened cuffs around his wrists. "Do you make a point of showing up for all the small fish your men bag for you these days?"

"You're hardly a small fish, Governor," Reivaro said, looking around as he strode toward the prisoner. "This way, please."

The Marine caught Corwin's shoulders and turned him around to face Reivaro. "And if you're impressed that *I* came to visit..." Reivaro paused and half turned toward the stairway. Jin keyed in her audios, caught the sound of three more sets of footsteps. Another Marine appeared, followed by a second—

Followed by Captain Joshti Lij Tulu himself.

Jin felt her mouth drop open. As far as she'd heard, Lij Tulu hadn't left the orbiting *Algonquin* since declaring martial law across Aventine. Corwin's face was turned away from her, but the stiffening of his back indicated that he was as surprised as she was.

But he'd been a politician once, and he'd once told Jin that the first skills a politician developed were quick thinking and even quicker recovery. "Why, Captain Lij Tulu," he greeted the newcomer. "This *is* an unexpected pleasure. Colonel Reivaro and I were just debating what size fish I was. I concede the argument."

"As well you should," Lij Tulu agreed, looking around the basement. His eyes rested on the kiln a moment, then returned to Corwin. "Your name alone raises you to giant trout status. *This*—" he gestured toward the kiln "—brings you to the very top rank of Cobra World traitors."

"I don't know how a harmless hobby makes me a traitor," Corwin said mildly. "I've been experimenting with ceramics for years. You can ask anyone."

"We have," Lij Tulu said. "Unfortunately for you, we've also seen your latest project in action. Are you aware that under Dominion martial law we could try you for sabotage and accessory to sedition this afternoon, convict you by this evening, and execute you by dawn tomorrow?"

"Sounds like Dominion martial law is barely one step removed from complete *lack* of law," Corwin said. "Consider me impressed or intimidated or whatever. Shall we move on to the *or*? Threats like that usually have an *or* chasing after them."

Lij Tulu smiled thinly. "You should probably know that I've dealt with my share of glib politicians back at the Dome. The *real* Dome, not this pathetic colonial caricature you have here. You should also know that I despise every one of them. I suggest you not try to sound like them."

"Point taken," Corwin said. "Can we get to the *or* now?"

For a long moment Lij Tulu just stared at him. "*Or* you can help me defuse the situation that's threatening to boil over into the streets of Capitalia," he said. "The Cobras will listen to you. Your niece and great nephew in particular will listen."

"I'm honored that you think so," Corwin said. "However, I'm sure they'll listen even harder to Paul Broom, whom you already have in custody. Why don't you try to persuade *him* to calm things down? Oh right," he continued, as if the thought had just occurred to him. "He *did* try to calm things down, at the Yates Fabrications plant in Archway. You rewarded his efforts by gunning down three Cobras in cold blood."

Reivaro stirred—

"It was hardly cold blood," Lij Tulu said, interrupting whatever the colonel had been planning to say. "But I'm not surprised that the reports you've heard were biased. As to Cobra Broom, yes, he's still in custody. But he's no longer in the Aventine system. Commodore Santores took him aboard the *Megalith*, which has gone to Caelian."

"Really," Corwin said, sounding intrigued. "Not exactly the vacation spot of the Cobra Worlds, so they'll probably be back soon."

"I doubt it," Lij Tulu said. "You see, we had a visitor yesterday: the *Iris*, one of the *Dorian*'s courier ships." He paused. "Which brought us the coordinates for Qasama."

Jin felt her breath catch in her throat. Barrington Moreau had found Qasama?

If Corwin was as stunned as Jin by the news, he recovered much faster. "So you're assuming the commodore will be heading there next?" he asked calmly. "Well, best of luck to him. I hope he hasn't bitten off more than he can chew."

"The *Megalith* chews just fine, thank you," Lij Tulu said. "But let's not drift from the point."

"I'm not," Corwin said. "The point, or the topic anyway, is biting off more than you can chew. You want me to help defuse things? Fine—we can talk about that. The bigger question is whether *you've* bitten off too much, and if so what *you're* willing to do in the cause of peace and domestic tranquility."

"The Dominion is at war, Governor," Lij Tulu said coldly. "So are you, or will be soon. My orders are to bring you to a war footing as quickly as I can, and I intend to do precisely that."

Corwin shook his head. "Then we have nothing further to discuss."

"Oh, on the contrary—we have a great deal to discuss." Lij Tulu shifted his eyes to Reivaro. "Take him to my shuttle. Then find everything he was using for those—" he jabbed a finger at the handful of neckband sections Corwin had left on the table "—equipment, raw materials, everything. Collect it, catalogue it, and take it to the Dome."

He turned and strode toward the stairs. His two Marine guards fell into step in front of him, while Reivaro, Corwin, and Corwin's guard fell into step behind him. The other two Marines waited until the rest of the parade had left, then began a methodical search of the items on the shelves and cabinets. From above her, Jin heard the indistinct sound of Lij Tulu giving more orders, followed by the thudding herd of footsteps she'd expected earlier as the Marines up there started searching the rest of the house.

She checked her nanocomputer's clock circuit. Just after three in the afternoon. The Marines hadn't bothered to turn off the kiln, possibly because they didn't realize it was still running. Sooner or later, though, they were bound to notice, and since Lij Tulu had ordered them to bring *everything* associated with Corwin's neckband factory they would probably consider the kiln to be on that list.

For the moment, the thing was too hot to be easily moved. Once they shut it off, though, it wouldn't take long for it to cool to the point where it would no longer shield her from whatever infrared sensors they had in those helmets. She had until then to figure out what to do.

Whatever she came up with had better be good. She hadn't witnessed the brief battle between the Marines and Cobras in

Archway, but she'd been through all the reports Corwin had been able to pull together, and it was obvious that the lasers built into the Marines' epaulets had both power and pinpoint accuracy. The only weakness she could see was that the lasers couldn't fire straight up or down, which still left the question of how an attacker could get into one of those positions in the first place without getting killed.

For the next half hour she watched the Marines search through cabinets, bins, and stacks of odds and ends. Along the way they collected tools, bags of ceramic powder, molds and, of course, the neckband sections Corwin had already made. All of it was duly noted, catalogued via some internal system, and then added to a growing pile near the base of the stairs. The sounds of footsteps from overhead gradually decreased as the Marines up there finished going through the rest of the house, and Jin kept expecting a few of them to come downstairs and assist the two already working the main center of contraband.

But no one appeared, and gradually it dawned on Jin that while this raid was important it was surely not the only situation the Dominion forces in Capitalia had on their plate. As the Marines finished their assigned task upstairs they were apparently leaving the house and heading elsewhere.

She'd assumed Lij Tulu's warning to Corwin that the situation was about to boil over onto the streets was simply overdramatic hype. Maybe it wasn't.

The Marines were nearing the end of their search when one of them discovered that the kiln was still on and shut it off.

And with that, the clock was ticking.

Jin watched as they tackled the final two cabinets, listening to the silence from overhead. If the situation elsewhere in Capitalia was as dire as she hoped, maybe these last two would decide to take their collection of loot and head back to the Dome. The kiln would be too hot to move for at least another hour, and Reivaro didn't strike her as the type to let two of his men sit idle when there was other work to be done. They could always come back later and get the kiln if they really wanted it.

Unless, of course, the two Marines didn't bother to tell the colonel they were finished.

It didn't exactly fit the image of the stolid, professional Dominion warrior that Reivaro and the rest of the Dominion force had

tried so hard to project. But Jin had seen enough organizations
to know that there were slackers in every group. She could certainly see how these Marines might prefer hanging around an
empty house, obeying their orders to the letter, instead of going
outside to face whatever mischief Lorne and the other Cobras
might be hatching.

The Marines finished with the cabinets and gave the room
a final visual sweep. Jin pressed one ear to the door, mentally
crossing her fingers as she keyed her audios to full power...

"Guess that's it," one of the Marines said. "Want me to go
get the cart?"

"In a minute," the other answered. "What about that?"

Jin shifted her attention back to the eyehole just in time to see
the Marine's hand come up and point to the kiln. She turned
her ear back to the panel. "—forever to cool down," the first
Marine groused.

"Oh, I don't think so," the second said, a malicious edge in
his voice. "Hang on—there was a bucket in one of these cabinets
over here."

Frowning, Jin looked back through the eyehole. One of the
Marines was heading toward the set of cabinets beside the deep
utility sink while the second one watched. "What are you going
to do?" the second one's voice came faintly.

"You want it cooled down?" the first called back. "Fine. I'll
cool it down."

"You pour water in it, you'll wreck it," the second warned.
"Probably split it wide open."

"So? The colonel just said to collect it. He didn't say what
condition it had to be in."

Jin mouthed a curse. So much for her hope that they might
be slackers.

So much, too, for the security of her hiding place. Left to cool
down on its own, the kiln could have masked her presence for
another half hour or more. With cold water dumped into it, that
cover would vanish within a couple of minutes.

Desperation, her late father had often said, was the true mother
of invention. By the time the Marine had located and filled the
bucket Jin had a plan. Not a great one, but it was the best she
could come up with.

The second Marine had taken a couple of cautious steps back, taking up a position about five meters away from the kiln and the table it was sitting on. Carefully, Jin put a target lock on the inside edges of each of his epaulets, where the sensors and targeting computer were located. Then, easing one hand up to rest lightly against the wall just above her head, she got a grip on the door's release with the other. The Marine with the water reached the table, raised the bucket over the top of the kiln, and poured a hefty slosh onto the hot metal.

And as a violently hissing cloud of steam billowed into the air, Jin popped the release and shoved open the door, dropping onto her butt with her legs stretched straight along the basement floor. Giving the wall behind her a shove, leaning back to give the push extra strength, she lurched out of the hole and slid on her back under the table and squarely beneath the legs of the closer Marine.

With the roiling white cloud obscuring the back wall and the hidden door, it was doubtful either Marine even saw was happening until Jin slid out from under the table and into their view. But if they were surprised, they were also quick on the uptake. Jin had barely come to a halt beneath the closer Marine when the more distant one snapped out some kind of warning, the exact word muffled by his helmet and the hiss of the steam.

But Jin was also ready. She triggered the antiarmor laser in her left leg, and her nanocomputer instantly took over her body's servo network, swiveling the leg to blast a pair of rapid-fire shots into the Marine's epaulets. The same movement of Jin's leg also shoved the right leg of the Marine standing over her, nearly knocking him off balance as the water bucket went flying off to the side. Even as he tried to get away from her, she lifted her right leg, cocked her knee to her chest, and shoved upward against his crotch, sending him flying straight up. His head slammed into the ceiling, shattering the acoustic tile and thudding hard into the joists and subflooring. He dropped back, flopping onto the floor like a dead fish, and lay still.

The other Marine was charging forward, fumbling at the strap of his holster, when Jin leveled her right hand and sent a full-power arcthrower blast at his helmet.

He staggered, his head and shoulders sheathed in a brilliant coronal discharge. Jin fired again, and this time he twitched violently and then collapsed to the floor, sections of his helmet still sparking. Jin scrambled to her feet, fingertip lasers at the ready. But he didn't move.

Neither did the other one. His head and neck seemed straight enough, but there was no way to tell through the helmet and armor what kind of damage he might have taken. He could be severely concussed, or paralyzed.

Or dead.

For a moment she stared at the figure, her stomach tensed in a painful knot. This was *not* what she'd signed up for when she'd become a Cobra.

But there was no time for regret or reflection now. The two Marines had surely been linked to the overall Dominion communication network, and reinforcements were probably burning their way toward her. She had to get out, and fast.

The first task was to retrieve the bag of neckband segments Corwin had entrusted to her. Then, splashing her way across the wet floor, she grabbed the bucket the Marine had used to douse the kiln and hurried over to the stairway and the pile of contraband the intruders had collected. She eyed the pouches of powered ceramic longingly, but there was no time to gather all of that together.

But she could at least retrieve the rest of the neckband segments. She scooped them into the bucket, stuffed her bag on top of them, then hurried across the room to the furnace. The emergency escape route Corwin had mentioned was well hidden, but knowing what the catch looked like enabled her find it within a few seconds.

This door was thicker than the one on her hidey hole, with more mass of insulation attached to its back. Probably to make it harder for infrareds to pick the door out of the rest of the basement wall, she decided. Beyond the door was a narrow, rough-walled tunnel no more than a meter and a quarter high leading outward from the house. Wondering again when her uncle had put in all this cloak-and-dagger stuff, she worked her way into the tunnel and sealed the door behind her.

Whenever he'd done it, he'd taken the time to do it right. The door fit perfectly into its frame, not letting through even a glimmer for her opticals' light-amps to work with. She switched to infrared, found it almost as useless as the light-amps in the uniform temperature of the dirt around her.

Still, with the heat radiation coming from her own body, the infrareds *did* give her about a half-meter bubble of faint visibility. It wasn't much, but it should at least keep her from whacking her head on any protrusions that might be sticking out of the low ceiling along the way. Holding the bucket close to her chest, her knees forced to a ninety-degree angle, she headed down the tunnel in an awkward squatting walk.

The floor was as rough as the walls, with plenty of lumps and the occasional root or large rock or other hazard. But it was mostly flat, and with the IR glow of her body she was able to see most of the obstacles before she could trip over them. In the silence her breathing seemed extra loud and harsh, and her back tingled with the eerie expectation of the moment when the Dominion's backup force found the hidden door and started shooting. She had to keep reassuring herself that it would surely be another few minutes before they could arrive, land their aircars, get inside, and start a search. As long as she kept going, she ought to be reasonably clear before the shooting started.

Her back didn't care about logic. It continued to tingle.

She'd gone thirty meters when a hint of light appeared.

But not from behind her. From *ahead* of her.

She stopped short, her breathing sounding even louder as the sound of her footsteps ceased. The light was still faint, but it was slowly getting stronger. Someone was coming toward her.

She frowned. No, not *toward* her, but perpendicular to her. As the light intensity increased, she could make out a wall blocking the end of her tunnel about thirty meters ahead. A curved wall, made of a dirty-white ceramic or concrete. The light seemed to be coming from somewhere to the side of that wall.

And then, it clicked. The curved wall she was seeing was the far side of one of Aventine's storm drain tunnels. The light was someone moving toward her along the tunnel.

She clenched her teeth, painfully aware that she was in about the worst possible location for a fight. Her sonics were all but useless in an enclosed area like this—too much of the blast would bounce straight back at her—and the distance to the drainage conduit ruled out use of her arcthrower. Corwin's tunnel was straight enough for her to use her lasers, but line-of-sight weapons worked equally well in both directions, and in a tunnel that wasn't even tall enough for her to stand upright she would have roughly zero chance of dodging whatever the person or persons at the other end of the target gallery chose to throw back at her.

Still, if she couldn't maneuver, she could at least make herself as small a target as possible. Setting the bucket on the ground behind her, she eased herself down onto her back, her left leg and antiarmor laser pointed forward toward the approaching light.

Which was getting closer. *And* moving quickly: she could now see the slight variations in intensity caused by the movement of the owner's arms as he or she strode along, and she could see that the stride was just short of a full-fledged jog. He was in a hurry, and in Jin's experience people on urgent business often didn't pay as much attention to their surroundings as they should. *Fish in a barrel*, the old saying whispered through her mind.

She just wished she knew which of them was the fish.

The light was getting closer, and her audios could now pick up the sound of footsteps. There were at least three people, possibly more.

She took a deep breath and lifted her leg slightly. If they passed her by, great. If instead they turned into her tunnel, she would have to wait until all of them were in sight before opening fire. There was a flicker of a shadow, and a hunched-over human figure carrying a flashlight was suddenly framed in the opening.

And without pausing he stepped up into Jin's tunnel and headed straight toward her.

She clenched her teeth. Behind him, two more figures came into view and joined him in her tunnel. For the moment, the light was aimed mostly at the floor, which should leave Jin still in shadow. But that wouldn't last. Holding her hand up to block out most of the glow, she keyed in her light-amps and tried to see the person behind the glare. If that was a Marine helmet back there, she would have no choice but to take the first shot.

And then, the light swung upward, as if the person was checking to see if the ceiling was this low the whole way. For a second a muted backwash of light reflected off his face—

Jin caught her breath. "Lorne?" she called softly.

All three figures froze. The light swung down again—*"Mom?"* Lorne's voice came.

Jin exhaled in a huff. "Yes," she said. She scrambled to her feet, remembering just in time not to try to straighten all the way up, and grabbed the bucket. "I thought you were the Dominion," she said, hurrying toward them.

"Not yet, but they're not far behind," Lorne said, coming forward and meeting her halfway. "We got a tip they were going to raid Uncle Corwin."

"Too late," Jin said as they came to a stop facing each other. Her son's face was thin and tired-looking, she noted, but otherwise he seemed in good health. "They've already got him."

Lorne's gaze flicked over her shoulder. "Are they still there? Maybe we can break him out."

Jin shook her head. "Sorry, no. They're long gone."

"Damn." Lorne pointed at her bucket. "Are those his neckbands?"

"Yes, everything he had," Jin said, holding it up. "But we need to get out of here. I made kind of a racket getting out."

"On a couple of Marines, I hope," Lorne said. He threw another look past her, then abruptly spun around and headed back the way he'd come. "Too late," he called softly to the others, who had remained by the drainage conduit.

"You know these others well, I hope?" Jin asked quietly.

"Very well," Lorne assured her. "Badj Werle and Dill de Portola from DeVegas province. You remember them, right?"

"Yes, of course," Jin said, some of her anxiety fading. Not only had the other two Cobras been solid friends to Lorne, but they'd also done serious damage to the Troft occupation forces during that conflict.

She swallowed. And speaking of the Trofts... "Listen, there may be some more bad news. According to Lij Tulu, Barrington Moreau and his ship—"

"When were you talking to Lij Tulu?" Lorne asked, frowning over his shoulder.

"He was with the raiding party," Jin told him. "He and Reivaro both. Lij Tulu was trying to persuade Uncle Corwin to help keep the peace here."

Lorne snorted. "Like *that's* going to happen."

"That's what Uncle Corwin said, too," Jin said. "Lij Tulu also told him they've found Qasama."

She sensed his shoulders stiffen. "Did they get the location from Dad?"

"I don't think so," Jin said. "He said Barrington Moreau found them. Though I suppose he could be lying."

"Probably not," Lorne said sourly. "That would explain the courier ship we spotted coming in early yesterday. *And* why it took off again later in the day. Chintawa thinks it was going to Caelian—he said Lij Tulu told him Santores has gone there."

"That's what Lij Tulu told Uncle Corwin, too," Jin confirmed.

They'd come up to the other two Cobras now. "Well, if he's a liar at least he's a consistent liar," Lorne said.

"Persistent, too," Werle said. "Any idea what they even want Qasama for?"

"Not a clue," Lorne said. "Nothing good, though. Well, that one's out of our hands. I just hope the Trofts left Omnathi enough resources to take on the Dominion, too."

Jin winced. From the looks of Qasama when she, Paul, and Lorne had left, she seriously doubted it.

The floor of the conduit, as Jin had already surmised, was a few centimeters below the level of the one Corwin had dug. He'd probably done that on purpose, she realized as Lorne helped her down, in hopes of keeping water from coming up into his basement when the drainage system was doing its proper job. The ceiling was a few centimeters higher here, and there was more elbow room, but she could tell it wasn't going to be an easy trip. "You have someplace safe we can go?" she asked as they headed back the way Lorne and the others had come.

"I don't think any place in Aventine is really safe anymore," Lorne said. "But we've got a spot that should work for a while." He half turned and flashed Jin a tight smile. "Trust me, Mom. You're going to love it."

"And we should stop talking now," Werle warned. "Sound carries way too well in these tunnels."

Silence descended on the group. Jin kept her focus on her footing, and on trying to come up with some plan for fighting back against the Dominion. She tried very hard not to think of what Lij Tulu might be doing to Corwin.

She tried equally hard not to wonder what Captain Barrington Moreau and his war cruiser were doing to Qasama.

CHAPTER SEVEN

The data stream flowed past Captain Barrington Moreau's eyes, bringing him the latest news on the status of the *Dorian*'s repair work, the state of health of his crew, the conditions on the planet below, and the short-range and long-range data on the greater solar system around him. Anything Barrington wanted was there at his fingertips.

And he couldn't focus on a single bit of it.

Three days. That was how long it had been since Jody Moreau Broom and her companions took the *Squire* and headed out into Troft space, searching for clues as to the fate of Broom's brother Merrick. During every one of those days Barrington had thought about the flicker-mine net the *Hermes* had run into and wondered if Broom and the *Squire* had run into another of those deadly traps. If she had, she was already dead.

And even if she made it to her target coordinates unscathed, what then? A single Dominion courier ship against a Troft planet with even moderate defense capabilities was a recipe for quick and certain annihilation. She needed him and the *Dorian*, and she needed them to be waiting at her back when she arrived.

But the window for coordinating their efforts was rapidly closing. With Commander Kusari and ten other officers and crewmen still on the ground, Barrington had no choice but to stay here at Qasama.

"Captain?"

Barrington blinked away the data stream and turned. Commander Ling Garrett, the *Dorian*'s first officer, was standing beside the command station, a troubled look on his face. "Yes, Commander?" Barrington said.

"A question, sir," Garrett said. "I wonder if I might have a word with you in private."

"Of course." Barrington glanced around CoNCH, spotted Commander Castenello conversing with some of his staff at the tactical command station. "Commander Castenello, you have CoNCH," he called as he stood up.

Castenello looked back, a slight frown on his face. But he merely nodded. "I have CoNCH, aye, Captain," he called back.

The Duty Officer's room was only a few meters away from the command station, tucked along the side of CoNCH's upper level. Barrington led the way inside, eased through the cramped space around the small desk, and sat down. "Go ahead," he invited Garrett, gesturing the other to one of the fold-down seats.

"Thank you, Captain," Garrett said as he sat down. "I have concerns about Jody Broom and the others of her expedition."

"As do I," Barrington said. "What do you suggest we do about them?"

Garrett visibly braced himself. "I respectfully suggest, sir, that we go after them. Right now."

"With some of our crew still recuperating on Qasama?" Barrington shook his head. "You know we can't do that."

"We may have to risk it, sir," Garrett said doggedly. "I've been looking through the report the *Hermes* brought this morning. If Commodore Santores leaves Aventine according to his current plan, the *Megalith* could be here before our injured would be ready to rejoin the *Dorian*."

Barrington pursed his lips. Santores *might* head out immediately. But there was a good chance he wouldn't. *Hermes*' report had detailed rapidly deteriorating relations between the Cobra Worlds and the Dominion task force. Santores might decide to let Barrington handle the initial prep work on Qasama while he stayed to try to smooth things over.

He pulled up the data stream. Still, Garrett was right. The Qasamans' projected recovery time for the rest of the *Dorian*'s injured crewmen did indeed overlap the *Megalith*'s possible arrival time.

"Right now, you're the commander on the scene," Garrett continued. "You can modify or even ignore orders as you deem necessary for unanticipated situations. But once Commodore Santores arrives, you won't have that luxury."

Or the legal protection, Barrington thought cynically. But it was how military officers had to think these days. "What about the *Dorian*? We're still not back to full fighting capability."

"I've checked the repair logs, sir," Garrett said. "Most of the remaining work should be finished in six or seven days, well short of the ten it'll take to reach Broom's coordinates."

"And if we run into another flicker-mine net along the way?"

"Whoever owns that system probably won't expect traffic to arrive from Qasama," Garrett said. "The chances that they would set up a trap along that vector seem unlikely."

"That still leaves Commander Kusari and the other ten men in Qasaman hospitals," Barrington said. "We'd have to bring them back aboard to finish their recuperation."

"I think we'd do better to leave them where they are, sir," Garrett said. "There might be complications from their surgery we wouldn't know how to deal with."

Barrington felt a frown crease his forehead. Pressing for action was one thing. Pressing for action without the *Dorian*'s engineering officer was something else entirely. "What aren't you telling me, Commander?" he asked carefully.

Garrett hesitated. "I think you should talk to Commander Kusari yourself, Captain," he said, his eyes not quite meeting Barrington's. "Perhaps you could ask for his thoughts on the subject."

"Yes," Barrington said, studying Garrett's face. "All right." Reaching to the desk's small control panel, he keyed the comm.

He'd set up a secure radio link to Kusari as soon as the engineering officer came out of surgery, but at this point he wouldn't put it past Omnathi to have figured a way through the encryption. He'd have to make sure he didn't say anything he wouldn't want the Qasamans to hear.

There was the soft tone of a connection. "Commander Kusari," Kusari's voice came briskly. "Good morning, Captain."

"Good morning, Commander," Barrington said, tapping briefly back into the data stream. It was indeed mid-morning in the Qasaman city of Azras. "I was calling for a status report. How soon do you think you'll be ready to return to duty?"

There was just the briefest pause. "Are you planning to head off after Jody Broom, sir?" he asked.

Barrington frowned. How in the world had Kusari gotten *that* from Barrington's question? "Let's talk about your leg."

"It's much improved," Kusari said. "Thank you for asking. Sir, I'd like to request permission to stay here for the immediate future."

"In the hospital?"

"Or just on Qasama in general," Kusari said. "I'd like to help them design defenses for their planet."

Barrington shot a look at Garrett, noting the stiffness in the first officer's face. Creating actual weapons and defenses had never been part of the plan. "They have their own people for that, Commander."

"People who have never faced an orbital bombardment, sir," Kusari reminded him. "They don't even know the parameters of the weapons they'd be facing."

"If we do our jobs right, we'll stop the Trofts before they get that close."

"And if we don't?" Kusari countered. "If something gets through, people will die. A *lot* of people."

"That's not our concern."

"With all due respect, Captain, I believe it is."

Barrington fought down a sudden flash of anger. "Are you fit for duty or not, Commander?" he asked. "Do I have to order you to answer?"

There was a half second's pause. "I would ask you not to give me such an order, sir."

Barrington stared at the speaker, his anger disappearing into a sudden hollow feeling in the pit of his stomach. What the *hell* was going on?

The Qasamans had saved Paul Broom's leg after the Trofts had been thrown off the planet. He'd repaid them with unshakable loyalty, to the point of going under Lij Tulu's MindsEye brain sifter rather than give up Qasama's location. They'd saved Kusari's leg—and probably his life—and suddenly he was hinting that he would disobey orders rather than leave them helpless against the coming assault.

Was this just natural gratitude toward their rescuers? Or was there something more sinister going on? Some drug or hypnotic associated with the Qasamans' medical technique that bent their patients' mind that direction?

If so, had Kusari been the only target? Or had all of his men undergone the same conditioning? And if so, was that going to be a problem down the line?

Specifically, was it going to be a problem if and when the Trofts started bombarding surface targets and the *Dorian*'s crew was ordered to ignore the destruction?

And suddenly, the idea of taking his ship on a rescue mission far away from Qasama and the possibility of confused loyalties was looking better and better.

He tapped the mute button and looked up at Garrett. "Personnel check," he murmured. "See if we can do without the men still down there."

"We can, sir," Garrett said quickly. Too quickly. "Minus those ten men, we'll still be running at ninety-six percent efficiency."

"Without them *and* Commander Kusari?"

Garrett's lip twitched. "Eighty-nine percent."

Barrington scowled. Eighty-nine percent after a major battle was acceptable. Eighty-nine percent after the damage had been mostly repaired and the crewmen healed wasn't.

But the thought of those ten men—plus the other ninety who'd been healed, plus the *Dorian*'s engineering officer—all thinking more about Qasama's safety instead of concentrating on their jobs wasn't much better.

With a final glare at the speaker, he unmuted the radio. "Very well, Commander," he said, striving to keep his voice cool and emotionless. "Our orders are to prepare Qasama for combat, and guiding the preliminary work is a legitimate part of that. Will you need the assistance of the ten men still down there with you?"

"They could be very helpful, sir, yes," Kusari said. "At least four of them need to stay for medical reasons anyway. Fortunately, the Qasamans should have enough manpower to do the job. What they need is information and guidance, and we can supply that."

"Understood," Barrington said, gesturing to Garrett. "Under the circumstances, I think we'll head out after Ms. Broom, after all."

"I believe that would be the best use of the *Dorian*, sir," Kusari said.

"I'm glad you agree," Barrington said. "Before we go, I'll transmit some messages for you to relay to Commodore Santores when the *Megalith* arrives."

"Yes, sir," Kusari said. "Thank you, Captain. I'll try to have some preliminary concept plans ready before you go. Give you some idea what Shahni Omnathi and I are thinking about."

Barrington scowled again. Omnathi. He should have known the Shahni would be right there on top of this.

In fact, maybe he was a little *too* much on top of it. "Good," he said, doing a quick search of a particular section of the data stream. There it was. "As they say, if you set the queen upon the ramparts..."

"The bishop will bow to the knight," Kusari said without hesitation. "With your permission, Captain, I'll get to work on those plans."

"Go ahead, Commander," Barrington said. "Moreau out."

He keyed off the comm. "I presume that was his proper countersign?" Garrett asked.

"It was," Barrington said, eyeing the other closely. "You already knew about this, didn't you?"

Garrett's lip twitched. "I'd seen some signs," he admitted. "Nothing I could put my finger on. I thought it would be best if you talked to him directly. Maybe forced the issue of staying."

"And forced it in private, without any of my other officers able to put in their own thoughts or suggestions?"

"Especially those who would vehemently oppose this decision," Garrett said. "They would have insisted Kusari be brought aboard *and* that we stay here until the *Megalith* arrives." He nodded toward the comm. "If the Qasamans are playing with their drugs again, that could have been a problem down the line."

"It still might," Barrington said heavily. "But whatever Omnathi's playing at under the table, he can hardly have any objections to our backstopping Jody Broom." He took a deep breath. "Let's give some orders, Commander. I want the *Dorian* ready in three hours."

"Yes, sir," Garrett said, standing up briskly. He sidled to the door and left.

And with that, Barrington knew, the die was cast. The minute Garrett's orders hit the data stream it would be an official part of the *Dorian*'s log, open to scrutiny and speculation by everyone aboard.

As well as by people who would never be aboard his ship. Hard-eyed men in the future, perhaps, who Barrington might face across a table at a Board of Enquiry.

But there was no point in worrying about that now. His new

mission was to go to Jody Broom's aid, ideally stirring up the Trofts in the process, while at the same time fending off those of his officers who would see this as an opportunity to damage the captain's reputation in favor of their own glory and that of their patrons.

And speaking of Commander Castenello, it was time Barrington went back into CoNCH and resumed his watch. Castenello's expression as he saw the new orders would be priceless. Almost worth the fallout that was sure to follow.

Barrington could hardly wait.

"...then just key off the safety lock—" Plaine flipped up a transparent cover on the *Squire*'s portside gunbay control board and pressed the button beneath it "—and you're good to go. Auto-fire *here*; manual *here*; passive and active sensors *here* and *here*."

Leaning over Jody's shoulder as they stood just inside the gunbay door, Kemp gave a low whistle. "Wow," he said. "As easy as that, huh?"

Plaine swiveled around in his seat, a look of strained patience in his eye. "*Yes*, it's that easy," he said. "You—what do you call yourselves, anyway? Cobra Worldians?—you haven't had much experience with sophisticated tech, have you?"

"We're Aventinians," Kemp told him. "People from Caelian are Caelians. It's pretty easy once you get the hang of it. And, yes, we have plenty of tech." He paused, and Jody could visualize a slightly brittle twinkle in his eye. "It's just that most of it is Troft."

Plaine's face hardened, just noticeably. Then, the tension cleared and he smiled. "Of course it is," he said. "I guess none of you got the notice about trading with the enemy." He swiveled back to the board. "Okay, let's go through it again. We shut it down like *this*—"

"Kemp?" Smitty's voice came from the intercom speaker. "Where are you?"

Plaine reached over and keyed the mike. "Portside gunbay," he said.

"Tell him I need him in CoNCH," Smitty said. "Got a rogue electrical glitch to track down that requires two sets of eyes."

"You want Jody, too?" Kemp called toward the intercom.

"No—the second set of eyes needs infrared capabilities," Smitty said. "Just at your convenience."

The intercom clicked off. "Which means *right now*, I assume?" Plaine suggested.

"Pretty much," Kemp said reluctantly as he stepped out of the gunbay. "You might want to come anyway, Jody—they might need an extra set of hands. We can finish this later."

"No, that's okay," Jody said as casually as she could manage. To be left alone with a Dominion Marine . . . "I could use the extra rundown—my memory for this kind of thing is terrible."

"Well . . . okay," Kemp said, even more reluctantly. "I'll be back as soon as I can."

He turned and headed back down the curved corridor. "He's not happy about leaving you alone with me, is he?" Plaine asked dryly.

"He's a little overprotective at times," Jody told him. "He'll be okay."

"Because he's right, you know," Plaine continued as if she hadn't spoken. "A Dominion Marine and an average young woman without a scrap of military training." He cocked an eyebrow at her. "You *haven't* had any military training, have you?"

"We just fought a war against the Trofts," Jody said stiffly. "We all learned a little something about fighting."

"I'm sure you did," he said, clearly not believing it. "You hungry? Thirsty?"

Jody blinked at the sudden change in subject. "I'm fine, thanks."

"Don't mind if I get myself something, do you?" Plaine asked. Without waiting for her to answer, he swiveled his chair around and got up, the movement forcing Jody to take a quick step backward to avoid being bumped into. "We usually have a pretty good selection in these bays," he continued, going to a shallow cabinet on the wall beside the hatch. He thumbed the catch and swung the cabinet door open. "You sure you don't want something?"

Jody leaned toward him to peer around the door. Half of the cabinet's rows of shelves were empty, probably consumed by the gunbay's previous occupant. The rest of the space was taken up by orderly rows of meal bars and bottles of a pale red liquid, everything clamped to the back wall. Distantly, Jody wondered what kind of violent maneuvers the ship was capable of making that would require such precautions. "The different packaging indicates different flavors," Plaine said, pointing at the bars. "That red stuff looks scary, but it's just water with a broad spectrum of added vitamins and minerals and a little added taste. Want one?"

"I'm fine," Jody repeated.

"You can see how much longer Herczeg could have held out," Plaine commented, popping one of the bottles from its clamps. "He's the Marine you nabbed on the way to Qasama. But we figured that if we distracted you enough we might be able to get the *Squire* turned around. Didn't work, but it was worth a try. Hey, you want to see a magic trick?"

Jody frowned. She'd never seen Plaine bounce around so many topics in so short a time before. Had he been dipping into some secret stockpile of drugs or something? "No thanks," she said. "Can we just get back to—?"

Right in the middle of her sentence he lobbed the bottle gently over her head and out the hatchway.

Automatically, Jody's eyes flicked to the arcing bottle. An instant later, her brain caught up, belatedly warning her that the bottle was probably a diversion and wrenching her eyes back to Plaine.

Too late. She was still refocusing when he gave the back panel of the cabinet a sharp jab with the heel of his right hand. The panel split down the middle and flew open with spring-loaded speed, revealing another, equally shallow compartment behind it.

Only instead of food and water, this compartment held a row of compact handguns fastened to the back with more of the quick-release clips.

Jody gasped, her brain freezing. *Betrayed!* Just as Smitty had predicted, Plaine had taken advantage of Kemp's absence to turn the situation to his advantage.

As Smitty had predicted, and Kemp had warned, and Jody had confidently dismissed. She was a Cobra now, she'd assured them, and she could handle anything Plaine could throw at her.

But in that first second, caught completely by surprise, Jody's whole mind and body had gone paralyzed. Reflexes that Kemp and Smitty had—reflexes she'd thought she'd mastered, as well— simply weren't there. She tried to put a target lock on Plaine's forehead, changed her mind and decided to aim for the weapons instead, then realized that she had no choice but to shoot to kill and tried to focus on Plaine again.

But it was already too late. With a single smooth motion, the Marine grabbed one of the weapons, swung around toward Jody—

And spun the weapon a hundred eighty degrees around, pointing the muzzle at his own stomach and pressing the grip into her hand.

For a long, painful moment neither of them moved or spoke. "Is this what you were trying to prove?" Plaine asked quietly. "That the minute I had a chance I would grab you as a hostage and force a standoff?"

"There was some thought of that," Jody conceded, her voice shaking with adrenaline reaction.

"We tried that, remember?" Plaine said. "It got Herczeg hammered and halfway to dead." He snorted. "Besides, I thought we all agreed that we're in this together. My life depends on you, and vice versa." He considered. "Well, maybe not so much the versa. Your Cobras do pretty well for themselves. How does that feel?"

Jody blinked. With so many right-angle turns coming in such rapid-fire she'd completely forgotten that her hand was currently wrapped around the grip of a gun. "Okay," she said cautiously, consciously relaxing her fingers. "Finger grooves are a little too far apart for my hand."

"No problem." Plaine was still gripping the laser's barrel. Now, he let go. "Hold it up."

Jody did so. The weapon was heavier than she would have guessed just by looking at it. "There's a little indentation on the upper curve of the grip, just above the vee of your thumb and forefinger. See it?"

With an effort—was he trying to distract her again?—Jody lowered her eyes from his face to the laser. "Here?" she asked, pointing to the spot with her left forefinger.

"Yes," Plaine said. "Left thumb on the indentation; left fingers curled around the top of the chamber; right hand with fingers and thumb spaced however feels comfortable; right forefinger alongside the trigger. Got it? Now, press with your left thumb."

Jody squeezed the indentation. To her surprise, the grip softened beneath her right hand, then reformed to fit the positioning of her fingers. "When it feels good, let go with your left hand," Plaine instructed.

Jody eased back on the indentation and felt the grip solidifying again. She lifted her right-hand fingers away from the weapon, then tried moving them to different parts of the grip. The grip remained solid. "Nice," she said, letting her fingers settle back into the newly reshaped grooves. "I guess this one is mine now?"

"Once you learn how to shoot it," Plaine warned. "I mean that. If you're not willing to put in the necessary work, I don't want you carrying it around. I doubt any of your friends do, either. Giving an amateur a gun is about the most stupidly suicidal thing you can do."

"I'll remember that," Jody said. "Speaking of which . . . ?" She hefted the gun, which was still pointed at him.

"No worries—the Dominion teaches stupid-suicide avoidance," Plaine said. "No pack."

Jody turned the weapon over. Sure enough, the power pack slot in the grip was indeed open and empty. "Ah," she said.

"But these *do* have packs," he continued, gesturing to two of the other weapons in the hidden arsenal. "So your little catch-release experiment is still valid, since I still *could* have proved your friends were right about me if I'd wanted to. I just didn't want to get shot during the demo. You ready to learn how to shoot one of those things?"

"I thought we were going to start with the big guns," Jody said, nodding toward the gunbay control board.

"What, you think we can't do both?" Plaine countered. "Lower deck's probably the best place to set up a range—nice straight corridors, and no one's down there." He pursed his lips. "Except me, of course. Lucky for me I can't accidently walk out of my cabin into the line of fire."

Jody eyed him closely. Was he hinting that he wanted the lock removed? Because she knew Kemp would never agree to that. "If you're looking to have that changed—"

"Not at all," he assured her. "I've seen nervous Cobras. I'd rather you keep me tucked away, nice and secure, where you won't always be jumping at shadows." He leaned back to the control board and tapped the intercom switch. "Whoever was waiting to jump me once I proved how dangerous and stupid I am, you can relax—we're done here. Ms. Broom now has a request." He gestured toward the mike. "Ms. Broom?"

Jody took a deep breath. She didn't need to learn how to use any of these Dominion hand weapons, of course—she already had plenty of her own firepower at hand. But it couldn't hurt to have another string to her bow. "We need to find something we can use as a laser target," she said. "Sergeant Plaine is going to teach me how to shoot."

CHAPTER EIGHT

"No," Merrick said, shaking his head. "They're not coming out. Probably because they never went in."

"I do not think that conclusion, you can yet make it," Kjoic disagreed. "On what is it supported?"

"On the fact that nothing has changed over there in the past three days," Merrick said, nodding in the direction of the Troft building. It wasn't visible through the trees, of course, but he knew exactly where it was. Not to mention every tree, shrub, rock, and Troft guard around it. "Plus the additional fact that they're still going nuts searching the forest," he added. "If they had Anya and her parents, they would know that once they were conditioned they would be able to find me. Anya would, anyway. Once they have her, all of their flying around is a waste of time."

"You assume they will have learned that such prisoners were associated with you," Kjoic pointed out.

"Of course they'll know that," Merrick said. "Remember Dyre Woodsplitter? He's the one who betrayed me after a couple of shots of their juice, even knowing that it could hurt Anya." Who he was betrothed to, and clearly cared a great deal for. Merrick tried not to think too hard about that part. "He's sure not going to go shy on them once they've actually got her in hand. Especially since the alternative to the war drug is probably some kind of torture."

"Trof'tes do not use torture," Kjoic said. "Still, chemical truth evokements are said to be very unpleasant." For a moment he

93

seemed to ponder Merrick's analysis, his radiator membranes flut-tering. "If we accept this as working truth, what do you propose as our next action?"

"Nice term," Merrick said. "*Working truth.* I'll have to remember that one. Well, logically, if Anya isn't in there, she's somewhere else. If we want to get any help from her or her parents, we need to find her."

"A self-evident statement, it is one," Kjoic said, a little dryly. "Yet the forest and the planet, they are very large."

"But we can assume she's not just wandering around at random," Merrick said. "She'll want to find me as much as I want to find her. That means she'll go someplace where I'm likely to look."

"Such as the spacecraft wreckage?"

"That's one possibility," Merrick agreed. "Or there's the spot where you and she camped out while I went ahead to Svipall. I assume the shelter she made for that night is still there?"

"It was intact when we left," Kjoic said doubtfully. "But both journeys are long. Would she be able to safely travel that far?"

"Probably depends on whether she and her parents are still together," Merrick said. "Regardless, those are the two best places to start."

"Perhaps." Kjoic peered at the trees blocking their view of the warehouse. "Do you propose that we leave immediately?"

"I propose that *I* leave immediately," Merrick corrected him. "One of us should stay here and keep an eye on the building."

Kjoic's radiator membranes gave an extra-large flutter. "Joined forces, it was done for a reason," he reminded Merrick. "Breaking the alliance is not a useful plan."

"We're not breaking it, just bending it a little," Merrick said. "We may be at a dead end here and should try something new."

"Then let us travel together."

"No, because we may *not* be at a dead end," Merrick said. "If I'm wrong, and Anya or her parents come out, one of us needs to see what they're up to. They could start hunting for me right away, or they could pause to set up a trap. Either way, we need to know about it."

Kjoic digested that one. "If we do this, how do we later find each other?"

"We'll use this spot as our rendezvous," Merrick said. "If I find them, I'll bring them here. If they leave the base, you follow them, find out where they're going, and then return here. Whoever gets here first waits for the other."

"This forest is not safe," Kjoic pointed out. "Especially for you, who will likely be traveling the greater distance."

"I've spent a fair amount of time here," Merrick assured him. "I've got a good feel for whatever it can throw at me."

Which wasn't even close to the truth, of course. There were undoubtedly many nasties lurking in the shadows that he and Anya hadn't yet run into.

But he *was* confident that his Cobra equipment and reflexes could successfully take them on.

Kjoic's membranes flared once and then settled back onto his upper arms. "I do not think this is wise," he said. "But I agree that both objectives are important, and there are only two of us to accomplish them. If you are convinced that you must seek Anya elsewhere, you may go with my permission."

"Thank you," Merrick said, resisting the urge to point out that he didn't really need the Troft's permission to do anything. "I'll be back as quick as I can."

"Travel with caution." Kjoic pointed to the laser in Merrick's belt. "And be wary of firing at night. The flash, it can be seen for a great distance in darkness."

"I'll remember that," Merrick promised. "You be careful here. I'll see you in a couple of days."

The patch of bambus spikes in Dewer's Hollow where Anya had built their last shelter was several kilometers west of Svipall and the Troft warehouse. Merrick traveled that direction for about two kilometers, just in case Kjoic decided to follow him. But there was no hint that anyone was back there, and a quiet hundred-meter backtrack at the end of the two kilometers turned up no sign of Kjoic or any other tail. A distinctive tree towering over an equally distinctive hollow log made a convenient place to stash the laser, which Merrick didn't especially want to lug around and which he definitely didn't need.

And with that, he was ready to head for his true objective: the underground rebel hideout to the north where he and Anya had slept for a few hours after their hang-glider escape from the Trofts nearly two weeks ago.

Back then, the hideout had been deserted and empty. Now, Merrick suspected he would find things to be a bit different.

Also back then, it had taken him and Anya a solid three days' worth of travel time to get from the hideout to the wrecked ship and then to Svipall. But their speed had first been limited by Anya, and later by the even slower Kjoic, whose speed had later been further reduced by his self-inflicted leg wound.

But this time Merrick was alone, with no civilians to protect or Trofts to hide his true abilities from.

Those first two kilometers, the ones heading west, had taken him thirty minutes. The next two, heading north at full Cobra servo speed, took him five.

It was risky, and not just because he might run squarely into some nest of predators before he knew they were there. The vegetation was nearly as hazardous, with thorns, snarls, hidden insect nests, and other obstacles. On top of that, there were still Troft aircars wandering around, and while the earpiece Kjoic had given him provided some early warning, Merrick was hardly ready to put his full faith and trust in the device. That meant having to split his attention between the ground and the sky, leaving open the possibility that a threat from one direction would nail him while he was focused elsewhere.

He'd gone barely ten minutes when the odds caught up with him.

He had just passed through the edge of a small clearing and was giving the bit of open sky above him a quick look, when he ran smack into a group of raccoon-sized animals with long claws and quill-covered backs. He raked his legs across the quills of the first two before he even knew they were there, and the next pair managed to take a swipe at him before he could leap up into the nearest branch out of their reach.

Fortunately, the animals seemed as surprised by the encounter as he was, which slowed their response to his sudden presence. The pack seemed to be fairly small and contained, but Merrick nevertheless traveled the next hundred meters in the air, jumping from tree branch to tree branch, just in case the first group was part of a bigger herd. Just as fortunately, though that bit of luck didn't occur to Merrick until later, the raccoons didn't seem to have any particular tree-climbing skills. That could have been trouble, given that naturally arboreal creatures would have little trouble overtaking a human who had to pause on each branch to locate the next likely tree and limb.

As it was, he nearly ran into a group of fafirs before he dropped back to the ground. Three of the hairy ape/wolf creatures started after him, but a low-power fingertip laser burst into each discouraged them from further pursuit.

Merrick's boots had taken most of the damage from that first group of quills, and his speed, agility, and weaponry had gotten him through the rest unscathed. Still, there was a lesson there to be learned. From that point on he made sure to travel slowly enough to keep an eye on what was ahead.

It was the middle of the afternoon when he reached the hideout.

He stayed at the edge of the clearing for several minutes, not moving, his infrareds and audios at full strength as he watched and listened for any sign of human or Troft activity. But he could see nothing, and all the animal and insect sounds seemed normal. Finally, he eased his way to the hollowed-out rock that hid the entrance and moved it carefully out of the way. Again he paused, this time crouched at the edge of the shaft, watching and listening. Still no signs of life. With one final look around, he set his feet on the ladder fastened to the side of the wood-lined shaft and climbed down.

The hideout's construction was very basic. There were two short tunnels leading off in opposite directions from the bottom of the shaft, each tunnel leading to a smallish room. Both rooms had full wood-plank ceilings, but only partial wall shoring, which gave the impression that the place had been abandoned before it was fully completed. Both rooms were empty, with any equipment or food stores long gone, all of it looking exactly like it had the last time he was here.

But this time wasn't last time.

With a final look at the second room, Merrick returned to what he had mentally tagged as the main room: the larger one where he and Anya had caught a few hours of restless sleep on the hard dirt floor. He gave that room a final, careful survey, then stepped to a part of the side wall that had been more completely shored with the floor-to-ceiling wooden planks than most of the rest. "Hello," he said conversationally. "I'm Merrick Hopekeeper. I know you're there, and I assume you're listening. Please open the door so we can talk."

Nothing happened. It was, he thought, with a touch of dark humor, like talking to a wooden wall. "If you don't come out,

I'll open the door myself," he continued. "If you have doubts that I can do that—and you probably do—I suggest you ask Anya Winghunter."

Again, no sound and no movement. "Okay, I guess we do it the hard way," he said. "I'll give you to the count of ten."

He began counting aloud, three seconds per number. He'd reached eight, and was debating with himself whether he should start with his lasers or his sonics, when the section of wood gave a small tremble, and then swung silently outward on concealed hinges.

Framed in the center of the doorway was Hanna Herbseeker, Anya's mother. "Anya said you were clever," Hanna said disdainfully. "We didn't believe her."

"You should always believe in family," Merrick said, looking past her shoulder at the room behind her. It was only dimly lit, but quick boost of his light-amps showed that it was considerably larger than the one he was standing in. Unlike the rest of the hideout, its walls were lined with shelves that seemed to be well stocked with packages of various sizes and shapes. "And you shouldn't lie to your allies," he added.

She sniffed. "We have no allies."

"The way you treat people, I'm not surprised," Merrick said. "Shall we go inside? I've had a long walk, and I'm guessing you have chairs in there."

Hanna hesitated, then silently stepped back and moved out of the way. Merrick walked through the doorway, half expecting someone to try to jump him.

The expected attack didn't come. And as he came fully into the room, he saw why: aside from Hanna there was only one other person in the big, sprawling room.

Anya.

She was seated at a table halfway back toward the side wall. Her hands were folded on the table, her head bowed, her eyes focused on her hands. Merrick keyed up his infrareds, trying to read her emotions from her facial blood flow pattern. But while the pattern was definitely there, he couldn't tell whether the underlying feeling was anger, embarrassment, or shame. "Hello, Anya," he called, turning past Hanna and heading toward her. "Glad to see you're all right."

"I am likewise relieved to see you," Anya said without looking up.

"Your enthusiasm is gratifying," Merrick said with more bit-terness than he'd really intended. "So you want to tell me how this all went down?"

Anya remained silent.

"Fine," Merrick said. He looked at Hanna, then back at Anya. "I'll tell *you*, then. Show your mother a little more of my clever-ness."

"Leave her alone," Hanna growled. "She did not betray you."

"That first night we came here you were expecting to find people inside," Merrick said, ignoring her. "Which seemed ridiculous to me, given how empty and unequipped the place was—it wasn't set up to be anything but a temporary hiding place. Only there *were* people here, weren't there? They just weren't where I could see them. I assume you waited until I was asleep and then sneaked in the rabbit hole here for a strategy conversation."

"There was no one here," Anya said, her voice so quiet that Merrick had to notch up his audios to make out the words. "Only a few notes."

"Notes identifying Svipall as the place to go, I assume?"

Anya's throat worked. "They said my parents had gone to Svipall to investigate what the masters were doing there."

"Which you could have told me when I woke up," Merrick bit out. "We could have skipped the whole crashed ship and Kjoic detour and gone straight to Svipall."

"But the notes were written before the crash," Anya said, a note of pleading in her voice. "You had already said the crash was important. Commander Ukuthi had told me you were wise and that I was to follow your leading."

Merrick clenched his teeth. "Withholding information is *not* what following my leading means. That doesn't explain why the hell you didn't tell me after we got to the ship instead of pulling that lame 'we're from Svipall' thing on Kjoic."

"I was afraid of him," Anya said. Her eyes were glistening with tears now, Merrick saw. "I was afraid if I told you he would hear."

"You didn't have any trouble telling me other stuff that he might have had trouble with," Merrick countered. "What it boils down to was that instead of dropping him off someplace harmless and being rid of him, we ended up hauling him to the exact place we *don't* want a Troft looking over our shoulders."

"Leave her alone," Hanna ordered.

Merrick spun to face her, his hands curling into laser-firing positions. The last thing he wanted right now was interference from an ice-hearted woman who'd let her own daughter be taken offworld into Troft slavery. "I told you—"

"She was not afraid of the Trofts," Hanna cut him off. "She was afraid of *you*."

The words hit Merrick like a slap across the face. "Afraid of *me*?"

"She was told you were wise," Hanna said. "She was told you would lead her to victory. But you have not done so."

"I've been here less than three weeks," Merrick bit out. "How long have *you* been fighting the Trofts?"

"She was told you were wise," Hanna repeated.

Merrick turned back to Anya, wanting very much to remain furious at her even as he felt his anger and frustration fading away. He'd been so focused on trying to figure out how to complete his mission—and to keep himself and Anya alive while he did it—that he'd never stopped to really think how this all probably looked from her point of view.

And he should have. Because there'd been glimpses into her thoughts and hopes if he'd bothered to pay attention. Her borderline hero worship had been obvious. Her dismay whenever he admitted out loud that he wasn't always right was jarring. Her blind willingness to go along with anything he suggested should have been disquieting.

He'd learned the necessity for instant obedience from the Qasamans during the war. But Anya's obedience went far beyond that.

Huffing out a sigh, Merrick crossed to the table and sat down beside her. Her shoulders tensed, and her facial blood flow changed subtly, but otherwise she gave no acknowledgment of his presence. "I don't know what Commander Ukuthi told you, Anya," he said quietly. "It's true that I have some skills and abilities. It's also true that I've been through a war against some of these same Trofts. But I'm not perfect, not by a long shot. When it comes to figuring out what the Trofts are up to, I'm just as lost as you are."

He paused, waiting for a response. But she remained silent. "The point is that we're in this together," he continued, "and it's going to take both of us to make it through. We're wiser together than we are alone."

"Wisdom counts for little if there is no action," Hanna said accusingly. "Action counts for nothing if it's too late."

"What action are we not doing that's too late?" Merrick asked, looking back at her.

"The action of rescuing Anya's father," Hanna said. "Ludolf Treetapper has been in Svipall these three days. He has not emerged nor been heard from since he entered."

Merrick chewed at the inside of his cheek. He'd hoped that the presence of Anya and her mother meant that none of the family had tried to infiltrate the Troft hornets' nest he'd stirred up. But apparently Ludolf had ignored the risks. "How did he get in?"

"I don't know," Hanna said impatiently. "It was in the confusion of your escape—that's all I know. We must focus on the fact that his life may be in danger."

"Yeah, being a stranger in Svipall these days isn't much fun," Merrick agreed grimly. "And you have no idea how he got in?"

"Why do you care about that?" Hanna countered. "You were able to get in. Why do you need to know his method when you have your own?"

"Because my method probably won't work anymore," Merrick said. "After my last visit, I'm guessing they've tightened their security." In fact, he knew that they had, having just watched them running new perimeter foot patrols and low-altitude aircar patterns.

But this wasn't the time to bring up what he'd been doing for the past three days. It especially wasn't the time to talk about who he'd spent those days with.

"Then you must find another way in," Hanna insisted. "Our first task is to save him."

"No, our first task is to not blindly rush into anything," Merrick said, trying to think. He didn't have the faintest idea how he was going to get into Svipall again, or how he would find Ludolf once he got there. And whatever he did, he absolutely didn't want to do it with Hanna looking over his shoulder. "Let's start with the size of this resistance group of yours. How many people can you pull together on short notice?"

With his infrareds still on, he could see the blood flow in her face change. "Enough," she assured him. "What do you need?"

"Enough people for an excursion through the forest to get some weapons," Merrick said, watching her face closely. "I'm guessing you should bring twenty or more. Can you do that?"

"Of course," Hanna said, her infrared pattern not changing. "When do you need them?"

"*I* don't; *you* do," Merrick corrected. "Anya's going to take you to the wrecked Troft ship about fifteen kilometers south of here."

Hanna's eyes flicked briefly to Anya. "What do you expect for us to find there?" the older woman asked.

"Hopefully, something you can use against the masters," Merrick said. "Most of the lasers have probably already been removed, but there should be stunners and nets, or whatever they use to corral wild animals. Some of the smaller lasers might have been missed, too—you'll have to check and see. It won't be great, but it should be better than those bersark bombs you used the last time around."

"The bersark was effective everywhere we used it," Hanna said stiffly. "If more had come to our cause—" She broke off, her pattern changing again. "New weapons will be of great use."

"Good," Merrick said. Her pattern changed as the images of the painful past faded back into memory.

But the pattern she now settled into wasn't the same one that had been there when she told him about how many fellow rebels she had on call. That suggested that one of those times—then, or now—may have been a lie. And somehow, he doubted that the part about new weapons being useful had been the lie.

And suddenly, he was tired of this dance. Anya's blind trust in him was bad enough, but at least he had a Cobra's weaponry and some combat experience. For her to put the same trust in her parents, after all they'd done to her, verged on the insane. Especially since they'd clearly sat on their hands for the past eight years.

It was time to finally call Hanna's bluff. "On second thought, it would probably be better if Anya and I both accompany you there," he said. "Between the masters and the forest itself, there's a lot of danger out there. The bigger the group, the better."

Another flicked look between mother and daughter. "Unless the numbers are great enough to draw unwelcome attention from either quarter," Hanna said. "Don't concern yourself with us."

"Then allow me to concern myself with Anya," Merrick said. "I made a promise to look after her."

"I understand," Hanna said. "And I agree. Instead of going with me, she shall go with you."

Merrick scowled. That was *not* where he'd wanted this to go. "You'll need her more than I will," he said firmly. "The ship isn't easy to find."

"We will find it," Hanna said, equally firmly. "As for you, you're still a stranger on our world. Your lack of knowledge of our language and customs may yet betray you." Her throat worked. "Besides, Ludolf Treetapper's life may even now be encircled by danger. Further delay in his rescue could prove fatal. You must go to him. And Anya Winghunter, for her own safety, must go with you."

Merrick scowled. Ploy and counterploy; and he'd come out on the short end of the stick. Not only would Anya's presence slow him down along the way, but he wasn't at all sure how she'd react when she found out that he and Kjoic were working together. "What about your journey back to the villages to gather your people?" he asked. "We should all go together at least that far."

"No," Hanna said. "I know these forests far better than you. I'll be in no danger." She looked at her daughter. "But it's unbecoming to bargain with her as if she was a mere tool. Anya Winghunter? What of us do you choose to accompany?"

Anya looked at her mother, then at Merrick, then back at her mother. For a few seconds the two women locked eyes. Then, Anya lowered her gaze and she turned back to Merrick "I will go with Merrick Hopekeeper," she said, her facial infrared pattern shifting. "If he'll have me."

"Of course I'll have you," Merrick said, suppressing a sigh. So much for that approach. "Fine. So Anya and I will head back to Svipall and see what we can find out about Ludolf Treetapper while you gather your people and head to the wrecked ship."

"Agreed," Hanna said. "When and where shall we meet?"

"Let's say at the home of Alexis Woolmaster, where you took me after my accident," Merrick said, running a quick calculation. "We should be ready four days from now at sundown. Will that give you enough time?"

Again, Hanna's facial pattern shifted. "Yes," she said. "I will leave at once."

"It might be better to wait until morning," Merrick pointed out. "It's starting to get late out there."

Hanna shook her head. "Time grows short, and Ludolf remains in danger. I leave at once." She raised her eyebrows. "As do you?"

"I thought we'd wait until morning," Merrick said. Pretending to spend the night here would give Anya a safe place to wait while he tailed Hanna to see where she went and who she met up with.

"No," Hanna said, an edge of anger creeping into her voice. "I've told you already: Ludolf Treetapper is in danger. Surely a powerful warrior like you does not fear the nighttime forest."

"At this point a few hours are unlikely to make a difference."

"But they might?"

Merrick shrugged slightly. "They might," he conceded. "I was just thinking of your daughter and *her* safety."

"I do not fear for my daughter when you are at her side," Hanna said. "Anya?"

"I agree," Anya said quietly. "And my mother is right. I fear more for him than I do for myself."

Privately, Merrick conceded defeat. Hanna was on her own now, just as she'd wanted. She could round up her fellow rebels, hide alone in a village somewhere, or anything in between.

And Merrick meanwhile was exactly where he'd started this mission: working with Anya to eliminate the Troft threat. "Fine," he said, nodding toward a pair of backpacks leaning against the wall. "Anya, is one of those packs yours? If so, get it and let's go."

"One is indeed hers," Hanna confirmed, crossing to the backpacks. "Come, Anya Winghunter."

Merrick watched as they settled the packs over their shoulders, frowning as a sudden thought struck him. Anya had told him it usually took two to three men to move the stone that blocked the entrance, and even then it usually required bersarkis to give them the necessary strength. Certainly that fit with Merrick's own assessment of the stone's weight.

So how had Hanna and Anya handled it by themselves? "Once we're all out, we'll need to put the stone back in place," he said, focusing on Hanna. "I'm surprised you two were able to manage it by yourselves."

"We didn't use that entrance," Hanna said as she buckled her pack's straps across her waist. With her back to him her face was hidden, but her voice showed no indication of lying. "There's a tunnel entrance which is easier to use, though it's in a more dangerous part of the forest." She turned back around, frowning at him. "Yet you came in that way alone?"

"The masters gave me special bersarkis patches in Svipall," Merrick said, holding up his arm. "They're not pleasant to use, but they do the trick."

"I see," Hanna said, peering across the room as if by concentrating she could see through the material of his sleeve. "Do you have one you could give me? My people would wish to study it."

"Sorry," Merrick said. "I only have one left, and I'll need it to move the rock back."

"There's no need," Hanna said, gesturing toward a tunnel that led out of the north end of the room. "As I said, there's another way. You can leave with me."

"Leaving the shaft completely open to view?"

"We won't need this place again."

"Not a good idea," Merrick warned. "In my experience, resources shouldn't be abandoned unless absolutely necessary. Anyway, I already told you I can seal it."

Hanna's lips compressed, her facial pattern changing. "Very well," she said reluctantly. "Travel safely, Merrick Hopekeeper. Protect my daughter. Find my husband."

"I'll do my best," Merrick said. "You watch yourself, Hanna Herbseeker. We'll see you in four days."

"I'll be there."

Merrick paused at the top of the shaft and gave the forest a careful visual sweep. Everything looked just like he'd left it. He climbed the rest of the way out, waited for Anya to join him, then returned the stone to its place. "Where's the other entrance?" he asked, looking into the forest.

"There," Anya said pointing. "Back in the forest. Why do you ask?"

"I was thinking we might want to follow her for a ways," he said. "At least get her to a road or decent path."

"No," Anya said. "She must go her own way. We must go ours."

"There isn't any secret army of rebels, is there?" he asked gently. "She and your father are all that's left."

Anya's shoulders hunched. "I don't know," she said quietly. "She tells me there is an army. You tell me there isn't. I know no truth anymore."

Merrick winced. Anya had experienced a lot of jolts and disappointments since arriving back on her home world. But even after being sent into slavery by her parents, there was clearly a part of her that still wanted to believe in them.

Maybe it was *because* they'd sent her to slavery. Maybe she needed to believe there had been some meaning and some purpose to those twelve years of exile.

If so, it was hardly up to Merrick to destroy those last lingering hopes. "I don't know any truth either," he said. "Your mother may just be playing it careful to protect her group. It's not like *we're* telling her everything about us, either."

"Yes," she said, her eyes still lowered. "We're going to look for my father now?"

Merrick sighed, feeling worse than ever. "Yes," he said, taking her arm and heading across the clearing. Even at their best speed they weren't going to reach Svipall before nightfall. "Look, I'm sorry I yelled at you in there. I was angry and...and things aren't going as well as I'd hoped when I agreed to come here. I'm making this up as I go, and I need your help."

She was silent another moment. "I'll do whatever I can," she said at last. "Just tell me what you need."

"Right now, I need to fill in some gaps," Merrick said. "Tell me everything you know, starting with what happened back at Alexis Woolmaster's house."

"There's little you don't already know." She shot him a glance, looked quickly away again. "My father took me away soon after my mother led you to Svipall. He said that you would surely open a path into the village, and that we would then enter the masters' area and obtain their secrets. My mother joined us, and we waited."

"Until I escaped?"

"Yes," Anya said. "But the hoped-for path didn't appear. We waited and watched, and then my father told us to wait while he searched on his own for a way inside. He promised to be back in two hours. But he wasn't."

"When did you come here?" Merrick asked, nodding back toward the hideaway.

"We waited two days," Anya said. "My father had not returned, nor had we found any trace of you. I told my mother that you knew of this place, and that if you remained free you'd come here to search for me."

"Which I did," Merrick said, feeling a small twinge of satisfaction. At least he'd gotten *that* right.

"Yes," Anya said. "When we heard the stone move, my mother was afraid the masters had found us. So we hid in the secret room until you appeared."

"Right," Merrick said. "So what makes your mother so sure

your father is in Svipall? Couldn't he just have been captured by the Trofts out in the forest?"

"In which case, he's still in Svipall, is he not?"

"Probably," Merrick said. Technically, she was correct. But on a practical level, Ludolf hiding anonymously among the Svipall villagers and Ludolf a prisoner in the Troft warehouse were two very different scenarios. "I'll just have to get back in. And your mother's right—the sooner, the better."

"You have a plan to rescue him?" Anya asked hopefully.

Merrick pursed his lips as he gazed into the forest. *To rescue him.* To rescue the man who'd tried a blatantly underpowered revolt against the Trofts, resulting in dozens, maybe hundreds of his fellow slaves getting killed. The man who, when the revolt failed, had failed to protect his young daughter, but instead had allowed her to be taken offworld into Troft slavery.

But there was no point in mentioning any of that. Ludolf Treetapper was family; and in this case, for whatever tangled reasons, family trumped reason and logic. "I think so, yes," he said instead.

"Will you tell me?"

"Later," he said. "Right now, we need to be quiet and concentrate on not getting attacked."

He *did* have a plan, or at least the beginnings of one. But as always with such things, the devil was in the details.

And there was definitely a devil in this one. One massive hell of a devil.

CHAPTER NINE

Lorne had promised Jin that she would love the place he was taking her to. It was quickly apparent, though, that his promise was going to be on hold for a while.

It wasn't Lorne's fault. If anyone's, it was Jin's fault for escaping from Corwin's house in such a loud and destructive manner. The injured Marines she'd left behind gave the response team even more incentive to track her down, and it didn't take them long to find the hidden exit. At that point, Reivaro's predictable reaction was to flood the drainage conduits with angry Marines.

Fortunately, the system was more extensive and complicated than they'd apparently anticipated. It was also just as hard for them to get through the narrow passageways as it had been for Jin and the others.

In fact, it was probably worse. The Marines couldn't walk completely upright any more than the Cobras could, which left them three options. They could waddle along with bent knees, though without the assistance of servos or powered armor that would quickly fatigue muscles and joints. Alternatively, they could find or jury-rig some sort of wheeled carts—grav lifts were too big to fit through the manholes unless they were disassembled—on which they could kneel or sit, though the rough flooring would make for slow travel. The same rough flooring would also create enough noise and vibration to telegraph the carts' approach half a kilometer away.

Or, worst of all, they could lean forward as they walked. Worst, because with their shoulders angled down and forward, there would be a point somewhere directly ahead beyond which their epaulet lasers couldn't reach. An opposing force waiting beyond that point would get their first attack for free.

The Cobras wouldn't set that kind of ambush, Lorne assured his mother. Not unless it became absolutely necessary. He and the others were still hoping the confrontation could be resolved without additional bloodshed.

Fortunately, it didn't come to a life-or-death decision, at least not that first night. Werle found them a partially collapsed side tunnel that clearly hadn't seen use for years, and the four of them settled down to wait out the Dominion search. Above them, the day turned into night, and the group's watchful waiting turned into sleep.

Werle and de Portola were up early the next morning and headed out for a quiet recon. They returned with reports of no Dominion activity in the area, but Lorne decided to wait a little longer, just to be on the safe side. Finally, about midmorning, he decided it was safe and they set off.

As they traveled, he once again promised Jin that she would absolutely love their final destination. Having just spent a fitful night lying on cold ceramic without any blankets or pads, Jin assured him that she absolutely would.

The journey through the drainage system took twice as long as the previous day's trek, and with the ever-present threat of a sudden Dominion attack it was at least three times as stressful. Jin tried to keep track of their turnings with her nanocomputer's compass, but by the time Lorne called a halt she was thoroughly lost. He opened a camouflaged door to reveal a hidden stairway and led the way down about two floors' worth of stairs to the entrance of their final destination.

From Lorne's glowing description she'd half expected to find a five-star hotel waiting at the end of the tunnel. Fortunately, she'd only half expected that, or else would have been thoroughly disappointed. The structure they came to was composed of maybe a dozen rooms of varying sizes—most of them small—with plain and undecorated ceramic walls and only thin carpet to cushion the equally hard floor. There was a sleeping area filled wall-to-wall with cots, and separate corners devoted to kitchen and sanitary facilities.

One of the larger rooms had been equipped with long tables

and folding chairs, where eight women and two men were working with some kind of clay and what looked like ball bearings.
A number of industrial and craft-style items were laid out on
another table along the wall. Three of the people looked up as
Lorne and Jin stuck their heads in the door, but the rest ignored
them, their full attention on whatever they were doing. In one
of the other rooms four women and two men were cutting out
odd-shaped strips from sheets of soft-looking, flesh-colored cloth
or foam. Beside the table were two recliner type chairs that
reminded Jin of the types used for eye surgery.

Small, unadorned, and plain. But at least the ceilings were tall
enough for her to stand upright.

"Well, it's a step up from the Braided Falls cave," she commented as Lorne concluded the brief tour in the kitchen area.
"Probably *three* steps up from last night's accommodations. And
don't get me wrong—it's very cozy. But it's hardly the glorious
refuge you were promising."

"Oh, I wasn't promising luxury," Lorne said. "At least, I didn't
mean to. I was promising that you'd love the irony. You have
any idea where we are?"

"Not a single clue."

"Yeah, the system was sort of designed that way," Lorne said.
"Hard to navigate. Turns out we're directly under the Dome.
About fifteen meters below, to be exact. This place was supposed
to be our last refuge in case of a Troft attack."

Jin stared. "You're kidding. This was here during the invasion?"

"And for a lot longer than that," Lorne confirmed. "It didn't
get used because everyone had forgotten it was here. Just like
everyone had forgotten that the drainage system was designed to
be a secret personnel expressway in case of emergency."

Jin shook her head. "That's bizarre."

But now that she thought about it, she realized that not only
was it not bizarre, it was all but inevitable. The original Aventinian
colonists had arrived in the aftermath of the first Dominion-Troft
war, using an access corridor through Troft territory that had
been basically forced down the Trofts' throats during the peace
negotiations. Tensions had been high, on both sides, and with
the fledgling colonies far beyond quick communication with the
Dominion, the betting in the Dome had probably been that the
colonists would be wiped out within ten years.

The colonists themselves had undoubtedly given themselves even worse odds. And so, when it came to founding their first real city—Capitalia—they would have planned for the worst.

"Clever, I guess," she said. "A little more headroom in the tunnels would have been nice."

"Actually, I'm guessing they scaled the dimensions exactly the way they wanted," Lorne said. "I get that from some incomplete documents that Chintawa more or less accidentally dug up and handed over. The designers wanted the tunnel system to be hard to get through so that it would be more defensible for any survivors who made it down here." He gestured somewhere off to the side. "Unfortunately, somewhere along the line a later cadre of urban planners forgot about the system's secondary use, so when the city did its second big westward expansion they put in smaller conduits. I ran into that problem back when I was trying to get Governor Treakness out of town. Still, we've got access to the entire center of the city."

"Hopefully, that'll be enough," Jin said. "So the irony is that this was designed against a Troft attack, but we're using it against the Dominion?"

"Even better," Lorne said with a wry smile. "The real irony is that this whole thing was designed *by* the Dominion."

Jin blinked. "*They* designed it?"

"Lock, stock, and barrel," Lorne said. "Including the materials, the layout, the defense capabilities, even the stealth layering. Even better, I'd give you long odds that nothing Santores has access to even hints that this is here, or how to find it."

"But I thought the first big expansion from Old Town didn't start until after the Corridor had been closed."

"It didn't," Lorne said. "It was Great-Grandfather Jonny Moreau who brought the plans with him, just before the Corridor was closed. The records aren't clear, but they also hint that it might have been Jame Moreau who had the plans drawn up in the first place."

Jin nodded, her stomach tightening. Jame Moreau. Brother of Jin's grandfather Jonny.

Grandfather of Captain Barrington Moreau. Who was currently at Qasama.

"But that's all history," Lorne continued, motioning Jin out of the kitchen area. "Let's move on to current events. Specifically, our two-pronged plan to be as big a pain in the butt to the Dominion as we can."

"Without killing anyone, right?"

"Without killing unless we have to," Lorne amended grimly. Ahead was the doorway into the room with the long tables; taking his mother's arm, he steered her inside. "This is our mudball team. They're working on our latest attempt to mess with the Marines' weapons system."

Jin stepped to the table for a better look. Earlier, from the doorway, she'd guessed the assembly materials to be clay and ball bearings. Up close, they looked like exactly the same things. "Okay," she said. "So the idea is to throw a whole bunch of small missiles—the ball bearings—with the clay to hold them together?"

"Basically," Lorne said. "We're figuring the first laser volley will disintegrate the clay and leave the metal to swarm the target."

"You're *figuring*? Does that mean you haven't tried it?"

"Not yet," Lorne said. "We've had to fiddle with the composition—the things were falling apart before they even left our hands. This is the first batch that's held together in our tests."

"We're hoping to be ready for a field test in a couple of days," de Portola added, walking into the room behind them.

"Be careful when you do," Jin warned. "Uncle Corwin said the Marines have pulled the whole planet's personnel lists and are running facial recognition scans on everyone they see."

"So we understand," Lorne confirmed. "But we think we've got a way around it."

"Speaking of which, they're ready for us," de Portola said.

"Okay," Lorne said. "Got to go, Mom. There are meal bars and water in the kitchen if you're hungry."

"Sounds good," Jin said. Actually, it sounded awful. She'd been living on meal bars since arriving at Uncle Corwin's—there hadn't been time for any real cooking while they worked on the neckbands—and her stomach was going to have to growl a lot louder before she could face another one of them. "I think I'll look around here for a while first."

"Okay," Lorne said, eyeing her closely. "If you're not hungry, you should at least go lie down. I doubt you got much sleep last night."

"I will," Jin promised. "I'd like to watch the work here for a while first."

"A *little* while," Lorne insisted. "We may need you up top at any time, and if you fall asleep Reivaro won't even have to chase you."

"And that would hardly be sporting," Jin agreed. "Don't worry, I'll get some sleep. Three hours at least."

"Make it six and you've got a deal," Lorne said.

"Fine. Six." Jin reached out and took his hand. "Be careful, Lorne." She looked at de Portola. "All of you."

"We will," Lorne said, giving her hand a gentle squeeze. "And you," he added, leveling a finger at the people working around the table. "Don't let her offer to help. If you do, she'll be here until you run out of clay and she'll *never* get any sleep."

"Don't worry," one of the woman said dryly. "We'll make sure she learns how to sleep sitting up first."

"Good," Lorne said. "See you later, Mom. Let's go, Dill."

Jin watched them go, an all-too-familiar hollow feeling settling into the pit of her stomach. Her whole family, at immediate risk or facing unknown dangers...

But others had lost more. Forcing the fears into the back of her mind, she turned back to the table.

The work seemed straightforward enough. Each of the workers had a bowl filled with a brownish clay or stiff mud, plus a shallow plate of steel bearings. The method most of them were using was to lay out a thick strip of clay on the table, press bearings into it, then roll the strip up like spiral cake. A couple of the finished mudballs looked a bit different, as if one of the workers had experimented with the technique. But for the most part, they looked pretty much alike.

The woman who'd spoken earlier looked up at Jin. "Don't even think it," she warned. "Lorne would have our hides if we let you work."

Jin smiled. "That much of a taskmaster, is he?"

"He's Lorne Broom," the woman said. "We need him." She smiled suddenly. "And you're Jin Moreau Broom. We need you, too. I'm Leslie, by the way."

"Nice to meet you," Jin said. "So. Clay and ball bearings?"

"That's the plan." Leslie cocked her head. "Unless you have a better idea?"

"Oh, I wouldn't say that anything I came up with would necessarily be *better*," Jin assured her hastily. Clearly, Lorne was in charge here, and she would never do anything that would

undermine his authority or leadership. She'd learned the importance of that back on Qasama. "But *different* might not be bad.
Shaking things up might keep the Marines off-balance."

"Well, everything we've got is over there," one of the men put
in, pointing toward the table against the wall. "Go see what you
can come up with."

"Thanks," Jin said.

Lorne had ordered her to go get some sleep. And she would.

But it wouldn't hurt to have a look at the equipment first. Just
a quick look. That's all.

Werle was sitting in one of the recliner chairs in the makeup
room, being worked on by one of the women, when Lorne and de
Portola arrived. "How's your mom?" he asked, opening one eye.

"Tired, but functional," Lorne said, nodding at the woman
adding the artificial skin to his cheek. "Hello—I don't think
we've met. Lorne Broom."

"Kathia Rezondo," she said. "I'm one of Jennie's people. I
work—used to work—on Anne Villager."

"Jennie?" de Portola asked.

"Jennie Sider," Lorne said. "Chief makeup artist on Greendale."

"Ah," de Portola said, nodding to the woman. "Nice to meet
you. Sorry about you getting shut down—I really like the show."

"Thanks," Rezondo said. "To be honest, we got away with it
longer than I thought we would."

Lorne nodded, feeling a twinge of guilt. It had been his idea,
but James Hobwell and the people of Polestar Productions had
been the ones who'd carried it out, and in the process borne the
brunt of Lij Tulu's anger.

The plan had been simple. Back in Archway Lorne had learned
that Reivaro's men had downloaded all of Aventine's personnel
records and were able to do instant facial recognition scans
through their own computer system. Jennie Sider had sculpted a
new face for him that hadn't looked anything like his own, but
the very fact that it wasn't in the database had tagged him for
the Dominion as a dangerous stranger.

So Lorne had taken that disadvantage and turned it on its head.

The scheme had started on Anne Villager two days ago in an
episode called "Face of Defiance," with the title character wearing

makeup and facial overlays to confuse her enemies. The next day the same theme had figured in Polestar's other two shows, Greendale and Tribecca, followed by a live epilog from the actors and producers exhorting the public to regain their privacy by following Anne Villager's example.

The on-air appeal had been too much for Lij Tulu, who had instructed Colonel Reivaro to shut down the entire production studio and haul in anyone he could find for questioning. Fortunately, most of the key people had anticipated the move and already gone to ground, with Sider, Hobwell, and a couple of the others managing to sneak into Capitalia before the hammer came down.

"Do you know yet if it worked?" Rezondo added.

"Oh, it worked, all right," de Portola said with malicious satisfaction. "It worked beautifully. The reports I've seen say the Marines have stopped at least fifty people in the streets already this morning. And those are just the ones they thought looked suspicious enough to bother with."

"The report I saw said it was like Costume Day out there," Werle added. "Half of Capitalia is decked out in either heavy makeup, face sculpts, or just ordinary costumes." He smiled slyly. "He said the Anne Villager look was especially popular."

"Not bad for a show no one admits they watch," Rezondo said dryly. "I just hope they'll be as enthusiastic when they start putting everyone in jail."

"They can't," Lorne said. One of the other women stepped to the other chair and nodded. Lorne gestured de Portola to go over and sit down. "They may have enough room to put all of Polestar on ice, but they can't even begin to find space for all the people out there who are masked up. They probably don't even have enough manpower to check everyone who's off their database—there's no way they can lock them up, guard them, and feed them."

"Which isn't to say they won't try," Werle warned. "You're right—the real test will be when a few of the offenders are hauled off in sight of everyone else as an example."

"Of course, the fact that they're Anne Villager fans makes them predisposed to stand up to bullies and heavy-hand authority types anyway," de Portola said as he settled into the chair. "But we should at least have today. If we can use the cover out there to slap Reivaro hard enough, that ought to continue the momentum."

"Or so goes the theory," Lorne said. "We'll find out soon enough whether it works."

"I guess we will." Rezondo made one final adjustment to Werle's face and took a step back to study her work. "Okay, you're done," she told him. "Cobra Broom? Your turn."

The makeup process took nearly two hours. Possibly the most boring two hours in Lorne's life.

When it was over, he didn't really feel any different. His facial skin couldn't feel the air, of course, and his new hair was brushing at the tops of his ears. But aside from that, it felt like he was still the same as he always was.

Until he was offered a mirror.

He'd gone through this process once before, back in Archway, under the direction of some of these same people. It was just as unbelievable now as it had been then. He might feel unchanged beneath the makeup, but there was not a single familiar thing about his new face. His cheekbones, the curve of his jaw, even the shape of his eyebrows had been altered to something unrecognizable. "Nice," he said, handing the mirror back. "This anyone's face in particular? Or is it a Kathia Rezondo original?"

"A little of both," she said. "Cobra de Portola?"

"Our theory is that most of the people out there playing facial dress-up will be just using random overlays and makeup," de Portola said, standing up from his own chair. Lorne looked closely at him, but couldn't see a single recognizable thing in his face. "We presume Colonel Reivaro will eventually tumble to that. Ergo, someone who looks *almost* like one of their records, but not quite, will hopefully be assumed to be an ordinary citizen."

"For instance, you look a little like a guy I dated in high school," Rezondo added.

"I hope you parted on good terms," Lorne said.

"If we hadn't, I'd have included a black eye," Rezondo said with a wry smile.

"I appreciate it," Lorne said, smiling back. At least, he hoped it was a smile that came across through all the makeup. "So. Where are we going?"

"Well, *I'm* going to North Bridge," de Portola said. "You and your girlfriend are going to check out the new Marine garrison in East Mona."

Lorne raised his eyebrows. It felt as odd as the smile had. "My *girlfriend*?"

"Cobras are all male," a throaty female voice came from the doorway.

Lorne turned his head. The woman standing there was young, with wavy blond hair and a touch too much makeup for his taste. Her outfit was mostly conservative, all browns and tans, except for the bright red silk scarf knotted casually around her neck. She looked him up and down, a slightly amused, slightly mocking expression on her face. "Except for your mom, of course," she continued as she walked into the room. Her walk was smooth and just at the edge of being slinky. "So we figure the Marines will be mostly watching men who are single or in small groups."

She reached Lorne and held out her hand. "I'm Doris, your camouflage du jour. Your pictures don't do you justice, Cobra Broom."

"I should hope not," Lorne agreed, taking her hand for a quick shake. Her skin was cool, the muscles a little stiff. "This going to be your first trip up?"

"Hardly," Doris said, withdrawing her hand and lowering the arm to her side. "I've taken three others up on these surveillance missions. And I know how to talk to these people, so if there's trouble just follow my lead."

"Good," Lorne said, suppressing a flicker of annoyance. A civilian trying to tell him how to handle a combat situation.

But then, this trip wasn't supposed to *be* a combat situation. "So they've got a garrison in East Mona now?"

"They call them garrisons, but they're not much more than six- to eight-man outposts," de Portola said. "We haven't figured out whether this is Reivaro's idea of suppressing dissent on a neighborhood level or bait they're hoping will draw us out of hiding."

"Our job is to see if we can figure that out," Doris said. "And to figure it out before the nine o'clock curfew kicks in."

"We'd better get to it, then," Lorne said, checking his nano-computer's clock circuit. Just before two o'clock in the afternoon. Plenty of time.

"Whenever you're ready," Doris said. Turning, she walked briskly to the door. "Our exit's a little tricky, so try to keep up."

"Good luck," de Portola said as Lorne followed. "And be safe."

The district known to Capitalia residents as East Mona was nearly two kilometers away, and Lorne had resigned himself to another long and unpleasant frog-walk through the city sewer system. To his surprise, barely three minutes into their travels Doris stopped at a vertical shaft and pointed upward. "Here we are," she said. "You'll need to get the door."

Lorne nodded and climbed up the rickety ladder fastened to the side. The manhole cover at the top was sealed, but a closer look showed it was being held in place by three small spot welds. His fingertip lasers made quick work of them, and he carefully eased the cover up.

His first surprise was that the cover didn't come up clean, but had a square patch of something slightly floppy glued to its top that stretched out past the edge of the metal itself. The second surprise was that they hadn't come out in a back street or parking garage, but in an airy, brightly lit room whose walls were lined with shelves of fresh produce. "Where are we?" he asked as he climbed out and offered a hand to Doris.

"Badham's Market," she said, ignoring his hand and climbing out on her own. "Farmers and growers are in and out of here all the time, so we figured a few extra people coming and going won't raise any eyebrows."

"Not to mention all the customers," Lorne agreed. The covering on the top of the manhole, he saw now, was made of the same SoftStep industrial matting that covered the rest of the floor. "Never knew Badham's was built on top of one of these access covers."

"Why would you?" Doris countered. "No one paid any attention to such things until you and Aaron Koshevski used them to get out of the city after the Troft invasion." She gestured to the cover. "Make sure you get the mat edges lined up."

A minute later, with the manhole cover back in place, they made their way through the market and out onto the Capitalia streets. "So we're walking the rest of the way?" Lorne asked as Doris turned them east.

"We were always going to walk," she said. "I just figured it would be better to walk upright instead of hunched over." She nodded ahead. "Besides, this way we can walk past the Marines' Dome garrison on the way. See if we can spot any differences between that one and their East Mona version."

"Good idea," Lorne said. "Be interesting to see what Reivaro's up to now."

"And how best to interfere with that?"

Lorne smiled tightly. "Goes without saying. So where's this Dome garrison?"

"Not far," Doris said, pointing ahead. "Two more blocks, then half a block down on Piedmont."

Lorne kept most of his attention on the people around them as they walked, watching for Marine uniforms and wondering which of the buildings on Piedmont the Dominion could have commandeered to use as their garrison.

The answer, as it turned out, was none of them.

"What the hell is *that*?" he muttered as they passed the corner and came within sight of the gray structure that had been erected squarely in the middle of the street, leaving just enough room on either side of it for the walkways. Besides being wide, it was also tall, stretching upward a good two stories. Its sides were a uniform gray, but there were a large number of vents, small windowlike structures, and bulging lines that looked like external conduits or tubing. There was a single door at ground level, currently flanked by two uniformed Marines.

"Like it?" Doris asked. "It's apparently the latest in Dominion instant housing. The things pop up overnight, with none of the locals seeing or hearing anything in particular. Of course, if you're going to sneak something in, doing it while everyone's asleep only makes sense."

"True," Lorne said. "What are all the vents and windows and pipes for?"

"No idea," she said. "Near as we can tell, they seem to be sealed. Either they're to be opened at some future date, or else they were for something that isn't going to be used here."

"So the only door is that one?"

"Plus another one just like it on the other end."

"Interesting," Lorne mused, running his eyes over it. A strange-looking structure ... and yet, somehow, it reminded him of something he'd seen before. "And just who is this *we* you keep talking about?"

And then, before she could answer, a man crossing Piedmont toward them suddenly turned and broke into a loping run away from the Marine building.

"What is it?" Lorne asked, his whole body tensing for combat. Two more people broke out of their walks into jogs, heading after the first man.

He glanced at the Marines, expecting to see them in motion. But both were still just standing at guard by the door. He looked back, to find a half dozen more people had taken up the strange race. Meanwhile, the rest of the pedestrians were continuing on their way, as if this kind of sudden mass exodus was an everyday occurrence.

"Come on—you'll love this," Doris said. She slapped Lorne lightly on the arm, then turned her back on the Marines and started running after the others.

Lorne cursed under his breath, breaking into a jog of his own. Of all the stupid things to do, drawing a soldier's attention by suddenly running away was near the top of the list. "What's going on?" he demanded as he caught up with her.

"It's called a guilt trip," she said. Her voice, he noticed, had changed subtly as she focused more of her attention on her running. "Something else your Anne Villager friends dreamed up. If you see a Marine, and you feel like some exercise, you just start running. Anyone nearby who also feels like it can join in. The idea is to make them wonder what's going on, and get them used to seeing groups of people running."

"Messing with their minds, in other words."

"Basically."

"What happens if they decide to chase down one of the groups?"

"And charge them with what?" Doris countered. "Even the Dominion doesn't have a law against public running. As long as you're not wanted for something, what are they going to do to you?"

And suddenly, her newly undisguised voice clicked. Her voice, and her earlier mention of Aaron Koshevski's role in getting Lorne and Senior Governor Tomo Treakness out from under the Troft occupation of Capitalia—

"Halt!" a loud voice ordered from behind them.

Lorne threw a glance over his shoulder. Two more Marines had emerged from the garrison building and were charging after the jogging citizens. "I'm guessing they're going to start by scrubbing off everyone's makeup," he muttered. "So?"

She took a deep breath. "Scatter," she called. "Everyone scatter."

For a second Lorne thought none of them had heard her, or that it hadn't registered, or that fear of the Marines was keeping people from reacting. Then, all at once, the loose pack of runners started splitting apart as singles and pairs angled off into side streets or shops. Lorne grabbed his companion's arm and pulled her toward the side street coming up on the right. If he remembered this part of the city correctly, there should be a convenient shop just around the corner.

There was a sudden crackling of heat-stressed pavement in front of the runners as the Marines laid down a volley of warning shots. Someone screamed, someone else cursed, but everyone kept running. Lorne felt his back tense with anticipation, wondering if Reivaro had ordered his men to take it to the next level if the warning shots didn't work.

But there were no further shots. Lorne glanced back as they rounded the corner, to see that the Marines were slowing down, apparently content with delivering a lesson to future would-be runners.

"Don't."

Lorne looked back as the corner building blocked the Marines from his sight. "Don't what?"

"Don't try jumping," she said, pointing at the single-story building ahead sandwiched between a couple of two- and three-story structures. "They'll have aircars watching in case a Cobra starts showing off."

"I had no intention of jumping," Lorne assured her. "There's a bar here that goes straight through to the next street."

"O'Donnel's?"

"Right." Of course she would know the place. "Come on."

Even in the middle of the afternoon the bar was reasonably full. Some of the patrons glanced up as Lorne came through the doorway, but most of them ignored the newcomers. A brisk walk down the side corridor, a trip through the swinging serving doors, the kitchen, and the stock room, and they were once again out on the Capitalia streets. "So when were you going to tell me?" he asked.

She shrugged. "I assumed you'd figure it out along the way somewhere."

"Yes," Lorne murmured, looking sideways at her. Now that he knew what to look for, he could see the all-too-familiar face beneath the makeup and skin enhancements.

The face of Nissa Gendreves. Former aide to Senior Governor Treakness, currently a major force in Aventinian politics.

The woman who'd done everything she could to get the entire Broom family convicted on charges of treason. "So what's your game this time?" he asked.

"There's never been a game," Nissa said. "My goal has always been the same: to do everything I can to defend and protect the Cobra Worlds."

"Especially if it builds your reputation among the anti-Cobra politicians?"

"Your father and Governor Uy gave top-secret military equipment to the enemy," Nissa said flatly. "Sugar-glaze it all you want, but that's still treason."

"They're not our enemies anymore."

"I'm not convinced of that," Nissa said. "But even if it's true, it's irrelevant. They *were* our enemies at the time, and that's all that matters."

Which was arguable, of course. But at the moment none of that was important. "So why didn't you turn me in to the Marines?" Lorne asked. "It would have been the perfect way to get me out of the picture. Afraid you'd get caught in the cross-fire?"

She snorted. "You aren't listening, are you? I said my goal was to defend the Cobra Worlds. Right now, the Dominion and Colonel Reivaro's homicidal Marines are way more of a threat than you and your family. I offered my services to Governor-General Chintawa, he hooked me up with the Resistance leaders, and they accepted me. End of story."

"So your job is to play escort?"

"Escort, courier, intel gathering," she said. "Anything that doesn't involve straight fighting or anything else I've got zero training or skill in."

"And possibly sweet-talking Dominion forces when necessary?"

"If there's no other way out," she conceded. "I got away with it once. I'm not anxious to try it again."

"Hopefully, you won't have to," Lorne said. He still didn't entirely trust her, but right now he didn't have much choice but to give her the benefit of the doubt. "Fine—back to work. You said there were six to eight Marines in each of these garrisons?"

"Those are the numbers we've seen so far."

"So if they want to keep two on each door *and* go chase after a couple of these impromptu jogging groups, they'd have to empty the place?"

"If not completely, at least mostly," Nissa said, frowning suspiciously at him. "Why? Are you thinking of trying to get inside?"

"Has anyone else seen what's in there?"

"No," she said. "But so far nothing's come out except Marines." She leveled a warning finger. "Tell me you're not going to just walk up and knock."

"Oh, no," Lorne assured her. "Not going to knock." He considered. "And probably not going to walk up."

"Broom—"

"Come on, let's get over to East Mona and check out the garrison there," Lorne cut her off. "A quick look, then back underground. We've got a lot to do before curfew."

CHAPTER TEN

This current collection of the *Algonquin*'s corridors, Corwin noted, was much narrower than some of the others Colonel Reivaro had led them through since hauling him out of the ship's brig. Evidently, there was no need to bring heavy equipment through this particular part of the ship.

"We're almost there," Reivaro said as they turned yet another corner.

"Don't hurry on my account," Corwin said. It was all very psych warfare, of course: the overnight stay in the *Algonquin*'s brig, followed by this long walk through a confusing maze of elevators and corridors. Especially since there was almost certainly a faster route to their destination than the one they were currently following. All was clearly designed to give him time to think, and sweat, and worry.

There was certainly plenty for him to sweat and worry about. Aventine was a powder keg, and Reivaro and Lij Tulu seemed determined to see how closely they could lob live barbeque coals to the fuse. Why Commodore Santores had abandoned the Cobra Worlds to these fools he couldn't guess.

But even those worries couldn't keep Corwin's thoughts from the most important one of all.

Thena.

Where was she? What was she doing? *How* was she doing?

He had no answers.

The separation had been her idea. He couldn't decide if that made it easier or harder.

And not just for him. He'd seen the embarrassment and pity in Jin's face back in his basement. In her own way, he recognized, she was as upset by Thena's disappearance as he was.

Young people, he knew, tended to believe that the things they did affected only themselves. Corwin was old enough to know better. His actions—and Thena's—created consequences and feelings that rippled outward to family, friends, even the Cobra Worlds as a whole.

Thena knew that, too. She'd always had a very similar outlook on life as Corwin's. One reason they'd lived so long and so comfortably together.

He missed her terribly.

"We're here."

Corwin blinked away the depressing thoughts. The last door had opened up into a fairly large, very medical-looking room, with a large contraption with an attached chair in the middle.

They were here, all right.

Time to go to work.

"Let me guess," he said, nodding toward the machine as he continued walking. "The MindsEye?"

"The MindsEye," Lij Tulu's voice confirmed from behind him.

Corwin stopped in the doorway and turned his head. The *Algonquin*'s captain had come up unobserved behind the group and was now standing in the center of the corridor. Symbolically blocking any hope of escape.

Mentally, Corwin shook his head. They were laying this on *way* too thick.

"I presume I don't have to tell you what this will do," Reivaro continued, making Corwin turn his head back again.

"Cobra Paul Broom underwent the treatment," Lij Tulu said. Apparently, having people talk at Corwin from two directions was supposed to confuse or disorient him. "As a consequence, we now know Qasama's location."

"I see," Corwin said. One of the guards nudged him in the back, and he started forward again. "I suppose now you're going to tell me how stressful it was, and how it permanently muddled his mind."

Reivaro's gaze flicked over Corwin's shoulder to Lij Tulu. "Not his mind," the captain said, his tone darkening. "But it does seem to have had an effect on his nanocomputer. Not all his Cobra gear functions anymore."

Corwin felt a frown crease his forehead. Was that just one more psych attack? Or could Lij Tulu be telling the truth?

Because if the MindsEye could permanently damage a Cobra nanocomputer, then the Dominion had stumbled on the perfect answer to Aventine's best weapon. No need to kill or isolate the Cobras if they could be simply turned back into ordinary men.

The original Dominion designers had made the nanocomputers impossible to remove or reprogram without killing their owners. Apparently, and probably by complete accident, Lij Tulu had stumbled across a way to bypass those safeguards.

"Just as well I don't have any Cobra gear, then," Corwin said, keeping his voice casual. "I also don't know any Aventinian state secrets, so I have no idea what you're hoping to accomplish here."

"Oh, I'm sure you know more than you admit," Lij Tulu said, coming through the guard phalanx and into the room behind him. "You know where the rest of the Cobras are based, for instance. You know where you've hidden the rest of those ceramic neckbands. And you probably know where your niece Jin Broom ran off to after she wrecked your house."

"Jasmine," Corwin corrected. So Jin had gotten out of his house after Reivaro's raid? That was the best news he'd had today. "She's only *Jin* to friends and family. So really, she wrecked my house? Interesting. How many Marines did she kill in the process?"

"None," Reivaro said stiffly.

"I didn't think so," Corwin said. "See, that's the big difference between your Marines and our Cobras. You've turned the whole decision-making process over to your computers and your weapons, and more often than not the decision is to kill. We, on the other hand, have a lot more discretion as to where and how hard we hit."

"Which is no doubt a useful trait in a police force," Reivaro countered. "But Dominion Marines are soldiers. We operate under different rules."

"That's too bad," Corwin said. "Because that's exactly what you've now tasked them to do. How many civilian kills do you think it'll take before the whole planet rises up?"

"And does what?" Lij Tulu countered. "Charges our positions with sticks and rocks?" He snorted. "It doesn't matter anyway.

We can pull up stakes tomorrow, move our operation to the unoccupied parts of Aventine, and still complete our mission."

Corwin felt his ears prick up. This was the first he'd heard about a specific mission. "And that mission would be . . . ?"

Lij Tulu smiled. "Tell you what." He gestured to the MindsEye. "You tell us your secrets, and maybe I'll tell you mine."

Corwin shook his head. "Sorry, but that's a dead-end deal. Literally."

"Meaning?"

"Meaning you put me in that, and I'll die," Corwin said.

"Sorry, but you're not getting out of it *that* easily," Reivaro said. "The MindsEye doesn't put any extra strain on the subject's bio system. Any weak organs or physical ailments you might have would be completely unaffected."

"Good to know," Corwin said. "What about a bomb inside the heart muscle?"

Reivaro stiffened. "What are you talking about?"

"It's actually a leftover from the Troft invasion," Corwin said, tapping his chest gently. "Back then, unlike now, I *did* know things I didn't want them finding out. It was actually set up to be a defense against torture or drugs, but I dare say your higher-tech gadget will probably trigger it, as well."

"Colonel?" Lij Tulu murmured.

"He's bluffing, sir," Reivaro assured him. "We gave him a full scan before we brought him aboard. There's nothing like that anywhere in his body."

"This from people who can't even detect Cobra equipment?" Corwin asked pointedly.

"That's different," Reivaro growled. But there was a hint of hesitation in his voice. "Cobra gear was specifically designed not to be detectable."

"And where exactly do you think my surgeons got the bomb they implanted in my heart?" Corwin said. "I'll save you the trouble of guessing: it's one of the old Cobra nanocomputers with a built-in self-destruct. It was designed to obliterate the computer itself plus a lot of the surrounding brain tissue. I don't think it'll have trouble doing the same to my heart." He cocked his head. "In fact, now that I see how the MindsEye is set up, it's possible the blast will do some damage there, too. At the very least you'll have to wash off a lot of blood."

"Let's assume for the moment that what you say is true and not just some ridiculous bluff," Lij Tulu said. "What then?"

"Obviously, I'm telling you all this because I don't particularly want to die," Corwin said. "Let's bring it down to the bottom line. At the moment, I'm a hostage and possible intermediary. Put me in the MindsEye, and I become a martyr."

"We don't take hostages," Reivaro said stiffly. "And we don't need intermediaries."

"Really?" Corwin countered. "Cobra Paul Broom was taken and hasn't been heard from since. Sounds like a hostage to me."

"He's gone to Qasama with Commodore Santores," Lij Tulu said.

"So you say," Corwin said. "Regardless, you had him, and now you have me. If I'm also not heard from, people are likely to draw unpleasant conclusions."

"I already said we don't need people to be happy."

"Maybe not," Corwin conceded. "On the other hand, I doubt a world in open revolt is what Commodore Santores will want to see when he comes back." He raised his eyebrows. "Unless you're not *expecting* him to come back?"

"He'll be back," Lij Tulu said. But there was just a hint of hesitation in his voice. "Eventually."

"Well, when he does, I'm sure he'd prefer to find us working and playing nicely together," Corwin said, deciding not to press the point. "All the more reason to keep me in reserve as a negotiator."

For a long moment Lij Tulu stared at him. Corwin stared back, years of friendly card games with other politicians having given him insight into his tells as well as the ability to suppress them. "I think you're bluffing," the captain said at last. "But you're right. For the moment it may be wiser to keep you in reserve. *But.*" He raised a warning finger. "If your nephew and his friends start making serious trouble, that may change."

"Understood," Corwin said. "And for the record?"

"Yes?"

"For the record," Corwin said, "Lorne is my *great* nephew."

The sun had disappeared behind the western horizon, and the sky had darkened enough for a few of the brighter stars to be visible in the eastern part of the sky. People were still moving around Capitalia, but they were starting to hurry now that curfew was fast approaching.

One block straight ahead, the two Marines flanking the Dome garrison door were standing their impassive watch.

Jin eyed them between the tall shopping bags cradled in her arms as she and her small group continued walking toward them. Lorne had hoped to do this at the East Mona garrison instead, but the streets and buildings there hadn't been suitable for the plan he'd come up with.

The downside was that this garrison was closer to the Dome, the center of what was left of Cobra Worlds political authority, and was likely to be somewhat more alert than an outpost in a less important neighborhood. The upside was that Lorne had already seen today that the Marines here were willing to chase after citizens who were mocking them with the so-called guilt-trip fad. Jin hoped the guards were still feeling the need to express their power.

Half a block. Jin could see the rest of the team, drifting in among the pedestrians from both directions across the last cross street in front of the garrison. She presumed the Marine guards were watching everyone closely, though it was impossible to tell where their eyes were pointed behind their helmets' faceplates. While they looked alert, they paradoxically also looked relaxed.

And really, why shouldn't they be? Their armored combat suits were impervious to everything in the Cobra arsenal except a close-in attack with antiarmor laser or arcthrower, and their computerized laser epaulets were usually able to keep an opponent far enough back to make close-in shots impossible. Jin's sonic weapons had a somewhat longer range, especially with the surrounding buildings creating a waveguide, but the Marines' helmets protected them against that approach.

Still, the very fact of their invulnerability made them susceptible to overconfidence. Tonight, Jin and Lorne would find out how well that weakness could be exploited.

Jin reached the intersection . . . and it was time. Dropping her bags, hearing the multiple crunch as the bottles inside shattered, she did an abrupt one-eighty and started running away from the garrison building. Out of the corners of her eyes she could see that the other four in her group were doing likewise, and a glance over her shoulder showed that the six who'd come in from the sides were following.

The bait was set and wiggling. Now if the Marines would just behave as they'd done earlier this afternoon...

They did. "Halt!" one of them boomed, his voice coming from some kind of amplifier in his helmet.

Jin again looked behind her. Two more Marines had emerged through the garrison door and were jogging toward the fleeing civilians. Jin dropped her gaze to the puddle spreading rapidly from her dropped shopping bags and glanced a targeting lock on it. Turning back to face forward, she triggered her antiarmor laser. The brief burst of light reflected faintly off the buildings and windows in front of her—

And with a violent, rushing *snap* the puddle of fuel ignited, sending smoke and flames high into the air.

There was a chorus of screams and startled shouts from the pedestrians back there who weren't part of the plan. Jin winced, hoping none of them had been close enough to be burned or singed by the erupting flames. Regardless, it was a safe bet that *everyone* near the garrison was running now, giving the Marines a lot of choices as to who they chased.

Not that their target was really in question. Even if they hadn't gotten a clear view of Jin's shot, it was clear that the fuel had been ignited by either a Cobra or a civilian with a forbidden laser weapon. Whichever it was, they would be determined to run the perpetrator to ground.

The Marines were no longer the only ones in the game, either. Ahead and above her, Jin caught another flicker as the bonfire she'd created briefly lit up an aircar arrowing in on the running crowd.

Jin returned her attention to her running, concentrating on keeping pace with the rest of the group. *Okay, Lorne,* she thought back toward the flames. *We've got their attention. Your turn.*

Standing inside the half-open door of the rooftop elevator shed, Lorne's first warning was the roar of the igniting fuel and the flickering reflected light from the nearby buildings.

His mother had done her part. The question now was whether the Marines were doing theirs.

Unfortunately, there was no safe way to find out. With the Dominion controlling all the phone and radio systems on Aventine, the only secure communication was via Dida code, the semi-secret dot-dash code that Cobras who'd been assigned to Capitalia and other major cities were taught.

Unfortunately, Lorne had never learned the code. Even if he had, he wouldn't have wanted to risk putting another Cobra out here to act as an observer. This was his idea, and the only reason he'd even involved his mother was that Nissa had blabbed and Jin had insisted on helping.

If Lorne was more cynical, he mused, he might wonder if Nissa had concluded she would never get the Broom family convicted on her treason charge, and had therefore shifted her plan to trying to get them all killed in action instead.

Of more immediate concern here was the timing. If the Marines were too close to the garrison when Lorne made his move—or worse, if any of the nearby aircars was focused on anyone except the running civilians—this would be over very quickly. Forcing his muscles to relax, he counted down the number of seconds he and Jin had agreed on, painfully aware that the calculation was ninety percent guesswork...

Shoving open the door, he emerged from cover and sprinted across the rooftop.

No one shot at him. No one yelled at him to stop. He reached the end and leaped.

He had wondered if there might be any defenses or obstacles on top of the garrison building. Nissa had told him that civilian reports had said no; but given that the witnesses *were* civilian he hadn't necessarily trusted their powers of observation.

But as he arced through the growing darkness toward the roof one floor below him he saw that the observers had been correct. Aside from another line of vents at each end and a pair of short heat-exchange towers in the center, the rest of the roof was smooth and uncluttered.

There were also no signs of any access hatches. But that was all right. Lorne had always planned on making his own.

He landed midway between the towers and the front edge, bending his knees and letting his leg servos absorb the impact. The material gave a little as he hit, but otherwise seemed sturdy enough. Straightening up, he angled his left leg thirty degrees out from his body; and as he spun around, ballet-style, on his right foot he activated his antiarmor laser, burning a circle of destruction into the roof around him.

He'd expected to have to make at least two complete circles to cut all the way through. To his surprise, he hadn't even made a complete turn when the section of roof collapsed beneath him, sending him dropping into the building below.

The structure was a good two stories high, which had led him to expect there to be two levels to the interior. But there weren't. In fact, as he dropped toward the floor eight meters below him he saw that there was no interior structure at all. It was all a single, empty building, with nothing but a table, a few chairs, and a couple of cots clustered near the door he was facing.

Standing beside that table, hurriedly climbing into their armored suits, were two more Marines.

They were gaping up at their unexpected visitor, and Lorne himself had barely registered their presence when a barrage of laser fire spat upward at him from their suits' epaulets.

But once again, the reflexive attack was thwarted by the weapons' design flaw. Lorne wasn't directly above them, but he was close enough to vertical that the epaulet lasers couldn't *quite* target him.

Another half second of descent, though, and that temporary bubble of safety would be gone. Lorne's antiarmor laser was out of position to fire back, and he knew instinctively that he would never get his fingertip lasers up and in position in time.

But the Marines' helmets were still sitting on the table beside them. As the rapid fire from below started nipping at his boots, Lorne fired his sonics.

An instant later a flash of vertigo washed over him as he caught the weapon's bounceback. The Marines, caught by the full force of the blast, collapsed without a snarl or curse.

Fortunately, their laser fire went silent when they did.

Lorne hit the ground, staggering a bit as the aftereffects of the sonic threw off his balance. He spun around, snapping up his hands into firing position as it belatedly occurred to him that there might be a similar pair of Marines gearing up by the other door.

Luckily, there wasn't. He and the two unconscious men were alone in the building.

He frowned, looking around. The big, plain-walled, plain-floored, *empty* building. A huge structure that had apparently been built and dropped into the middle of a Capitalia street for the purpose of housing a few Marines and nothing else.

Paper tiger, the old phrase echoed through Lorne's mind. Was that really all this was? A big, obvious demonstration of the Dominion's power? Did Lij Tulu really have nothing better to threaten the Cobra Worlds with?

For that matter, why would the *Algonquin* even be carrying something like this? Surely they hadn't gone to the effort to build these things from scratch.

Unless they had some other purpose and had merely been pressed into this duty.

Unless they weren't buildings at all.

He crouched down and touched the floor. The material was soft and yielding, far more yielding than a building floor ought to be. A quick slash with his fingertip laser, and he'd cut himself a small sample. It was about ten centimeters thick, and flexible enough that he could fold it in half without even using his servos.

It made no sense. But he didn't have time to figure it out now. His mother and the others should have disappeared down the various rabbit holes prepared for them by now, and the Marines would be heading back. He had to be gone before they got here.

The original plan had been for him to leave the same way he'd entered. But that had assumed that there would be some interior structure to the building that wouldn't require him to make an eight-meter leap straight up to the roof. Such a jump was theoretically possible, but it would be tricky, especially if any of the Dominion aircars were still roaming around.

But now that he knew what this building was made of, there might be a quicker, safer way.

The schematics he'd studied before the mission had shown one of the sewer system access points under the northern edge of the garrison. Lorne found it on his second try. Fortunately, this one hadn't been sealed from below, and he was able to get the cover off with a little effort from his arm servos.

With the structure's floor cut open, of course, the returning Marines would know instantly how he'd made his escape. But since Reivaro already knew they were using the sewer system that wouldn't tell him anything new.

It was hardly the intel-rich report Lorne had hoped to bring back. But at least he should make it back in one piece. Stepping into the shaft, he found the ladder with his feet.

And paused, looking back at the unconscious Marines. Halfway into their armored combat suits, with their regular fatigue tunics draped across two of the chairs.

Both uniforms complete with combat epaulets.

Grinning tightly, Lorne stepped back out of the shaft. Nissa Gendreves and the still-unnamed people she answered to were going to love this.

Or possibly not.

"Are you *insane*?" Nissa demanded, staring wide-eyed at the Marine tunic propped up in the center of the underground room behind a double layer of copper mesh. "You brought Marine weapons *here*? What if they trace it?"

"That's why it's here," Jin said. She hadn't been any happier about this than Nissa, at least at the beginning. But she was slowly coming around. "If they can detect it through five meters of steel, concrete, and dirt *and* two Faraday cages, then there's probably nothing we'll ever be able to do to stop them."

"Which is also why it's this far away from all the rest of our operational areas," Lorne added. "But frankly, I don't think they've got a hope of finding it. You wouldn't put any kind of remote control tracking or control system into a weapon like this—too much risk that an enemy could intercept or hijack the signal."

"Unless it's by laser," Nissa growled. Still, she seemed to be calming down a little. "I know, I know—five meters of ground and concrete. You *do* realize, I hope, that reverse-engineering is probably out of the question. They'll have tech in there we can't even understand, let alone duplicate."

"Don't worry, we aren't looking to create our own Dominion Marines," Jin said. "But there's a lot we can learn without going that far. How the targeting system works, for example, or what the lasers' limits are, or whether they can be overloaded or overheated. That sort of thing."

"We're looking for anything that can give us a new edge or fresh approach," Lorne said. "But never mind that for now. We've got bigger questions. Those garrison buildings that no one saw the Dominion putting up? I know how they did it."

"Do you, now," Nissa said, frowning. "Let me guess: a huge, silent crane?"

"No," Lorne said. "A huge, silent air compressor."

Nissa blinked. *"What?"*

"You heard me," Lorne said. "Those so-called buildings are nothing but giant balloons." He dug the sample out of his pocket and handed it to her. "Here's a piece I cut out of the floor."

Nissa peered at the material, running her fingers over it and testing its flexibility. "But if it's a balloon and you cut a hole in it...?"

"Obviously, they did something to it after blowing it up to make the structure rigid," Lorne said. "I'm guessing some kind of spray coating, which might be why the floor wasn't affected."

"Or possibly exposure to sunlight," Jin said. "The point is that the garrisons aren't what they seem. The next question, then, is what are they for?"

"Intimidation, I assume," Nissa said. "They're there to look big and scary and keep the citizens in line."

"No," Lorne said. "If that was their purpose they should look more like military bunkers. But they don't."

"They look like factories," Jin said quietly. "Or sections of factories."

Nissa looked back and forth between them, her forehead wrinkled. "You've lost me."

"Let's start with what we know," Jin said. "The Dominion is fighting some alliance of Trofts at the other end of the Assemblage. That alliance, or some of their friends, were worried enough about the Cobra Worlds to try to take us out of the equation."

Nissa snorted. "We were never *in* the equation."

"Maybe *we* didn't think so, but the Trofts and Dominion sure did," Jin said. "Now add in the fact that the Dominion took three long-range warships out of their fleet—which they could surely have used somewhere else in the battle front—and sent them here."

"Loaded with inflatable dummy factories," Lorne murmured. He and his mother had worked through this logic on the way back from the raid, but thinking about it still sent a shiver up his back.

"But that doesn't—" Nissa broke off. "Are you saying—? No. They wouldn't. They *couldn't*. We're *them*."

"Are we?" Jin countered. "We haven't been part of the Dominion for three generations. Their laws, their culture—we hardly recognize them anymore, and vice versa."

"Even if that wasn't true, I doubt it would matter," Lorne said.

"If they're desperate enough to come all this way, they're desperate enough to sacrifice us to save themselves. Greatest good for the greatest number, and all that."

Nissa inhaled sharply. "Oh, my God," she breathed. "Qasama. *That's* why they were so focused on finding Qasama."

Lorne looked at his mother, another shiver running up his back. He'd hoped that particular conclusion was wrong. But if Nissa had reached it on her own... "Yes," he said. "Because if they can use the Qasamans as bait instead of us, so much the better."

"Bait," Nissa repeated, as if trying the word on for size. "So you think they're hoping to lure the Trofts here and into a trap?"

"Yeah, that's the other thing," Lorne said. "If that's their plan, they're not going to pull it off with just three ships. They must have another group on its way, maybe timed to arrive the same time they're hoping the Troft force gets here."

"Dogs fighting over a bone," Nissa said, her gaze drifting back to the Marine tunics inside the Faraday cages. "Whichever dog wins, it's pretty hard on the bone. So what do we do?"

"That part we haven't yet figured out," Jin said. "In theory, there's plenty of open space even on Aventine to put up a bunch of fake factories, and the other worlds are even emptier. In practice, though, I'm guessing that factories in the middle of nowhere with no populace nearby to supply workers will look highly suspicious."

"It's also probably why Reivaro went to such effort to commandeer Eion Yates's factory and start turning out armor plate for the *Dewdrop* and our other ships," Jin said. "Santores wants to make it look like we're turning out armored fighters."

Nissa huffed out a sigh. "We need to let Chintawa know about this right away. And the rest of Aventine, too."

"Chintawa, yes," Jin said. "Rest of the world, no. The last thing we need is panic and riots."

"The people need to know," Nissa insisted.

"They will," Jin said. "But when the time is right."

For a moment the two women locked gazes. Nissa looked away first. "All right," she said reluctantly. "We'll keep it quiet. For now."

"For now," Jin agreed. "You have a private way to contact Chintawa?"

"Yes." Nissa gave Lorne a strained smile. "You asked earlier who the *we* was that I listen to and get orders from. I assume you've figured it out?"

Lorne nodded. "Governor-General Chintawa."

"And a couple of others," Nissa said. "All of whom are walking the razor edge between cooperation and open revolt."

"As opposed to the razor edge between resistance and getting killed?"

"We all have our parts to play," Jin said, shooting a warning look at her son. "Yours is to guard our new toys; mine is to go hunt up some techs to start taking them apart."

"And hope we can find something useful," Nissa added.

"Oh, we will," Lorne said, smiling at her. "Because I know *exactly* what to look for."

CHAPTER ELEVEN

For the first half hour of their walk back toward Svipall Anya remained silent.

That was fine with Merrick. He was slowly getting a feel for the circadian rhythms of Muninn's animal life, but he was a long way yet from knowing which predators were most dangerous at which times of day. That meant he still had to watch everywhere and listen to everything, especially as the sun moved toward the horizon and they approached the transition period between diurnal and nocturnal hunters.

For the first ten minutes or so he'd continued to try to come up with a way to double back to the hideaway and at least get an idea of which way Hanna went when she left. The main stumbling block to that was finding a place where Anya would be safe while Merrick went off alone, and during the first part of their journey he kept an eye out for a cave or perhaps an abandoned thorn hut like the one Anya and their travel companions had built their first night on Muninn.

But there was nothing. There weren't even any of the thorny bamboo plants themselves, let alone a shelter made of them.

Eventually, reluctantly, he gave up on the idea. Hanna was well and truly on her own now.

"Is my father dead?"

Merrick felt his lip twitch. Anya's first words since leaving the hideaway, and *that* was what she'd decided to lead off with?

"I don't know," he said. "But I think there's a good chance he's still alive."

"Why?" she countered. "After all this time, he is surely not still free. He would have come to the stronghold if he was."

"*Not free* doesn't necessarily mean *dead*," Merrick pointed out, wrinkling his nose as they stepped out of the woods into a small clearing. Clearings had the advantage of being places where nothing would leap at them from the treetops. They had the disadvantage of being places where roving Troft aircars could more easily spot them. "If he's been captured, the masters may still want him alive," he added as he shifted his attention from the ground to the sky. Nothing up there that he could see, and his earpiece was being quiet.

"Why?" she repeated. "If my parents are indeed all that remains of their rebellion, there's nothing useful the masters can learn by questioning him."

Merrick felt his throat tighten. What could he say?

Back when he thought the whole family might have been caught, he and Kjoic had speculated that the three captives would be conditioned and sent out to hunt for the two fugitives. If the only one the Trofts had was Ludolf, they had even more reason to pump him full of their war drug. Not only would they want him to lead them to Merrick, but also to Hanna and any remnant of their rebellion that still existed.

Anya didn't know about the Troft drug, and the thought of her father undergoing such a treatment wasn't going to do much for her already somber mood. But she needed to know where they stood. "Actually, there is," he said. They made it through the clearing and he shifted his attention again from the sky to the ground and lower tree branches. "When I was in Svipall—"

"Merrick—look!" she gasped.

Merrick spun around, hands snapping up into firing position, eyes darting around in search of whatever predator she'd spotted. But there was nothing.

"Up there!" she said, pointing a rigid finger up at the sky over the treetops on the other side of the clearing.

Rising mostly vertically in the gentle breeze was a pillar of black smoke.

Merrick felt his breath catch in his lungs. Unless the forest itself had caught fire, the only thing he knew that was in that direction was—

"It's the safehold," Anya breathed. "It has to be. Oh, Merrick."

"Did your mother get out?" Merrick demanded, trying to bring his frozen mind back on line. "Anya, was your mother ready to go? Did she leave the same time we did?"

"I don't know," Anya said, her voice as rigid as her face. "We must find out." She tore her gaze away from the sky, jerking her head around to face him. "*You* must find out. Please."

Merrick hissed through his teeth. He could certainly travel there faster by himself than he could with Anya in tow.

But that would mean leaving her here, alone and defenseless. Did he dare take that risk?

"Please," Anya repeated. "I'll be all right here. Please." She looked around, pointed at a patch of the thorny bamboo by the edge of the clearing. "There—I can make a thorn mace and a barrier to protect myself. Please, hurry. Before it's too late."

Merrick winced. If it wasn't too late already. From the looks of the smoke pillar the hideaway had been burning for a while. If Hanna was still inside, it was unlikely he could do anything for her.

But he had to try. "All right," he said. "I'll be back as quick as I can."

"I know." Anya squeezed his arm. "Be safe."

Traveling quickly through unfamiliar forest, as Merrick had discovered on his trip from Svipall, was a risky proposition, with predators and unfamiliar terrain demanding his full attention. The predators were still a problem; but now, having just walked this path, the terrain was fresh in his mind, allowing him to travel much faster.

And he did. He sprinted through the woods, relying on memory and instinct to guide his feet away from pits and root tangles, trusting in luck and his admittedly distracted vigilance to avoid predators and potential Troft observers.

Soon—far too soon—he began to smell the acrid scent of burned wood and plastic.

There were a few tendrils of smoke seeping out from under the stone when he arrived at the clearing. But the main cloud was rising from somewhere in the forest beyond, presumably from the other entrance.

Clenching his teeth a little harder, he charged across the clearing and into the woods on the other side. He'd helped with a couple of rescues during the war on Qasama, but dealing with an underground fire was far beyond his experience. This whole thing would have to be done on the fly.

He was nearly to the site, and in fact had gotten his first glimpse of the base of the smoke column through the trees, when there was a brilliant flash of light and a violent explosion from somewhere in front of him.

Computerized reflexes took over, twisting him around to put his back to the blast and throwing him face-down on the ground. A second flash lit up the forest, and a second thunderclap rolled through the trees, as he hunched up on elbows and knees and waddled as quickly as he could toward cover. He hit the ground again behind the bole of a large tree just as a third shot hammered at the ground.

But this time, as the echo of the blast faded away, he heard something new: the drawn-out crackle of tearing wood.

And suddenly, he understood.

Carefully, he lifted his head and peered around the tree just as a fourth shot lit up the area. He was right. The Troft aircars hovering overhead weren't attacking the hideaway, or targeting someone trying to escape the fire, or even shooting at Merrick. They were methodically blasting away the nearby trees, creating a new clearing where they could land.

Merrick pressed a little closer to the ground as a smaller blast took down a smaller tree. So that was that. Whether or not Hanna was still in there, his part in this was over. The Trofts had the entrance nailed down, and even with the obscuring smoke there was no way Merrick could get into the tunnel unobserved. The only other way in was via the shaft, and the minute he moved the rock a second column of smoke would be visible to any vehicles watching from above.

All he could do was get back to Anya and get as far away from this place as they could while the Trofts were still concentrating on the fire and the hideaway. Carefully, taking as much advantage of cover as he could, he backed away from the commotion.

It had taken Merrick and Anya half an hour to cover the distance from the hideaway to where he'd left her. His return trip just now, done at a dead run, had taken him less than five minutes. This third trip, with the extra caution required by the presence of Trofts and Troft aircars in the area, took nearly an hour.

But the vigilance paid off. He reached the spot where he'd left Anya without incident.

To find that Anya was gone.

"Anya!" he called as loudly as he dared.

No response. He activated his infrareds and keyed his audios to full power. Nothing but the heat signatures and sounds of forest animals. He did a spiral search of the area, starting with the thorn bamboo plants where she'd said she would barricade herself. He gave up after scouring a full half kilometer without finding even a trace of her.

She was gone.

He returned to the thorn bamboo, his heart thudding, his brain spinning with fear and guilt. What could have happened to her? There was a freshly broken branch on the bamboo, which implied she'd had time to make herself a thorn mace, and he'd seen her skill at driving off small predators. Something bigger might have made it through her defenses, but such a battle should have left some evidence behind, whether blood or broken branches or bits of torn clothing.

But there was nothing.

The Trofts? He'd already seen that they were out in force today. But the clearing by the thorn bamboo had no broken bushes or signs of aircar skids, and the trees everywhere else were too thick for a vehicle to have put down. How could they have gotten to her without leaving some trace behind? In theory they could have killed her with a laser blast from above and rappelled her up, but again there should be some telltale burn damage. And if they'd attacked and she'd run away, shouldn't she have left Merrick some indication or returned once her attackers were gone?

There was only one option he could think of. Anya had vanished because she *wanted* to vanish.

For a long moment he stared into space, trying to make sense of it. Why would Anya leave him? Where would she have gone that she didn't want him tagging along? Back to the hideaway? To the wrecked ship? To Svipall?

His eyes fell on the thorn bamboo. He'd been watching for such bushes ever since they left the hideaway, hoping to leave Anya so that he could return and follow her mother. But he hadn't seen any.

Until this one. The very first thorn bamboo they'd encountered, the first bush that Anya could argue would provide her with a weapon and soothe Merrick's conscience about leaving her.

And while the smoke had clearly been rising for several minutes, it was only then that Anya happened to spot it.

Happened to.

This was no spur-of-the-moment decision. This whole scenario had been carefully planned.

And Merrick had no doubt as to who the architect had been.

"Damn," he muttered, looking back at the still-rising smoke. Anya had told him that she and her mother had stayed in the hidden room because they thought the Trofts had found them. Now, it was obvious that the person they were actually hiding from was Merrick.

Hanna had cooked up some kind of scheme, probably something involving infiltrating or raiding Svipall to rescue Ludolf. Merrick apparently wasn't part of the plan.

He scowled at the column of smoke still rising in the distance. So Hanna didn't want his help? Fine. He had his own mission on Muninn anyway. To hell with her, Ludolf, and their imaginary rebellion.

For that matter, if it came down to that, to hell with Anya, too.

Merrick had been working on a Plan A for getting into the Trofts' Svipall warehouse. Now, thanks to Hanna and Anya, a brand-new Plan B had suggested itself.

He nodded firmly to himself. Plan B it was.

The sun had set and the sky was starting to darken by the time Merrick made it back to the hideaway. The Trofts had long since finished knocking down all the trees they needed, and three armored aircars had settled into the newly formed clearing.

Given the circumstances, of course, it wasn't the best job of space-clearing in the world. All three vehicles had ended up canted at varying angles on the downed trees, two of them with one landing skid on the ground and the other on a trunk, while the third was precariously straddling two of the trees. About a dozen Trofts were visible, all in full armor and helmets and carrying heavy lasers. Four were standing near the tunnel entrance, the others walking a perimeter patrol. The smoke plume had mostly disappeared, probably an indication that other Trofts were down the rabbit hole putting out whatever fires still remained.

For a few minutes Merrick lay in the grass behind one of the bigger trees, studying the aliens' patrol pattern. The looseness of the roving formation seemed to indicate they weren't expecting any active opposition, but were mostly on guard against Muninn's assortment of predators. Given the fading light, they were also probably using infrareds or light-amplification.

He looked at the three aircars, studying their design. They seemed to be halfway between troop carriers and full-blown gunships, larger than fighters but with heavy lasers mounted up front. They had hatches near the bow on both sides, just behind the flight deck, and all the ones in his current sight lines were currently closed. Their landing skids were about a meter high, allowing the aircars to put down on uneven or debris-scattered terrain. At the stern were a pair of oversized thrusters and a high-low rudder that stretched from half a meter above the vehicle's top nearly to the ground, allowing for quick and violent turns and other maneuvers. On the hull in front of the thrusters were a pair of smaller hatches, though whether they were for maintenance access or external storage he couldn't tell. Running nearly the full length of the underside were a pair of grav lifts with a radiator grille between them.

Merrick turned his attention to the carrier nearest him. It was one of the two that was canted up on one side, with Merrick on the upslope. Like all the other hatches he could see, the one on his side was closed, and a quick light-amp check showed that there was a Troft seated on the flight deck. Even if the hatch wasn't sealed, he probably couldn't get in that way without making some noise or triggering some indicator lights that would alert the pilot. The hatch on the aircar's other side could conceivably be open, but given the haze of smoke still drifting across the area, it made sense for the Trofts to want to keep all the hatches closed.

Besides, getting inside the main compartment probably wouldn't gain him anything. It was unlikely there would be any place where he could hide long enough to get back to Svipall. The storage/maintenance hatches were too small for easy access, and the space behind them was even less likely to provide any hiding places.

Which left the aircar's outer surface. Or, more specifically, its underside.

It would be tricky. The parallel lines of grav lifts wouldn't be dangerous to an unprotected hitchhiker, but there was nothing there for him to hang onto. The grille was more promising, though it was still running hot enough to give off a solid infra-red glow. At the aircar's fore and aft ends were protrusions and indentations that were probably sensors or cameras, placed along the center line where they'd be as far away from the grav lifts' electronic distortion as possible. Most likely they did double duty as surveillance gear and targeting assistance for the lasers.

Lasers which were aimed outward from the clearing, Merrick noted with a small shiver, just like the lasers of the other two aircars. If a jormungand or some other large predator ambled into range, the Trofts clearly wanted their heavy weapons pointed the right direction. Just another reminder of the nastiness lurking all around them.

He looked again at the radiator grille. The louver slats were wide and thick, the metal surfaces probably doing as much to disperse the power system's heat as the forced air being blown through the narrow spaces between them. Comparing those spaces to the leaves on nearby branches, he estimated that the vents were no more than a couple of centimeters wide. That should be wide enough for him to slip his fingertips into, and his servo locks would make the grip secure.

The problem was that the slats were likely to get dangerously hot when the aircar was running full thrust. If whoever was in charge decided to take a turn around the forest before heading for home, Merrick could conceivably end up with some serious burns. Using strips of cloth from his shirt as insulation would help, but it might not be enough.

He looked at the ground around him. In the process of knocking over the trees, the Trofts' laser blasts had also created a lot of large wood splinters.

A minute later, he had them: four stress-ribbed slabs of torn wood that should work perfectly for what he needed. At least, he hoped so.

Now all he had to do was figure out a way through the cordon.

There, he hit an unexpected roadblock. The patrols were clearly on the alert, their pattern didn't leave any obvious holes he could exploit, and the Trofts gathered around the smoking hole had an annoying tendency to glance behind them at the forest at random intervals. Clearly, they'd all had enough experience with Muninn predators that they weren't inclined to be casual about it.

There was only one option. Sooner or later, the Trofts would pull back to the aircars and head for home. Once they were all out of view, Merrick would have a brief window to get himself over to his target vehicle and into position.

It wasn't the greatest plan he'd ever heard. In fact, the more he thought about it the more he realized just how heavy with risk this entire Plan B was.

But considering what his Plan A had been, it was worth the gamble. Slipping the wood shards into his shirt where they'd be handy but out of the way, he began to mentally map out the route he would take when the time came.

It came fifteen minutes later, and it happened so suddenly that Merrick was nearly caught off-guard. A handful of Trofts emerged into the smoky gloom from the tunnel, loaded with various scorched or burned objects. The Trofts waiting by the entrance took the debris from them, and the whole group split into three parts, each heading for one of the aircars. As the hatches opened to admit them, the perimeter guard began closing their circle, keeping their eyes on the forest as they backed inward toward the clearing, also distributing themselves among the various aircars. The last one on Merrick's side took a final look around the forest and then walked around to the other side of his aircar.

The instant he was out of sight, Merrick hunched up on elbows and knees and headed in.

The first three meters were the most perilous. Up to that point he was still in the pilot's line of sight, though the Troft would need to be looking the right direction and be running infrareds. Fortunately, he seemed to be concentrating instead on his pre-flight prep. Seconds later, Merrick reached the shadow of the downed tree, and from that point on his crawl was under at least partial cover. He reached the vehicle's midsection, rolled up over the log and landing skid to the other side. Another few meters, and he was lying beneath the center of the grille.

He had positioned himself on his back and pulled the first two wood chips from his shirt when the lines of grav lifts on both sides of him blazed to life.

Quickly, he wedged the two chips into the slits near his feet, angling them down and outward. He jammed his ankles sideways into the space between grill and wood, using his servos to lock his legs firmly in place—

Abruptly, the aircar lifted into the sky.

He barely had time to grab at the grille, getting his left fore-finger into one of the slots more by luck than by skill. He locked the joint, wincing at the heat blowing past his hand, as the forest dropped away beneath him. He got one of the other two chips out of his shirt and jammed it into the grille on the right side above his head. Making sure it was solidly wedged in, he got a grip on it with his right hand. Then he unlocked his left forefinger and got the final chip positioned where he could grip it with that hand. Raising his torso and hips close to the grille, pressing his body against it to make his profile as small as possible, he locked the hip and thigh servos into position.

And with that, there was nothing more he could do except hope. Hope that the grav lift glow shielded him from sight as the aircar came in for a landing. Hope that the radiator grille similarly masked his heat signature. Hope that the wood chips he'd chosen didn't break or work themselves loose.

Hope that the aircars were going to Svipall.

He winced. That one hadn't even occurred to him until just now. If the Troft response team had instead come from the city of Runatyr, which Anya had said was the region's major population center, he would end up forty kilometers from his goal. If had been sent from a full-fledged Troft military base, he was going to be in serious trouble.

But the aircars' direction seemed right, as near as he could tell with nothing but dark forest and an occasional tendril of road to orient him. He held on, tensing every time one of the other aircars dipped low enough that their pilots might be able to see him . . . feeling the cool wind rushing past his back even as his front grew uncomfortably hot pressed against the radiator . . . alert for any sign that the wood chips were on the verge of breaking or coming loose . . .

And then, suddenly, they were there.

It was Svipall, all right—the plain, boxy Drim warehouse build-ing was so far outside the norm of anything else he'd seen on Muninn that it was instantly recognizable. Merrick hadn't visited very much of the village on his two brief times inside, but with his light-amps active he could clearly make out the surrounding fence and the bersark field he'd pole-vaulted over.

Hopefully, he wouldn't have to face that challenge again. If he was able to stay hidden while the aircars maneuvered though the warehouse's cargo-sized doors and to wherever they would be parked for the night, he should be able to get his hands on some of the drug samples and get out before anyone could stop him.

If he was spotted... in that case, it would probably be time to show them who and what he really was.

The aircar continued to descend. It reached the level of the warehouse roof.

Only they weren't headed for the building. Instead, they were aiming toward a landing spot inside the village itself.

Inside the village, and inside the additional line of fence he and Kjoic had seen from their observation tree.

Only now, with his new angle, Merrick could see that it wasn't just a line of fence. It was, in fact, a complete ring, enclosing four houses plus a large expanse of what he vaguely remembered as cropland at the northeast part of the village between the houses and the warehouse. The new fence didn't connect with either the warehouse or the village's outer fence, but was set several meters inside both structures, completely isolating the houses and open space.

And as the aircar continued to descend, Merrick saw the reason why. The open space was the new landing field for Troft vehicles, and the aliens were clearly intent on making sure their human slaves didn't get anywhere near their flying weapons.

Why the enclosure was also isolated from the warehouse, and why it also included four houses, was still a mystery.

The other two aircars were already settling to the ground, once again exposing Merrick to observation from their cockpits. He tensed, pressing himself a little closer to the radiator as his aircar maneuvered to a spot beside the nearest of the houses. Why the pilot was landing so close to a building when there seemed to be plenty of open space was quickly apparent as Merrick caught a glimpse of three more sets of grav lifts cutting across the sky toward Svipall. Apparently, the Troft commander had been suspicious enough of the fire that he'd put all his birds into the air.

It was unlikely that he was bringing in his entire contingent, either. In his place, and under the circumstances, Merrick would want at least two vehicles flying high cover over the area at all times.

It was something he would need to keep in mind when he made his move.

Though he was no longer sure what exactly that move would be, or how it would work out. As his aircar settled to the ground he keyed in his telescopics, studying what he could see of the fence.

It was a basic chain-link design, with a tight weave similar to that of the village's perimeter fence. But a closer look with light-amps and telescopics showed a major difference: this fence had tendrils of some other wire or cable woven into the pattern. Sensors, undoubtedly, probably of the contact or proximity variety.

The Trofts didn't want Svipall's citizens getting in. Unfortunately, their electronic vigilance was also going to make it hard for Merrick to get out.

For the next half hour he stayed where he was, watching sets of Troft feet first cross the open space toward the warehouse as the aliens left the aircars, then watching different sets of Troft feet enter the enclosure as another group of the aliens came in for a quick maintenance check and to retrieve the burned objects the response team had brought back. It was clear from the traffic pattern that the main gate—maybe the *only* gate—was near the warehouse, but from Merrick's position that part of the fence was blocked by one of the other vehicles. He tried to listen for sounds of locks or latches that might give him a clue as to how the gate was secured, but even with his audios turned all the way up those sounds were lost amid the alien conversation and the noise of wind through the forest beyond the outer fence.

Listening to the rustling of leaves, he found himself wondering what Kjoic was doing right now, and whether the day's aircar activity had forced him into hiding. Or worse, gotten him captured or killed.

But Kjoic's life and safety were Kjoic's problems. Merrick had plenty of his own. For the first part of the aircar maintenance cycle he listened tensely to the cattertalk conversations going on around him, wondering if the grav lifts or radiators would come under scrutiny and what he would do if they did. Fortunately, from the chatter it appeared that the vehicles had recently had full checkups, which hopefully meant they wouldn't be going under the microscope for a while.

Finally, the parade ended, and all the Trofts headed back to the other end of the enclosure and out the gate.

Merrick stayed where he was for a few more minutes, listening to the night sounds and trying to figure out his next move.

This inner fence, like the one around the village, was about three meters high, which Cobra-powered servos should have no trouble clearing. The problem was the sensor threads he'd spotted, plus the fact that the fence was in full view of the sentries at the inner warehouse doors.

At least, most of it was. Not the section that went behind the four enclosed houses.

He turned his head around, frowning at the base of the house a few meters from his hiding place, wondering again why they were here. Isolating armed aircars from the Svipall humans made sense. But why isolate these four houses as well? Had they been turned into maintenance centers? Equipment and supply dumps?

Crew quarters?

He winced. Of course—that was it. For whatever reason, the aircars had been deliberately isolated from both the village and the warehouse. It only made sense to isolate the crews, as well.

And if that was the case, the enclosure could fill up with Trofts again at any moment as the crews finished their debriefing in the warehouse and headed to their quarters for food and bed. If he didn't move soon, he was likely to end up stuck here with enemies on two sides.

Once again, he keyed up his audios. There was no sound of movement nearby. Carefully, he unlocked his servos and lowered himself to the ground, huffing out a grateful breath as he was finally free of the radiator's heat. He took a moment to remove the wood chips—no sense leaving evidence that someone had infiltrated the village—and stuck them back into his shirt. On elbows and knees he eased his way past the line of grav lifts to the edge of the aircar nearest the house and farthest from the warehouse. He keyed in his infrareds and gave the entire house a long, careful look.

So far, so good. This side, at least, didn't seem to be occupied. The house was only a single story high, which didn't leave a lot of room inside, but if he could get in without being spotted by the Trofts guarding the warehouse door he should hopefully be able to find someplace to hide while he worked out a plan for getting back into the warehouse. Certainly there should be more options than he had out here. He slid out from under the aircar and rose into a crouch, focusing on the door and wondering briefly if it was locked—

There was a hint of movement just inside the door. Merrick dropped flat on the ground and froze.

Three men emerged from the house, their faces wrapped in scarves, their clothing a mottled pattern of black and gray. Each had a small flat bag looped around his shoulder and hanging at his side. Crouching low, they started across the field, two of them aiming past the bow of Merrick's aircar toward the other vehicles lined up along the field.

The third man headed straight toward Merrick.

Merrick stifled a curse. Whoever they were, he couldn't afford to let them catch him here. But there was no time to get back under the aircar, and there weren't any other hiding places he could get to without being seen.

Which left him no choice. Rolling up onto his side, he arched his back so that his torso was pointed directly at the men and fired his sonic.

The two men nearest him went down with gratifying speed and even more gratifying silence. The third man, partially shielded by one of the others, wobbled violently but stayed on his feet. "Jash!" he stage-whispered, clawing off his mask and gulping in air. It seemed to help. "Emkre!" He staggered toward the nearest of the men.

Rolling back onto his stomach, bracing his feet against the landing skid, Merrick threw himself forward in a low, flat dive.

His target might have seen him coming. But he wasn't in any condition to dodge. Merrick's hooked right arm caught him across the chest, slamming him backwards off his feet. At the last second Merrick twisted around toward him, catching the back of his head with his left hand to cushion it and taking the brunt of the impact on his own left shoulder and side.

For a moment they just lay there together, the man still breathing heavily, Merrick waiting tensely for signs that the incident had been noticed from the other end of the field. The man started to speak; Merrick shifted his right hand to cover his mouth.

He stiffened. Now that he had a good look at the man's face...

"Hello, Ludolf Treetapper," he murmured into the man's ear. "Your wife and daughter are very concerned about you."

CHAPTER TWELVE

Merrick lugged the two unconscious men back into the house, being careful not to make it look too easy. Ludolf managed to make the trip on his own.

The house, as Merrick had noted, was only one story tall. But it also had a small basement area that was being used for storage, with boxes of various sizes piled in haphazard stacks against two of the four walls. Ludolf led them to one of the empty walls, the wall facing the fence, and sat heavily down on a concrete floor composed of half-meter-square blocks. At the top of the wall, just above ground level, were a pair of narrow windows that let in just enough diffuse light from the rest of the village for illumination.

They would also let any wandering Troft patrol see in. The contrasting light levels should make it difficult for anyone to see inside, but it wouldn't be impossible.

"Put them down—there," Ludolf ordered in a low voice, pointing at the base of the wall. "What in the name of the Holy did you *do* to us?"

"Don't worry, it was just a sonic weapon," Merrick assured him. Carefully, he laid the two men on the floor where Ludolf had indicated, fighting back a trickle of misgivings. The stacks of boxes theoretically made this a good place to hide, but the very obviousness of it meant the basement would be the first place the Trofts would search if they suspected they had intruders. And with only a single set of rickety stairs leading in or out, the place was a highly effective trap. "It just scrambled their balance and inner ear. They should be fine in a few minutes."

"I don't see any weapon," Ludolf said, running suspicious eyes over Merrick's clothing. "The only arms are with the masters at the building."

"The only *obvious* arms, maybe," Merrick said. He reached into his shirt and pulled out one of the wood chips. "The best weapons are those that don't look the part."

Ludolf snorted. "A piece of *wood*?"

"Would you like me to demonstrate?" Merrick offered, leveling the chip at him.

Ludolf's lip twitched. "No," he muttered. "What are you doing here? Why did you intrude upon our mission?"

"For starters, I'm here to find *you*," Merrick said. "As for intruding on your mission, I was concerned it would intrude on *my* mission."

"Your mission was to find me," Ludolf said, pushing himself back to his feet. "You've done so. Now move aside."

"Not so fast," Merrick said, stepping between him and the stairs. "One, you're in no shape to go skulking around out there. Two, I said finding you was just for starters. Let's hold off any heroics for a minute, and while you finish recovering you can tell me what this is all about."

Ludolf snorted. "What happens on Muninn is none of your concern," he said, trying to circle around Merrick.

"And if I choose to make it my concern?" Merrick asked, again moving to block him.

Ludolf spat out a couple of words Merrick hadn't heard before. "I make it clearer: we don't want you here. You have no concept of our fight. No stake in our struggle. You are a weak spot, and a liability. I curse the fate that enticed Anya Winghunter to bring you here."

"You'd rather she have come back alone and empty-handed?"

"I'd have rather she brought an army," he retorted. "Why else do you think she was sent?"

Merrick stared. "What?"

"I've said enough," Ludolf growled. "Too much. Move aside."

"Not until you tell me what you were planning to do out there."

Apparently, Ludolf meant it when he said he'd said enough. He lowered his head and charged, aiming his shoulder at Merrick's stomach with the clear intent of bowling him over.

Unfortunately for him, Merrick had anticipated the move. Instead of hitting Merrick's torso, Ludolf ran his shoulder into Merrick's right palm, with a servo-locked arm behind it. The impact threw the older man off balance and sent him tumbling to the floor. "Keep it up, and someone's bound to hear us," Merrick warned as Ludolf rolled back up into a crouch, scowling in pain and anger as he clutched his shoulder. "I want to hear the plan. *All* of it."

"They will take you," Ludolf ground out. "They will sift you like wheat, and it will all have been for nothing."

"I may be harder to sift than you think," Merrick said. "But fine, try it this way. You need my help. You may think you don't, but you do. At the very least, you need me to get out of your way. And I'm not going to do that until I know what's going on."

"Anya said you thought you knew everything," Ludolf growled. "She said you believed yourself unbeatable."

"That sounds more like how *she* thinks about me," Merrick said. "Bottom line is that, like I said, I have a mission of my own. Unless I know yours, there's a good chance we'll run into each other."

"Then tell me *your* plans," Ludolf said. "I'll do what I can to avoid them."

"I'm the one still standing," Merrick reminded him. "And in about ten seconds I'm going to knock you out and leave all three of you here. Is that what you want?"

Ludolf curled his hands into fists. Merrick waited, and after a moment the man hissed out a sigh. "You will destroy us all," he muttered. "Very well. The fire at the stronghold. It was a signal for all to gather for the final battle."

Merrick frowned. "All who? Are you saying you really *do* have an army?"

"We do indeed," Ludolf said firmly, a hint of pride briefly peeking through his anger and resignation. "An army that will rise up against our oppressors in both city and villages."

"Right," Merrick said. Whether this alleged army could do any good against armed Trofts was another question, of course. But even if they failed, they might at least be able to create a decent diversion.

A second later he winced as his brain belatedly caught up with that thought. Was he *really* starting to think of people as nothing more than pieces in strategic plans?

Maybe he was. Maybe in this case he had to. "And your job here tonight?"

Ludolf eyed him. "We've seen how the masters in the large building can corrupt and control people. We need to see how they are doing this, lest they do it to us all."

"I agree," Merrick said, feeling a frown crease his forehead. So why hadn't the Trofts already done that? He'd seen how effective their war drug was. Why weren't they doing mass injections?

Because it wasn't ready, apparently. Which meant he still had time to get in and collect some for himself.

For himself; and *by* himself. The last thing he wanted was Ludolf and his private army getting in his way. "So again: what was your job here?"

"We came to cripple the vehicles," Ludolf said. "When the battle begins, the masters will draw all their resources together to defend and counterattack. I do not intend for these vehicles to join in that action."

Merrick focused on the bag still slung over Ludolf's shoulder. "We're talking explosives?"

"Yes," Ludolf said reluctantly. "And the time for affixing them is nearly past. Soon the masters who fly the vehicles will return here to their beds. You must allow me to finish my task before they reappear."

"You haven't thought this through," Merrick said. "You said the battle was supposed to draw your people to a single place. But unless they all have vehicles of their own, they can't possibly be in position for another day or two at the least. If you disable the aircars now, the masters will have time to fix them before the battle starts."

"Do you think us fools, Merrick Hopekeeper?" Ludolf said scornfully. "The disabling won't occur until we're ready to execute the attack."

"The bombs have remote controls?"

"Of course."

"Ah," Merrick said, eyeing him. Equipment like that seemed a bit sophisticated for a group centered in a farming village. Especially a farming village that had been under enemy control as long as Svipall had. "How long until the attack?"

"When all is ready," Ludolf said.

"That doesn't tell me anything."

"It wasn't meant to."

Merrick grimaced. Stalemate. "Fine," he said. "But you're still too wobbly on your feet. You wait here, and I'll go plant the bombs."

For a long moment, Ludolf gazed at him in the dim light. Trying to read his face, Merrick guessed. Maybe thinking about what Anya had told him, and wondering how much of it was true. "Very well," he said. "I'll wait. But not here." He got back to his feet and lurched over to the wall near his unconscious companions. He reached to the floor and fished out a set of thin wires nestled into the cracks between the concrete blocks. Setting his feet, he got a grip on the wires and pulled.

And to Merrick's amazement, the entire concrete block swung up on invisible hinges to reveal an opening hidden beneath it.

Ludolf looked sideways at him, his lip curling in a cynical smile. "You believe us to be savages," he said. "Anya warned us of that, too."

"I never said that," Merrick protested, moving closer and peering into the opening. The shaft was short, only a couple of meters long, with a wooden ladder along one side and a dark opening that seemed to lead into a tunnel running under the basement wall toward the Trofts' new fence. Very much in the style of the forest hideaway, he decided. "You have a lot of these scattered around, don't you?"

"We've been slaves for a long time," Ludolf said pointedly, unslinging his explosives bag from his shoulder and setting it on the floor beside the opening. "I'll go down. You will hand Jash and Emkre to me."

He climbed down the ladder. Merrick went to the first unconscious man, slipped off the shoulder bag containing his explosives, and got a grip under his arms. He carried him to the shaft and lowered him down to Ludolf, then did the same with the second man. "Any particular section of the aircars you were planning to blow up?" he called down softly as Ludolf manhandled the second man into the tunnel.

"They were designed to fit into the vents of the heat radiators," Ludolf called back. "Hurry and place them, then return here. Do *not* let the masters follow you."

"Yeah, thanks, I got that part," Merrick growled. He lowered the trap door into position and slid the lifting wires back into their cracks. It would take an extra few seconds to pull them out again, but he didn't want to leave any clues to the exit if he had to get out of the compound some other way. He grabbed the straps of the three bags and headed up the stairs.

The landing field was still deserted. Keeping low, Merrick ran to the first aircar, the one he'd ridden in on, dropped to the ground, and rolled over the skid and to the center. The explosives in the bags were better designed than he'd expected: compact and engineered to fit snugly into the gaps between the radiator louvers.

Whether they would pack enough punch to take down the radiator and the vehicle was another matter, of course. But he had no way of testing that. A quick inventory showed there were enough bombs in the bags for two per aircar, so he slipped two of them into the radiator, just to give it whatever edge he could. Rolling out the other side of the vehicle, he headed for the next one in line.

The aircars near the house end of field were relatively safe to get to. But as he moved ever closer to the warehouse building the risk grew progressively greater. The guards at the warehouse doors stood at attention with weapons ready, the slight flutter of their radiator membranes indicating they were fully alert. Merrick's job would probably have been easier last night, he reflected, before Hanna's fire had stirred up the hornets' nest. But there was nothing he could do except make sure he didn't kick the nest any more. Keeping one eye on the guards and the warehouse door, keeping the aircars between him and the guards as best he could, he kept going.

He'd finished the second-to-last aircar and was preparing to roll across the ground to the final one when the clock ran out. The person-sized warehouse door swung open, spilling a wedge of light onto the field.

Cursing under his breath, Merrick grabbed at the radiator louvers with his fingers and the tips of his boots and hauled himself off the ground, pressing as close as he could to the still-warm radiator. He held on awkwardly, his feet pressed hard against the edges of the slats as he tried to keep them from slipping off.

He'd expected a parade to come marching out the open door, in particular the Troft soldiers who'd been at the clearing and fire. But only three Trofts sauntered out, all of them in tech coveralls, rolling a tool cart in front of them. As he watched, they angled off to their left and headed toward the closest aircar to the warehouse, the one Merrick hadn't yet mined. They stopped beside it, and as the warehouse door closed they began pulling portable floodlights from the cart and setting them up around the vehicle.

And with that, Merrick's mission was over. He'd already seen from the open door that light from that direction would make any ground movement near the warehouse instantly visible to the guards. If he didn't leave now, he would be begging to be caught.

Even without the lights, it would probably be useful to make sure the guards' attention was elsewhere for a couple of seconds. Merrick pulled the biggest of his wood chips from his shirt, aimed at the section of fence thirty meters past his aircar's bow, and threw it as hard as he could.

The angle was awkward, and Merrick's range of movement pulled up beneath the aircar was severely limited. But Cobra servos were up to the task. The chip sailed through the air and landed in the grass right at the base of the fence. Merrick got a glimpse of Troft helmets turning that direction as he dropped back to the ground, rolled out from under the aircar, and headed as quickly and silently as he could back toward the house.

He was slipping through the door when the warehouse door again opened and the expected line of Troft soldiers began filing out, marching across the field in single file.

The house was still silent, which probably meant it was unoccupied, which probably meant it was the destination of the approaching soldiers. Merrick made his way down to the basement, wondering briefly if Ludolf's men had awakened in time for them to get through the tunnel under their own power or whether Ludolf had had to carry them the whole way. He located the proper concrete square, crouched down and fished the wires out of the cracks—

"Interesting," a soft Troft voice came from behind him.

Merrick spun around, snapping his hands up into firing position and kicking in full light-amps. There was a shadow of movement from behind one of the stacks of boxes—he twitched a target lock onto the figure—

"Your allies, they are more clever than I expected," Kjoic said, stepping out from concealment behind the stacks of boxes. "As, too, are you."

Merrick caught his breath. *Kjoic*? What in the Worlds was *he* doing here?

Too late, he understood. Kjoic had been here the whole time he and Ludolf were having their conversation. He'd heard the plan, and watched silently while Merrick went off to sabotage the aircars. Now the trap was sprung, and Merrick had walked straight into it.

He frowned. So where *was* the trap? This basement was as perfect a spot for an ambush as anyone could ever ask for. What was Kjoic waiting for?

Unless it *wasn't* a trap.

Kjoic was standing motionless beside the stack of boxes, his radiator membranes doing a slow flutter. Waiting for Merrick to work it through? "You're not so bad yourself," Merrick commented. He shrugged the bags and the remaining two bombs off his shoulder and laid them on the floor, then rose slowly to his feet. "How did you find this place?"

"The inner fence, I noted it had been constructed at an odd angle," Kjoic said, his radiator membranes settling back onto his shoulders again. Maybe he'd been more than a little concerned that Merrick would take his presence badly and try to do something about it. "I enquired and was told that the occupants of this house had insisted it be left outside the new compound. Suspiciously loud, that demand seemed to me."

"And of course the commander, not wanting to look like he was being bossed around by a slave, kicked out the occupants and reconfigured his fence line," Merrick said, nodding.

"Manipulation, it is sometimes easy to accomplish," Kjoic agreed. "Importance, I suspected the house had it, so I determined to explore. I was examining the boxes when your allies made their unexpected appearance from the ground."

"Ah," Merrick said. "Just to be clear, *allies* isn't the word I'd use with Ludolf Treetapper. I don't think he likes me, and he certainly doesn't trust me."

"Affection and trust are not necessary for allies," Kjoic said. "A common goal, it is all that is required."

"Maybe that's how it works for you," Merrick said. "We humans like at least a little trust in the mix. Speaking of common goals, what happened to the idea that we would work out a plan together before we made any move?"

"That question, I could ask it also of you," Kjoic said pointedly. "The smoke, I saw it from the observation post. The Trof'te response, I also saw that. I believed you had set the fire to draw a response you could use to enter the Drim building."

"I presume you know better now?"

"I have heard Ludolf Treetapper's statement," Kjoic said. "I have no reason to distrust it. So you merely took advantage of the fire?"

"Exactly," Merrick confirmed. "I was going to go to the crash site to look for Anya, as we agreed, but along the way it occurred to me that there was another place she might go instead where it would be safer for her to wait. I was on my way when I saw the smoke, and continued on to see if she was in danger. Once I got there, as you say, it seemed like a good opportunity to get into Svipall and possibly into the Drim'hco'plai warehouse itself. So I took it."

"And if you had succeeded in obtaining the Drim'hco'plai war drug with this plan?"

"We would have worked it out," Merrick said. "Just as you no doubt also planned to meet with me once you left Svipall."

Kjoic's radiator membranes twitched. "The drug, you believe I already have it?"

"Don't you?" Merrick countered. "You're here. Speaking of which, how *are* you here?"

"I believed you had dissolved our alliance," Kjoic said. "I knew I must move quickly if I were to forestall your anticipated attempt to obtain the drug on your own. I therefore determined to approach the Commandant of the Drim'hco'plai facility and reveal my identity."

Merrick felt his mouth drop open. "You *what*?"

"Calmness, regain it," Kjoic said. "I revealed only my identity as representative of the Kriel'laa'misar. My true mission, I did not reveal it."

"So what, you told them your demesne-lord sent you to look in on his investment?"

"Essentially," Kjoic said. "Though I made my demands somewhat more forceful than you perhaps might think."

"Oh, no, I've seen Troft arrogance and demands," Merrick assured him. "How did you explain suddenly showing up out of nowhere? Didn't he want to know how you got here to Muninn?"

"The question, he did indeed ask it," Kjoic said. "My answer, it was veiled. I stated I had been on Muninn for several weeks inspecting the other facilities."

A shiver ran up Merrick's back. "There are other places like Svipall?"

"Not to my knowledge," Kjoic said, his voice going a bit drier. "Nor do I expect it likely. But seldom is a Trof'te commander told the entire truth. Doubt of my word, he will have none."

"Unless he talks to whoever's running the planet."

"Who also will not doubt my word," Kjoic said. "The with-holding of truth, there is a long tradition of it."

"Okay," Merrick said cautiously. To him, it seemed an insane way to run a war. But then, he already knew that Trofts were seldom closer than mere allies of convenience.

And really, if it came to that, he and Ludolf's group were pretty much running things the same way. "And yet you claim you don't have the drug?"

"If I did, I would not still be here," Kjoic said. "There are many space-worthy vessels on Muninn I could steal or commandeer."

"So what happened? Don't they trust you?"

"Trust, it is not the issue," Kjoic said. "I am a representative of the Kriel'laa'misar, but a representative without the funds or authority for payment."

"Ah," Merrick said, nodding. Of course the Drims wouldn't hand over the drug without getting paid for it. That was the whole point behind Kjoic's presence here in the first place. "But they *did* at least show you the lab and storage facilities, right?"

"They did not," Kjoic said, his voice going dark. "Your escape, the result of it was the tightening of all defenses. The center floor is now home to guards and weapons. The test subjects, they are also no longer brought into the Drim'hco'plai building."

Merrick winced. Infiltrating the village and the drug test had seemed like a good idea at the time. It had gained him impor-tant information, but at a cost that might turn out to be higher than they could afford. "I wondered why they'd enclosed *four* houses. So this is where they're keeping the gunship pilots *and* the human test subjects?"

"Additional soldiers, they have also been bivouacked here," Kjoic confirmed. "They are those who are assigned to guard the village and the outside perimeter. All who are not already well known to the Commandant are sequestered in this village within a village. Further chances, the Commandant does not wish to take any."

"Wonderful," Merrick growled. "So you have no idea where the drugs are being manufactured and stored?"

Kjoic's radiator membranes vibrated slightly. "*That* statement,

I did not make it," he said in an almost-innocent tone. "The drugs, they are being stored and created in the northeast corner of the building."

Merrick frowned. "You're kidding. How do you know *that*?"

"The location, it was obvious from the pattern of guards and barriers," Kjoic said. "The logic, it is interesting, is it not?"

"The logic, it stinks," Merrick said with a snort. "Putting it in that corner means it's right by an outside wall. An attacker wouldn't even have to go through the village to get to it."

"Yet the outer wall, we *will* have to go through it," Kjoic warned. "It is not as easy to breach as you might think. The soldiers guarding the perimeter, they are also present and alert. The Commandant, he undoubtedly expects a thief to believe the goal is deeper in."

"Thereby giving the soldiers more time to take him down while he's searching in the wrong place," Merrick said. "Okay, maybe it's smarter than I thought. It might still come back to bite them."

"We shall hope," Kjoic said. "But the pilots, they will soon arrive. You must depart."

"Yeah," Merrick said, eyeing him closely. "One last question. You knew I was going to sabotage the aircars out there. You also know that Ludolf Treetapper is planning a revolt in Runatyr. Are you going to do anything about either of those?"

"The Drim'hco'plai, they are not my allies," Kjoic said, sounding vaguely surprised that Merrick would even ask. "Nor is Muninn a world of the Kriel'laa'misar. What the humans do to them is not my concern. Indeed, their revolt may assist us in our own task."

"That it may," Merrick said. Above him, he could hear the sounds of footsteps as the line of Trofts he'd seen emerging from the Drim building reached the house. "I'll be in touch," he murmured, heading back to the hidden trap door. He lifted it—

"You will keep me informed?" Kjoic asked.

"I'll do my best," Merrick promised, frowning as something suddenly struck him. If he modified his original Plan A... "Tell me, can you fly one of those aircars out there?"

"Yes."

"You may need to take one up to help battle a threat some-time in the next couple of days," Merrick said. "When you do, remember that the one currently closest to the Drim building is your best bet. Sorry—I didn't get its number."

"The number, I will obtain it," Kjoic said, his radiator membranes fluttering. "Your plan, can you explain it?"

"No time," Merrick said, lowering his voice to a whisper and pointing to the ceiling. "But if I can work it out, you'll know it when you see it."

"Very well," Kjoic said. "Be safe, Merrick Hopekeeper."

The tunnel Merrick had seen at the bottom of the hidden shaft wasn't very long, really only long enough to reach the house next door, the one directly across from the Trofts' new fence. But the tunnel's middle section had been widened into a room that was in many ways a smaller version of Hanna's forest hideaway.

Waiting there for him was Ludolf.

"You were gone a long time," the other said, his voice heavy with suspicion.

"I wanted to do the job right," Merrick said, looking around. The room had floor-to-ceiling wood shoring but, like the outer room of Hanna's base, was largely devoid of equipment, weapons, or even adornment. Fleetingly, Merrick wondered if there was another hidden room lurking behind it. "As it was, I had to skip one. Some techs came out to work on one of the aircars before I could get to it."

"Just that one?"

"Just that one," Merrick confirmed, watching his facial infrared pattern change. "But you already knew that, didn't you?"

"You were watched from outside," Ludolf said calmly. "Why did you hesitate so long after entering the house before coming here?"

"I wanted to look over the boxes in the basement," Merrick said. "I figured I had a few minutes before the masters arrived, and I wanted to see if there was anything there we could use."

"Was there?"

Merrick shrugged. "I really couldn't tell. It was too dark to read most of the markings, and I didn't want to risk making noise by opening any of them."

He held his breath. But there was no twitch in Ludolf's infrareds. Apparently, he was satisfied with the explanation. "So what is this place?" he continued before Ludolf could speak. "Svipall's version of your forest hideaway?"

"Yes," Ludolf said. "Though smaller and less elaborate, as you can see. It was designed mainly to store equipment and weapons for when the time came to rise against the masters."

"Which will soon be upon us."

"Yes," Ludolf said. "Tell me, what will be *your* part in that struggle?"

"I have a plan," Merrick said. "But to make it work I'll need to talk to some of the villagers. Especially people who've worked and traveled extensively in the forest. Are there men and women like that you can trust?"

"There are a few," Ludolf said, his forehead creasing. "If you wish merely to travel to Runatyr, there are many who can guide you."

"Oh, I'll be going to Runatyr soon enough," Merrick said. "But I have a couple of stops to make first." He gestured toward the other end of the tunnel. "Let's go find some of these trusted friends of yours and I'll tell you all about it."

He would, too. Or at least, he would *mostly* tell them about it.

CHAPTER THIRTEEN

The laser in Jody's hand flashed, and at the end of the *Squire*'s lower-level corridor the target Sergeant Plaine had set up on the bulkhead answered with an echoing spark of its own. "Number-two ring," Kemp announced from behind her.

"I *know* it's the number-two ring," Jody growled, activating her telescopics.

She'd tried firing with the telescopics running. It just made her dizzy. She'd tried extending her little finger along the side of the laser's grip, hoping her nanocomputer would take the hint and run a target lock for her. Apparently, it had never even occurred to the computer's designers that a Cobra might occasionally want to fire an actual weapon. All that was left was to try to learn how to shoot by sheer dint of effort.

And that wasn't going so well, either.

"You'll get it," Kemp soothed. "Learning a new skill takes time."

"Tell that to Rashida," Jody said.

"Tell what to Rashida?" Rashida's voice came from behind them.

"Tell you that learning new skills takes time," Jody said, feeling a fresh wave of annoyance as she turned around. Even focused on her practice, she should have had her audios high enough to spot Rashida's approach. "He's trying to make me feel better."

"And it isn't working," Kemp added.

"He's right, though," Rashida said, lowering her hand to rest

167

on the laser belted at her side. Apparently, she'd come down for some practice of her own.

Not that she needed it. "Then how come *you're* so good so fast?" Jody countered.

Rashida shrugged uncomfortably. "The same reason I learned so quickly how to fly a Troft ship."

"Fast-learning drugs?"

"Yes," Rashida said, sounding even more uncomfortable. "I have a small selection that I brought with me." Abruptly, she straightened to her full height. "And no, I will not give you any," she said firmly. "They are powerful and dangerous, and you have not been screened or tested for safety."

"Getting shot at by Trofts is also dangerous," Jody pointed out. Still, she could feel some of her frustration fading. She could hardly compare her progress to the learning curve of someone on one of Qasama's repertoire of useful but risky chemicals. "Don't worry—I wasn't going to ask. My mother delivered enough tirades against the use of shortcuts while we were growing up. Especially chemical ones."

"She is wise," Rashida said, peering at the laser in Jody's hand. "May I make a suggestion?"

"Sure."

Rashida glanced at Kemp, then drew her own weapon. "You have a targeting lock that controls the laser in your little finger. Can you not align that finger with the target and activate it?"

Jody stiffened. "It's okay," Kemp said quickly. "Plaine's up in CoNCH with Smitty."

"Yeah," Jody said. "Listen, there's something I've been meaning to ask all of you. Plaine said he'd been listening to us for a while before his grand entrance. Do any of you remember mentioning that I was a Cobra?"

"Smitty and I have been thinking about that, too," Kemp said. "Neither of us can recall it ever coming up in conversation since we've been aboard."

"And Smitty and I have closed down that system since Sergeant Plaine joined us," Rashida added.

"Good," Jody said. "I couldn't think of any conversations, either, but I wanted to check with you. If he's planning some kind of mischief, I may be the only hole card we have."

"Agreed," Kemp said. "And we definitely want to keep it that way. So, back to the question about using your laser targeting system. I see two problems, Rashida. One, the trigger requires her to press on the nail with her thumb."

"Which doesn't really work with a trigger stud," Jody said.

"Right," Kemp said. "And two, having *two* laser shots come out of one gun would kind of tip off the Trofts that something odd is going on." He cocked an eyebrow at Jody. "Unless the laser was at full power and your fingertip on low," he offered. "In that case, they might not even notice the softer shot."

"At least until they took a good look at the target," Jody pointed out. But he had a point. "Though if they're wearing battle armor...?"

"In that case the fingertip shot might only leave a minor distortion anyway," Kemp said, nodding thoughtfully. "Let's give it a try."

"Okay," Jody said, frowning in thought. She rested the laser across her left palm and eased her right hand tentatively across the grip. If she stretched her little finger straight out like Rashida had suggested...

"Let me help you," Kemp offered. "At least we can see how it looks."

"Okay," Jody said, getting a proper grip on the laser with her right hand and putting the tip of her forefinger a bit awkwardly on the firing stud. "If you press the fingernail firmly enough, it should fire the laser and gun together."

"Right." Kemp stepped close to her side and wrapped his left hand around her right hand.

"Okay," Jody said, an odd feeling running through her. This wasn't the first time their hands had touched, but somehow this one felt different. "Ready?"

"Ready."

Peering down the corridor, Jody twitched a lock onto the center of the target. "Now." Kemp squeezed her finger—

The corridor lit up with a double flash, and the target gave a corresponding double spark. "Fingertip dead center, gun about ten centimeters higher."

"And both flashes very noticeable," Jody pointed out, wrinkling her nose. "So much for that approach."

"Not necessarily," Kemp said. "Remember, the gun's on practice setting—much lower than full power. The bigger flash might hide it better. *And* the Trofts will probably also be scrambling for cover at the time."

"Even if they see the second shot, it may not matter," Rashida added. "They will be dead. And as Kemp has already said, a following examination may only see an unexpected distortion."

"I wonder what it looks like when the gun's at full power," Kemp mused. "It's bound to look different—question is, how *much* different? Shall we give it a try?"

"Let's make sure it won't be a problem first," Jody said, holstering her weapon. "You said Plaine's in CoNCH?"

"Yeah," Kemp said. "Want me to go with you?"

"That's okay," Jody said, heading down the corridor. "Rashida can probably use someone to spot for her. I'll be right back."

Plaine was indeed in CoNCH when she arrived, sitting in one of the monitor seats and gazing at a screen that seemed to be made up of false-color images. "Where's Smitty?" she asked.

"Went to get some water," Plaine said, his voice oddly preoccupied. "Said he didn't want to take any of the emergency bottles in here. Come here a second, will you?"

"What is it?" Jody asked, crossing the compartment to his side. "Is that something outside?"

"You don't get images from outside when you're in hyper," Plaine said. "This is a view of the Troft ship that accompanied Captain Moreau and the *Dorian* to Qasama."

"Okay," Jody said. To her, it didn't look so much like a Troft ship as it did some three-year-old's efforts at finger-painting. "Something wrong with it?"

"I don't know," Plaine said, scratching his cheek. "This is one of the images the *Squire*'s sensors took of it while we were leaving Qasama." He touched a spot on the image. "According to the manual, these are the active sensors up here."

"Okay. So?"

"So we're leaving Qasama, and the *Dorian* isn't trying to stop us," Plaine said. "Shouldn't the Trofts be wondering what's going on?"

"Why should they care?" Jody asked. "We weren't heading toward them, so it clearly wasn't an attack."

"Soldiers—*real* soldiers—care about *everything*," Plaine said, as if that should be obvious even to an Aventinian. "As for us not attacking, how do they know we aren't planning to circle around and get them in a cross-fire?"

"Okay," Jody said, eyeing the picture. "So how *do* they know that?"

"That's my point," Plaine said with exaggerated patience. "However you slice it, they should be watching us as closely as they can." He tapped the sensor spot on the image. "Only they aren't."

Jody chewed at her lip. "What about his weapons? Can you tell anything about them?"

"The lasers' active targeting systems are as quiet as the rest of his sensors," Plaine said, pointing to another spot on the image. "The lasers themselves seem to be on standby. Missile launch systems are also showing cold."

"So they really *aren't* expecting trouble," Jody concluded. "Sounds like they must have come to an agreement with Captain Moreau."

"Yeah, you'd think so, wouldn't you?" Plaine set his finger on the image one final time. "Only there's this. These are the engines... and that's *not* the IR profile for systems on standby."

Jody frowned. "What are you saying? That the Trofts are getting ready to leave Qasama?"

"That's how it looks," Plaine said. "And I still think they should be more interested in where we're going."

"Unless they already know," Smitty commented quietly from behind them.

Plaine looked over his shoulder. "You thinking that, too?"

"Thinking what?" Jody asked.

"That we've been set up," Plaine said flatly. "Or you have, anyway."

"Don't flatter yourself, Plaine," Smitty said. "If we've been set up, I'd say we've *all* been set up. *We* may have forgotten you were still aboard, but I doubt Omnathi or Captain Moreau did."

"Good point," Plaine said, glowering at the aft bulkhead. "The Qasamans would have had a job getting me out of the gunbay, but Moreau could have done it with a single order. Point conceded. The question is, why have we been set up? And for what?"

"For whatever and whoever's at the far end of this trip," Smitty said. "Which is making me feel a lot like bait."

"Or like a canary," Plaine said.

"Canary?" Jody asked.

"Old pre-space practice of taking a small bird into a mine to warn when the air's getting bad," Plaine explained. "If the bird conks out, the miners know to get out."

"So if we get blasted into atoms ten minutes after we arrive, Moreau and the Trofts will know to stay away?" Smitty asked.

"Something like that."

"Lovely," Jody murmured.

Plaine shrugged. "Don't blame the messenger. I'm just pointing out the facts. This trip was *your* idea."

"*Our* idea," Smitty corrected. "No one got dragged into this. Not even you."

"Whatever," Plaine said. "My point is that we've got seven days before we reach our end point. We need to be as ready as possible." He raised his eyebrows at Jody. "Which is a polite way of telling you to get the hell back to your marksman practice."

"On my way," Jody said stiffly. "The reason I came up here was to ask if there would be a problem if we fired the lasers a couple of times at full power. There's something we want to check out."

Plaine's eyebrows went up again. But he didn't ask. "Shouldn't be a problem as long as you keep the target range where I set it up. If you want to move it, check with me first so we can make sure there's nothing sensitive behind it."

"It's fine where it is," Jody assured him. "Thanks." She looked at Smitty. "You want to come watch?"

"I'll be down in a bit." Smitty nodded toward the false-color display. "I think I'll see first if Plaine can give me a quick course in reading this kind of sensor image."

"Sure," Plaine said. "Grab a chair, and I'll pull up the manual."

Jody needed only four shots, albeit with lots of accompanying discussion and analysis, to prove to everyone's satisfaction that the higher laser setting did indeed partially mask the lower-power shot from a Cobra fingertip laser.

But only partially. Someone who knew what to look for would have no trouble spotting the smaller blast.

"But like I said earlier, we can assume that the Trofts *wouldn't* know to look for a second blast," Kemp said. "And you can see the lower shot hardly even scarred the metal."

"Though I doubt the enemy will be wearing Dominion bulk-heads," Rashida pointed out.

"Yeah," Kemp agreed reluctantly. "I guess until we try this on some actual Trofts we're not really going to know one way or the other."

"Yeah," Jody said, thinking back to Plaine's disturbing data and even more disturbing conclusions. "Don't worry. I'm pretty sure we're going to get that chance."

Reivaro put up with the masks, the makeup, and the randomly running civilians for two days. Then, without warning, he struck back.

"It started at their Mabry garrison about three hours ago," Werle said grimly, as he skimmed through the video of the incident. "They moved in a bunch more Marines overnight, and the minute the first group of morning joggers got started they came charging out like crazed spinies. They grabbed everyone who was running, told them they were under arrest, and hauled them back to the garrison."

"Scooping up a few more along the way," Jin said, feeling her lip twist as she watched a pair of Marines detach themselves from the prisoner escort group and chase down a man and woman who'd been walking along minding their own business. "What are they charging them with? Or is Reivaro not even bothering with appearances?"

"Don't know," Werle said. "De Portola's been hanging around the neighborhood—"

"Discreetly, I hope."

"Believe it or not, Dill can be discreet when he wants to be," Werle said. "So far no movement or comment from that quarter. Nothing from Lij Tulu or Chintawa, either. Best guess is that the prisoners are being detained without charge while their identities are being confirmed, or some such nonsense. We'll probably see people dribbling back out over the next few hours."

"Harassment for harassment's sake."

"So we assume," Werle said. "Though I suppose that if we're going to be completely honest, we *did* start this one."

"No, *they* started it when they invaded us and declared martial law," Jin said. This wasn't a game, and she had no intention of letting Werle take even a single step in that direction. "I trust we're not going to let this go without a response?"

"I'm told there are discussions underway," Werle assured her. "No decisions yet."

"After three hours?"

Werle shrugged. "Chintawa's a civilian. He's not used to making quick decisions. And I assume Commandant Dreysler is waiting for him to figure out his response before he does anything."

"Really," Jin said, watching the display as the last of the Marines and civilians disappeared into the garrison building. "Too bad we're out of communication with them."

She raised her eyebrows at Werle. He looked back, frowning. His eyes flicked to the display—

His face cleared. "Damn shame, yeah," he agreed. "So it's up to *us* to do something?"

"Looks like it," Jin said. "How many Cobras do we have available?"

"You, me, Lorne, and a couple of others," Werle said. "And we can pick up de Portola along the way unless he'll need more than a quick briefing."

"A quick briefing should do him all right," Jin assured him. "Get everyone you can grab in the next ten minutes and bring them to the makeup room."

It took another two hours to get the plan ready and everyone in position. By then, as Werle had predicted, the citizens who'd been hauled into the Mabry garrison were starting to emerge.

According to the observers de Portola had left on the scene, some of them looked angry. Others looked frightened. Nearly all seemed shaken to one degree or another.

But the majority also seemed determined to carry on. A few of them, mostly women, were already reapplying the makeup that had disguised their features and gotten them arrested in the first place.

Still, Reivaro had made his point. While there had been no reports of mass arrests elsewhere in the city, there were only a handful of other impromptu jogging incidents after the Mabry incident, most of them perpetrated by teenagers. The general populace had been poked, and some percentage were undoubtedly rethinking their whole commitment to civil defiance. Especially since the Cobras seemed to have sat out the whole thing.

Jin meant to change that perception.

"Everyone in position?" she asked Werle as they walked together toward the Dome garrison. No one knew exactly where Reivaro was right now, but if he was in one of the garrisons her guess was that he was in this one.

"Looks like it," he murmured back, glancing casually around. "There's Dill and Lorne and—whoa."

"What?" Jin asked, feeling her heart pick up its pace.

"Emile's here," Werle said. "Emile Chun-Wei, one of the Capitalia Cobras."

"I know who he is," Jin said, peering in the direction Werle had been looking when he spotted the other Cobra. Even with her telescopics she couldn't see anyone who looked familiar. Whoever the Polestar Productions make-up artist had been on Emile's current transformation, he or she had done a superb job. "What's he doing here?"

"Hopefully, looking to join in," Werle said. "We told Chintawa about the plan, of course. I guess he or Dreysler decided to send backup."

"Or a few roadblocks," Jin said, her thoughts flashing back to the Dome's dithering non-opposition stance during the Troft invasion. "Can you tell how many of Emile's friends have come along?"

"Nope," Werle said, giving the area another casual sweep. "I don't know any of them well enough to pick them out under their makeup. I only know Emile because of that quirky little walk of his."

"Mm," Jin said. "Luckily, that works both ways. If we can't tag them, they shouldn't be able to tag us, either."

"Probably not," Werle agreed. "Though it'll be a little more obvious once we swing into action." He threw her a sideways look. "Though I doubt they'll *ever* recognize you."

"Thanks," Jin said dryly. As a woman, she should theoretically be completely off the Marines' radar as far as Cobra hunts were concerned.

Unfortunately, her very uniqueness as the only female Cobra turned that theory the other direction. Reivaro had seen her on many occasions, and had undoubtedly issued orders for his men to take a close look at every middle-aged woman who crossed their path. The obvious solution was to change her face to something much younger, which had been her plan when she walked into their base's makeup room.

To her mild annoyance, Kathia Rezondo had had other ideas. She'd patiently explained that making someone look significantly younger was very difficult to pull off in an uncontrolled environment like a city street, especially when people were undoubtedly watching for that kind of transformation. It was far easier and more convincing to go the other direction.

And so, with Werle holding her arm like an attentive grandson, she walked along the street as a slightly unsteady, slightly muddled ninety-year-old.

A ninety-year-old *man*.

Rezondo had had to argue long and hard on this one. But in the end, Jin had reluctantly agreed that it made sense. Lij Tulu and Reivaro had seen the records, both those back in the Dominion and the ones here, and they knew full well that the anemia and arthritis created by the bone laminae and servos drastically shortened Cobras' lives. There were no ninety-year-old Cobras on Aventine, period.

Of course, it was entirely possible that Lij Tulu had already thought of the possibility that Cobras might try to use old age as a cover. But Rezondo had assured Jin that the presence of wrinkles and gray hair wasn't all there was to old age. Jin was already starting to show the slight hesitation and carefulness of advancing years in her normal walk, and her growing Cobra arthritis merely enhanced that. If the Marines were smart enough to watch for such things, Jin should be able to successfully pull off the masquerade.

Lorne hadn't been convinced. But Jin had—eventually—and had talked him into it.

Now, though, as they approached the garrison building half a block away, second thoughts were starting to seep through her determination. Even knowing the huge structure was all illusion didn't mean it wasn't intimidating.

Besides which, she didn't actually *know* that the whole thing was still just the hollow shell it had been when Lorne checked it out two days ago. Reivaro had sneaked extra Marines into the Mabry garrison; what was to say he hadn't done something similar here? More Marines, more weapons, maybe even a ground tank or aircar or two—any or all of those would make a huge difference to the plan. Worse, by the time she knew for sure what Reivaro had up his sleeve, it would be too late to change course.

"There he is," Werle murmured. "At your nine—Ben Saller. See him?"

"Yes," Jin said. The young civilian—a city pipe inspector, she vaguely remembered, a friend and co-worker of Aaron Koshevski's—was coming toward her from the left, on a vector that would cross her path a couple of meters in front of her and about sixty meters from the two Marines standing stiff guard duty at the garrison entrance.

"Okay, this is it," Werle said. "Last chance to abort."

Jin took a deep breath. She'd had some of these same doubts during her part in the defense of Qasama, and there'd certainly been times when she or another combat squad had found themselves in way over their heads. But the Qasamans had always persevered, and even when they were surprised in battle they kept going. And more often than not they'd achieved their objective.

She wouldn't let Lij Tulu and Reivaro scare her away. She wouldn't give them the satisfaction.

"Ready," she said.

"Okay." Werle's chin dipped slightly in signal, and out of the corner of her eye Jin saw Saller brace himself. He crossed in front of her and Werle without a glance at either of them—

And abruptly launched himself into a full-fledged sprint, aiming for the temporary cover of the building on the corner.

Jin stopped, turning to look after him, hoping her look of surprise was visible through all the makeup. She held her breath, hoping this part of town hadn't been intimidated by the Mabry incident.

It hadn't, at least not completely. A young woman broke into a fast jog as Saller passed her, heading after him. Two men, one a teen, the other a respectable-looking businessman type, followed. Two more women, middle-aged with floppy hats half covering their faces, joined in at slightly slower paces.

And as the garrison door flew open and a dozen Marines charged out, Jin shook off Werle's arm and took off with an crazy ninety-year-old's what-the-hell enthusiasm to join the growing crowd.

She got nearly fifty meters before the Marines caught up with her, one of them grabbing her arm and forcing her to a halt while his companions continued the pursuit. The ladies with the hats got another twenty meters, the businessman thirty, and the teen fifty. Saller himself, who was clearly in good shape, made it nearly a hundred meters past Jin before he, too, was run to ground.

"Come on," the Marine holding Jin's arm ordered, turning her around and giving her a small shove back toward the garrison.

"Why?" Jin demanded, giving token resistance. A second wave of Marines behind them had fanned out into the crowd of onlookers, she saw now, grabbing a few more citizens for their collection. There was no sign of Werle; hopefully, he'd been able to slip away before the Marines arrived. "What's going on?" she persisted, continuing to tug weakly at the Marine's grip. "Where are we going?"

"You don't scan, Gramps," the Marine said. "We need to find out who you are."

"You don't need to take me somewhere for *that*," Jin scoffed. "I'm Jeb Stuart Jones. I live on... well, my grandson knows the address. He can tell you. Where is he, anyway? Corky? *Corky? Where's* that little spitter gotten to?"

"Yeah, don't worry—we'll bring him to you," the Marine said. They passed the edge of the corner building, and he gave her another small shove to turn her toward the garrison. "You can wait for him in there."

"I don't *want* to wait for him there," Jin protested. "He promised to take me to the park."

"Just go," the Marine growled. Two more Marines had emerged from the garrison, and Jin's guard gave her a last shove toward them. "Go. They'll show you where you can wait."

A minute later, still protesting, Jin was guided through the door into the garrison.

Earlier, she'd wondered if Reivaro had done more with the empty structure than simply stock it with extra Marines. He had, but it wasn't as bad as she'd feared. There was a row of lockers near both entrances, clearly for the use of the extra troops. In the center of the building, easily accessible to either end, was a sprawling analysis center, complete with bioscanners, an array of bottles that were probably makeup and synthetic skin dissolvers, and a couple of machines whose function she couldn't even guess at. Four techs in white coats were standing ready by the equipment. Set along both sides of the analysis equipment were detention areas enclosed by meter-high mesh fences.

There were already eight citizens inside the detention areas, most of them showing a mix of anger or nervousness, with a line of seven Marines escorting another dozen protesting citizens toward the cages. Six other Marines were standing rigid guard, making sure their captives stayed where they'd been put and turning the intimidation factor up to full strength.

Colonel Reivaro was nowhere in sight.

Too bad. Jin had hoped he might be supervising this person-ally, but she wasn't all that surprised that he wasn't.

She glanced casually around as she continued to dribble out confused protests to her escort. Right now, the thirteen Marines inside the building were far too big a plate for her to handle alone. Hopefully, Lorne and the other Cobras could even those odds a little.

Even more hopefully, Emile and his Capitalia contingent wouldn't try to stop them.

Lorne watched tensely as his mother was half led, half pushed into the garrison building. Seven Marines had now gone in, with six still outside herding the last remaining prisoners. There were probably another pair guarding the door on the garrison's opposite side, plus an unknown number inside.

Though there probably weren't too many of the latter. The more people they dragged off the street, the more successful this kind of intimidation was. Reivaro would have largely emptied the garrison in order to scoop up as many citizens as possible, which suggested there would be no more than a total of twenty Marines for the Cobras to contend with.

Of course, that was an assumption. It was also an assump-tion that they could get this done quickly enough that Reivaro wouldn't have time to airlift more troops to the scene. And if there was one thing the war on Qasama had taught him, false assumptions could be quickly lethal.

Jin disappeared through the doorway...and the countdown began.

Lorne eased his way forward through the pedestrians, uncom-fortably aware that most of the people were heading *away* from the garrison instead of toward it. The remaining Marines, focused on herding their prisoners, didn't seem to notice the oddity of Lorne's movement, but he knew that such unawareness wouldn't last long. Thirty meters to his left, Werle was also heading inward, with de Portola the same distance to Lorne's right.

The last Marine in line was twenty meters ahead. Lorne glanced targeting locks onto the inner edges of his epaulets, feeling the sense of walking onto thin ice. The Dominion's epaulet lasers had been rigorously tested and had proved their ability in combat. The Cobras' mudballs had been neither. If this trick didn't work, Lorne and the others were looking at death or at the very least an excruciatingly painful capture.

But there was no way around it. Lorne was close enough now to the rearmost Marine, and Werle and de Portola were in range of the next ones up the line, for their antiarmor lasers to take out the epaulets' targeting system. But the other three Marines were far enough away that there was no guarantee the Cobras could neutralize them with a single pair of shots, especially since the first attack would alert them.

And if their computers were still functional, that one volley was all the Cobras would get. The Marines' counterattack would be swift, accurate, and most likely delivered at full power.

His nanocomputer countdown ran to zero.

And simultaneously, all three Cobras pulled a pair of mudballs from their pockets, leaned back as they swung up their left legs, and fired antiarmor laser bursts into their targeted Marines' epaulets.

The control edges flashed into small clouds of vaporized metal and ceramic, taking the Marines' autotarget system with them, though not before one of the epaulets got a shot off that sizzled a handful of tiny burns across Lorne's leg. But the lasers were set to the Marines' stage-two riot-control level, and the ablative material hidden beneath Lorne's trouser legs absorbed the heat of the shots. He hurled his two mudballs at the next Marine forward in line and broke into a full-speed dash toward the line of enemies.

All six Marines spun around, fully alerted, the ones with the damaged epaulets staggering a little as the fragments from the destruction caromed off the sides of their helmets. Laser shots flashed out toward the charging Cobras; but with their targeting systems gone, the Marines were on manual, and their shots went wide of their zigzagging opponents. The unaffected Marines' fire was better, slashing across the incoming Cobras with deadly precision.

But their auto-target systems were also set to riot level, and again Lorne's protective wrappings blocked most of the fire. He winced at the small flickers of pain from the energy that made it through, knowing full well that the Marines were even now shifting to higher power. A split second later the mudballs the three Cobras had thrown crossed the edges of their respective Marines' automatic defense perimeters.

And to Lorne's vast relief, the damn things actually worked.

The first shot from each Marine shattered the incoming clay, releasing the ball bearings to continue on in a narrow cone. Faced with the suddenly revealed threat, the targeting systems kicked into overdrive, the epaulets erupting into an awesome light show as each ball bearing was targeted and blasted into vapor.

Lorne hurled two more mudballs at his target Marine in rapid succession, his nanocomputer's throw-targeting system enabling him to keep his eyes focused on the first Marine, the one he was currently running down.

The irony was the fact that the bearings would cause little or no damage to the armored suits if they got through the laser defenses. But that was irrelevant to the Dominion computers. Fast-moving objects were approaching, and the defenses' number-one obligation was to stop them.

The Marine Lorne was charging at probably felt much the same way about the incoming threat, certainly with far better cause. But with his lasers on manual, and his target dodging and evading, he was unable to neutralize the threat. Behind Lorne, de Portola reached his own attack distance, and the flash of his arcthrower lit up the sky. Lorne's target Marine fired one more useless shot, and then abruptly turned and ran.

Sprinting up behind him, Lorne sent an arcthrower blast into the back of the man's helmet. The Marine gave a violent twitch, staggering as the current ran through him and his suit. Lorne fired again, and the Marine dropped face-first onto the ground and lay still.

There was another flash at the edge of Lorne's vision, and he looked over to see Werle's Marine also slump to the ground. Three down; three to go. He shifted direction toward the Marine still fighting off the mudballs and picked up speed. To his sides, Werle and de Portola were keeping up the barrage on all three Marines, hopefully distracting their computers enough for Lorne to get in range.

Once again, hope and plan came together. Lorne hit the twenty-meter mark, threw himself forward in a twisting dive that ended with him on his back with his left leg pointed at the loose group of enemies. Six antiarmor laser blasts later, the last three sets of epaulets had lost their autotarget ability.

He bounded back to his feet and charged forward. But Werle and de Portola were already pounding ahead of him. They reached arcthrower range, and a moment later the three Marines had joined their comrades on the pavement.

"Wow," de Portola said as they came to a halt. "That was easier than I expected."

"Only because there were just six of them," Werle warned. "There are probably twice that many left, who'll be coming out any second."

"So let's keep them bunched at the doorway," de Portola said. He took off again, sprinting toward the garrison door, Werle right behind him.

Lorne followed, glancing around. With his full focus on attack and defense he hadn't had a chance to see what had happened to the civilians the Marines had been escorting.

Fortunately, there were no bodies strewn across the pavement, but only men and women running from the battle scene as fast as their legs could carry them. Many of them were still in range of Dominion weaponry, but as long as the Cobras were Reivaro's primary targets the Marines should leave everyone else alone.

Now if only Lorne and the others could reach the door and bottle the rest of the Marines in a choke point...

They were still thirty meters away, still out of guaranteed kill range, when the door was flung open and three Marines charged through.

Werle and de Portola were ready. Each of them threw a quick one-two barrage of mudballs, picking up their pace and going back to zigzag. Lorne locked onto the Marines in the back and hurled two mudballs of his own, painfully aware that he had only six left. The Marines' epaulets exploded in defensive fire as the troops fanned out to the sides, trying to make room for the others behind them. Something caught Lorne's peripheral vision as it flew toward the Marines from his left—

And a split-second later the street was rocked with a violent explosion.

CHAPTER FOURTEEN

With the garrison door open, the explosion from outside was startlingly loud.

Far louder than the mudballs should be. For that matter, far louder than *anything* Jin had worked on should be.

She slapped her hands over her ears as her heart leaped into her throat. Had the blast been some sort of accident—stray laser fire into a tank of flammables, maybe? Had Reivaro decided to abandon even the pretense of civility and restraint?

Another blast echoed through the building. What the *hell* was going on out there?

But there was no time to figure that out now. She still had a job to do.

A job that was getting easier by the second. Three of the thirteen Marines in the garrison had already made it through the door, out into whatever was happening out there, and the bits of flickering light she could see showed that they were fully engaged in combat. The four who'd been following them were momentarily stalled, the vanguard holding their ground halfway in the doorway. The six other Marines around her were standing motionless, their helmets turned toward the battle, apparently waiting for information or orders. Another pair of blasts came from outside—

Abruptly, four of the remaining Marines turned and bolted toward the garrison's far door.

Leaving only two behind to guard the prisoners.

Jin smiled to herself. Perfect.

There was another explosion from outside. Jin again lifted her hands to her ears, staggering a little as if the sudden noise was giving her vertigo. She turned toward the two remaining Marines, one of them standing a meter back from the other, both of them facing the group of nervous civilians. "Please—what's going on?" she called. There was another blast, and she again put her hands over her ears.

The Marines didn't respond. "What are you people *doing* out there?" Jin asked again, lowering her hands. She continued toward them, keeping her walk unsteady. Sooner or later they would probably order her back, but if she looked harmless enough they might let her get close enough.

Almost there. "Move back, sir," the nearer of the Marines ordered, the voice coming from the helmet's speaker sounding hollow and artificial. The Dominion could surely make better speakers than that; the mechanical effect was probably a deliberate attempt at intimidation.

"Why are you always making noise?" Jin asked plaintively, again clapping her hands over her ears. Another two steps. She lowered her hands, flicking a target lock onto the control edges of their epaulets. "Some of us have enough trouble sleeping with the traffic noise—"

"Sir—"

Another blast came from outside, and again Jin swung her hands toward her ears.

But this time, as her hands went up, she curled her fingers into firing position, squeezing the fingernails with her thumbs.

The nearer of the two Marines was caught completely by surprise as Jin's first two shots took out his epaulets' control edges. She leaped toward him—

And twisted sideways as a double flash from his laser sizzled through the air around her.

With his control edges fried, she knew, he was reduced to manual targeting. But she was still a huge target at this range. She did another quick hop to the side as a second pair of blasts shot past, stretching out her arm toward him and cancelling the target lock on the second Marine. The latter was rapidly backing away and to the side; Jin countered by taking another side step of her own to put the first Marine between them. The first Marine got off one more useless volley right as Jin's arcthrower blasted across the gap to his helmet.

He staggered back as she leaped forward, firing a second shot that dropped him toward the floor. Jin lunged forward and managed to slide her hands beneath his armpits, catching the limp body before it could collapse all the way.

And now, with him held before her like a shield, she turned her attention to the second Marine.

He was backing up, a stream of hissing curses coming from his helmet speaker. Jin target-locked his control edges and, with her hands still tucked beneath the unconscious man's arms, fired her lasers. He dodged to the side—too late—and Jin sent a second pair of shots into his epaulets. Then, shifting her grip on her human shield, she threw him with all her strength toward his partner.

The Marine again tried to dodge, and this time almost made it. But not quite. Even as he fell backward with the impact, his fall taking his epaulets out of firing range, Jin sent a pair of arcthrower shots into his armor, taking him out of the fight for good. She took a half second to make sure both were down, then swiveled around to face the open door.

Her biggest fear was that her attack had been heard and that she would now be facing another four to seven Marines. But all seven had made it outside and seemed to be fully occupied. Turning back, she headed toward the techs.

They were still frozen in the same spots where they'd been sitting or standing, all four of them staring at her with a mixture of shock and fear. "Get away from the equipment," Jin ordered, pointing her fingertip lasers at them for emphasis. "If any of you have comms to the Marines, I strongly suggest you don't use them."

Silently, the techs scrambled up from their chairs and backed up a few steps toward the opposite door. "They'll get you, you know," one of them warned. "They're Dominion Marines. They're the best."

"I'm sure they think so," Jin said. "Lie down on your stomachs, faces toward the far door."

Again, they did as ordered. Briefly, Jin considered blasting the equipment, decided she didn't want to risk the extra noise, and turned to the prisoners.

All eyes were on her, as she'd expected. A number of mouths were hanging open, as well. "Everyone all right?" she asked.

"Who are you?" a woman asked, her voice shaking a little. She hadn't been one of the people who'd been running, Jin noted, which meant she was one of the ones the Marines had snatched from the crowd at random.

"Who cares?" an older man cut in. "He's a Cobra. You're getting us out, right?"

There was another explosion, and Jin took another look at the door. There was a lot of laser fire going on out there, most of it not directly visible but inferred from the flickering reflections off the neighboring buildings. The explosions had settled into an almost rhythmic pattern, one coming every ten seconds or so, and from the sound and reflected light pattern she could tell that particular attack was coming from the right side of the door. If the four Marines who'd taken off through the far door were trying to counterattack at the Cobras' rear, they should also have gone down that side of the building.

Which should, logically, leave the other side of the building unguarded.

"You're getting us out, right?" the man repeated. "The back door, right?"

"No," Jin said. "Follow me. Quick and quiet."

She stepped over the two Marines she'd stunned and headed toward the wall. Along the way she noticed a patch in the floor that probably marked the access shaft that Lorne had used in his own earlier escape. For a moment she was tempted, but this really wasn't the sort of crowd she'd feel comfortable taking down a rickety ladder. She passed it by, throwing a quick look behind her to make sure the rest of the prisoners were following.

They were. The older man had taken the lead, while the woman who'd apparently been too confused or startled to realize she was facing a Cobra was bringing up the rear. Jin reached the wall and swung her left leg up and around in a sweeping arc, activating her antiarmor laser and slicing an opening in the wall.

She slipped through, fingertip lasers at the ready, wincing at the sudden arthritic pain the maneuver had sent throbbing through her hip joint. She'd guessed right: the narrow space between the garrison building and the walkway was deserted. Stepping to the side, she gestured the prisoners to join her. "There," she murmured to the leader, pointing to a service alleyway leading off the street a few meters to the side, her words punctuated by another explosion from the front of the building. "Get them to the next street and then send them all home."

"Aren't you coming with us?" he asked, frowning.

"I'll see you out," Jin said. "Then I have other work to do."

The man's eyes flicked over her shoulder toward the flashes of reflected light. "Right. Good luck." He gave her a brisk nod and then headed at a fast jog toward the alley.

The rest of the prisoners followed, a couple of the older men and women being helped along by some of the younger ones. Jin set her back to the garrison building wall, turning her head back and forth and up, watching tensely for the inevitable counterattack. Even if Lorne had all the local Marines pinned down, the techs must have called for help by now. Reivaro surely had a fast-response team standing ready to be airlifted anywhere in the city.

For that matter, even the local Marines might be free soon. The explosions were becoming increasingly sporadic, suggesting the battle was coming to an end, one way or another. As soon as the last civilian was out of her sight, she would fire off the prearranged triple antiarmor laser shot off the edge of the garrison building, and she and Lorne's team would do their best to get the hell out of here.

Hopefully, they would all get out alive. This whole thing had been a risk, and a potentially disastrous one. But it had been important to show Capitalia's citizens that the Cobras weren't going to let the Dominion simply walk all over them.

Back on Qasama she'd seen how important civilian support was to a fighting force. It was a road that went both ways.

"Cobra?"

Jin turned. The woman who'd been at the rear of the line was standing in the opening in the wall, a pained expression on her face. "What are you doing?" Jin demanded, glancing at the alley. The last of the line of prisoners was just disappearing. "That way. Go on. *Go.*"

"I'm sorry," the woman said.

Before Jin could respond, the woman's collar exploded into a cloud of cold, sweet-smelling mist.

Jin threw herself backward, her leg servos turning the panic jump into a full five-meter leap. But it was too late. Already her vision was wavering, and as her feet hit the ground her legs collapsed beneath her. She stretched out her hands to break her fall.

And the world went black.

The first explosion had caught Lorne completely by surprise. From the reflexive backward jerking of the Marines, it seemed the blast had taken them off guard, as well.

Luckily for them, their defense didn't depend on their attention or lack of it. Even as a second object came hurtling in from the side, the air once again was filled with a blazing fury of laser fire.

Unluckily for them, Lorne's response also didn't depend on him knowing the details of what was going on. With the Marines' auto-fire once again fixated on whatever the explosion had unleashed toward them, they were vulnerable to attacks from all other directions. Putting on a burst of speed, Lorne charged toward them, target-locking all the epaulet control edges in his field of view. There was another blast as a laser shot hit the latest flying object, followed by two more of the objects and two more explosions.

It was as Lorne reached range and threw himself onto his back in laser-firing position that he finally got the last piece of the puzzle. Even as his antiarmor laser blasted the Marines' epaulets something hit his leg, sending a flash of pain through his calf. He finished his firing, rolled up into a crouch, and checked the spot.

Sticking out of his leg was what looked like a small metal nail.

He looked up again as another explosion thundered across the area, swearing softly under his breath as he pulled out the nail. So that was what Emile and his fellow city Cobras had come up with. Instead of another form of mudball, they'd created shrapnel bombs.

But this wasn't the time or the place to deal with the complications of such a weapon. The first three Marines out of the garrison were disarmed and Werle and de Portola had sent two of them to the ground with arcthrowers blasts. But that left five Marines still standing, their epaulets blazing at the renewed barrage of shrapnel bombs, and there were undoubtedly more behind them. The Cobras had to draw out the whole garrison if Jin was going to have her chance to free the prisoners.

"Incoming!" someone shouted from Lorne's left. He glanced that direction, just in time to see more reflected laser fire coming from the far side of the building's corner. More Marines, probably having come from the garrison's far door to try a sortie at Emile's rear.

Briefly, Lorne wondered if he should send Werle to assist Emile's group, decided he and his team would do better to keep the Marines on this side tied down. Another Marine had appeared through the door, jumping to the side and opening up with a flurry of laser fire, much higher power this time. His first shot sliced through Lorne's ablative insulation and burned across his rib cage, but his programmed reflexes managed to dodge the others. There was no chance for Lorne to target anything as small as epaulet control edges while in violent motion; instead, he did a quick lock on the Marine's helmet and threw his last mudball.

For half a second the incoming threat took over the Marine's firepower, redirecting the lasers toward the ball bearings instead of Lorne. Lorne took advantage of the momentary reprieve to target-lock the Marine's control edges and fire. The epaulets' fire faltered, then resumed toward Lorne at a slower rate as the Marine switched to manual targeting—

An arcthrower blast split the air, and the Marine dropped to the ground.

"Come on!" someone shouted.

Lorne jumped back to his feet, looking around. The street was littered with Marines, some of their epaulets trailing wisps of smoke. Presumably all unconscious, though there was no way to know if there'd been any fatalities.

The Cobras, unfortunately, were another story. Two of them lay unmoving, crumpled on the ground.

"Come on!" the order came again, more urgent this time, accompanied by a shake on Lorne's shoulder. This time he was able to identify the voice: Emile. "Come on, Broom—we got aircars coming in."

"What about the signal?" Lorne asked, looking up toward the building's corner. There was no sign of his mother's laser fire, or any evidence she'd sliced through the material there. "Anyone see the signal?"

"I didn't," de Portola said. "But he's right. We have to go."

Lorne clenched his teeth. If his mother hadn't gotten the prisoners out... but Emile and de Portola were right. Getting the rest of them caught wouldn't gain anyone anything. "Go."

Steeling himself, he reached down and picked up one of the dead

Cobras. Emile already had the other and was heading for the nearest access shaft. The rest of the Cobras, Lorne noted, were dispersing toward the various shafts they'd mapped out for the escape.

"Here they come," Emile muttered.

Lorne looked up.

Overhead, the Dominion aircars were starting to appear.

And suddenly, the high-minded demonstration of Cobra support for the citizenry was about to turn into a slaughter. Lorne winced, his stomach twisting, waiting for the barrage to begin.

But to his surprise, it didn't. The aircars' occupants merely watched as he and Emile reached the shaft unhindered and escaped back underground.

Perhaps Reivaro was hoping to find their headquarters by mapping the locations of their bolt-holes. Perhaps he or Lij Tulu had decided to be content with delivering yet another lesson in Dominion superiority. Perhaps their goal now was simply to drive the enemy from the field.

Having first, of course, killed two more of them. Part of the whole superiority lesson.

"You all right?" Emile grunted as they reached the bottom of the shaft.

"Yeah," Lorne said. There was no light at all down here, and he keyed in his infrareds. Emile and the two bodies gave off the usual glow, lighting the couple of meters of concrete immediately around them but leaving the rest of the area in darkness. "You?"

"Mostly."

"Good," Lorne said as they headed off down the conduit. Moving in the cramped space with a body on his back, he quickly discovered, was a whole new level of difficulty than doing it alone. "What the hell were those?"

"You mean our little distractions?"

"I mean your damn shrapnel bombs," Lorne shot back. "In case you hadn't noticed, there were civilians in the area."

"Oh, relax," Emile said scornfully. "They were shaped charges. The only ones in danger were the Marines."

"That's ridiculous," Lorne growled. "You can't make a shaped charge that you throw."

"You can if you're throwing at Dominion Marines." Emile huffed out a sigh, and Lorne had the annoyed impression that the other Cobra was rolling his eyes. "Look. We coat the bombs with a hard shell. Well, hardish, anyway. We throw one at a Marine, and his laser punches through the shell, igniting the explosive. The intact part of the shell holds things together just long enough to direct the main blast and shrapnel through the hole straight back at him."

"Most of the shrapnel, anyway," Lorne muttered. "I got one of your nails in my leg."

"Yeah," Emile said. "Well, it was our first try." He threw a look over his shoulder. "What's *your* excuse?"

"My excuse for what?"

"This whole boneheaded stunt," Emile bit out. "Two more Cobras dead; and for what? Reivaro would have let all the civilians go in a few hours anyway."

"And what would have happened the next time we asked Capitalia to help us out with something?" Lorne retorted. "We can't do this alone, Emile. We need the whole planet behind us if we're going to get the Dominion off Aventine."

"If you think we can get rid of them on our own, you're dreaming," Emile said flatly. "The only way to do that is to get the Trofts in on the job."

Lorne felt his mouth drop open. "The *Trofts*? Are you *crazy*?"

"Oh, relax," Emile said. "I'm talking about *our* Trofts. The Tlossies and Hoibies. If we can get them to push back against the Dominion, even Lij Tulu might be persuaded to go home."

Lorne shook his head. "Not a chance. Whatever they're here for, they're not going to go away just because a few Trofts ask them politely."

"Who said anything about asking?" Emile countered. "We know Captain Moreau took the *Dorian* to the Hoibic homeworld. I can't see their demesne-lord being happy that there are alien warships in his neighborhood."

"*I* can't see him being stupid enough to line up with the group fighting at the other end of the Assemblage," Lorne said. "Especially when he probably has no independent way of knowing how their side of the war is going."

"I guess we'll see which one of us is right," Emile said. "Starting...oh, about a week from now. Maybe less."

"What happens in a week?"

Emile threw a sly smile over his shoulder. "You'll see," he said. "Here's a hint: it'll start in DeVegas province."

Lorne frowned. DeVegas was where the first shots had been

fired in this simmering resistance against the Dominion. It was where the first blood had been drawn. Was Commandant Ishi-kuma planning something dramatic?

He caught his breath. "The *Dewdrop*?"

"Yep," Emile said with obvious satisfaction. "The armor plating that Santores insisted on—"

"And got by wrecking every metal-working machine in Eion Yates's factory."

"If it makes you feel any better, it's nothing personal about Yates or DeVegas," Emile said. "Lij Tulu's in the process of wrecking two other factories in Willaway province to get armor plate for the *Mensana* and *Southern Cross*."

"Terrific," Lorne said, making a face. Three factories wrecked. Even if by some miracle the Dominion left tomorrow, the consequences and costs would linger for years to come.

His stomach tightened as he focused on the body slung over Emile's shoulder. Not to mention the costs in human life. "So Chintawa's plan is to send the *Dewdrop* to the Hoibies to beg them for help? And you really think Lij Tulu will be careless enough to let it get out of the system?"

"Don't worry—we haven't forgotten your big plan," Emile soothed. "The idea is for it to wreck the Dominion's relay satellites on the way out. That *was* what you wanted Chintawa to do, wasn't it?"

"Yeah, about five days ago," Lorne said. "I'd say events have kind of passed that one by."

Emile snorted. "Events like sacrificing more Cobras so that civilians can run around thinking they're helping us? Not to mention your bellwether back there?"

"What are you talking about?" Lorne asked, frowning.

"Bellwether," Emile repeated. "That's a sheep that leads the others—"

"I know what it is. What do you mean, *not to mention*?"

"That hundred-year-old guy you sent in to lead the civvies out of there," Emile said with clearly strained patience. "I assume he was one of your DeVegas Cobras under a kilo of makeup?"

"No, *he* was my mother under a kilo of makeup," Lorne bit out. "What happened? Did something go wro—?"

Emile stopped short, spinning around so abruptly that Lorne nearly ran into him. "That was your *mother*? Jasmine *Broom*?"

"How many mothers do you think I have?" Lorne shot back,

a sudden horror jabbing through him. Even with just infrareds the shock in Emile's expression was clear and terrifying. "What's happened?"

"She didn't make it out," Emile breathed. "My east-side spotter signaled that the last two civilians got caught in some kind of gas trap and didn't make it out."

Lorne hissed out a curse as he dropped to one knee and slipped his burden onto the conduit floor. "I have to go," he said. "Sorry—you'll have to get him back on your own."

"Hold it," Emile said, grabbing Lorne's wrist. "There's no point. By now they're long gone."

"You don't know that," Lorne countered, shaking off his grip.

"Of course I do," Emile gritted out. He grabbed Lorne's wrist again, and this time locked his finger servos in place. "Reivaro's not going to kill her—she knows too much stuff about us. But he's also not going to sit her down and question her here. They're long gone, probably straight back to the *Algonquin*."

"You don't know that," Lorne repeated.

But down deep, he knew Emile was right. The civilian grabs had been a trap all along, designed by Reivaro and Lij Tulu to draw out someone they could pump for information.

"Of course I do," Emile said. "So do you, if you'd be honest with yourself for two seconds. You go back now and odds are they'll grab you, too. Though *you* they might just kill."

Lorne stared down at the body he'd unceremoniously dumped on the cold conduit floor. Its infrared glow was fading as the residual body heat slowly radiated away. Emile was right on that score, too. "So what do I do? Just sit here and do nothing?"

"No, you get your butt back to your base and start clearing everyone out," Emile said, releasing Lorne's wrist. "Sooner or later they're going to get its location out of her, and you need to be gone before then." He hissed out a curse. "I guess you can bunk in with us until you can find a new place of your own."

"You don't seem thrilled by the prospect."

"Eggs and baskets," Emile said as Lorne picked up the dead Cobra again. "Nothing personal. I was going to take us back to our place and deliver the fallen, but I think we'd better head to your people first and get them started packing. Which way?"

"Straight ahead," Lorne said. "There's a junction about fifty meters ahead where we can switch places if you want me to lead."

"That'd be handy," Emile said as he set off again down the tunnel. "And while you're enjoying our hospitality you can teach us your new trick."

"New trick?"

"You and your buddies were throwing your mudballs way too accurately," Emile said. "Even for country boys who don't have anything to do in their off-hours except throw rocks at trees."

"Oh—*that* trick," Lorne said, nodding. "Nothing mysterious there. Turns out to be some nanocomputer programming that everyone's forgotten about."

"Figured that," Emile said with a grunt. "Should come in handy."

"More than you know," Lorne assured him. "And while we work on that, we can discuss how to make those shrapnel bombs of yours safer for any civilians in the area."

"Sounds like a plan," Emile said, picking up his pace. "Sounds like a really long night, too. Let's get to it."

CHAPTER FIFTEEN

For the entire trip from Caelian Paul had hoped that Santores had been bluffing about Captain Moreau having already found Qasama. He'd hoped this was some elaborate ploy to trick him into giving the Dominion that information.

But it wasn't. There was Qasama, just as Paul remembered it from his last trip here, filling the *Megalith*'s main CoNCH display.

"Congratulations," he said, trying to keep the bitterness out of his voice. So it was true. He'd been crippled for nothing. "Now what?"

"I don't know," Santores said, an odd tension in his voice. "What do you see? Or rather, what *don't* you see?"

Paul frowned at the display. What *didn't* he see?

And then he got it. Moreau's ship, the *Dorian*, was nowhere to be seen. "Maybe it's on the other side of the planet."

"No," Santores said. "Standard orbit would have brought it into view at some point during our approach. Captain Moreau would also have routinely put comm-sensor satellites in place to cover his blind spots. They're not there."

"He must have decided to go somewhere else."

"Or he didn't have a choice in the matter," Santores said. "I'm going to hail the Qasaman leadership now. I'd like you to open the conversation."

Paul nodded. He'd wondered why he'd been so abruptly summoned to CoNCH. Not that he really felt like doing the Dominion any favors. "And you think I'll be willing to do that *why*?"

"Because these are your friends," Santores said. "I imagine you'd prefer that the conversation remains cordial."

Paul raised his eyebrows. "Is that a threat?"

"Not at all," Santores said. "I'm simply suggesting that they may be more willing to tell *you*—politely—what's happened to the *Dorian* than they would me."

Paul sighed. No, he wasn't interested in helping Santores.

But the Qasamans had already been through hell. If he could keep the Dominion from delivering another helping, he needed to try. "Fine," he said, holding out his hand. It still felt leaden without his servos, but he was starting to get used to it. "Microphone?"

"Just speak toward here." Santores pointed to a spot on the control panel and tapped a key. "Go ahead."

"This is Paul Broom of the Cobra Worlds," he said. "I'd like to speak to Shani Moffren Omnathi. At his convenience, of course."

Given that the *Megalith* had been visible from the planet for a solid hour, he expected that Omnathi would be right on top of it. He was right. "I greet you in the name of the Qasaman people, Cobra Paul Broom," Omnathi's voice came from the CoNCH speaker. "Welcome back. Who, may I ask, is your traveling companion?"

Paul gestured to the panel. "I think he means you."

"Commodore?" one of the nearby officers murmured as a flashing circle appeared on Santores's landscape display.

A circle that was nearly five hundred kilometers west of Azras, the southwest-most city of Qasama's Fertile Crescent region. "What's that?" Paul murmured.

Santores tapped the mute key. "It's the transmission's location."

"Doesn't seem to be much civilization there," the officer pointed out.

"There doesn't, does there?" Santores agreed. "Broom?"

Paul frowned. As far as he knew, none of Qasama's towns or villages were nearly that far away from the main Crescent settlements. Had the war damaged the area so much that Omnathi had decided to move some of the populace elsewhere? "Sorry. No idea."

"I suppose we'll just have to ask." Santores tapped the key again. "This is Commodore Rubo Santores, commanding the Dominion War Cruiser *Megalith*. I understand that Captain Barrington Moreau and the *Dorian* preceded me here. Were they here?"

"They were," Omnathi said. "We spent several days healing their wounded, and then they left."

"When?"

"Four days ago."

"Bound for where?"

"The answer to that question is somewhat complicated," Omnathi said. "I believe your Lieutenant Commander Kusari would be best equipped to offer the explanation."

The CoNCH officer sent Santores a startled look. Santores himself, as far as Paul could tell, didn't react at all. "Are you speaking of the *Dorian*'s Second Officer and chief engineer Lieutenant Commander *Eliser* Kusari?" he asked.

"Yes, Commodore, this is Commander Kusari," a new voice came briskly on the speaker. "Welcome to Qasama, sir. Captain Moreau's compliments, and his apologies that he couldn't be here to greet you in person."

"Thank you, Commander," Santores said, his voice cool. "May I ask *why* Captain Moreau was unable to be here?"

"He felt it would be most useful to follow the *Squire* to its destination," Kusari said. "I have his report here, whenever you're ready to receive it."

Again, Santores touched the mute key. "Atchkinson, do we have a secure transmission?"

"No, sir," one of the crew reported. "Directed signal, but easy enough to tap into."

"And not encrypted, I assume."

"Yes, sir."

Santores again tapped the key. "We'll hold off on that for the moment, Commander," he said. "A more important question right now is why he left you behind."

"I was still undergoing treatment when Captain Moreau left, sir," Kusari said. "As were ten other officers and crewmen still with me. As of now, though—"

"Are you saying Captain Moreau left *eleven* of his men behind?" Santores cut in harshly.

"We were injured, sir—"

"Were the *Dorian*'s medical facilities destroyed?" Santores demanded. "All the medics killed by violence or plague?"

"No, sir, not at all," Kusari said. For a man clearly at the focus of official displeasure, Paul thought, he was taking this all very calmly. "Partly, as I said, Captain Moreau deemed the local doctors and facilities more capable of bringing us to full health. More importantly to the captain, he thought we could assist the Qasamans in preparing a proper decoy for the Trofts. Shahni Omnathi—"

"*Silence!*" Santores snapped. "You're speaking of classified material on an open channel."

"And with Omnathi standing right there," Paul murmured.

Santores threw him an ice-edged glare. "What?"

"The transmission circle didn't change position when Kusari came on," Paul explained, pointing to the landscape display. "I assume that means the two of them are together?"

For a moment Santores held the glare. Then he turned back to the board. "Commander Kusari," he said, his voice under rigid control. "Is Shahni Omnathi with you?"

"Yes, sir," Kusari said. "Sorry, Commodore, I should have mentioned that earlier. The Shahni and his top people have been fully informed about the Dominion decoy plan."

Paul felt a tingle up his back. "What decoy plan?"

"Whose decision was that?" Santores asked, ignoring Paul's question.

"Mine, sir," Kusari said without hesitation. "After the *Dorian* left, it seemed to me that the Qasamans' record of resourcefulness and courage made it logical to bring them into our confidence so that we could more effectively combine forces."

"Did it, now," Santores said. His tone was still under control, but it was becoming progressively darker. "*Logical*, you say."

"Logical and productive both," Kusari said. "Shahni Omnathi has come up with a plan to draw the Trofts to their destruction while still minimizing civilian casualties."

For a moment Santores was silent. Watching him out of the corner of his eye, Paul could see a battle of emotions going on there. "I see," he said at last. "That will be all for now. A shuttle will pick you up within the hour and bring you aboard for a full debriefing."

"Understood, sir," Kusari said. "If I may suggest, though, you might find it more instructive to come down here for the debriefing. That way you could see the terrain and the Qasamans' plan for yourself."

"I'll rely on you to apprise me of that information," Santores said. "One hour, Commander. Santores out."

He touched the switch again. "Commander Darrow? Do we have anything more on the terrain around that transmitter?"

"Putting it in the stream now, Commodore."

"And?" Paul prompted.

"And what?" Santores asked.

"And what's there?"

Santores glanced at him, perhaps belatedly remembering that he couldn't tap into the data stream like everyone else aboard. "It's mostly forest," he said. "Relatively flat, with a few low hills. No major rivers; a couple of small streams. Some large rock formations that might be useful for cover or as the core for defense emplacements." He shook his head. "Only it's too far away from the main population centers. The Trofts will never believe that's where—" He broke off, glancing at Paul again.

"That's where what?" Paul prompted.

"Though there seem to be enough people there at the moment, sir," Darrow spoke up. "I'm reading heat signatures of... must be a good five thousand people there right now."

"In the middle of a *forest*?" Santores asked, frowning. "What are they all doing there?"

"Looks like they're clearing ground," Darrow said. "We've got some heavy machinery—small but well powered. We've also picked up—there's another one."

"Yes, I see it," Santores said, nodding.

"What was it?" Paul asked.

"Laser flash," Santores said. "Horizontal."

"They're cutting down trees," Darrow said. "Clearing land for us to lay out our factories."

Paul blinked. Their *factories*?

"Ah—*there's* where they all came from," Darrow continued. "We've got a tent village under the trees about half a klick to the south. Plus... looks like mess tent and sanitary facilities, as well."

"Unbelievable," Santores murmured. "And all this in only four days?"

"Sir?" Darrow said, his voice suddenly odd. "I've tagged something you might want to look at."

"The mountain due west of the encampment?"

"Yes, sir," Darrow said. "Only if the deep-radar scan is accurate..."

"Damn," Santores breathed. "It's a *volcano*?"

"Yes, sir," Darrow said grimly. "It's not dormant, either—you can see steam tendrils at the edges."

"How close is it to the workers?" Paul asked.

"Too close," Santores said grimly. "About ninety klicks away. *And* upwind."

Paul's stomach tightened. "So if it blew...?"

"Smoke and ash over the whole place," Santores said, his voice suddenly thoughtful. "I wonder if that's what Omnathi and Kusari have in mind. Darrow, what would it take to punch a hole in that crater?"

"It would take a good tap, sir," Darrow said. "But it sure looks primed and ready to go. *And* there's a massive amount of magma underneath the rock crust on top. We'll need to do more detailed scans before we know the full parameters."

"Get busy," Santores ordered. "While you're doing that, get with Crivkovich and see what it'll take to blast out the plug and bring it full active."

"Wait a second," Paul said, staring at the spot on the landscape display. "You want to set off a *volcano*? With all those people in the way?"

"Hopefully not," Santores said. "The idea would be to wait until the Trofts had invaded." He looked sideways at Paul. "Don't worry, we should have enough warning to get most of the civilians out of the way first."

"*Most* of them?"

"And hopefully evacuate the population centers further east," Santores added. "We'll certainly do our best."

An eerie sense of unreality seeped into Paul's heart. So that was what Kusari had been talking about. The plan was to draw some of the Dominion's enemies here, bait them into attacking the planet, and then destroy them. Had that been the plan all along?

But it couldn't have been. It wasn't until Santores and the Dominion ships arrived at Aventine that they knew Qasama even existed.

Which meant that if the bait-and-kill *had* been the plan, it must have been the Cobra Worlds that were the planned decoy.

The decoy. The killing ground.

Slowly, Paul looked around CoNCH. How many of these men, he wondered, knew what the Dominion of Man had sent them here to do to their distant cousins? Was it something only the senior officers were privy to?

Or did everyone know and simply not care? Was the Dominion of Man in such a desperate situation that they would try anything to survive?

It was a chilling and terrible thought. And yet, Paul had to admit that if their positions were switched the people of the Cobra Worlds might be capable of doing exactly the same thing.

In fact, from some of the things he'd heard after the Troft invasion, a sizeable percentage of Aventine's populace had been perfectly willing to throw Qasama to the wolves if it would get the aliens off the Cobra Worlds. "And if your best isn't good enough?" he challenged.

"You're angry, of course," Santores said. "I can't say I blame you. The Qasamans have been good to you and your family. You naturally don't want to see them caught in the middle of a war, especially one that's not of their making."

"They're not being *caught* in a war," Paul bit out. "They're being *put* there. By you. Fellow humans, and you're cold-bloodedly setting them up to be invaded. That doesn't bother you?"

"What bothers me is that the Dominion of Man is facing destruction," Santores said bluntly. "If there was any other way, I'd be happy to consider it. But I have my orders. My people—my worlds—my oath—those are my first priority. Would you behave any differently?"

"I would at least look for an alternative."

"Would you?" Santores gestured to the map screen. "Because I see the evidence of great destruction down there. Far more than I saw on Aventine or Caelian."

"It was the Trofts' decision to focus their attention here."

"Was it?" Santores countered. "Because I've read the reports. You didn't take the Isis Cobra factory to Aventine or any of the other Cobra Worlds. You brought it here."

"Because the Qasamans had the best chance of defeating the invaders and thereby persuading the local Troft demesnes to come in on our side."

"Was that the only reason? Or were you also thinking that, win or lose, this way Qasama would take the brunt of the war damage, not Aventine."

"The Qasamans accepted Isis gladly and enthusiastically," Paul insisted. "They were the ones making the plans and leading the resistance."

"As it would appear they're doing again."

"Because you gave them no choice."

"They wanted their world free of Troft threats," Santores said. "You helped them accomplish that. Now they want that same freedom, and it's the Dominion of Man who's giving them the necessary assistance."

Paul glared across CoNCH. Except that Qasama wouldn't be in danger if it hadn't been for the Dominion ships. Santores was completely mislabeling cause and effect.

But there was nothing to be gained by pointing that out. Even if Santores recognized his hypocrisy—and Paul wasn't convinced he would—it was clear the commodore was uninterested in hearing anything that landed outside the narrow parameters of his orders.

And if Santores decided that blowing a volcano was the best way to carry out those orders, the devastation could end up being worse than a dozen Troft invasions.

Paul had to come up with an alternative. Somehow, he had to come up with an alternative. "You need to tell me everything," he said. "The whole plan. All of it."

"Of course," Santores said, a faintly condescending smile on his face. "Dominion officers are quite casual about violating Standing Orders."

"You don't know this world or its people," Paul said. "I do. That's why you brought me up here to talk to them. You can't trust Commander Kusari or Shahni Omnathi or anyone else to give you a straight answer."

"And I can trust you why?"

Paul lifted his arm. "Because I'm totally dependent on you," he said. "I can't move quickly or for any great distance. My hearing and sight are severely limited."

He watched Santores's face carefully on that one. But if the commodore spotted Paul's half-truth, there was no sign of it in his expression. "My fate is tied to you and the *Megalith*," Paul went on. "Not to belabor the point, but I'm literally the only one in a million-kilometer radius you can trust."

For a long moment Santores studied him. Then, his eyebrow twitched. "Very well," he said. "The corpsman will return you to your cabin. The general plan will be on your computer by the time you arrive."

"Thank you," Paul said. "After I've read it, I'll start thinking of how the Qasamans can help." He raised his eyebrows. "*And* how, if they choose, they can hinder."

✧   ✧   ✧

The Troft cordon around Svipall had been designed to keep people out of the village and, more importantly, out of their research and manufacturing facility. In theory, such a cordon should be equally effective at keeping people *in*.

But in practice, Merrick knew, that wasn't always the case. Even with modern sensor arrays, soldiers with their attention turned outward weren't nearly as aware of things going on behind them. If Merrick was careful and patient, he should be able to slip through the ring.

The real trick would be making his escape without revealing his abilities to either Ludolf or Kjoic.

A distraction would be handy. Fortunately, the Trofts had already arranged one for him: another evening test of their obedience drug, this one set for two days after his secretive arrival. If it followed the same pattern as the one he'd gone through, a good percentage of the village would probably be there to watch. Kjoic, as a visiting Troft from an allied demesne, would also undoubtedly be invited to wherever had the best view.

That solved the Kjoic question. The Ludolf part followed directly: Merrick simply persuaded him that Kjoic needed to be watched. As it turned out, that persuasion took very little effort.

Merrick had entered Svipall twice through the bersark field on the village's western border, one time with no adverse consequences, the other with a whole raft of them. The similar field on the eastern border was narrower, which would mean less time in the open, and he spent some a couple of hours during his first day at the top of one of the meeting hall's twin bell spires, studying the field with his telescopics and infrareds. There were fewer patches of non-dangerous plants intermixed with the bersark than in the western field, but there was a decent line of them that he should be able to follow. Even better, the patches weren't so far apart that he would need to resort to the pole-vaulting charade that he'd used before. Here, any chance observers should simply conclude that he had exceptionally good jumping skills and was extremely lucky as to where he landed.

And once Merrick was out of the village and past the Troft cordon, he would get started on Plan A.

The second contest of the evening was in full swing when Merrick did a high-jump roll over the eastern fence and slipped across the bersark field to the relative safety of the forest beyond.

Another half hour spent halfway up one of the trees using Kjoic's fancy sensor earpiece to study the Trofts' patrol pattern, and he was able to slip through the cordon.

Traveling the Muninn forest at night could be dangerous. But he had to risk it. A growing number of people had now seen him, even if they didn't know what he really was, and the more who knew about him the bigger the chance that one of them would let information slip that would enable the Trofts to find and capture him. Worse, with Kjoic having now revealed his identity to the Drims and working to cozy up to their inner circle there was an increasingly good chance he would find a way to steal a sample of the war drug on his own.

And that would be disastrous. Not just because he wouldn't need Merrick anymore, but because Kjoic was Merrick's best—possibly only—way off the planet. With Kjoic's original ride into Muninn lying wrecked in the forest, he would need to finagle himself an alternate transport, and it would be far easier for Merrick to negotiate a ride with him than to try to steal a spacecraft of his own. Especially since he had no idea how to fly a Troft ship.

But hitching a ride required a bargaining chip, which meant Merrick had to get to the drug first. Plan A should accomplish that.

Hopefully without getting him killed.

CHAPTER SIXTEEN

The first thing Jin noticed as she drifted back to consciousness was that her arms wouldn't move.

Her first thought was that she'd fallen asleep on them somehow and the nerves simply weren't responding to her brain's commands. Her second thought was that somehow her servos had failed.

That was the horrifying thought that snapped her out of the fog. With a quick shake of her head, she opened her eyes.

To find herself sitting in a padded contour chair, her legs held down by a pair of massive metal bars, her arms held crossed against her chest by another set of bars. Across the room from her—and it wasn't a very big room—was a ship-style hatch flanked by two glowering Dominion Marines.

"She's awake," a voice announced from her left.

"Yes, Doctor, thank you—I *did* notice," a dark voice replied from the same direction.

Jin turned her head toward the voices. There was a young man sitting at a display that looked like a medical monitor panel, his face carefully neutral. Beside him, standing stiffly and staring back at Jin—

"Captain Lij Tulu," she greeted him, keeping her voice cool and professional even as she felt her heart seize up inside her. Her last thought as the gas attack took her was a desperate hope that Lorne or one of the other Cobras would see what had happened and whisk her away to safety.

Clearly, that hadn't happened.

One of the lines on the display the two men were sitting beside gave a little twitch in response to Jin's suddenly enhanced heartbeat.

Lij Tulu noticed. "Calm yourself, Cobra Broom," he said, standing up and walking around her one-chair prison to a spot between the two Marines, presumably so he could stare at her more efficiently. "If I'd wished you dead, you'd be dead."

"And of course, we can't have *that*," Jin said. "You'll want to run me through your mind-sifting machine before you drop me out an airlock."

"I *did* think about that, yes," Lij Tulu said with a casual shrug. "There must be a whole collection of tidbits inside that armored skull of yours that would prove interesting, embarrassing, or both."

"Along with a few choice opinions about you and the whole Dominion of Man."

"I'm sure," Lij Tulu said. "Fortunately for you, at this point it's probably not worth the effort. It would take at least a few hours to locate and retrieve information on your resistance friends, and by that time they would surely have relocated and changed their faces." His lips compressed briefly. "And we seem to be rapidly moving beyond the point where political pressure or even blackmail is of any use."

"That's what happens when you start using scare tactics that inflame the populace," Jin pointed out. "Is that how you got that woman to help you? Blackmail?"

"Woman?" Lij Tulu asked, frowning.

"The one who gassed me."

Lij Tulu's frown cleared. "Oh—her. No, no—there was no blackmail involved. She's one of us."

"Really?" Jin asked, thinking back. As far as she could remember, there hadn't been a single women among the various Dominion troops that she'd seen. "I didn't realize there were any women aboard your ship."

"Of course there are," Lij Tulu said. "We'd hardly take a voyage this long without them. As for inflaming the populace, don't be ridiculous. The populace is composed of sheep. Always has been, always will be. Civilians can be as outraged and angry as they want, but rarely will they ever do anything to significantly change their circumstances."

"You might be surprised at what a frontier people are willing to do."

"You mean run away from our garrisons and troops to provide cover for you?" He shrugged. "A passing fad, already starting to fade."

"Maybe," Jin said. "Maybe not. Even if most of them bow out, there are still the Cobras."

"The same Cobras who didn't lift a finger to fight against the Troft invasion?"

"A lot of them did," Jin said firmly. "And those who didn't took a fair amount of scorn for that. That embarrassment will probably factor into their actions under this current invasion."

Lij Tulu smiled thinly. "We'll see how brave and self-sacrificial they are once they're all wearing loyalty collars."

"You have to catch them all first."

"We're working on that," Lij Tulu assured her. "Though even that may not prove necessary. You say the Aventinian people are more apt to act than those of civilized worlds. But even frontier people need leaders." He gestured toward her. "And it seems to me they're rapidly running out of them."

"You're joking, of course," Jin said. "Just because you have a matched set of Brooms you think the people are going to give up?"

"Oh, we have more than just you and your husband," Lij Tulu assured her. "We also have your uncle. And of course, we can have Governor-General Chintawa and the rest of Aventine's leadership whenever we want them."

"Except that Chintawa and the leadership are the ones who ordered the Cobras to sit on their hands the last time," Jin said. "Taking them away isn't going to solve your resistance problem. It's more likely to exacerbate it."

"You must have missed my earlier comment about our loyalty collars." Lij Tulu raised his eyebrows. "Or are you expecting your uncle's little ceramic inserts to protect them? Because that's not going to happen."

Jin's eyes flicked to the Marines standing behind him. Unlike the combat-suited ones she'd faced down in Capitalia, this pair were wearing the simpler shipboard uniforms. But the deadly epaulets were still there, riding their shoulders, ready to spit death and destruction at anyone or anything at a moment's notice.

At anything. At a moment's notice...

It took all her strength to keep her face impassive. Even so, the medical readout must surely have caught the hidden signals of her sudden cautious excitement.

She didn't dare turn her head to see. If Lij Tulu hadn't already noticed the blip in the display, such a movement on her part would surely draw his attention.

Because if she was right, she'd just found a potentially devastating gap in the entire Marine combat setup.

But that revelation wouldn't do the Aventinian Cobras any good locked away in her brain up here. Somehow, she had to get the word down to Lorne.

Escape was out of the question. Not only was she pinioned like a Christmas turkey, but she had no idea where on the *Algonquin* she was. Finding a transmitter and figuring out how to work it was equally problematic.

She would have to send the message with someone else. And there was only one person aboard who might be able to pull that off.

She focused her attention back on Lij Tulu. "You're very confident," she said, adding just a hint of mocking to her tone. "But I think you'll find we still have a few surprises to throw at you."

"If you're referring to those bombs, rest assured we're already working on a counter."

"Maybe," Jin said. "As to the inserts, I think you dismissed them a bit too quickly."

"You think I'm wrong about them?"

"Well, *one* of us is wrong," Jin said. "We'll find out soon enough."

Lij Tulu shook his head. "You really are an arrogantly stupid people, aren't you? Fine. Let me spell it out for you."

He lifted a hand, started ticking off fingers. "One: we have the pieces of the inserts your Cobras had in Archway. Reverse-engineering them gave us your Uncle Corwin's manufacturing process. Two: the raid on his house confirmed our analysis and also provided us with the heat signature of the firing furnace. Three: approximately two hours ago we raided the other four locales in Capitalia where the inserts were being made, confiscated the equipment and inserts, and arrested the men and women involved."

He raised his eyebrows. "And four," he said, ticking off a final finger. "We know exactly how much explosive pressure the inserts can handle. Our latest batch of collars have been constructed with just enough extra explosive to render the inserts useless."

Jin shrugged. They were efficient enough. She had to give them that. "I don't believe you."

"I didn't expect you to," Lij Tulu said. "Corpsman, bring in Governor Moreau. Tell him I'm granting his request."

"His request?" Jin asked.

"He wanted to see you."

"How did he know I was here?"

Lij Tulu smiled. "I told him."

Jin felt her throat tighten. "Of course you did."

Behind Lij Tulu, the hatch slid open. The captain stepped aside, revealing Uncle Corwin, flanked by two more Marines. "Are you all right?" Corwin asked as he stepped into the compartment.

"I'm fine," Jin assured him. "You?"

"I haven't been mistreated." Corwin looked at Lij Tulu. "Well?"

"Well, what?"

"You didn't bring me here out of the goodness of your heart. You want something. Let's get on with it."

"As you wish." Lij Tulu held out his hand, and one of the Marines who'd been escorting Corwin handed him a small case. "I have two items here," he continued, setting the case on Jin's lap and opening it. "Well, three, technically."

Jin swallowed hard. Inside the box was one of the Dominion's loyalty collars, along with the two halves of one of Corwin's ceramic inserts.

"Your niece doesn't believe that our new collars are strong enough to shatter your inserts," Lij Tulu continued, taking the items out of the box. "Would you care to express your opinion?" He held out the items toward Corwin.

"I have no idea what you're talking about," Corwin said calmly. "I already told you that working toward a replacement for Cobra bone laminac has been my hobby for many years now. As you may know, the ceramic has been linked to heightened incidence of—"

"You're saying you have no idea whether or not your ceramic will protect against an explosion?" Lij Tulu interrupted.

Corwin spread his hands. "Explosions really aren't my area of expertise."

"Of course," Lij Tulu said, nodding. "Well, when theory fails, as the saying goes, one must return to the lab." He moved the collar a few centimeters closer to Corwin's face. "Shall we try it on you? Or your niece?"

Jin felt her mouth go dry. But Corwin merely smiled. "Really, Captain," he chided. "You aren't actually going to try such a clichéd bluff, are you?"

"I'm not bluffing."

"Of course you are," Corwin said. "There's no possible way to justify the murder of a helpless prisoner to Commodore Santores when he returns."

"*If* he returns," Lij Tulu said. "We're at war, Governor, in case you've forgotten."

"Doesn't matter," Corwin said. "Whether to Santores or someone in the Dominion of Man, you'll eventually have to account for your actions. And that wonderfully two-edged sword known as your MindsEye means you can never falsify the facts. Not forever."

"There are safeguards against its use against senior officers," Lij Tulu said. But he nevertheless lowered the collar back to his side.

"I would hope so," Corwin said. "Really, though, instead of threatening to blow our heads off you should be considering which of us you want to send back to Capitalia."

"He wants to send one of us back?" Jin asked, frowning.

Lij Tulu gave a little snort. "Your uncle thinks Colonel Reivaro needs to have a—what did you call yourself? An impartial observer?"

"That was my original suggestion," Corwin acknowledged. "However, I now accept your counterargument that I'm hardly impartial." He lifted a finger. "Allow me therefore to recast my suggestion. I may not be completely impartial, though as a former politician I believe I'm more capable than most of seeing both sides of a situation. But I *would* be an observer who couldn't be bullied or otherwise ordered to keep silent if the colonel or his men crossed the line."

"What line would that be?"

"Whatever line is specified by the Dominion of Man rules of engagement," Corwin said. "Moreover, you mentioned safeguards against using the MindsEye against Dominion officers. Since those safeguards don't apply to me, it would be much easier and quicker for a Board of Enquiry to use the device on me and learn the truth."

He raised his eyebrows. "Unless you don't *want* Santores and the Dome to know the truth."

"I have no fear of the truth," Lij Tulu said stiffly. "Nor do I expect Colonel Reivaro or any of his men to overstep their proper bounds."

"I'm pleased to hear that," Corwin said. "Then you'll send one of us down?"

"And with such smooth words you invite me to place a potential spy into the center of Colonel Reivaro's operation?" Lij Tulu suggested.

"Not a spy," Corwin corrected. "Think of me more as a negotiator. Someone Reivaro can have on hand in case he needs someone to act as a go-between with the opposition."

"A negotiator, you say."

"Yes." Corwin's lip twitched in a half smile. "And, should he need one, a hostage. You seem to think I'm an important figure. It might be interesting to see if that importance translates to an unwillingness on the Cobras' part to put me in the middle of a cross-fire."

"Interesting point," Lij Tulu said. "I'm surprised that a man of such bluntness actually survived a life of politics."

"There's some debate as to how well I survived it," Corwin conceded. "So which of us are you going to send to Colonel Reivaro? Cobra Broom, or me?"

"You still assume I'll send either one of you."

"It's in your best interests, Captain," Corwin said quietly. "If Reivaro steps over the line, you'll want it clear that the fallout came from *his* decisions, not your orders."

"You'd hardly be a credible witness at an Asgard court martial, with or without the MindsEye," Lij Tulu said. "But your hostage suggestion has merit. Very well. A shuttle will be prepared for you." He turned an ironic smile to Jin. "Anything you'd like to say to your son? I'm sure Governor Moreau already has a plan for slipping messages past his guards."

Jin nodded to herself And finally, there it was. Permitting this meeting had been an obvious setup right from the beginning—no military man with a shred of security training would put two prisoners together this way by accident. The purpose was equally obvious, and Jin had already concluded that Corwin's persistent persuasion was a waste of breath. Lij Tulu had already decided to send him down in hopes that his presence would flush out whatever group of Cobras still evaded the Dominion's net. All the captain's hesitation and verbal doubts were just window dressing for backwater politicians who might be naïve enough to take his game at face value.

But to brazenly invite Jin to give Corwin a message in hopes that he would deliver it, thereby risking the Cobras' information channel, was pushing it.

"Really, Captain," Corwin said, sounding wounded. Apparently, he'd decided to play to Lij Tulu's expectations. "I wouldn't dream of betraying your trust that way."

"You were the one who suggested acting as a go-between," Lij Tulu reminded him. "I'm offering you the chance to deliver a mother's message of hope and strength to her son." He gestured to Jin. "So. Cobra Broom?"

Jin looked at Corwin. From his expression she could tell he expected her to graciously decline the invitation, emphasizing by contrast just how naïve her old uncle was. It was a small ploy, but worth trying. And under other circumstances Jin would have been happy to play along.

But for once, she was going to have to disappoint him.

"Thank you," she said. "He can tell Lorne that I'm alive, well, and not being mistreated in any way."

Corwin's expression slipped, just for a split second, as Jin failed to play the role he'd anticipated for her. But an instant later it was back, not disappointed but quietly alert as he realized she'd just changed the game. Recognizing that what she was about to say was vitally important.

She just hoped she could pull it off. The trick was to choose her words carefully, without looking like that was what she was doing, and give Corwin something that would go over Lij Tulu's head. "Remind him to exercise restraint and professionalism, and to remember that we're trying for freedom, not mass slaughter. And warn him to stand tall, and watch his own back, because no one else will do it for him."

Another almost-flicker of an almost-frown. "If I have a chance," Corwin promised, nodding. "If not, you can tell him yourself when this is over."

"I hope so." Jin looked at Lij Tulu. "And warn them about the new explosives in the collars. I don't want people getting killed out of a false sense of security."

"Neither does Captain Lij Tulu, I'd guess," Corwin said.

"Indeed," Lij Tulu confirmed. "As your niece said, no one wants a mass slaughter."

"Good," Jin said. "What now?"

"Governor Moreau will be delivered to Colonel Reivaro," Lij Tulu said. "As for you, I'm still trying to decide."

"Don't take too long, please." Jin looked down at her folded arms. "I know it's hard to believe, but this position isn't nearly as comfortable as it looks."

On Muninn, Merrick had discovered, it always came down to a balance between risks.

On the one hand, he didn't want to spend the night too close to Svipall and the Troft warehouse. But at the same time, traveling the forest at night could be problematic. Catching a few hours of sleep wedged into the higher branches of a tree opened him to fafir attacks and aircar detection, but taking the time to build a bamboo shelter on the ground would take time, create noise, and possibly attract other predators.

In the face of all that, Merrick opted for compromise. He traveled five kilometers from Svipall, then began hunting for a bamboo patch.

Half a kilometer later he found one. It was about five meters across, dense enough to keep out any large ground predators and tall enough to discourage attacks from above. He forced his way through the stiff plants to the center, cleared away enough of them to make himself room to lie down, then positioned the pieces he'd broken off into a kind of crisscross shield over his head. It wasn't nearly as comfortable or secure as the shelters he'd seen Anya build, but it was faster and should be good enough for a single person.

The sun was already up by the time he awoke. For a few minutes he stayed where he was, his audios at full power, his infrareds peeking between the bamboo plants surrounding him, searching for potential danger. But for all the evidence, both the forest and the Trofts might have completely forgotten about him. He got up, pushed his way back out through the patch, and started a spiral search pattern.

So far, Plan A was working as anticipated. Now came the tricky part.

Or rather, the tricky *parts*, plural.

First on his list was to find a burrow. Ludolf had told him what to look for, but the signs were more subtle than he'd expected.

Finally, just after noon, he found it: the underground lair of one of Muninn's deadly and nearly unkillable jormungand snakes.

A big one, too, judging from the sixty-centimeter entryway. Merrick studied it and the surrounding territory for a few minutes, wondering if there were more burrows hidden beneath the bushes or inside root tangles.

But he didn't see anything. Besides, it didn't matter, security-wise, whether there were more jormungands in the area. There were enough dead leaves matted around the bushes that he should be able to hear another snake coming in time to get out of its way. What he needed for Plan A was a larger jormungand, like the one whose burrow he was already standing in front of.

Looking for more burrows would be nothing but stalling. Scowling, he listened to Kjoic's sensor earpiece to check for Troft aircars, gave the sky one final visual scan just to make sure, then got to work.

The first job was to get the jormungand out onto the surface. Ludolf had told him that the big snakes typically gorged themselves and then retreated to their burrows to spend a few days digesting. As far as anyone knew, no one had ever tried to lure one back out during that time, mainly because lying dormant out of sight was exactly where everyone preferred them to be.

Gingerly, Merrick eased his left leg into the burrow mouth. Time to see how much aggravation a jormungand could take. He gave the sky one final scan, then fired a laser burst into the burrow.

In the brief flash of light he saw the rough ridges on the tunnel's inner surface, hardened perhaps by some kind of secretion. No jormungand, but the tunnel had a gentle curve to the side that might be hiding the creature. He fired again, angling his aim as best he could into the confined space to send the shot a little farther around the curve. Another brief glimpse of the tunnel, this time with a hint of smoke from spot he'd burned on his first shot.

So whatever the jormungand had lined its burrow with, it did indeed burn. If Merrick's laser didn't do the trick on its own, maybe he could try smoking it out.

Though that carried its own set of risks. He'd seen how fast the Trofts reacted when Hanna torched their hidden base, and he didn't want that kind of company. He fired again—

In the flash he saw the jormungand, already halfway up the tunnel, the wide slit of its mouth gaping open.

Without his servos, and with only one leg planted on solid ground, Merrick would have lost a leg at the very least. But while the jormungand was fast, Cobra reflexes were faster. Merrick shoved hard off the ground with his right leg, sending himself arcing backward five meters to carom off a tree. The bounce half spun him around, sending him tumbling to a face-first landing on one of the bushes. He fell off that, rolling again onto his back as he finally hit the ground. He shoved himself back to a standing position, knees bending automatically in preparation for another leap.

The jormungand was out of its lair now, charging faster than Merrick had ever seen one move. Again he shoved off the ground, this time jumping sideways out of the snake's path. A glance that direction showed another tree looming in his path; this time he managed to grab a branch and change course before slamming into the trunk. He regained his balance, dropped to the ground, and started backing away.

To his surprise and annoyance, the jormungand didn't follow. It just lay there, its tail end still in the burrow, its tiny eyes trained on Merrick, its mouth half open as if daring its attacker to take another shot. Apparently, it was satisfied with driving away the intruder who'd assaulted it in its own nest.

Merrick would have to persuade it otherwise. He lifted his left leg...

And reluctantly lowered it again. With Troft aircars on patrol, firing with his leg halfway down a jormungand hole had been risky enough. Firing a shot through five meters of clear air was begging for trouble.

"So you don't want to come out and play?" Merrick muttered under his breath, studying the creature. Like all jormungands it was shaped like a tapered cylinder five meters long, its diameter ranging from a third of a meter at its head, to nearly half a meter across at its center, then to a slender tail at its rear. Despite the jormungand's apparent annoyance at being shot at, Merrick knew from experience that the creature's thick scales were both dense and ablative, a combination that robbed even an antiarmor laser shot of much of its penetrating power.

If the jormungand wouldn't chase him, he would have to try something else.

He pursed his lips, studying the snake again. The tapering on this specimen didn't seem quite as pronounced as it had been on the others he'd seen. Did that mean it was nearly done with the digestive process and was ready to go hunting again?

More flies with honey than with vinegar, the old adage whispered through his mind. "Fine," he said. "If you don't want to play, maybe you'd like to eat. Wait here a second—I'll see what I can whip up."

He leaped into the nearest tree, making sure he was out of the jormungand's vertical reach, and keyed in his infrareds. They weren't as effective in full sunlight as they were at night, but they should be good enough to find him a target.

They were. Six more trees away, clumped together in a tangle of branches, was a group of eight fafirs.

The jormungand hadn't moved. Keeping an eye on it, Merrick dropped out of his tree again and slipped across to the fafirs' roost.

From the ground, the leafy branches beneath the creatures made them nearly invisible. Once again, Merrick's infrareds made the difference. A minute and six fingertip laser shots later, there were half a dozen dead fafirs lying at his feet.

None of it had escaped the jormungand's attention. The snake was still lying where Merrick had left it, but its front segment had angled up a little from the ground as if it was trying to get a better view. Picking up one of the fafirs, Merrick retraced his steps back to the snake.

This trick had worked once before. Time to see if that had been a fluke. "Lunch," he said softly, lobbing the fafir to land a meter from the jormungand's mouth.

For a long moment the snake just lay there, regarding the fafir as if wondering why it wasn't moving like they usually did. Then it eased forward, opened its mouth the whole way, and took a bite.

Even scorched by laser fire it apparently tasted good. Three more bites and it was gone.

"There you go," Merrick said. "See how easy that was? You want more?" He backed up to where he'd left the rest of the fafirs and picked up another one. He tossed it toward the jormungand, this time aiming it to land three meters away.

Again, the snake hesitated. But it didn't hesitate as long this time. Slithering forward, it again gobbled up the free meal.

"Okay, let's see if you learned," Merrick said. He picked up the remaining four fafirs—

A rustling in the bushes to his left was his only warning. Dropping the fafirs, he threw himself forward in a flat dive, rolling back to his feet with his fingertip lasers ready.

And launched himself into a second dive as a second jormungand charged straight at him. He again hit the ground and rolled back up.

To see both snakes gorging themselves on the remaining fafirs.

Apparently, there *had* been another burrow hidden under the bushes.

And if there were two, could there be more?

Now that he could get a better look, he saw that the newcomer was considerably smaller than the first snake he'd lured out of its hole. Was it younger than the original? Had he stumbled on some kind of family or communal nest?

Plan A had involved a single jormungand. But a whole group of them would be even better.

Provided he could get them all back to Svipall.

He squared his shoulders. If he was going to lure a whole family of snakes to the Trofts, he was going to need a lot more bait. "You two enjoy," he told the jormungands as he leaped up into the nearest tree and keyed his infrareds. "Let's see what else is on the menu."

CHAPTER SEVENTEEN

Lorne had first discovered, then quantified, the forgotten Cobra throwing programming out in the open fields of Dushan Matavuli's ranch.

There, it had been largely a matter of trial and error. Here in Capitalia's tunnel system, it was more a matter of finding enough space for the other Cobras to learn how to do it.

But Emile and his group were determined, and in the end they had a reasonably good grasp of the technique.

Which didn't mean they didn't need additional practice out in the open air. Fortunately, Emile knew of a secluded alleyway and largely unused building complex on the northern side of the city that should give them the necessary space.

To Lorne's annoyance, he wasn't invited to go along.

"Because you're needed here," Emile explained with a calmness that did nothing but add to Lorne's frustration. "You still have data to dig out of that Marine tunic you swiped, right?"

"There are techs working on it who have way more knowledge than I do," Lorne pointed out.

"But they don't have a soldier's point of view," Emile said. "You could see something they don't, or ask a critical question that would never occur to them."

"We'd be gone less than three hours. They wouldn't even miss me."

Emile sighed, a sound that managed to be patient and theatrical at the same time. "Don't be dense, Broom. The Dominion has

219

your mother, father, and great-uncle. Maybe even your sister, too. Your family is a big deal on Aventine. You know it, I know it, and they know it."

"By that logic you should stick me in a hole somewhere and never let me out," Lorne growled.

"Where do you think you *are*?" Emile countered, waving a hand around him. "Oh, don't look at me like that. It's not that we're not going to let you get out and fight. We just don't want to make you too easy a target until we have to."

Lorne glared at him. But unfortunately, he made sense. "Fine," he said. "Go have your little field trip. But if you get ambushed and captured don't come crying back to me."

For a second Emile just stared. Then he got it. "Don't worry, I won't," he said with a grin. "See you later."

De Portola and Werle were sitting at the worktable, poking at the partially disassembled guts of one of the Marine epaulets, when Lorne arrived. "Where are Will and Christy?" Lorne asked, looking around for the two techs.

"Catching some sleep," Werle said. "So how did the training go?"

"Fine so far," Lorne said, wincing as he pulled up a chair and sat down. In theory, he'd been up and down these tunnels enough times that he really ought to have figured out how to handle himself to avoid back pain. In practice, it hadn't worked that way. "Emile's taking them someplace in Bonneville district to try it in the open air."

"You're not going with them?" de Portola asked.

"Emile won't let me," Lorne said, glowering at the table. The epaulet's components, he noted, had been laid out in Christy's usual precise order. Some of the pieces looked familiar, but others were complete question marks. "Something about being too valuable to risk unless there's a real chance that I'll be shot at."

"That sounds like him," de Portola said. "Never mind. You can help us bash our heads against this brick wall instead."

"No progress?"

"Not so's you'd notice," Werle growled. "The power supply is sewn or woven into the tunic—all along the back here, here, and here. No idea how it works. Laser capacitors *here*; optical sensors *here*, targeting computer *here*—that one we already knew—and microgimbals for aiming *here*."

"But no transceivers."

"Nothing we can identify as such." Werle peered closely at Lorne. "You're sure they have to be here?"

"There has to be *some* kind of friend/foe ident system," Lorne reminded him. "Their computers have to know to shoot at us and not at each other."

"Maybe it's in their helmets," de Portola suggested.

"We've seen them fight without helmets," Lorne reminded them. "No, the epaulets and tunics are the only consistent part of their outfits. The IFF system has to be in there."

"Okay, but would it really be a transceiver?" Werle asked, scratching his cheek thoughtfully. "Seems to me a radio signal could be hacked and either duplicated or jammed."

"Unless it's a constantly changing code," de Portola said.

"Still should be jammable," Werle said.

"So if it's not a transceiver—" Lorne broke off as a sound caught his ear. He keyed up his audios.

Someone was coming down the tunnel toward them. Someone clearly moving as fast as the low ceiling allowed.

Werle and de Portola were already out of their chairs, slipping opposite directions around the room and converging on the door from both sides. Lorne stood up and faced the door, ready to act as diversion if necessary. The footsteps came closer...

And Nissa Gendreves ducked into the room.

"Broom," she said as she caught sight of him. She glanced to the side, twitching a little in reaction as she spotted Werle a meter away from her. "Come on—we need you topside."

"What is it?" de Portola asked from behind her.

Nissa gave another twitch as she spotted him, as well. "A shuttle's just landed outside the Dome. It's carrying a passenger: former Governor Corwin Moreau."

"Uncle *Corwin*?" Lorne echoed, feeling his throat tighten. "What's he doing here? How did he look?"

"I don't know," Nissa said. "Governor-General Chintawa was called to Colonel Reivaro's office—maybe he'll get some answers. I was asked to bring you to Eagle Three so he could brief you."

"Yeah, sure," Lorne said, starting toward her. Eagle Three was one of the five spotter nests Chintawa and the Cobras had set up to keep an eye on what was happening with Reivaro and the rest of the Dominion HQ forces. Lorne didn't know where any of them were, but he'd been assured they were as secure as any place in Capitalia.

"We'll come with you," Werle said.

"There's no need," Nissa said shortly. "You have work to do here."

"I think we're about to have a lot more work to do there," de Portola said. "Which way to Eagle Three?"

Nissa sighed. "Follow me."

Eagle Three was in a fifth-story apartment in a complex about two blocks away from the Dome and the rest of Aventine's main government center. Reivaro had set up his HQ in a warehouse two blocks away, and most of the Dominion's space-to-ground traffic landed in the Dome's landing area. With a view of all three of those points, Eagle Three had been an obvious place to set up an observation post.

Lorne could only hope it wasn't equally obvious to Reivaro and Lij Tulu.

The young woman who answered the apartment door didn't say anything, but merely stepped aside to allow the four of them in. Clearly, she was used to having her privacy invaded. She led them to a small bedroom where another woman was sitting beside an old tabletop comm that had been set up on a dresser against the wall. "Ducha," Nissa greeted her gravely. "Any word?"

"He's waiting for you now," Ducha said, running a measuring eye over Lorne and then tapping a switch on the comm. She looked vaguely familiar, but Lorne couldn't place her. One of the civilians he'd seen on the street prior to last night's attack, perhaps? "We're here," she announced.

"How secure is the signal?" Lorne murmured.

"Very," Nissa murmured back. "Hard-wired—special cable run through the city's wiring matrix. No chance of anyone tracing it without tipping us off."

"Cobra Broom?" Chintawa's voice came softly through the speaker.

"Here," Lorne said, stepping forward. Ducha stood up, gestured him to her chair. He nodded his thanks and sat down. "I'm told my great-uncle's been brought back from the *Algonquin*?"

"Yes, he has," Chintawa said. "And no, I wasn't informed about this until he arrived."

"Why is he here?"

"According to him, Lij Tulu sent him back to keep an eye on Reivaro's activities."

"Really," Lorne said, throwing a frown at Werle and de Portola. "Does that mean Reivaro's planning to ramp things up?"

"Possibly," Chintawa said. "I should add that Governor Moreau's watchdog role is solely the opinion of Governor Moreau. Reivaro himself was noticeably silent on the reason for his return." There was a soft snort from the speaker. "Knowing your great-uncle, I'd guess he spun Lij Tulu some vague warning about possible excesses and the need for the captain to make sure his own rear was covered."

"Sounds like Uncle Corwin," Lorne said. "I can't see Lij Tulu agreeing unless he had his own agenda, though."

"Clearly," Chintawa said. "I see his likely goals as twofold. First, to locate you or your resistance cell by tracking this current communication."

The hairs on the back of Lorne's neck prickled. "Which isn't possible. Right?"

"So I've been assured," Chintawa said. "Hopefully, our experts are right. His second goal, I believe, is to lure you and your friends into a rescue attempt, which he expects will end with you as his prisoner."

"Trading a pawn for a knight," de Portola murmured.

Lorne nodded grimly. That definitely sounded like Reivaro. "Did Uncle Corwin seem to have been mistreated? Any injuries or indications of psychological torture?"

"Nothing I could see," Chintawa said. "Oh, and he said your mother looked fine, too."

Lorne felt his mouth drop open. "Lij Tulu let him see *Mom*?"

"So he says," Chintawa said. "Not only that, but Lij Tulu apparently let him bring you a message from her, as well."

"Which was?"

"He was to tell you that she was alive, well, and not being mistreated in any way," Chintawa said. "He was also to remind you to exercise restraint and professionalism, and to remember that you're trying for freedom, not mass slaughter. And he was to warn you to stand tall and watch your own back, because no one else would do it for you."

Lorne frowned. "That's the message?"

"His exact words," Chintawa said, a hint of dark humor in his voice. "I've had enough dealings with your family to know that phrasing and word choice can be important. What does it mean? Aside from the obvious warning aspects, of course?"

"I don't know," Lorne said. "Anything else?"

"Just one item," Chintawa said, the humor vanishing. "Not from your uncle, but an ultimatum from Reivaro. He says the rest of Capitalia's Cobras have three days to come in and be fitted with loyalty collars. If they don't, he'll start putting collars on Aventine's political and industrial leaders."

Lorne hissed between his teeth. "Starting with you?"

"He didn't say, but I assume so," Chintawa said. "He also said—and Governor Moreau confirmed this—that they're making a new version of the collars with enough extra explosive to break the ceramic inserts you've been making down there."

"Or at least what we were making before the raids," Nissa murmured.

"Raids?" de Portola asked.

"The kiln groups were hit a few hours ago," Nissa told him. "All four were put out of operation."

"Why didn't you tell us?" Werle demanded.

"To what end?" she countered. "There was nothing you could do about it. The point is that we already didn't have enough inserts for all the Cobras. And if they're adding extra punch to the mix..." She shook her head.

"No, the point is that we're not giving up," Lorne said. "We still have our stockpiles, right?"

"Yes, and we were collecting the new ones every hour, so we didn't lose all that many," Nissa said. "But without the kilns this is all we're ever going to have."

"Unless we can track down more kilns somewhere," Chintawa said. "I'll send out enquiries. In the meantime...I don't know. Probably you should all lay low for a while."

"We'll do what we have to," Lorne said. "Thanks for the information."

"No problem," Chintawa said. "Good luck."

Lorne looked up at Ducha and raised his eyebrows. Silently, she reached past him and turned off the comm.

"Hell in a handbucket," de Portola said. "I guess Reivaro *is* ramping things up."

"You mean collaring Chintawa and the rest of the politicians?" Werle said. "Kind of surprised they hadn't already done that."

"We're still the main threat," de Portola said. "Losing the kilns is going to be a problem, though."

"*If* we let them collar all of us," Lorne said. "We still should be able to hide out awhile longer."

"Which will mean more collars for the politicians," Nissa said.

"That's their problem," de Portola said. "I'm more interested in what your mother said."

Out of the corner of his eye, Lorne saw Nissa bristle at de Portola's casual dismissal of the threat to Aventine's leaders. But she didn't say anything, and Lorne decided to do the same. "Anything in particular?" he asked de Portola.

"The part about watching your back because no one else would do it for you," the other said. "Even if she wasn't a Cobra herself she'd know that's not true."

"Which means it was code," Werle agreed. "The question is, code for what?"

"I wish I knew," Lorne admitted. "It doesn't make any sense to me."

"It has to," Werle insisted. "She wouldn't waste her one shot at sending you a message."

"What about the part about not slaughtering the Marines?" Nissa asked.

"That one's obvious," Werle said. "Probably cover for the last one."

"Unless it's the other way around," Nissa pressed.

"Not guarding each other's backs is the line that's clearly false," Werle said patiently. "Ergo, that's the one that has to be the hidden message."

"Could it be a quote, or a line from a book?" de Portola asked. "Something she would read you at night, or something you two discussed or argued about?"

"Nothing comes to mind," Lorne said, trying to think. "But why send anything through Uncle Corwin in the first place?"

"Because Lij Tulu wouldn't let her use the comm?" De Portola suggested tartly.

"I mean why didn't she talk to someone before she was captured?" Lorne said. "Or leave a note or something."

"Ah," Werle said in a voice of sudden understanding. "Because it's something she learned *after* she was captured."

"Right." Lorne turned to Nissa. "Did anyone talk to the civilians the Marines snatched up that my mother freed?"

"I'm sure *someone* did," Nissa said, frowning in thought. "I know the Cobras are looking for every scrap of intel they can get on the Marines, their bases, and their equipment. But I don't know who's in charge of that."

"We can ask Emile when he gets back," Werle said.

"But now we should leave," Nissa warned. "The Governor-General doesn't want extra people crowding in here anymore than necessary."

"Understood." Lorne nodded to Ducha, standing quietly off to the side. "Thank you. For everything."

"You're welcome, Cobra Broom," she said gravely. "Make them pay."

Lorne frowned. "Excuse me?"

"Make the bastards pay," she said. "All of them."

"This is Ducha Jankos, Lorne," de Portola said softly. "I'm not sure you've ever met."

Lorne felt his stomach knot up. Ducha Jankos, mother of Taras Jankos. One of the three Cobras killed by the Dominion Marines in Archway in Reivaro's manufactured riot.

"No, we haven't," Lorne said, nodding to her. "But I saw your picture once, Ma'am. Taras thought the world of you."

"And I of him," she said simply. "Be safe, Cobra Broom. And bring him justice."

Lorne swallowed. Justice, or revenge? Or was it even his place to make that judgment?

Remember you're trying for freedom, his own mother had admonished him. *Not mass slaughter.* Not everyone on Aventine, he suspected, held that attitude.

"I'll do my best," he promised. "We all will."

The walk back to the examination room was very quiet.

It had taken a lot of work, and quite a few of the *Squire*'s supply of weapon power packs, but Jody had finally gotten pretty good at marksmanship. Now came the hard part: hitting the target quickly, and without the luxury of careful aiming and a two-handed stance.

It was so much easier with her own built-in weapons. A flick of the eye, a quick target-lock, a thumb on the fingernail, and her nanocomputer and servos did the rest.

Unfortunately, the only grip she'd come up with to let her

bring that system into play required two hands, with her left forefinger resting on her right forefinger's nail. That made for a somewhat awkward grip and took a potentially dangerous half-second or more to set up, along with still delivering a telltale double laser shot. Her reluctant conclusion was that she needed to look exactly like a normal Dominion-trained human right up to the point where she became a Cobra.

It was solid tactics, and had both Kemp's and Smitty's approval. Unfortunately, it meant a lot of extra work.

But this was a matter of life and death, not only for her and the rest of her friends, but possibly for Merrick as well. She'd come this far, and would do whatever else it took to find him and bring him home. Including hours of target practice.

Bracing herself, she snatched the laser from her holster, leveled it at the target, and fired twice.

"Not bad," Plaine's voice came from behind her.

Jody gave a little jerk, as if she'd been startled. In fact, her audios had picked up his footsteps ten seconds ago. "Anyone ever tell you it's bad manners to sneak up on people?" she asked reproachfully, turning to him and keying her infrareds. If he knew she was a Cobra, he would probably guess that she was lying about being surprised. If she was lucky, that knowledge would show up in his facial blood flow.

She was ninety-nine percent sure that he didn't know. But that stray one percent still nagged at her.

Still, she could see nothing in his face to indicate any emotion. At least not right now. "Sorry," he apologized, walking up to her. "On second thought, no, I'm not sorry. You need to work on being alert at all times."

"Even when I'm in a safe and secure place?" she asked, shutting off her infrareds.

"Never assume any place is safe and secure," he said flatly. "We've learned that in the Dominion of Man. Usually the hard way."

"Mm," Jody said, wondering if she should follow up on a line like that. Probably not. "So you here to offer advice?"

"If that's what you want," Plaine said. "Show me what you've got."

"Okay." Jody holstered her laser again, braced herself—

"Stop," Plaine ordered. "Don't expect you'll have time to prep, because you probably won't. Draw, spin to your left to face your target, and shoot. *Now.*"

Jody yanked the laser out of her holster, spun around, and squeezed off a shot.

She keyed her telescopics. Ring four on the target. A terrible shot.

"Not bad," Plaine said, craning his neck. "Not good, either, but not bad. Ten more shots, then we'll switch to spinning around to your right. Trust me—there's a big difference."

"Okay." Jody holstered the gun and turned to face him again. "What are you here for, anyway? You come down to watch me practice?"

"I was mostly just wandering around," he said. "We've only got a few days before we reach this planet of yours."

"And your conscience was bothering you?" Jody asked jokingly.

He stiffened, just noticeably. "What do you mean?"

"I asked if your conscience was bothering you," Jody repeated, frowning as she again keyed her infrareds. There it was: the increased facial blood-flow that indicated an emotional surge.

Only what emotions was the extra heat mirroring? "It's okay," she said quickly, throwing a verbal net that had more than once ensnared her brothers when they were growing up. The trick of looking like you knew more than you really did . . . "No one else is here. We can talk freely."

For a moment he stared at her, his enhanced infrared slowly fading. "You're blowing smoke," he said. "But sure, why the hell not? We're all in this together, right?"

"Right," Jody said. The conscience line had been nothing more than a weak, throwaway joke. But it had clearly touched a nerve. "And we need to be on the same page."

"Don't know if it's a page, exactly," Plaine said. "But . . . hell, maybe it is. Fine. The reason I'm here—*and* the reason you didn't get blown out of the sky when you left Qasama—is that Captain Moreau and your friend Omnathi made a deal."

Jody stared at him. She'd wondered at the time about the *Dorian*'s restraint, but since then other matters had pushed it to the back of her mind. "What kind of deal?"

"You don't know where we're going," Plaine said. "I know, I know—we're looking for your brother. But all we know for sure is that someone involved in the attack on Aventine was hauling animals from Qasama to this unidentified system. That means they're either enemy Trofts, or involved somehow with enemy Trofts."

"There's a difference?"

"Trust me," Plaine said sourly. "You'd need a five-dimensional matrix to sort out how all the demesnes work and play together. Or don't. The point is that our task force was sent to Aventine to make trouble and, hopefully, draw off some of the forces standing against the Dominion. Popping up unexpectedly in a system the Trofts don't think we even know about could help that along."

"Even if we get ourselves slaughtered in the process?" Jody asked. "Is that why you wanted us to learn how to use the gunbays?"

"Well, it can't hurt," Plaine said, a ghost of a smile tweaking his lips. "But it may not come to that." He considered. "Or it could be even worse," he amended. "The thing is, Captain Moreau's plan was to bring the *Dorian* in behind us."

Something tingled on the back of Jody's neck. "You mean they're out there right *now*?"

"That's the question," Plaine said. "It's also the problem. See, the *Dorian*'s engineering officer is still recovering on Qasama, and Moreau could get in a pit of trouble if he took off without him. But if he waits too long, the *Megalith* could arrive and Commodore Santores might order him to stay put."

"Either way, he's a bunch of days behind us," Jody muttered.

"Not necessarily," Plaine said. "The *Dorian* can travel faster than a courier ship. They could make up a lot of time. Maybe even all of it."

"So in other words, they either show up in time to rescue us, or else they hit the Trofts with a sucker punch after we've got them all conveniently bunched up."

"We'll hope for the former," Plaine said. "But hey, don't be so optimistic. It could be that Captain Moreau will succeed in losing us *and* the *Dorian*."

"That would be the *even worse* part, I take it," Jody said, wrinkling her nose. "You think the system we're going to will be that well-defended?"

"We have no idea how well-defended they'll be," Plaine said patiently. "Unknown system, remember?"

"Yeah," Jody said. "I guess maybe we shouldn't have rushed out so quickly. Might have given Commander Kusari enough time to heal."

"Would you have waited if the captain had asked you to?" Plaine asked pointedly. "You'd already dithered about it for five days."

Jody scowled. She'd hardly been dithering—she'd been under-going the surgeries involved in making her into a Cobra. But of course Plaine didn't know that. "Probably not," she conceded, noting the bitter-edged irony. If it hadn't been for the efficiency of the Isis system, her transformation would have taken consid-erably longer. Long enough, maybe, that the *Dorian* would have been ready to come with them.

Or maybe long enough for the *Megalith* to arrive and forbid Captain Moreau from assisting.

Or, for that matter, long enough that she would have arrived at the Troft system to find Merrick already dead.

She sighed. A person could run that circle forever without finding a place to stop. Answers only came in hindsight, and by then it was too late to fix the wrong decisions that had gone before. She could only do what seemed right and hope it worked out. "Is there anything different we should be doing?" she asked.

"Nothing I can think of," Plaine said. "Finding your brother's going to make all the noise Captain Moreau could possibly want. I figure we'll just play it out and see what happens."

"Okay." Jody frowned at him. "So if the plan isn't changed, why are you telling me all this?"

Plaine shrugged. "You guessed something was wrong. *Not* telling you would have created a distraction. And yeah, that means you can tell the others, too." He looked past her down the corridor toward the target. "Besides, when you're in the middle of a bad situation, it's good to know there's help waiting just around the corner."

"*If* that help arrives in time."

"Don't think of it like that," he said firmly. "Always remember that help is on its way. You just have to hold out for a few more minutes. Just a few more minutes."

"Right." And if the hoped-for help never arrived, a little self-deception would hardly make much of a difference. "I guess I should get back to work."

Slowly, Plaine drew his eyes back from the target. And, per-haps, from distant memories. "Yeah, I guess you should," he said. "Okay. Draw, spin left, and fire. We'll do it ten more times, then shift to spin-right."

CHAPTER EIGHTEEN

Merrick had hoped to get back to Svipall just after dark. Finding the jormungands so early in the afternoon had threatened to put him ahead of that schedule.

Theoretically, that wasn't a big deal. With Troft military helmets utilizing both infrareds and light-amplification, night and day should be effectively equivalent.

But in practice, as Merrick had learned during the Qasaman war, every laser shot—from friend or foe—necessarily blanked out the optics for a split second. The enhancements kicked back on almost immediately, of course, but for that brief time the Troft was partially blind.

And at umpteen to one odds, Merrick needed all the advantages he could get. Even small ones.

As it turned out, though, the vague timeline he'd plotted for Plan A hadn't taken the jormungands' own quirks into account. They wanted the free food he was tossing to them, but they also had a tendency to pause while they fed, either savoring every bite or making sure they didn't miss anything. Even worse—or in this case, really, even better—was the fact that within the first couple of kilometers he'd lured out over ten of the big snakes, and there were often occasions when the whole entourage paused to squabble over a share of whatever animal had come up next on Merrick's menu.

The delays were frustrating. But on another level, they were necessary. Merrick had figured he would be lucky to pull even one jormungand, and he was being hard-pressed to find enough tidbits to keep them all in line. The fafirs were starting to notice the new predator working his way through their territory, and were making themselves scarce. Sometimes Merrick needed ten or fifteen minutes to find a new supply of food, and every such delay held the risk that the jormungands would get tired of waiting for their two-legged benefactor and go home. At one point, Merrick toyed with the idea of going after larger prey and cutting them into smaller pieces, despite the risks that such blatant use of his lasers would entail.

Fortunately, by that time the jormungands had learned to be patient with his sorties. Even more fortunately, about two kilometers out from Svipall he ran across a whole nest of quail-sized creatures crammed into a hollow tree. They weren't much more than a mouthful to the larger jormungands, but they were easy to kill and the snakes seemed to like them. There were too many to simply carry in his arms, but using his shirt and a couple of branches he was able to rig a travois to carry them.

A couple of the smaller jormungands, with perhaps less patience than their elders, moved in close to the travois as they continued on, clearly intent on helping themselves. A quick burst from his sonic sent them slithering back again.

The sun was down and the sky fading into blackness when they reached Svipall.

The final leg of their journey had not gone unnoticed, of course. During the last kilometer or so aircars began to appear overhead, first one, then two, and finally four, drifting slowly across the forest canopy. Fortunately, Kjoic's sensor earpiece gave Merrick warning when one was on the way, and he was able to turn the Pied Piper procession into an innocent jormungand group meal by tossing the meat into the middle of the procession instead of in front of it. There wasn't much he could do about his own heat signature, but if the Trofts noticed a lone human on the edge of the jormungand gathering they apparently didn't worry about it enough to investigate closer.

Hopefully, by the time they realized what was actually happening it would be too late to do anything about it.

That moment came somewhere during the last twenty meters of the journey. The aircars were no longer drifting past but were

hovering directly overhead, pacing the jormungands, clearly trying to figure this out. A few tentative shots were taken, but the
combination of dense canopy and jormungand hide made such
aerial attacks useless. Until the procession came out onto open
ground, the Trofts would just have to wait.

Complicating matters was the fact that they also had to weigh
the possibility that this was nothing but an elaborate diversion
designed to draw the bulk of their forces while the real attack
was launched elsewhere.

Which meant that when Merrick reached the last row of trees by
the north end of the building he found barely ten Trofts waiting:
five kneeling, five standing, their lasers trained across the fifty
meters of open space between them and jormungands' likely exit
point. Above them, two of the four aircars who'd been dogging
him had taken up backup positions. The other two had vanished,
perhaps to perimeter patrol. Behind them and to Merrick's left
was the northeast corner of the building.

Behind that blank wall, if Kjoic hadn't lied to him, was the
room where the Drims' war drug was stored.

Smiling tightly, Merrick collected the last five quail from his
travois and hurled them across the gap toward the Trofts.

The quail were big enough that the soldiers could easily see
them arcing toward them. A couple of reflexive shots sliced across
the barrage, but most of the Trofts apparently suspected the quail
were a diversion and kept their weapons leveled at the forest.

Unfortunately for them, the quail were big enough for the jormungands to see, too. The last bits of free food had barely landed
when the snakes burst out of the forest and slithered toward the
defense line, each intent on being the first to reach the buffet.

For a long second nothing happened. Perhaps the Trofts were
momentarily stunned by the enthusiasm with which the snakes
were charging them, or perhaps they were simply waiting for a
closer and clearer shot. The jormungand in the lead had covered
ten of the fifty meters toward the line when the clearing lit up
with laser bursts as the Trofts opened fire.

They were still blasting away, trying to penetrate the jormungands' incredibly tough scales, when Merrick stepped out from
behind the trees and grabbed the tail end of one of the biggest
snakes as it passed him. He locked it firmly in his elbow, spun
himself around a couple of times until he had the creature

completely off the ground and spinning with him, then hurled it across the gap, hammer-throw style, into the Troft lines.

And in that instant the orderly laser fire collapsed into complete chaos as the soldiers scrambled madly to get away from the creature.

Given time, plus the massive firepower available, they would eventually have gotten on top of the unexpected threat. Merrick had no intention of giving them that time. Even as the soldiers scattered, firing madly at the thrashing jormungand, he grabbed another of the snakes and hurled it at his target wall. It bounced off the ceramic and twisted around to face a pair of Trofts whose frantic retreat had taken them in that direction.

One of the Trofts managed to dodge out of the way. The second wasn't as lucky. The jormungand raised its front segment and lashed out, its teeth digging deeply into the solder's armor. Someone bellowed something, and the wall behind them lit up with multiple flashes as both the victim and his companion poured laser fire into the snake. One of the aircars swooped down from its high-cover position and added its own fire to the soldiers' desperate defense.

It was still hovering there, its pilot's attention on the attacking jormungands, when Merrick grabbed one final snake and threw it across the aircar's bow. The vehicle jerked with the impact, its pilot instinctively rolling it to the side to drop off his unwanted passenger. Unfortunately for the soldiers he was trying to help, his maneuver unintentionally dropped the snake right on top of them.

And with confusion now engulfing the entire guard contingent, Merrick sprinted out into the open. One of the Trofts had lost his laser during the struggle with the jormungand; if Merrick could get to it without being stopped, he might be able to cut a hole in the wall without revealing who and what he was.

He was halfway across the open ground when an aircar that had been hovering out of sight over the forest dropped below treetop height and screamed up behind him.

Merrick flinched, his programmed reflexes throwing him to the side in a tight hit-and-roll. But no laser fire blazed out at him. Instead, the pilot charged into the fray, blasting away at the jormungands and trying to help his comrades.

And not doing it very well. Even as Merrick regained his feet and resumed his run, the aircar unleashed a withering volley of

fire at the side battle, half of the blasts overshooting the jormungands and tearing into the building wall. Either the pilot was an
incredibly bad marksman—

Abruptly, Merrick got it. That wasn't an incompetent or petri-
fied pilot. It was Kjoic, using Merrick's actions and the resulting
chaos as cover to help pave the way for his partner's evening
raid. A couple more volleys, and Merrick might not even have
to bother with that discarded Troft laser—

A second later his servos again threw him into a sideways dive
as Kjoic's aircar tilted violently and lurched backward straight
toward Merrick. He made a second swerving dive as the aircar
almost straightened out, then rolled half onto its side again. It
checked its backward motion and lurched forward, picking up
speed as Kjoic continued to fight the sideways instability. Passing
low over the soldiers and their battle with the jormungands, it
slammed hard into the building, tearing a jagged gash in the wall.

Mentally, Merrick flipped Kjoic a salute. The Troft had played
the incompetent pilot perfectly, pretending to first weaken the
wall, then demolish it.

And Merrick had his opening.

He put on a burst of speed of his own, glancing up at the
gathering swarm of aircars, wondering if any of the pilots would
spot him through the haze of laser fire. With the ground troops
fully engaged with the jormungands, the aircars were the only
force on the scene who could stop him or save their comrades.

Except that right now they didn't seem capable of doing either.
All the vehicles he could see were weaving around, crabbing
sideways, drifting backward or forward, and otherwise having
serious problems.

Ludolf had triggered his bombs.

Briefly, Merrick wondered if Kjoic perhaps hadn't been faking
ineptitude at all, but that instead of grabbing the single unsabo-
taged aircar he'd accidentally taken one of the others. But it didn't
really matter. Whatever the mechanics of the move, Kjoic had put
the aircar exactly where Merrick needed it: lying canted on the
debris from the wall, its nose half inside the room. Leaping on
top of it, Merrick eased through the ragged tear in the ceramic.

No lights were glowing in the room beyond. But there was
enough reflected laser light from outside to show the basics.

From what Kjoic had said, Merrick had expected the room to

be a standard storage facility, with lockers or cabinets or at least stacks of crates. Instead, it was laid out more like an assembly room, with six long tables loaded with small boxes, chemical glassware, and diagnostic and mixing equipment.

At first glance the place looked chaotic, with no pattern as to which pieces of equipment were lined up on which table. But as Merrick studied the arrangement, he realized there was indeed a clear direction from mixing to heating to assembly and onward to a single table at the end which held a final set of scanners and a neat stack of narrow boxes about twenty centimeters long each. Hopping down from the aircar's nose, he crossed the room to that last table and opened one of the boxes.

Inside were a long line of about a dozen small round patches, each with a small nub in the center. The material was thinner than the tan and red patches the Trofts had used on him during the Red Patch drug test he'd been part of, but the overall shape and the placement of the nub were the same. The nub was the same color red as he remembered, too.

That was hardly definitive, of course. But Kjoic had pinpointed this room, and it was hardly in his best interests to steer Merrick wrong.

Besides, there was no way Merrick could search the whole building, especially when there was no guarantee he would recognize the drug anyway. These patches were as good a candidate as any.

And right or wrong, he was running out of time.

A pair of gray lab jackets were hanging on wall hooks near the table. Merrick grabbed both, putting on one as a replacement for the shirt he'd left on the travois and using the other to wrap up six of the boxes. He crossed the room, hopped up onto the aircar's nose, and peered cautiously outside.

The battle was still raging, but it was rapidly coming to an end. Two more aircars had joined in the action, and only two of the five snakes Merrick could see were still moving. He slipped down the side of the aircar to the ground, visually picked out the closest edge of the forest, and ran.

He did the first thirty meters at a regular sprint, mimicking the distinctive Troft gait, hoping that anyone who spotted him would think he was a terrified lab tech running from the jormungands. Once he was clear of the glare of the laser fire, he dropped the pretense and put on a burst of full-power Cobra servo speed.

Rather to his surprise, he made the forest without being shot at. Apparently, the Trofts were *really* focused on destroying the jormungands.

He ran another two kilometers without stopping, ducking tree branches with the aid of his light-amps and avoiding tree roots through his slowly gained experience and a lot of luck. His earpiece detected two Troft aircars during that time, but both seemed to be running a patrol pattern and neither came very close to him. He slowed to a walk and shifted to a more meandering route, and after another half hour finally began to breathe easy.

And even, cautiously, to congratulate himself.

He'd done it, just as Commander Ukuthi had recruited him to do way back on Qasama. He'd infiltrated the human slaves on Muninn, figured out what the Drims were up to, and even had a sample of their new toy for Ukuthi to take back to the Balin demesne-lord.

If he could figure out a way off Muninn, *and* then get back to Qasama.

And unfortunately, Kjoic was still the key to both. Which meant he had to find a way to hook up with the Kriel spy again.

Which was going to be tricky.

Merrick obviously couldn't go back to Svipall. He'd already pushed his luck there way too many times. Besides, going to Svipall would probably bring him into contact with Ludolf again, and he still didn't trust the man.

But there were two other places Kjoic might think of for a rendezvous. First was the wrecked Troft spacecraft where Merrick and Kjoic had first met. Second was Alexis Tucker Woolmaster's house out in the forest, where Merrick had spent a fair amount of time and where Kjoic had first revealed his true identity and purpose.

Alexis's home was considerably closer than the spacecraft, which would mean less time either he or Kjoic would need to spend in the forest. The downside was that the Drim Trofts knew the place, too...except that they knew it as the place where some of their soldiers had been gunned down by either stealth or treachery. If they figured that to be Merrick's next landing spot, they would come in force.

On the other hand the spacecraft could be crawling with Trofts at this point, as well. Or Anya and her mother could be there, with or without any other wide-eyed revolutionaries in tow.

After Anya's little disappearing act Merrick wasn't sure he wanted to see her again this soon. He definitely didn't want to see her while carrying his current cargo. It was clear that Ludolf and Hanna *really* wanted to get hold of the war drug, and until Merrick knew what they wanted it for he had no intention of giving it to them.

But he couldn't sit out here in a random patch of forest and hope Kjoic somehow stumbled on him. He had to go *somewhere*, and Alexis Woolmaster's house was the closest of the likely meeting spots.

So he would go there, find a place to hide and observe, and give Kjoic a day to find him. If he didn't, Merrick would switch to the spacecraft.

And if Kjoic didn't come there, either...

Merrick grimaced as he looked at the stars overhead through a gap in the trees. But there was no point borrowing trouble. Not yet, anyway. If Kjoic didn't show, Merrick would simply have to find another way off the planet. Until then, he had places to go.

Checking his nanocomputer's compass, he turned south. A nice, long circle around Svipall's southern edge, he decided, and an equally long, leisurely approach to Alexis's house.

Fortunately, he had the whole night to do it.

And finally, the data stream included the report that Barrington had been awaiting for days.

The *Dorian* was back to full battle capability.

He scowled as he skimmed the report. Or at least it was back to the fullest capability possible while missing its chief engineer and ten other officers and men.

There was a movement beside him, and he disengaged from the data stream to see Commander Garrett walking across CoNCH toward him. "Captain," Garrett greeted him.

"Commander," Barrington said, checking the time. Garrett wasn't due on watch for another hour. "I see you have the ship fully up to speed a full day ahead of schedule. Congratulations."

"Thank you, sir," Garrett said. "I wonder if I might have a moment of your time."

"Of course," Barrington said, feeling his eyes narrow. Once again, there was something way too casual about his first officer's manner and tone.

"It concerns the missile tracking system," Garrett continued, nodding across CoNCH toward the weapons monitor station. "It would be easier to show you."

"Of course," Barrington said, rising from his chair. The cluster of weapons, engineering, life-support, and damage-control monitor stations was typically unoccupied when the ship was at low-alert status. A good place for a private conversation. "Lead the way."

"Yes, sir."

A minute later they were at the weapons monitor. Garrett sat down and punched in a code, and a diagnostic tree began writing itself across the main display. "I thought I should warn you, sir," Garrett said quietly. "Commander Castenello has been sounding out the officers about seating another Enquiry Board."

"Has he, now," Barrington said, a knot forming in his stomach. Castenello's move was hardly unexpected, but he'd assumed the tactical officer would launch his latest attack within a day or two after leaving Qasama, when it would still be convenient to turn around and go back. Now, with the *Dorian* nearly at the halfway point, seemed the worst possible time to try a political coup. "And what reception is he getting?"

"I don't know for sure, sir," Garrett said. "But without Commander Kusari, I'm afraid the majority may side with him."

"If the majority think I'm unfit for command, then that's the way the vote *should* go," Barrington said.

But the stomach knot tightened another turn. Was he really about to lose command of his ship?

"Well, that *is* the question, isn't it?" Garrett said. "Whether they truly think you're unfit, or whether they're playing their own political games."

"And how would you suggest we disentangle those motivations?"

"I don't know, sir," Garrett conceded. "Frankly, I've never known how all that worked."

"That's because you made it to the top without a patron," Barrington said. "I admire you for that, Commander. And I'm not the only one who does."

"Thank you, sir." Garrett smiled wryly. "But there's no need for excessive praise. I'm already on your side."

"It was genuine, Commander," Barrington assured him. "And hardly excessive. The big question now is whether you're ready to take command."

A muscle in Garrett's cheek twitched. "So that's it?" he demanded softly. "You're just going to give up?"

"Oh, I'll fight as best I can," Barrington said. "But you said it yourself. Without Kusari, I'm balanced on a knife's edge. I'm just surprised it took Castenello this long to take action. Now it's going to cost him that much extra time to get back to Qasama."

"Except that he's not planning to take us back to Qasama," Garrett said. "Not until we've checked out Broom's system."

"He wants to keep *going*?"

"Yes, sir," Garrett said. "He's pitching it as a broad reading of Commodore Santores's mission statement, just as you did, with a hinted undertone that following your lead would give a formal Board on Asgard one less charge to hit you with. I think that's his way of soothing any wavering consciences."

"But it still leaves you in command," Barrington pointed out. "Given that you're likely to follow my plan completely—" He broke off. "Or *will* he be leaving you in command?"

"Well, that's the other question," Garrett said. "Kusari isn't here, which leaves Filho next in line. We both know that he's very much in Castenello's camp on most things. If he were in command I don't doubt Castenello would effectively be running the ship."

"But again, that assumes he's got a card that can take you out." Barrington raised his eyebrows. "*Does* he?"

Garrett gave a little shrug. "Everybody has things in their past," he said. "But I doubt there's anything sufficiently damning in mine."

"Which isn't say he couldn't twist a minor key into a major one," Barrington said. "Nothing we can do until he shows his hand, I suppose." He nodded toward the display. "Is there really a problem with the missile tracking system?"

"Of course, sir," Garrett said. "I assumed someone would check." He touched a handful of keys, and one of the boxes on the display tree flickered amber and then went green. "There. It's fixed."

And if Castenello checked, there would be a reasonable data trail for him to follow. He might suspect a clandestine meeting, but he wouldn't be able to prove it. "Excellent."

"Thank you, sir," Garrett said. "With your permission, there are some other matters I need to attend to. I'll return in an hour to stand my watch."

"Very good," Barrington said. "Carry on."

He returned to the command station, watching out of the corner of his eyes as Garrett left CoNCH. *But I doubt there's anything sufficiently damning in mine*, Garrett had said. He'd said it calmly, too, as a man would speak truth.

Or a very well-rehearsed lie.

Barrington didn't know which it was. But he would find out. Probably very soon.

Merrick had budgeted himself the entire night to make his way through the forest to Alexis's house. It was just as well that he had.

The river running south of Svipall was the first obstacle. The initial crossing, far out in the forest, was trickier than he'd expected, ultimately requiring him to drag a couple of half-rotten trees to the bank and build a jump-off spot for himself. But at least he didn't have any roving Trofts to deal with. The next place where the river was narrow enough for him to recross it without that kind of potentially conspicuous activity was too close to the village and would have brought him into range of patrols and aircars. He was forced to travel further south and west than he'd intended to find a decent crossing spot, with the result that he ended up approaching the house from due west instead of from the southeast as he'd planned.

And of course, the whole way he had to deal with Muninn's nocturnal predators, and to do so without using his lasers.

It was an hour before dawn when he finally reached the ring of bersark that surrounded Alexis's ranch. The house itself was dark, but his infrareds indicated that there was someone home.

Unfortunately, at this distance he couldn't tell whether that resident was human or Troft. The only way to be sure would be to get closer.

For a moment he was sorely tempted to find the nearest sizeable bamboo patch and lock himself inside for a few hours' of sleep. He was exhausted, hungry, and grimy, and it would be safer to put off whatever confrontation he was facing until he'd taken care of at least one of those three.

But time wasn't his friend here. If the Drims hadn't already discovered the theft, they would soon. And the minute they did, they would undoubtedly launch a manhunt that would make the one they'd sent after him and Anya after their wing escape look like an afternoon stroll. If he and Kjoic didn't make themselves scarce before then, they were going to have serious trouble finding and stealing transport.

Unlike the bersark barriers at Svipall and Anya's own village of Gangari, Alexis's was intended only to keep out large ground animals. She therefore hadn't bothered removing the trees where the fafirs and other arboreal creatures lived and traveled. Once again, for the umpteenth time that night, Merrick jumped up into one of the trees and made his way through the network of branches to the other side of the barrier. He dropped back to the ground and moved carefully toward the house.

He was within fifty meters by the time he was able to confirm that the heat signature from inside was human. It was ten meters more before he realized that it wasn't one signature, but two.

As near as he'd been able to tell the last time he was here, Alexis lived alone. Did she have company?

Or was this someone else? Anya and Hanna, maybe, fresh from their search for weapons on the downed spacecraft?

Only one way to find out. Watching the corners of the house for unexpected surprises, he walked up to the front porch and climbed the steps toward the front door—

"I knew you would come here," a whisper came from behind him.

Merrick spun around, jumping off the side of the porch and landing on the ground in a crouch, his hands snapping up into firing position.

Anya stood a few meters behind him, her arms at her sides, an expression of utter weariness on her face. Where in the Worlds had she been hiding?

He never had a chance to ask. Without warning the edges of the eaves over the porch exploded in white powder, spraying it across the whole area around the door.

Again, Merrick leaped away. But it was too late. Even as he hit the ground he could feel the bersark starting to take effect, to cloud his vision and confuse his mind. He tried to run—tripped and fell on his side as gravity abruptly seemed to change direction—shoved himself off the ground only to see the forest and Anya herself wavering as if they were underwater—fell onto his other side as his legs collapsed beneath him—

And then, all was blackness.

CHAPTER NINETEEN

"We'll never have a better shot," Nissa insisted. "This is our chance to go on the offensive."

"Or our chance to get ourselves killed," Emile countered.

"Or at least get *Lorne* killed," de Portola added.

"Or anyone else," Emile said, glaring at de Portola. "Some of *my* Cobras, for instance."

"Not arguing," de Portola said. "It's just that Lorne is the likely spearhead on anything we do. So, yeah, I'm thinking he's at the top of the worry list."

"I'm not trying to get anyone killed," Nissa insisted. "I'm just pointing out that having Governor Moreau joined to Reivaro at the hip could be a one-time opportunity."

"Only if Reivaro actually lets someone in to see him," de Portola warned. "If he doesn't—and I think he'd have to be an idiot to do that—then any plan either dies on its feet or walks some of our last ghosts into a trap."

Lorne winced. The ghosts were the Cobras like him, who'd so far avoided getting slapped with the Dominion's loyalty collars. There had never been very many of them, and their numbers had already shrunk more than anyone liked. No matter how well they hid, or however much makeup they wore out on the streets of Capitalia or Archway, the Marines were slowly but steadily picking them up and forcing collars on them.

And once that happened, that particular Cobra was lost to

them. Especially since these were the Dominion's new collars, the ones with enough explosive packed inside to break through Uncle Corwin's ceramic inserts.

"So we just don't let that happen," Emile said.

"Preaching to the choir, friend," Werle said. "So we either need a plan that's a guaranteed success or we scrub the whole idea."

"That's a little extreme, don't you think?" Nissa said, glaring at him. "You know there are no guarantees in warfare. All I'm asking is that we take this chance while we have it."

"I'm willing to drop it to eighty percent," Emile said equably. "It'd be nice if we had that tunic completely scoped out first, though."

"We're working on it," Werle said. "But the IFF system is key, and we still haven't nailed that down."

"Plus they've probably changed it by now," de Portola pointed out. "So even if we find the system, we probably won't be able to duplicate it."

"Keep working on it," Nissa said. "Do you need any more help?"

"Thanks, but we've already got the best people for the job," Werle assured her.

"Fine," she said. "Just remind them that our clock is counting down. There's no way to know how long before Reivaro gets tired of having Moreau underfoot and sends him back up to the *Algonquin*."

"We're working as fast as we can," Werle said, a little stiffly.

"And we'll try to come up with that attack you want," de Portola added.

"Thank you," Nissa said. "But it's not just for me. It's for all of Aventine."

"Right," de Portola said. "We'll try to remember that."

Nissa's eyes narrowed. "So I guess we're done here," Lorne spoke up before she could reply. No one in the room liked her, but there was nothing to gain by pushing her into a glaring contest.

"I guess we are," Emile said. "By the way, Broom, did you get the message that Chintawa wants to see you?"

"No," Lorne said, frowning. "Is it about Uncle Corwin?"

"How should I know?" Emile countered. "You're supposed to meet him at—oh, hell, never mind; I'll walk you over there. Got a couple of questions for him anyway. Assuming you can fit it into your schedule."

"I'm all yours," Lorne said, suppressing the impulse to roll his eyes. Between Nissa and Emile, he was being seriously rubbed the wrong way today.

Of course, the two of them probably saw it the other way around. Emile he'd flattened with his stunner while trying to get Governor Treakness away from the Troft invasion; Nissa he'd committed high treason in front of. They probably considered his presence as much of an irritation as he considered theirs.

But they were all in this together. Like it or not, they were allies, and Lorne intended to act like it.

A minute later he and Emile were once again walking their bent-back way down the tunnels. "How far is this place?" Lorne asked.

"Not very," Emile said. "You trust her?"

"Who?"

"Nissa Gendreves. Do you trust her?"

"I don't know," Lorne admitted. "Probably depends on what I'm trusting her to do."

"You're a better man than I am, then," Emile said. "I don't trust her as far as I could spit her." He looked half over his shoulder at Lorne. "I especially wouldn't trust her if I was a Moreau or a Broom."

"Maybe," Lorne said. That thought *had* occurred to him. Many times. "You think she's angling to take out Uncle Corwin and me together?"

"If she could also gain some kind of victory or advantage for the Cobra Worlds while you went down?" Emile snorted. "In a heartbeat."

"It would have to be a seriously major victory for her to trade away my potential use in future operations," Lorne pointed out. "I'm counting on the hope that she loves Aventine more than she hates us."

Emile grunted. "Or at least that she loves her own future career and glory. Just watch her, that's all I'm saying. Okay, we're here. How are your rock-climbing skills?"

"Decent enough, I guess," Lorne said, frowning. "We going up or down?"

"We start by going down," Emile said. "We'll end by going up."

Lorne rolled his eyes. "Yeah, thanks. I'll manage."

"Good," Emile stopped beside an alcove that contained a shaft leading down from the floor. "It's about twenty meters," he added as he positioned himself over the shaft with his feet and hands pressed against opposite sides of the ceramic like a four-pointed starfish. "Give me a three-meter head start and then follow. *Don't fall on me.*"

The technique was a little tricky, but Lorne picked it up quickly enough. "Cute setup. I'll bet the Trofts can't do this."

"Not without redoing their knee joints," Emile agreed. "In fact, I'm guessing the only ones who *can* do this are Cobras. Everyone else has to be lowered on ropes. Okay, we're coming to the end—wait until I tell you I'm clear, then target-lock the floor and drop. Your servos should land you on your feet."

Putting a target lock on the floor while he was facing upward wasn't easy, but Lorne managed to roll over far enough while suspended to get a clear view. The distance was only about four meters, and he wasn't entirely certain his servos could react in time. Still, Emile had done it, and they both had the same programmed reflexes. He did as instructed, and to his mild surprise landed upright exactly as Emile had promised.

They had arrived in yet another of the low-ceilinged conduits. Unlike the ones a level up, though, this one was laid out almost like an office hallway, with four doors leading off the sides at fifty-meter intervals. "You look at the history books, you'll see that the whole city building project back then is described as Aventine's most massive and shameful boondoggle," Emile said as he led the way down the conduit. "Cost overruns, time overruns—the works." He tapped the conduit roof. "Now you know why."

"So why is Chintawa down here?" Lorne asked as they approached the first doorway.

"Chintawa?" Emile walked past the doorway and turned around to face Lorne. "Oh, right. Sorry—I lied." He nodded his head toward the room. "In here."

Lorne's first impulse was to fire his stunner and get the hell out of there. But it would be a useless gesture, and they both knew it. If it was a trap, Emile already had people stationed to intercept him. Silently, he continued forward, his eyes on Emile's self-satisfied smirk the whole way, and stepped through the doorway.

The room he found himself in was larger than he'd expected, nearly thirty meters long and twenty wide, with a ceiling thankfully high enough to permit him to stand upright with half a meter to spare. Eight long tables filled the room's center, each with three men and women seated on each side. Lorne couldn't tell what they were doing, but each person was surrounded by large bowls, measuring bottles, a pair of heavy-looking bread-loaf-sized containers, and a stack of smaller boxes with colorful and familiar snack-bar logos on them. More of the latter boxes were stacked along both of the room's side walls. A woman standing behind one of the workers on Lorne's side of the room turned around to face him.

Lorne stiffened. Of all the people he hadn't expected to see—

"Hello, Lorne," Thena Moreau said quietly. "It's good to see you."

For a frozen moment Lorne was at a loss for words. Aunt Thena. Uncle Corwin's wife.

Or rather, his estranged wife. The woman who, with crisis looming with the Dominion, had simply walked out on him.

"Hello, Aunt Thena," he managed. *Allies, like it or not.* "I'm surprised to see you."

"Oh?" She glanced over his shoulder. "Emile didn't tell you where you were going, I take it?"

"No," Lorne said. "He said he was taking me to Chintawa."

"Did he, now." She looked at Emile again, a mildly annoyed look on her face. "Really, Emile."

"He would have worried the whole way," Emile said calmly. "Besides, a surprise is good every once in a while. Keeps the heart pumping. You going to keep trying to stare a hole through her, Broom, or are you going to ask what they're doing in here?"

With an effort, Lorne turned his eyes to the tables. The workers were measuring out a powdery material from their bowls into the larger boxes, adding some liquid from their bottles, then closing and pressure-sealing the boxes. They would then open the second box, pull out a slab of brown material, and put it into one of the snack boxes. More powder and liquid into the now empty box, and the operation would repeat.

"Actually, Emile, I think Lorne and I need to clear the air before we do anything else," Thena said. "The break room's over there, Lorne, and I think it's empty at the moment."

"That's okay," Lorne said, folding his arms across his chest. "Whatever talking you want to do, you can do it right here."

"All right," Thena said. "Sounds like I'm starting. Fine. You're angry at me for walking out on your uncle. You're especially angry about the restraining order I asked for. You want to know what on earth he might have done to make me take such a drastic and humiliating step."

"Yeah, that about covers it," Lorne growled. "Plus the fact that he was already under heavy stress from the whole Dominion invasion thing. He didn't need this."

"I know," Thena murmured.

And to Lorne's surprise a flicker of pain crossed her face. He keyed his infrareds, wondering if the ache was just an act. But her facial warmth indicated the emotion was real.

Not that it mattered now, really. "Well, if you were trying to stay out of it, you succeeded brilliantly," he said. "In case you hadn't heard, he's a Dominion prisoner."

"Yes, I'd heard." She studied his face. "You don't get it, do you?"

"Get what?"

"That keeping me out of the Dominion's line of sight was *exactly* what we were trying to do." She gestured at the tables behind her. "So that we could do *this*."

Lorne looked back at the tables, a sudden uncertainly washing over his anger and resentment. What the *hell*...? "And what is *this*, exactly?"

"This is the collar insert manufacturing facility," Thena said. "The *real* one, not those little kiln things Corwin set up around Capitalia. Those were the diversion. This is where we either make or break freedom for the Cobra Worlds."

Lorne focused on her. On her stiffness, and determination, and pain... "It was his idea, wasn't it?" he said. "Uncle Corwin's. Make himself the bait so that they could snatch him up and you could keep working here."

Her lips compressed. "Actually, it was my idea," she confessed. "But my plan would have had us both disappearing to different places in the city. He said the Dominion expected us to be naïve primitives—his term—and that they'd be content if they thought they'd ruined our pathetic little operation. He also insisted they needed a prize, and that he was the biggest one we could afford to lose." She sighed. "Also his term. And he thought they'd be suspicious if I just disappeared. So we concocted this big fuss, I made it, and I moved out." She waved at the room. "I've been here ever since."

Lorne looked at Emile, fully expecting to see another of his famous smirks. The country bumpkin Cobra, so thoroughly taken in this way.

But for once, the other Cobra wasn't looking amused or superior. In fact, he looked almost sympathetic. "Okay," Lorne said, turning back. "So how does this work? I thought you needed a kiln to bake the inserts."

"That's true," Thena said. "Unless you have one of two catalysts that harden the ceramic at room temperature. That was what Corwin really wanted when he set off on this hobby: a ceramic that could be applied to a potential Cobra's bones in paste form and then solidified in situ. He was hoping that would be less traumatic in application, and less likely to create anemia and arthritis down the road."

"I gather you were able to dig up a supply of those catalysts?"

"Everything inside the city limits," Thena said, nodding. "Possibly everything *outside* the limits, too. I haven't asked where our suppliers have been scrounging."

"Yeah," Lorne said, sighing. They seemed so satisfied with their work. Bursting their bubble was going to be painful. "There's just one problem. Reivaro's added more explosive to the collars."

To his surprise, Thena simply nodded. "Yes, we know," she said calmly. "In fact, we were expecting it. That's why the ones we're making here are thicker and stronger than Corwin's original set. Another reason to use the kilns, by the way. They could only handle the old size, and we hoped that would convince Lij Tulu that we *couldn't* make anything stronger."

"And of course the old inserts will work just fine with the old collars," Emile added. "Unless Reivaro wants to make enough new collars to upgrade everybody, we can still use the old inserts on those."

"He won't upgrade," Thena said, her voice going grim. "He's already given notice that he'll be putting collars on Chintawa and the other leaders once he's finished with the Cobras."

"Yeah, we heard that, too," Lorne said. "We need to stop this nonsense before it goes any further."

"Which is the main reason I asked Emile to bring you here today." Thena smiled faintly. "Aside from hoping to repair my reputation, of course. As you can see by the stack by the wall, we have almost enough inserts for all the Cobras. Certainly everyone in Capitalia. Which means...?" She held out a hand to Emile.

"Which means we don't have to guard our ghost Cobras anymore," he said. The smirk was back, Lorne noticed. Only this time it wasn't directed at him. "Which means we can let Nissa throw them at whatever goat-brained scheme she wants. As long as we make sure they get captured and not killed, we're good."

"Because when the time comes all the Cobras will be given inserts that'll protect them from the collars anyway," Lorne said, nodding. "And the more Cobras Reivaro has wearing his collars, the calmer he'll be."

"And the more careless, we hope," Emile said. "When he starts relaxing is when we hit him." He eyed Lorne. "Still be handy if you could finally get those epaulets figured out."

"Working on it," Lorne said. "As long as we're on the subject, of mysteries, Aunt Thena, I need to ask you about a question Mom supposedly sent me via Uncle Corwin after she got captured. The message told me to exercise restraint and professionalism, and to remember that I was trying for freedom, not mass slaughter."

"That sounds like your mother," Thena said, nodding.

"Agreed," Lorne said. "But then there was this part: I was to stand tall and watch my own back, because no one else would do it for me."

"Really," Thena said thoughtfully. "Your mother said *that*?"

"So I'm told," Lorne said. "Which we all know isn't true. Cobras always have each other's backs."

"So you think there's a hidden message?"

"Exactly," Lorne said. "I was hoping there might be something that struck a chord with you. An incident from her childhood, maybe, where someone blindsided her or betrayed her trust or something?"

"Nothing comes to mind," Thena said, her forehead wrinkled in concentration. "But it won't be anything like that anyway. She knew Corwin was a prisoner, and she couldn't assume I'd be available for you to talk to. It has to be something that you yourself would pick up on."

Lorne grimaced. "I was afraid of that."

"Could it be something from Qasama?" Emile suggested. "There's got to be a lot of stuff that happened there that you never put into any of the reports Reivaro can tap into."

"Oh, there was plenty," Lorne said, scowling. "And yes, I've been wracking my brain to come up with something. But everyone on Qasama had everyone else's back, too."

"No operational or jurisdictional disputes?"

"Nothing that rose to that level," Lorne said. "There were occasional disagreements on tactics, but those were always resolved higher up the ladder than I was. Mostly the fighters at my level got orders and followed them."

"I meant if there was something your level," Emile persisted. "Like here, when you had orders to get Treakness off Aventine and I had orders to stop you."

"I hadn't heard about this," Thena said, frowning. "When was this?"

"Right after the Troft invasion," Lorne told her. "Turned out there was more to it than that, which neither of us knew at the time."

"How did you resolve it?"

"He blasted me on my butt with his stunner." Emile cocked his head. "For the record, if I'd been really hell-bent on following Chintawa's order I could've taken you."

"That's what my dad said," Lorne said calmly. "Mom disagreed. But no, the Qasaman leadership never had that kind of a schizophrenic split. Like I said, we had each other's..."

He trailed off as a sudden thought thunderbolted into his mind. On one level, it made no sense. But on another, it made perfect sense.

Was *that* what his mother had been trying to say?

"Lorne?" Thena prompted carefully.

Lorne found his voice. "Emile, did you talk to any of the prisoners who got out of the garrison before Mom was captured?"

"We talked to all of them," Emile said, eyeing Lorne as closely as Thena was. "All we could find, anyway. You got something?"

"Maybe," Lorne said. "Did any of them say whether or not Mom got shot during the rescue?"

"You mean by the Marines?" Emile shook his head. "I don't remember anyone mentioning injuries. My spotter didn't mention seeing any burn marks, either."

"What does that get us?" Thena asked.

"Maybe the edge we've been looking for," Lorne said, heading for the door. "Come on, Emile. See you later, Aunt Thena. Emile, can you track down one of those prisoners and talk to him or her again? I want someone who was paying good attention during the battle."

"Yeah, I can find someone," Emile said. "What do you want me to ask them?"

"I'll tell you on the way," Lorne said, ducking back into the corridor and heading for the shaft. "Come on, move it. Like Nissa said, this may be our chance."

Taking the Marine epaulet apart had been tricky. Putting it back together, especially when Lorne told them he wanted it connected to the tunic's power supply but not remounted in its seating receptacle, was even trickier.

But the techs were good at their job, and Werle and de Portola had been taking extensive notes. By the time Emile returned, everything was ready.

"Okay, I talked to the guy who was first in line out the door," Emile said, peering past de Portola at the tunic and the epaulet sitting half a meter away on the table, connected to the tunic by jury-rigged power cord extensions. "He said she stepped up to the two Marines, lasered both epaulets on one of them, ducked to the side and lasered the other's, then blasted them both with arcthrowers."

"Did the Marines fire back?"

"At least one of them did," Emile said. "Maybe both. It happened fast, and he wasn't expecting it. He wasn't sure if she was hit, but he doesn't remember seeing any burn marks, even up close." He snorted. "He also said he hadn't expected there to be a quiz."

"That's okay," Lorne said. Nothing in the testimony contradicted his theory. That was a good first step.

Now it was time to find out for sure.

"So what's all this?" Emile asked, pointing to the tunic and detached epaulet.

"An experiment," Lorne said. "Everyone ready?"

"As ready as we're going to be," Werle said. "Hang on while we get our shields."

"Shields?" Emile asked, frowning.

"We're going to fire the epaulet lasers," Lorne told him as Werle and de Portola slipped through the mesh overlap in the double Faraday cage and headed for the two slabs of ceramic Lorne had scrounged for them. "I don't want to risk making holes in the cage, so Werle and de Portola have volunteered to play target."

"Volunteered," de Portola said with a sniff as he handed one slab to Werle and picked up the other one. "Right. You, and you."

"Hey, Emile, you want a job?" Werle asked hopefully.

"Thanks," Emile said. "I'll just watch."

A minute later everyone was in position.

And this was it.

"Okay," Lorne said, carefully picking up the epaulet and a small push-button dangling from it on a couple more small wires. "Is this the firing button?" he asked, looking through the mesh at Will and Christy standing along the side of the room with their recording gear.

"Yes, sir," Christy confirmed. "Really, we can do this if you want."

"Thanks, but we'll handle it," Lorne said. There was still a risk here; and while Aventine was low on Cobras, it was even lower on techs who could figure out Dominion equipment. He would have sent them both out of the room if they hadn't flatly refused to go.

Holding the epaulet in front of him, pointing it at the center of the slab in Werle's hands, he gently squeezed the trigger.

The familiar blue needle flashed out, hitting the slab near the edge. Apparently, the particular cell the techs had connected to had been slightly misaligned on its gimbals. Shifting his angle, he tried again, and this time the beam hit dead center. "Okay, it works," he called back to the techs. He switched aim to de Portola's slab and again fired, for a second bull's eye hit.

"Still waiting to be impressed," Emile prompted.

"We're getting there," Lorne assured him. "Okay, pick up the tunic."

"Who, me?" Emile asked.

"Yes," Lorne said. "And be careful not to pop off the power cord."

"Sure." Gingerly, Emile got a grip under the tunic's arms and lifted it off the table. It sagged a little in his hands, but was rigid enough for the top section to stand mostly upright.

"Now hold it in front of de Portola," Lorne instructed. He waited until Emile was in position, then turned his epaulet until it was pointed at the tunic. "Hold still—"

"Hold it," Emile said hastily, shifting to the side and holding the tunic as far away from him as he could. "You sure you know what you're doing?"

"We're about to find out," Lorne said. Mentally crossing his fingers, he pressed the button.

And twitched as a blue beam shot out of his epaulet and into the tunic.

"Damn," Emile snarled. "You idiot—you almost hit me."

"Don't worry, it's on low power," Lorne said mechanically, staring at the spot where the shot had hit. No—that shouldn't have happened. He looked up at de Portola, then at Werle, seeing his own surprise and disappointment reflected in their faces.

He'd been so *sure*.

"So what exactly was that supposed to prove," Emile asked, dropping the tunic back on the table.

"Hey—be careful with that," Will admonished.

Emile ignored him. "Well?" he demanded.

Lorne took a deep breath, suddenly feeling like a fool. Of course it couldn't be that simple. "Mom said I needed to watch my back," he said. "Your witnesses to her attack said the second Marine hadn't shot back. And I was thinking about the time I hit you with a stunner." He hissed out a breath. "I thought maybe that Marine lasers were programmed to not fire at other Marines."

"We've seen them blasting away all the time in firefights," Emile said. "Having other Marines around never bothered them before."

"Are you sure?" Lorne countered. "Because if your witnesses were right, Mom's encounter was the first time we really had a situation where the lineup was a more or less controlled situation. I think she recognized that, figured out what the second Marine's lack of counterattack meant, and tried to send us that message."

"Good for her," Emile said. "Except she was wrong."

"I guess so," Lorne conceded. "Or else we just read it wrong."

Emile raised his eyebrows. "*We?*"

"Fine—*I* read it wrong," Lorne bit out. "Happy?"

"I'd be happier if we actually had something," Emile countered. "Call me back when you do. I'm going to check in with Chintawa." Turning, he pushed his way out the metal mesh—

"Wait a second," Werle said.

Lorne turned. Werle was staring at the tunic, an intense look on his face. "Maybe none of us is wrong," he said slowly. "Maybe we're all just stupid."

"Meaning?" de Portola asked.

"That isn't a Dominion Marine," Werle said, nodding toward the table. "It's a Dominion Marine *tunic*. Maybe there's a difference."

"Oh, so you're saying one of us should put the damn thing on and let Broom take pot shots at him?" Emile asked.

"No," Lorne said, setting down the epaulet. "He's saying *I* should put the damn thing on and let one of *you* take pot shots."

"Whoa!" de Portola protested. "That wasn't what I was saying at all."

"Too bad," Lorne said. "Also too late. Emile, get over here and pick up this epaulet before I knock it loose."

"Lorne—" de Portola began.

"Don't bother," Werle said. "You know what he's like in this mood."

Lorne had lifted and carried the tunic enough times to know how heavy it was. To his surprise, though, once it was settled on his shoulders and the front sealed it actually felt lighter. Some trick of weight distribution, probably. "You ready?" he asked Emile.

"Yeah," Emile said, an odd look on his face. "You know, this probably isn't the smartest move you've ever made."

"Don't worry, I've made plenty of dumber ones," Lorne assured him. "Okay. Start with a shot at Werle's shield to get the aim. Careful—it angles to the left."

"Yeah, I saw." Emile lined up the epaulet and carefully squeezed off a shot.

It hit just above the center of the slab. "Good shot," Lorne said. "Okay. Center of my chest, right over the breastbone."

"Where you've got laminae protection in case this doesn't work," Emile said, nodding, as he again lined up his shot. "Ready?"

Lorne braced himself. "Go."

Emile squeezed the firing button.

Nothing happened.

"You push it?" de Portola asked.

"Yeah," Emile said. He squeezed the button again. Nothing. He turned it back to Werle's shield and squeezed—

And once again the blue flash blasted out.

"My God," de Portola murmured. "Did we really do it?"

"Looks like it," Lorne said, feeling the tension fading from his muscles. "Okay. So let's—"

"Wait a minute," Will spoke up from the side. "Don't stop yet—we need to get some border parameters."

"He's right," Werle agreed. "Does it only block a direct shot, or will it also avoid a near-miss?"

"De Portola, move around a little to Broom's right," Emile ordered. "I'll start by shooting into his slab just past Broom's shoulder and keep moving outward until it fires."

It took several more minutes, a few more laser shots, and a lot of non-laser shots. But in the end, they had it. "So the no-fire bubble is about five centimeters around every Marine," Lorne said thoughtfully. "So if we can get right up into someone's face and stay there, we should be relatively safe."

"Only from the Marines behind him," de Portola said. "And that assumes we can get that close without already getting shot."

"Okay, so there's still a *little* challenge to it," Lorne conceded. He reached up to the tunic's collar and started to unfasten it—

"No—wait," Christy called. She had her face pressed against the eyepieces of a tripod-mounted optical scanner. "Don't take it off. All of you—run your telescopics up and tell me what you see on Cobra Broom's collar."

"My *collar*?" Lorne asked, craning his neck and trying to look down.

"I'll be damned," Emile breathed. "There's microengraving on it. Why didn't we ever see that before?"

"Probably because we never looked," Werle said.

"No, it wasn't there before," Will said. "Christy and I went over everything with a microscope. Must be heat-triggered."

"Could this be the IFF system?" Lorne asked.

"It looks like it," Christy said. "The epaulets' optical sensors are certainly good enough to read it at a distance of at least a hundred meters. Maybe more."

Lorne stared at the epaulet Emile was holding. If they really had scoped this out... "Can you duplicate it?" he asked.

Will and Christy exchanged looks. "We can try," Will said. "The microengraving we should be able to copy. The material is a different issue."

"But we can give it a shot," Christy said.

"Even if it just disables the autotarget system without us having to get close enough to blast the epaulet computers, it'll be worth it," Werle said. "We're already evading most of their manual fire."

"I get the feeling they don't work as hard on that as they should," de Portola agreed. "Too used to their computers doing their work for them."

Lorne nodded, his mind racing. If they could even slow down the Marines' attacks... "Emile, what's the status on the *Dewdrop*?"

"It should be fully armored in five days," Emile said. "Maybe four."

"And we'll need to do a shakedown trip, right?"

"With all that extra armor weight on it? Of course."

"You still thinking about taking down the Dominion's relay satellites?" Werle asked. "Because with this we might not need that."

"Right," de Portola agreed. "Who cares if they recognize us if they can't shoot us?"

"One thing at a time," Emile admonished them, frowning hard at Lorne. "You've got something. What is it?"

"Something we need to think hard about," Lorne said. "You said you were going to talk to Chintawa. Mind if I tag along?"

"Be my guest." Emile shifted his eyes to Will and Christy. "And *you* two figure out how to copy these collars. Fast."

CHAPTER TWENTY

The vote among the *Dorian*'s senior officers went as Barrington had expected.

"For disobeying standing orders and leaving a system of vital interest without explicit orders," Castenello intoned, "we, the senior officers of the Dominion of Man War Cruiser *Dorian* find Captain Barrington Moreau unfit for command. Captain Moreau is therefore relieved of command, and is to be confined to quarters until such time as a full Enquiry Board headed by Commodore Rubo Santores can be convened."

He looked at Barrington. "Captain Moreau, have you anything more to say into the record?"

"Not at this time," Barrington said. Castenello didn't have a very solid case, and he suspected several of those who voted on his side knew it. But the tactical officer's patron was powerful, and there was likely more politics going on behind the scenes than anyone would ever admit to. "I look forward to facing Commodore Santores and receiving actual justice."

For a moment Castenello eyed him. But apparently the dig hadn't quite reached the level where he felt he had to respond. Instead, with a small snort, he turned to Garrett.

Barrington felt his throat tighten. What he *hadn't* expected was the vehemence with which the officers would also turn on the *Dorian*'s first officer.

"In addition," Castenello continued, "for the manipulation and

259

withholding of critical data from the rest of the senior officers, Commander Ling Garrett is also relieved of command. Have *you* anything more to say into the record, Commander?"

"If I thought it would make a difference, I would," Garrett said calmly. "I would, however, suggest to the assembled officers that facing combat immediately after so drastic a shakeup in leadership could be disastrous. I further suggest that, should the *Dorian* survive such an encounter, the assembled officers will face far worse charges than Captain Moreau and I have been convicted of."

Barrington held his breath. The underlying message was clear: change your vote *now*, reinstate the captain and first officer, and some very bad trouble waiting down the road would go away.

Technically, an additional Enquiry Board would have be called before anyone could change his vote. But given the irregularities already in evidence, Barrington wouldn't put it past any of them to try to call for a second vote here on the spot.

But apparently they were solidly in agreement with Castenello. That, or bending the rules more than once per day was too uncomfortable to consider. The group remained silent.

"We'll see," Castenello said. "Regardless, you'll also have your chance at a further Enquiry Board after we've returned to Qasama."

"You apparently missed my comment about the *Dorian* not surviving the upcoming encounter," Garrett reminded him. "If that happens, we'll all be dealing with a much higher court than anything Commodore Santores can convene."

"Yes," Castenello murmured. "Scare tactics aside, Lieutenant Commander Filho is perfectly capable of successfully taking this ship into combat."

"Especially with you there to guide him?" Garrett suggested. "You *are* planning to usurp a portion of his command, aren't you?"

Castenello's eyes narrowed. "Have a care, Commander," he warned softly. "Such talk will not be permitted. A Dominion ship has just one captain, and that captain is Commander Filho."

"Ten minutes ago it was Captain Moreau," Garrett pointed out. "If Commander Filho does something you find unacceptable, will you also relieve him of command?" He looked at Filho. "Or are you convinced, Commander, that without your vote he won't be able to do that?"

"Commander Castenello is right," Filho said. But there was a hint of uncertainty in his eyes. "We'll see this operation through, because our mission statement *does* permit investigation of unknown Troft regions. However, your suggestion that we may face a dangerous combat situation assumes a commitment I'm not currently ready to make."

"Wait a minute," Barrington said, frowning. He hadn't heard this part. "You're continuing on to the system, but you're *not* planning to assist Ms. Broom and the others?"

"I merely said I'm not committed to that path," Filho said. "If it seems safe to do so, I will. But I make no promises."

"I see," Barrington said between stiff lips. So that was the rest of Castenello's plan. If there was any Troft opposition at all, Filho and Castenello could turn tail and run, then use the Troft military presence to bolster their contention that Barrington had been leading them into disaster.

Barrington had no power to alter that decision. But maybe there was still a way for him to influence it.

"That's your decision, of course," he said. "I simply suggest you bear in mind that Jody Broom's crew includes a Dominion of Man Marine."

He had the satisfaction of seeing backs straighten and jaws drop along the full length of the table. "Who?" Castenello demanded.

"Gunnery Sergeant Fitzgerald Plaine of the *Algonquin*," Barrington said. "He was in the *Squire*'s starboard gunbay when Broom and the others took the courier off Qasama."

"Why weren't we told about this?" Filho asked.

"We didn't know ourselves until the *Squire* had already left," Garrett spoke up.

Which was a lie, of course. Barrington and Omnathi had specifically agreed on Plaine's continued presence aboard the *Squire* as part of the Dominion's price for letting the courier leave Qasama unhindered.

But of course, no one else in the room knew that.

"Why didn't he disembark at Qasama?" Filho persisted. "More to the point, why didn't the Qasamans *make* him disembark?"

"I presume he stayed aboard because he'd been ordered to man the gunbay and had received no orders to the contrary," Garrett said. "I'm hoping we'll have a chance to ask him."

"I assume you're not suggesting we endanger the entire ship to rescue a single Marine," Castenello warned.

Barrington smiled. There it was again: that *we* endanger the ship.

And he had no doubt Filho and the rest had heard it, too. "I have no authority to suggest anything," he told the tactical officer. "I simply wish to have all the facts in evidence."

"I'm sure we all appreciate it," Filho said.

"Yes," Barrington murmured. So too, he suspected, did the pair of Marine guards flanking the hatchway.

Three more days to Jody Broom's destination, assuming Filho didn't reduce the *Dorian*'s speed. Plenty of time for the word to spread to the rest of the ship's Marine contingent that one of their own was in danger.

And unlike the Navy's senior officer corps, most Marines didn't have patrons behind them, confusing military issues with political fog.

This could, Barrington thought as he was escorted to his cabin, prove to be a very interesting three days.

Merrick's first realization as he clawed his way back to consciousness was that he was terribly thirsty.

His second was that his arms were being held along his sides, there were straps over his chest and thighs, and his head was being rigidly held in place.

Damn.

He opened his eyes, expecting to be facing a high, gray ceramic ceiling. He was right, except that the ceiling was lower than he'd thought it would be. Instead of being in the central room of the Drim warehouse, he was apparently in one of the smaller side rooms.

"You're awake."

The voice was familiar. But it was so quiet, so dead, and so hopeless that it took him a moment to realize that it was Anya. "Is that you, Anya?" he asked, trying to turn his head. But again, the padded brace resisted him.

Well, he could change that. His neck had servo enhancements, too, and a little extra power to them ought to break him out of this stupid thing.

He paused, belatedly focusing his attention on his hands. They were resting at his sides, unblocked or fettered or secured in any way.

Which meant his fingertip lasers were still functional.

Which meant his captors still didn't know he was a Cobra.

And until he knew more of what was happening, he didn't dare do anything to indicate otherwise.

"Where are you?" he said instead. "I can't see you."

"I'm here," she said, stepping to his side and into his view. Her eyes were as dead as her voice. "I am sorry, Merrick Hopekeeper. I am so very sorry."

"I'm sorry, too," Merrick said. "What exactly happened back there?"

"Betrayal, it was done to you," a new voice came in.

And Kjoic stepped into view on his other side.

"Yes, I see," Merrick said, keeping his voice calm. "Betrayal, it was certainly done to me. Do I stand in the presence of my betrayer?"

"In a way." Kjoic looked across Merrick at Anya. "But it was not by her choice or volition."

Merrick looked at Anya. Her eyes still looked dead. "Anya?" he prompted.

"Ludolf Treetapper suspected you had obtained the war drug," she said. The words came out flat and monotone, as if she was reading from a page she wanted to be done with. "He guessed you would go to Alexis Tucker Woolmaster's home to look for me."

Merrick's eyes flicked to Kjoic, noted the slight fluttering of his radiator membranes. So Anya still didn't know he and Kjoic had been working together?

Not that it mattered. Kjoic had clearly seen his opportunity and changed sides.

On the other hand, Kjoic didn't know he was a Cobra either. "And?" he asked.

"He prepared a trap with bersark powder," Anya said. "He expected you would approach without caution. You did."

"And the drug patches I took?" He looked back at Kjoic. "I presume your friends have them?"

"You presume incorrectly," Kjoic said. "Ludolf Treetapper escaped with them." His membranes gave a little bounce. "The patches, he is now using them to create rebellion in Runatyr."

"*Rebellion?*" Merrick looked at Anya. "Does he have enough people for that?"

"Of course not," she said with an edge of bitterness. "That is why he needs the drug."

Merrick winced. "So he's taking Troft slaves and making his own slaves out of them."

[Wakefulness, the prisoner has achieved it?] a new Troft voice came from somewhere behind Kjoic.

[Wakefulness, he has achieved it,] Kjoic confirmed, switching to cattertalk.

A second Troft strode into view, his membranes fluttering as he gazed down at Merrick. He wore a gold sash across his torso, probably an indication of high rank. [A slave of Muninn, you are not one,] he declared, his voice accusing. [A spy, you are one. That truth, do you deny it?]

[That statement, I *do* deny it,] Merrick said. If Kjoic had indeed betrayed him, denials were a waste of breath. But it couldn't hurt to try to sow a few seeds of doubt between Kjoic and his Drim allies. [The statement, whoever spoke it is untruthful.]

[Your protest, there is no use to it,] Kjoic said. [Further truth, I may now reveal it to you.] His membranes stretched out a few centimeters. [An agent of the Kriel'laa'misar demesne, I am one.]

Merrick stared up at him, his still-groggy brain suddenly spinning. [An agent, you are one?] he repeated, trying to buy time to sort all this out.

Because he already knew who Kjoic was. More to the point, Kjoic knew that he knew. This might be news to Anya, but Kjoic was addressing his comments to Merrick, not her. A big, impressive revelation that was meaningless.

Unless it was all an act. Had Kjoic *not* told the Drim that he and Merrick had been working together?

Merrick keyed his infrareds, studying the heat from Kjoic's radiator membranes. Kjoic was concerned, all right. But was he concerned about what Merrick might do? Or was he concerned about what the human might say?

Maybe a little experiment would shed some light. [Such a lie, I should have guessed it,] he said, putting some bitterness into his tone. [A Drim'hco'plai, you seemed even less competent than one of them.]

The Drim officer's membranes flared with annoyance. But the heat from Kjoic's membranes faded noticeably. So he *had* been worried that Merrick wouldn't catch on to the ruse and say the wrong thing.

Which meant...what? Was Kjoic still Merrick's ally? Was he just toying with him? Or was he playing both sides for his own advantage?

[Insults, a human in your position should not deliver them,] the Drim said stiffly. [The demesne-lord who sent you, who is he?]

Merrick frowned. Why would the Troft think he'd been sent from some other demesne instead of the Dominion? [A demesne-lord, none sent me,] he said. [The Dominion of Man, my loyalty is to it.]

[A Troft slave transport, you arrived aboard it,] the Drim countered. [Your companion, a slave of the Balin'ekha'spmi demesne she was. The Balin'ekha'spmi demesne-lord, does he now threaten the Drim'hco'plai demesne with war?]

Merrick suppressed a grimace. Great. What was he supposed to say to that one? [The Balin'ekha'spmi demesne-lord, he and I have never met,] he said. That much, at least, was perfectly true. [War, I do not threaten it. My fellow humans, to free them is why I have come.]

[Your fellow humans, to die with them will be your end,] the Drim bit out, his membranes fluttering with agitation. He looked somewhere outside Merrick's field of vision. [His preparation, inform me when it is complete.]

[The order, I obey it,] another Troft voice came from across the room.

The Drim looked back at Merrick. [Your service, I will eagerly await it,] he said. [Your death, I will await it even more.]

Turning, he stomped out of sight. Merrick keyed his audios, and a moment later heard a door close.

[Unpleasantness, I seem to have landed in it,] Merrick said quietly. [The situation, what is it?]

Kjoic glanced over at the other, unseen Troft. "The situation, it is volatile," he said in Anglic.

Merrick frowned at the language switch. Then his fogged mind again caught, and he realized that the other Troft in the room probably wasn't nearly as versed in the human language as the rest of them.

Just the same, it would probably be good to keep their voices low. "How volatile?" he asked.

"Very volatile," Kjoic said. He paused, and Merrick saw the Troft turn his head a few degrees toward Anya.

This time Merrick was a little faster on the uptake. "Anya, is there any water in here?" he asked. "I'm really thirsty."

"I will get it for you." She eyed Kjoic a moment, making it clear that she wasn't fooled in the least by the ruse, then walked out of Merrick's view.

Kjoic waited another couple of seconds, then leaned in a little closer. "Ludolf and his humans are doing well," he said quietly. "But they have neither the power nor the resources for a sustained battle. In the end, they will lose. But damage, they can inflict it upon the masters before that."

"And the masters can inflict even more on them?"

Kjoic's membranes twitched. "Yes," he said. "Especially with you on their side."

Merrick stared at him, his stomach knotting up. Of course. "The war drug," he murmured. "They're going to inject me with it and send me to attack Ludolf's rebels."

"Yes," Kjoic said again. "They await only your full recovery from Ludolf Treetapper's bersark trap."

Merrick grimaced. But at least that gave him a little time to come up with something. The last time he'd inadvertently sampled raw bersark he'd slept for three days, woken up long enough to talk to Alexis and Ludolf for a bit, then gone back to sleep for two more days. Assuming he was running the same pattern, he should now have two more days to sleep.

Hopefully, his subconscious mind would be working on the problem during that time. "How long have I been here?"

"Two days," Kjoic said. "The treatment, you will begin receiving it tomorrow."

"*Tomorrow?*" Merrick echoed, staring up at him. "Did Ludolf use a weaker strain or something?"

"The bersark, the Trof'te have methods of flushing if from a human system," Kjoic said.

Merrick winced. Of course they did.

And with that, he'd just lost two days. Or rather, Ludolf had. The Drims presumably had no idea the kind of destruction they were about to unleash on the rebels.

But they would see. They would all see.

Unless Merrick could figure out an escape plan.

"What about you?" he asked.

"My arrangement with you, they do not know of it," Kjoic said, lowering his voice even further. "I still seek to obtain the drug and make my departure."

"And me?"

Kjoic's membranes fluttered. "Your departure, I do not foresee it happening," he said reluctantly. "Your death, it will occur in Runatyr."

"If it doesn't?"

"It will."

"But if it doesn't?" Merrick pressed. "I'm very lucky, you know."

For a moment Kjoic eyed him. "If you survive," he said at last, "we will seek an accommodation for us both. But your luck, I do not believe it can carry you that long."

"Good enough," Merrick said. "As to my luck, let's wait and see."

Colonel Reivaro finished gazing off into space with that whole *data stream* thing the Dominion people used instead of actually talking to each other. He blinked once, then walked to the table where Corwin was finishing his lunch. "You look very catly," Corwin commented.

"Catly?"

"As in the cat that ate the canary," Corwin said. "Common local idiom." It wasn't, of course, but with little else to do he'd taken to messing with the invaders' minds as best he could without pushing them so far that they'd catch on and slap him down. "News about the *Dewdrop*, I presume?"

Some of the satisfaction left Reivaro's face. "And how would you know that?" he asked.

Corwin shrugged. *Messing with their minds.* "People talk," he said casually. "Even Dominion of Man Marines sometimes say things they shouldn't to people they shouldn't."

Reivaro gave him a thin smile. "Really. And you expect me to believe my Marines have broken protocol rather than accept the far more likely scenario that you saw me mouth the *Dewdrop*'s name while I was checking the data stream?"

"I suppose it could have been that," Corwin conceded. Sometimes the mind-messing worked, sometimes it didn't. "So why the catly look? Let me guess: things are going according to your plan?"

"Exactly," Reivaro said. He started to turn away—

"I don't suppose you'd care to share that plan with me," Corwin said. "That way I can be just as impressed as you are when it happens."

Reivaro turned back, and for a long moment gazed hard into Corwin's face. Then, he shrugged. "Why not?" he said. "It's not like you have any contact with the outside world."

"Exactly," Corwin agreed. "And I know you're dying to tell someone. That's how it is with secrets."

"Another Aventinian saying?" Reivaro asked. "Because we have a similar one: *three may keep a secret if two of them are dead.* But as I say, why not?"

"Why not, indeed," Corwin said. It wasn't nearly that simple, of course. The only reason Reivaro might agree to detail his great plan was the hope that he would be able to read something in Corwin's face that would indicate whether or not his own intel on the resistance's plans was accurate.

Corwin wished him luck on that one, given that he didn't have the slightest idea what Lorne and the others were up to.

Reivaro pulled over a chair and sat down. "As you've already surmised, the news I received was about the *Dewdrop.* Its armor plating is complete."

"At the cost of how many factories' worth of ruined equipment?"

"Just one," Reivaro said without embarrassment. "Though armoring your other three ships will probably cost at least two more. No matter. The point is that once the systems have been checked and the gravs balanced it'll be ready for a test flight."

"And you're expecting them to sabotage it?"

"Not at all," Reivaro said. "My sources indicate the rebels will attempt to take over the transport and use its test flight to destroy the relay satellites we have orbiting Aventine."

Corwin frowned. "What in the Worlds for?"

"They seem to think our facial-recognition records are aboard the *Algonquin* and that those of us on the ground must access that database whenever we want to check on a random citizen walking down the street. Ergo, they think knocking out the satellites will rob us of that ability whenever the *Algonquin* itself is out of the line of sight."

"Sounds a bit naïve," Corwin murmured.

"Not only naïve, but completely wrong," Reivaro assured him.

"So what are you going to do? Make sure none of the resistance gets aboard?"

"On contrary," Reivaro said. "The Dome government has already been invited to select a crew and put aboard as many observers as they'd like."

"Seriously?" Corwin asked, frowning.

"Seriously," Reivaro assured him. "Part of Captain Lij Tulu's ongoing effort to involve the people of the Cobra Worlds in our work. I'd be the first to admit that our public relations efforts have been less than stellar."

"Yes, martial law will do that to people."

"At this point I suspect that the disruptions caused by the renegade Cobras are more annoying to the average citizen than the mild restrictions of martial law," Reivaro said. "Be that as it may. The *Dewdrop*'s maiden flight will hopefully demonstrate the progress that we can make if we all work together."

"Passing over the fact that that our share of the operation was made under extreme duress?"

Reivaro smiled cynically. "Come now, Governor. This is Capitalia, and the main duress happened in DeVegas Province. There's nothing like physical and cultural distance to make old news age even faster. No, the focus here is going to remain exactly where we want it: showing them what we're doing to prepare for future Troft incursions."

"You might also find your focus shifting to the latest in Aventinian sabotage techniques," Corwin warned. It wasn't like that was giving anything away—Reivaro had surely already thought of that possibility.

"Doubtful," Reivaro said. "Especially as I've already informed the Governor-General that there would be a contingent of Marines aboard to keep order."

"You think that will scare off the Cobras?"

Reivaro snorted. "Come now, Governor. Surely this isn't *that* complicated. If there are Marines aboard . . . ?"

"Ah," Corwin said, nodding. He'd had it a couple of exchanges ago, actually, but he liked being underestimated. "If they want to take out the satellites, they'll need to first neutralize the Marines. That means adding a few Cobras to the crew or the observers."

"Very good," Reivaro said, his tone that of a teacher whose student has finally given the correct answer. "And not just *any* Cobras, but Cobras who we haven't caught and collared yet. Their so-called ghost Cobras. Once they're aboard—" He shrugged. "We'll have them."

"Minus the ones you lose in the fight," Corwin warned. "As well as the Marines they'll take with them."

"Oh, there won't be a fight," Reivaro said. "That's the real beauty of the plan. Your resistance comrades will pack the crew with Cobras, but there won't be any Marines aboard for them to fight with."

"Interesting," Corwin murmured. Yes, that was just twisty enough for Reivaro's twisty mind. And possibly alluring enough to sucker Lorne into falling for it. "Of course, once they're in the *Dewdrop* nothing prevents them from heading anywhere they want to go."

"Hardly," Reivaro said. "We'll have fighters standing by. Anywhere they go on Aventine we can follow and capture the Cobras before they can get away."

"And if they take the *Dewdrop* out-system?"

"To where? Caelian? Qasama? One of your so-called friendly neighboring Troft demesnes?" Reivaro waved a hand. "If they want to leave, they're more than welcome. Getting a few Cobras out of my hair is an acceptable endpoint."

"Except you'll lose the use of the *Dewdrop*."

"With all that armoring the ship will still look like a threat to any Troft scouts who might be nosing around," Reivaro said. "That's really all the upgrade was intended to accomplish in the first place. Come to think of it, having them head out on a grand tour of the region might work better than having them sit here at home. The enemy Trofts might see it as the Dominion's attempt to recruit allies, which may draw even more of their focus and forces here."

"Maybe *you* see that as a good thing," Corwin said. "I doubt anyone else would."

"*Good* is a slippery concept," Reivaro said. "I prefer to focus on something more well-defined: the defense of the Dominion of Man."

"So what exactly do you defend? Just the land?"

"And the people."

"What about the deeper aspects of humanity?" Corwin pressed. "Morality and ethos, for instance?"

Reivaro shrugged. "Two more slippery concepts."

"Some would say they're the foundation on which everything else stands."

"I'm sure some would," Reivaro agreed. "But those are mostly people who sit in sunlit towers with the time and leisure for deep thoughts. People who seldom recognize or acknowledge those of us standing between them and death. Or worse."

Corwin frowned. "What's worse than death."

"What the Trofts offer each planet they overrun," Reivaro said bitterly. "Invasion. Conquest. Slavery."

"Yes, we're getting to know about those things," Corwin murmured.

"Because of us?" Reivaro asked with a tight smile. "Don't you believe it, Governor. We moved in to save humanity, with or without your help. The Trofts move in to reduce humanity to its lowest survivable level." He snorted. "Sorry if I sound simplistic, but when you're fighting for survival, morality is a luxury. You do the job, however you must, and you win or lose. Period."

"I'm sorry for you," Corwin said quietly. "It's hard to imagine a victory less hollow than that."

"Perhaps," Reivaro said. "But a hollow victory still beats the hell out of any flavor of defeat. Someday, you in the Cobra Worlds will understand that." His eyes unfocused as he looked somewhere past Corwin's shoulder. "Or not. No. To be honest, I hope you don't ever understand. If the Dominion falls, it would be nice to know there was still an outpost of humanity remaining."

"Careful, Colonel," Corwin said, forcing some lightness into his voice. Was Reivaro really giving him a look into the soldier's soul? "Your men will think you're going soft."

"Hardly," Reivaro said. His eyes came back to Corwin's; and as they did, the veil dropped across his face again. "Besides, words are meaningless. Actions are what count. Very soon, Governor, you'll see those actions."

"Along with a few more Cobras under your power?"

"Let's hope it'll soon be *all* of them." Reivaro's expression hardened. "Then maybe we can finally get back to fighting the *real* enemy."

With a suddenness that somehow surprised Jody more than it should have, they were there.

"Doesn't look like much, does it?" Kemp murmured from behind her, his breath brushing through her hair.

"Troft planets never do," Plaine said grimly. "But trust me, they'll have a warship or two stashed away somewhere. Every important Troft system does." He looked over his shoulder at her. "You ready?"

Jody took a deep breath. *Was* she ready? She had no idea.

But however ready she was, this was as good as it was going to get. "Let's do it," she said.

She reached blindly down, found Kemp's hand and squeezed it. "Showtime."

CHAPTER TWENTY-ONE

Kjoic had told Merrick the war drug conditioning would begin the next day. But as far as Merrick could tell, nothing had happened. Early in the day the Drims had come by and taken some blood and tissue samples, and in the late afternoon they'd returned and removed his shirt for a close look at the veins in his arms. But after that, they disappeared, leaving him and Anya alone.

Merrick stayed awake for the next couple of hours, partly in case they tried to blindside him while he was sleeping, partly to study the sounds of the building with an eye toward making a break for it.

Escaping his bed, at least, should be easy enough. His finger-tip lasers were in perfect position to take out the straps across his thighs; once his legs were free, he should be able to pull his knees up to his chest, angle his left calf to the side, and take out the strap securing his left wrist. And once that hand and laser were free, the rest of the straps could be dealt with in seconds.

But of course that would only be the beginning. Back on Qasama he'd seen how clever Commander Ukuthi could be with defenses even against Cobras, and just because the Drims here didn't know who he was didn't mean they hadn't prepared for every eventuality.

He also had Anya to consider, which effectively negated any chance for him to utilize the more flamboyant Cobra maneuvers. Unless he was able to carry her bodily through those actions, he needed an escape plan that she could follow with normal human abilities.

Adding to the difficulty was the fact that he also had no idea how much time he had to come up with his plan. Kjoic had said the conditioning would begin immediately; but it was now the second day since his recovery from the bersark and still nothing had happened. If his blood work showed some trouble, he might have another day or two; if it was simply bureaucratic dithering or fine-tuning, the project could start at a moment's notice.

But something was definitely happening out in the main building area. There was a lot of cattertalk going on, with half a dozen voices represented. He tried keying his audios, but even at full power he couldn't make out any of the words.

There was the sound of another door opening, and hurrying Troft footsteps coming toward him. Merrick braced himself—

"You must hurry," Kjoic said, his face popping into view over Merrick's pinioned head. His voice was tense, his radiator membranes fluttering.

And to Merrick's surprise, the Troft began unfastening his restraints. "What is it?" Merrick asked. "What's going on?"

"A spacecraft, it has appeared over Muninn," Kjoic said. He paused a moment, possibly listening to the voices outside, then continued releasing Merrick's straps. "An unfriendly spacecraft, it is one." He paused again. "I believe its goal may be rescue."

Merrick felt his heart seize up. *Rescue*? But no one even knew he was here. Who could possibly be looking for him?

Of course. Commander Ukuthi, fourth heir of the Balin'ekha'spmi demesne and the Troft who'd talked Merrick into this lunatic mission in the first place, wouldn't simply have abandoned his spy. Somehow, he'd learned Muninn's location and had come to break Merrick out. "Do we know which demesne it's from?" he asked. If it was a Balin ship, it would confirm Ukuthi's hand in this.

"You misunderstand," Kjoic said. "A Trof'te ship, it is not one. It is a Dominion of Man war-class courier."

Merrick felt his mouth drop open. "A *Dominion* ship?"

"Deserters from the Dominion, the commander claims they are. Damaged, he further claims his vehicle to be."

"You keep saying *he claims*," Merrick said. His hands came free, and he reached up to finally wrench away the clamp holding his head. "You don't believe him?"

"I do not," Kjoic said flatly, moving down to work on Merrick's thigh straps. "I believe it has come for reconnaissance."

Merrick scowled. That was possible, all right. Ukuthi was clever enough to use Merrick to get the Drims' attention while he sent in a probe for a *real* look. And what better way to keep the Drims thinking the wrong direction than by using a captured Dominion spacecraft for his probe?

But really, those details didn't matter. Whoever was in that ship, Merrick's job was the same: to get aboard it.

He sat up and looked across the room. If they'd taken Anya away . . . but no. She was right there, hunched over in a chair in the corner, her eyes gazing at the floor in front of her.

Good. Once he made contact with the ship it should be an easy matter to get Anya aboard too. "Is there a radio in this building that can reach the courier?" he asked, swinging his legs off the table and easing himself into an upright position. Days of lying down had left his muscles a little uncertain, but it was easy to compensate with his servos. "We'll also need to know the frequency they're using."

"No need," Kjoic said stepping back. "The courier ship has been ordered to land outside of Runatyr. An armed aircar, we can travel there in it."

"You mean *together*?" Merrick asked, frowning in sudden suspicion.

"My time to leave, it has arrived," Kjoic said. He touched a thick belt around his waist. "The war drug, I have obtained a sample of it."

Merrick felt his stomach tighten. If Kjoic already had the drug, he had no reason to help Merrick any further. "They might be willing to give you a ride, too," he offered.

"It matters not," Kjoic said. "Spacecraft, there are several in Runatyr. I will take one and make my own way." His membranes flared once. "Do not fear, Merrick Hopekeeper. Our alliance remains until we are fully prepared to depart this world. We may yet need each other's assistance."

"And my drug sample?"

For a second Kjoic just stared. Then, he gestured to a table beside the head of Merrick's bed.

Merrick looked. Sitting along the edge were a pair of the small boxes like the ones he'd stolen from the building a few days ago.

He picked up one and popped it open, to find a dozen of the familiar patches inside. "Take as many as you wish," Kjoic said. "But come now. Time, we rapidly run out of it."

"Understood," Merrick said, frowning as he scooped up five of the patches. Just like the ones he'd stolen, except that the nub in the middle was a lighter shade of red than he remembered. A variant of the original drug, tweaked to his specific body chemistry? Was that why it had taken this long to get started?

"Come *now*," Kjoic repeated, his membranes quivering with agitation.

"Yeah," Merrick said. His borrowed lab jacket was hanging on a hook on the table; pulling it on, he stuffed the five patches into one of the pockets. "Come on, Anya. Time to get out of here."

[Runatyr, there is a small spaceport at the southern edge of it,] the thickly accented cattertalk came through the CoNCH speaker. [The westernmost part, you will land in it.]

"What did he say?" Kemp muttered.

"I think he said we are to land at the west edge of that spaceport," Rashida said, pointing to the main display.

"You mean right where that battle's going on?" Kemp asked.

Jody winced. They'd spotted the signs of guns and laser fire about ten minutes before the Trofts finally acknowledged their hails.

Unfortunately, there was no way to tell who was fighting whom, or which side she and the others should be on. If any of them.

"Not *in* the battle, no," Rashida assured him. "They directed us to the western edge. The battle is mostly in the northeast sector."

"I was joking," Kemp assured her.

"Joking or not, it may not be possible to avoid the trouble," Plaine's voice came from the starboard gunbay speaker. "I'm picking up a lot of spillage from the main lines."

"Spillage?" Kemp asked.

"I think he's talking about flanking fire moving along the edges," Smitty's voice came from the portside gunbay. "You seeing all that?"

"A moment," Rashida said. She tapped a couple of keys, and one of the side displays changed to what seemed to be an enhanced IR image.

There was spillage, all right, Jody thought grimly. The faction that had thrust toward the spaceport was now being flanked on both sides by the other faction.

"Whoa," Plaine said. "Did you see that?"

"See what?" Smitty asked.

"Three of the lasers on the left flanking just went out simultaneously."

"So the attackers there aren't just using lasers and firearms?" Jody asked.

"Looks like it," Plaine said. "No idea what, but there were no IR readings except those from the fighters. We may know more when we get closer."

"So what do we do?" Kemp asked. "Land near the fighting and see what's going on, or get as far away from it as we can?"

"Well, it's not two Troft demesnes fighting," Plaine said thoughtfully. "There'd be an air component and probably a space component, as well."

"Or the wreckage where air cover used to be?" Smitty suggested.

"Right," Plaine agreed. "Best guess is it's Broom's brother and some allies trying to get to a ship."

Jody felt a flicker of cautious hope. After all this time—after all this effort and concern and putting her friends in horrible danger could they finally have succeeded? Was that really Merrick down there, alive and well and kicking Troft butt?

There was hope. But there was also a freshening of fear. With her expectations now raised, even by a little, it would be that much more devastating if they were dashed.

"So; right in the middle of the fight?" Kemp asked.

"Not the middle," Plaine said. "Let's put down behind one of the flanking groups. I see a couple of likely spots—I'll mark them for you."

"Just bear in mind that the Trofts won't be happy if we land anywhere except where they told us to," Smitty warned.

"Have no worries," Rashida said. She flexed her fingers and resettled them on the controls. "And strap in, please. This landing may not be very smooth."

"Where are they now?" Merrick asked, trying to ignore the speed—and extremely low altitude—at which Kjoic was burning across the forest toward Runatyr. "Can you see them?"

"My piloting, I am focused on it," Kjoic ground out, his radiator membranes fluttering rapidly against his shoulders. Apparently, this wasn't as easy as it looked.

"There," Anya said, pointing past Merrick's shoulder. "Low in the sky. Do you see it?"

Merrick keyed in his telescopics, fighting against the sudden dizziness as the image bounced crazily before he could zero in on it.

It was a spacecraft, all right. A reasonably big one, too, somewhat larger even than the Cobra Worlds' own transports. He couldn't completely make out the shape, but from his angle it looked odd, rather like a triangular slice from the side of a melon. It was nothing like any Dominion ship he'd ever seen in the old records, but that didn't mean much—a hundred years of progress and development would have rendered everything the Cobra Worlds had ever known of their homeland completely unrecognizable. "Any idea where it came from?"

"The Dominion of Man, I already told you that it had."

"I meant whether it had come directly from the Dominion or from the Cobra Worlds," Merrick backpedaled. Kjoic didn't know about Ukuthi and the Balins, and that was a card he had no intention of showing. "Or even Qasama."

"That truth, you must seek it for yourself."

"Trust me," Merrick assured him. "We will."

"Perhaps you should talk to them," Anya suggested. "If they seek to rescue you, you should report your presence."

"The frequency of their communications, I have already programmed it into the comm," Kjoic added.

Merrick hesitated. If that was a Balin force lurking in there... but if they'd already fooled the Drims once as to their true identity, they could certainly fool Kjoic. And if they'd revealed themselves, it didn't matter whether or not Kjoic also knew who they were.

Or did it? Kjoic was playing an entirely different side of this game than either the Drims or the Balins. Would he take it badly if he found out a third demesne had dealt itself in?

He might. But Merrick didn't have a choice. No matter what the Balins were here for, he needed to let them know he was still alive, he had the intel they'd sent him for, and he was ready for a pickup.

"Thanks," he told Kjoic, snaring the headset hanging on a hook beside his right knee and putting it on. He adjusted the microphone close to his lips, then keyed the comm. "Hello, Dominion of Man courier," he called. Might as well continue the charade. "This is Merrick Moreau Broom of Aventine. Please respond."

The words and the voice came from the CoNCH speaker, flowing over Jody's ears like a cool summer breeze over her face. Dimly, she was aware that Kemp was squeezing her hand, and that she was squeezing his just as hard; that Rashida was smiling back at her with a glistening of tears in her eyes; that even Plaine was offering his professionally correct congratulations over the speaker.

None of it mattered. None of it really even penetrated the sense of disbelief and victory.

Her brother was alive.

Merrick was on his third repetition of his hail when the warm cloud of euphoria abruptly popped back into the frost of reality. Merrick was here and alive, but they still had to get him safely aboard the *Squire*. Things still hung in the balance, and she was damned if she'd come all this way just to watch him die within her sight. Fumbling at her control board, she found the comm switch. "Merrick, this is Jody," she said. "Where are you?"

For a handful of seconds she thought they'd lost the connection. "Merrick?"

"Jody?" Merrick called, his voice as flabbergasted as she'd ever heard it. "What in—? Where *are* you?"

"Where do you think? The treehouse?" she countered. "Come on, come on—we haven't got all day. Are you in that battle?"

"No, but we're heading toward it," Merrick said. There was a half-heard comment from somewhere on Merrick's side of the connection. "And I'm guessing we can only get so close before we're stopped."

"Wait a minute," Plaine cut in. "Was that a *Troft* voice I just heard?"

"Yes," Merrick said. "I've picked up an ally. Too complicated to go into now. Where are you planning to land?"

"Anywhere you want," Jody said. "Where are you?"

"About twenty klicks east of you," Merrick said. "We're over forest, but we can veer to the main road heading east from the city."

"Great," Jody said. "We'll be right there."

"No, we won't," Plaine said firmly. "We change course now and they'll know what we're doing."

"What?" Jody asked, frowning.

"Head in the game, Broom," Plaine bit out. "We're falling out of the sky, remember?"

Jody blinked. What the *hell*—?

"You're falling out of the *sky*?" Merrick demanded. "*What?*"

"It's okay," Kemp said quickly. "That's just the line Rashida's fed them, that we're having engine trouble and are going to have to crash-land."

"Crash-*land*?" Merrick echoed. "Where?"

"Eastern edge of the battle," Kemp said. "Just outside the fighting."

"Unless we get more spillage," Plaine put in. "That's probably what the Trofts are counting on, that we'll splat some of the rebels."

There was a pause from the comm, and Jody could hear a quiet conversation going on. She keyed in her audios, but the *Squire*'s own background noise overwhelmed her efforts to eavesdrop. "Okay," Merrick said. "Put down wherever you need to. We'll come to you. And be careful."

"You, too," Jody said. "See you soon." There was a click as the comm disengaged. "You sure you can't just tell them you fixed whatever was wrong?" she asked hopefully.

"No." Kemp's tone left no room for argument. "The way she set it up, there's no way to magically change things."

"She had to do it that way," Smitty said, just as firmly. "They wouldn't have bought it any other way."

"Assuming they *did* buy it," Plaine muttered.

"I am so sorry," Rashida apologized. "I thought it would be for the best."

Jody clenched her teeth. "It's okay, Rashida," she said. "We'll make it work."

"We will," Kemp confirmed. "Absolutely."

"Abandon us, you were prepared to do it," Kjoic said. His voice suddenly sounded very alien.

"I wouldn't have abandoned you," Merrick assured him. Nevertheless, he felt a shiver run up his back. Kjoic had killed a whole shipful of his own species when he first arrived on Muninn in order to carry out his mission. What he would do to an alien wasn't something Merrick wanted to think about. "Anyway, it's a moot point. You heard what Jody said about having to continue to the spaceport. There should be more than enough confusion for you to score the ship you want."

"And what of me?" Anya asked.

"Maybe we can take you with us," Merrick said, feeling the uncomfortable sensation of a box being closed around him. A promise to Kjoic; a promise to Ukuthi; and now a half-promise to Anya.

And then there was Jody. What in the *Worlds* was she doing here? How had she even found him?

"There," Kjoic said, taking one hand off the controls to point. "Do you see?"

"I see," Merrick said, his hands closing into fists. The courier was coming in fast—too fast, maybe—cutting low over the southern end of the city. He watched as it dipped ever lower...

And then, suddenly, it was gone, disappearing from sight behind the trees surrounding the city.

"Drim'hco'plai attack aircars, they approach," Kjoic said. "Their arrival, it may occur before ours."

"Let them try," Merrick said darkly. "Just don't let them succeed."

Jody had seen aircraft crashes before. And right up until the moment that the *Squire* came to a slightly angled halt amid the ruins of some kind of small sheds she couldn't tell whether this one was a real crash or only looked like one.

It took Plaine to fully convince her. "Nice," the Marine said from his gunbay. "Seen 'em better, but not very often."

"You've *seen* fake crashes?" Jody asked.

"Oh, yeah," Plaine said. "Great way to sucker the Trofts into thinking they've got a wounded bird ripe for plucking. Speaking of which, I've got five chicken-beaks in sight behind the last line of rubble we threw up when we hit. Smitty?"

"My side's got humans," Smitty said. "We seem to have landed smack-dab on the front."

"Or the front adjusted to accommodate us," Plaine said. "Waiting on a plan, Broom."

Jody scowled as Rashida brought up both gunbays' image feeds.

They were wedged in between the two sides, all right. "Any sign of Merrick, Rashida?"

"No," Rashida said. "They are traveling very low to the ground, and I lost view of their aircar as we came down."

"Far as I'm concerned, your brother and his new best buddy can stay out there until we get this ground thing sorted out," Plaine said.

"Got three humans—males—approaching," Smitty reported tightly. "Plaine?"

"Trofts still holding back," Plaine said. "Are those *rocks* your natives are holding?"

"Or grenades," Jody said. Though they sure *looked* like random, fist-sized stones.

"Don't underestimate rocks as weapons," Kemp warned. "Put Cobra strength behind them, and they carry a hell of a lot of stopping power."

"And might be able to do a job on our external sensors if they get close enough," Jody said, coming to a decision. "I'd better go out and talk to them."

"Okay," Kemp said. "Let's go."

For a second Jody considered telling him she could do this alone, and that he needed to be ready to protect the ship against the Trofts if necessary. But a second later common sense kicked in. She could take care of herself; but the people out there didn't know that, and she didn't want to have to prove herself at the cost of someone's life. Having a glowering companion along might slow down any aggression long enough to at least gain them a hearing, especially with laser pistols strapped to their sides. "Okay," she said. "I'll do the talking."

The three men had made it almost to the *Squire*'s side by the time Jody and Kemp popped the hatch. Two of them were hanging back a couple of meters, still gripping their rocks, while the older man in the lead held a small Troft-style laser pistol. The ones in the rear lifted their rocks warningly as Jody and Kemp came into view—

"*Humans?*" the man in the lead said in oddly accented Anglic, his eyes widening.

"And friends," Jody said, hoping that was true. They still didn't have a clue as to what was happening here.

The man's eyes widened even more. "Your voice," he said disbelievingly. "You are kin of Merrick Hopekeeper?"

Jody caught her breath. These people knew Merrick? "I—"

She stopped as Kemp touched a subtle warning on her arm. "Who are you?" she asked instead. "What do you know of Merrick Hopekeeper?"

"I am Ludolf Treetapper," he man said. "Merrick Hopekeeper is an ally of my daughter, Anya Winghunter."

"An ally in this war?"

"He has served," Ludolf said. "Do you come to serve, as well?"

"We've come to find him," Jody said. There was a flicker of something suspicious in Ludolf's face—"so that we can hear his report on the situation," she added quickly.

"He is not here," Ludolf said. "But we expect him soon. Until then, you will help us battle the masters?"

"The masters? You mean the Trofts?"

"I mean they who enslaved us," Ludolf bit out. "They will all die—"

He broke off, dropping into a startled crouch as a stutter of laser fire blasted from Smitty's gunbay, blasting a building to Jody's left into a pile of rubble. "Smitty?" Kemp murmured.

"Trofts trying to flank you," Smitty's voice came through Jody's comm. "Whatever business you've got with these guys, get it over with fast."

"He says they worked with Merrick," Jody said.

"You believe them?"

Jody looked back at the men, keying in her infrareds. Hopefully, she was getting better at this whole lie-detecting business.

She frowned. Ludolf's facial heat signature was a little elevated, not unreasonable in the middle of a battle. But his two companions were practically blazing.

Were they ill? If so, they had to have the kind of fever that was normally extremely debilitating in adults. Yet they were not just alert and walking around, but fighting.

She focused on the rocks they were holding, a cold sensation on the back of her neck. *Put Cobra strength behind them*, Kemp had said. These men weren't Cobras, but maybe they had the equivalent of Cobra strength.

The Qasamans used a wide range of enhancement drugs for everything from quick healing and learning to deep thinking and planning. Apparently, these people had something similar.

"I don't know," Jody told Smitty, easing back on her infrareds.

"But Merrick will be here soon. Until then, we need to keep the Trofts back so that he's got a place to land." She gestured to Ludolf. "What's your plan here? What are you trying to accomplish?"

"No plan," Ludolf said. "We kill the masters. As many as we can, to drive them from our world."

"Got it," Jody murmured, another shiver running through her. Wholesale slaughter. Terrific plan. Useless and completely counterproductive.

But Ludolf's rebellion was his problem. Merrick was hers, and she needed to clear the area for him. "All right, we'll do what we can to help. How long does that drug last?"

"Drug?"

"The drug that makes a rock a useful weapon against armored Trofts," Jody said. "I need to know it won't peter out halfway through a rush."

"It will last," Ludolf said. His eyes had narrowed, a sudden woodenness to his face. Maybe the combat drug was supposed to be a secret? "But we need weapons," he added, looking pointedly at her holstered laser. "Do you have more?"

"Behind you!" Smitty snapped.

Jody spun around, dropping into a crouch as she yanked her laser from its holster. A pair of Trofts had emerged from one side of a broken wall, their lasers swinging around as they spotted the cluster of humans. Jody snapped her own weapon up into position, shifting to the two-handed grip she'd practiced so long aboard the *Squire*. She flicked a target-lock onto each of the two Trofts and fired.

As it had aboard ship, the fainter echo of her fingertip laser was painfully visible to her. But she was looking for it, and she doubted anyone else was. Regardless, both Trofts twitched and dropped with gratifying ease, their weapons clattering to the ground.

"On your three!" Smitty called.

Jody jerked her head around to see three more Trofts coming around the other side of the broken wall. Again, she target locked them.

But Kemp was already on it, spinning on his right foot, his left leg sweeping the aliens. Three flashes from his antiarmor laser, and the Trofts were down.

"Good shooting, Broom," Plaine said.

"Thanks," Jody said, turning back to Ludolf.

He was staring at Kemp, his eyes gone wide again. "What was—what was *that*?" he managed.

"Leg laser," Kemp said before Jody could answer. "Strapped under my clothes."

"But—"

Ludolf broke off as a multiple flicker of reflected light came from the wreckage around them. "Plaine?" Jody called.

"Yeah, they're on the move," Plaine confirmed grimly. "I had to brush them back. Bringing up the heavier stuff now."

"Aircraft?" Kemp asked.

"Not yet," Plaine said. "Don't know what they're waiting for. I'm talking about barrel guns."

"You've seen them?" Jody asked, a knot forming in her stomach. Plaine had given them several lectures aboard the *Squire* about Troft field weaponry, and barrel guns were one of the nastiest. Each was basically a fat cylinder, two meters in diameter, full of caseless armor-piercing ammo belts wrapped around an axial gun. With a cyclic rate of thirty rounds per second they could do serious damage to slow or stationary targets.

"Two of them, yeah," Plaine confirmed. "I lost them behind that smashed hangar-looking thing that's in front of you and to your right, but I'm thinking they'll stage them from that line of storage sheds on your two. They can send the barrels rolling on the ground behind the sheds, targeting the *Squire* the whole way."

"Firing through one gap and rolling under cover to the next," Kemp said grimly. "Best plan is to get there before they send them off?"

"Best plan, sure," Plaine said. "Not necessary the safest."

"Close enough," Kemp said. "I'll take it."

"*We'll* take it," Jody corrected firmly. "Ludolf, we're going to check out those sheds. You can go back to doing whatever you were doing when we landed."

"Do you seek to send us away?" Ludolf demanded, his eyes narrowing. "Do you plan—?"

"There!" Kemp cut him off, pointing to the sheds. "Come on—I saw a barrel."

He set off toward the sheds at a zigzag run. Jody followed, her heart pounding. Her first battle as a Cobra. She hoped desperately she wouldn't let Kemp down.

They reached the nearest of the sheds. Kemp glanced behind him, probably making sure Jody was still there, did a quick three-sixty, then slipped around the shed. Resting her thumbs gently on her ring finger nails, ready to fire her lasers at an instant's notice, Jody followed.

Straight into a hornet's nest.

There were a couple of dozen Trofts in the space behind the sheds, some of them prepping a pair of barrel guns, others standing a loose perimeter guard.

And as Kemp and Jody came into sight, every one of the aliens turned toward them.

Jody jolted to a halt, her first impulse to back up into the partial protection of the nearest shed and try to fight from there. But Kemp didn't even hesitate. He fired a full-power blast from his sonic, then threw himself forward into a twisting dive that landed him on his back with enough sideways momentum to start him spinning.

A second later, the area lit up as he opened fire with his antiarmor laser.

The three nearest Trofts jerked and toppled over. The laser flicked on and off and on again as Kemp's target locks and nano-computer calculated, aimed, and fired. As his spin slowed to a halt, he half rolled onto his side, tucked his knees to his chest, and continued firing at the next group of Trofts.

But there were too many for him to take down before they recovered from their surprise and started firing back. Too many for him; too many, Jody knew, even for the two of them.

But they had to try. *She* had to try. Her brother's life was on the line, and she hadn't come all this way to leave him hanging now. The barrel guns could wreck the *Squire* and completely demolish Merrick's aircar, and it was up to her and Kemp to neutralize the weapons before either of those happened.

Setting her teeth firmly together, throwing target locks onto the nearest three Trofts outside Kemp's fire zone, she charged into battle.

CHAPTER TWENTY-TWO

Suddenly, sooner somehow than Merrick had expected, they were there.

The spaceport was a mess. Not the kind of mess where there was fighting and destruction everywhere, but the kind where the fighting had mostly come and gone, leaving pockets of wrecked buildings and small, smoldering fires scattered randomly across the landscape.

The battle hadn't completely stopped, though. Here and there he could see the sporadic fire of lasers or the muted flash of firearms as Ludolf's rebels continued their struggle against their enslavers. With the war drug Ludolf had stolen boosting the strength and stamina of his forces, the fight would probably drag on for quite a while.

Though a few combat aircars like the one they were currently riding in could bring things to a much faster end. Distantly, Merrick wondered why the Trofts hadn't deployed fighters, or even aerial spotters. Were they hoping to capture Ludolf and his people alive for questioning? That might explain the lack of fighters, but not the lack of spotters.

But Ludolf's private war wasn't his concern. Ahead, at the edge of the spaceport and right in the middle of some of the heaviest fighting, was the Dominion ship he'd seen going down. "There," he said, pointing it out to Kjoic as he keyed in his telescopics. The ship had crashed with its bow pointing toward them, which limited how much Merrick could see. Still, while it had definitely hit the ground hard, there seemed to be less damage than he'd expected from the way it had been arrowing down from the sky. Hopefully, it was still spaceworthy. "Looks like there's enough room to the left of it for us to put down."

"Safety, that place does not have it," Kjoic said, his radiator membranes fluttering. "To the left of the ship, behind the line of storage huts—the two large cylinders?"

Merrick shifted his gaze that direction. The cylinders were big, all right: two meters tall and four long. They were behind one of the sheds, pointing directly at it. "What are they?"

"Antiarmor rollers, they are them," Kjoic said. "The warriors are preparing to roll them past the huts to fire at the Dominion ship."

Merrick winced. Rolling the cylinders just a few meters to the side would clear the shed and leave them pointing directly at the ship. "How do they work?"

"Belts of explosive shells, they have them," Kjoic said. "The shells, an axial gun fires them."

"Protection?"

"Heavy armor, the front has it. Less armor, the sides and rear have it."

"Loading?"

"From the rear."

So that would be the weakest point. "How good are the shells? How badly could they damage the Dominion ship?"

"Very," Kjoic said. "We must land on the other side to be safe."

The words were barely out of his mouth when the area around the rollers erupted with laser fire. Laser fire coming from the heel of a barely seen figure on the ground.

Jody had brought along a *Cobra*?

"The danger, it is that the Dominion ship may fire on us—"

"Never mind that," Merrick cut him off, searching for inspiration. A second Cobra had now joined the battle, but that seemed to be all. With over a dozen Trofts still on their feet, even a pair of Cobras would be hard-pressed. Merrick needed to find a way to whittle down the odds, and he needed to find it fast.

There it was. Maybe. "That half-broken wall over there," he said as he unstrapped from his seat. "Four meters high, directly behind that first cylinder. You see it?"

"Yes," Kjoic said, his membranes fluttering a little more. "The far side of the wall, do you wish to land there?"

"No, you're going to land on the far side of the Dominion ship like you said." Merrick stepped to the side hatch and got a grip on the release. "But first you're going to come in low—ten meters up should do—directly over the wall, flat on to it, holding your current speed. Can you do that?"

"An attack, do you intend to make one?"

"Just do what I said," Merrick said. "I'll catch up after you've landed."

"But—"

"Just *do* it," Merrick snapped.

The wall was coming up fast. Merrick watched, hoping there was enough structural strength left in the masonry for what he needed, and wishing fleetingly there was a program in his nano-computer that could handle the speed and distance calculations for him. Theoretically, this should be just like a wall bounce, the kind he'd done a hundred times.

Except that a wall bounce usually required *two* walls. Here, Merrick had only one.

Almost time...and as his mental countdown ran to zero, he flung open the hatch and leaped out. He flicked a targeting lock on the shed wall, and let his muscles go limp.

He'd hoped that his nanocomputer would classify this as a wall bounce and respond accordingly. To his relief, it did. Even as he arced downward the servo system took full control of his body, twisting and flailing his arms and legs in precisely the right way to line him up feet-first with the broken wall. An instant later he slammed into it, his knees bending as his leg servos absorbed the impact.

The wall creaked in protest, but held. As Merrick's body started to rotate into a fall, his knee servos reversed direction, shoving him off the wall and starting him on a quick spin that would normally bounce him to the next wall over, repeating the maneuver until he was safely on the ground.

Only in this case, there was no second wall.

What there was, instead, was a two-meter-high Troft roller.

Merrick had no idea how much a roller weighed. His main goal, aside from getting to the ground quickly so he could help the other Cobras, was to skew the roller just enough out of line with the Dominion ship that some of the Trofts would have to stop their side of the fight long enough to get it back into position.

But either he'd overestimated the roller's mass or underestimated his own momentum. To his surprise, the weapon yawed a solid thirty degrees off line as he slammed feet-first into the rear part of the cylinder wall. His servos straightened again, shoving the big cylinder another few degrees over, leaving its axial gun pointed well off target.

And leaving its rear loading area pointed directly toward a cluster of Trofts.

Mentally crossing his fingers, Merrick triggered his antiarmor laser.

Kjoic had said the cylinder's rear wall was less well armored than the front. But it was armored enough. Merrick kept his laser trained on that same spot as his servos pushed him back off the weapon; continued firing as he arced through the air; even kept at it as he landed hard on the jagged debris scattered on the ground at the base of the wall. But the cylinder remained intact. His only hope now was to get around behind the roller and try his luck with the back endcap. He slid to a halt and started to scramble to his feet—

Without warning a laser lashed out from his right, blasting into the roller's rear endcap.

Reflexively, he ducked, his nanocomputer throwing him to the side. An instant later he ducked again as a pair of Trofts appeared in the reflected glow of the beam and fired their own lasers at him. He sent them a blast from his sonic, hoping to jar their aim, and flicked a pair of target locks on their helmets. Snapping out his right hand, he pointed at the nearest Troft and activated his arcthrower, sending a lightning bolt into the alien's helmet.

Just as the roller endcap disintegrated in a massive blast of fire and shredded metal.

Even with the explosion pointed away from Merrick there was enough shockwave bounce-back to throw off his balance. He twisted around, trying to stay on his feet, and was losing that battle when a pair of strong hands grabbed his upper arms from behind.

Instinctively, he tried to twist away. But the grip was too strong and held him solidly. One of Ludolf's drugged men? He twisted his forearm up, cocking his hand over his shoulder for an arcthrower shot at his assailant—

"Merrick!" Jody's voice gasped in his ear.

An instant later she'd let go of his arms and thrown herself on him in a full-body bear hug. "I knew we'd find you," she said, her voice barely understandable with her face buried in his shoulder. "I knew we would. Are you all right?"

"I'm fine—" He broke off as a laser blast came from the rear of the second roller.

"That'll be Kemp," Jody said, finally pulling away. "Come on— we need to get to the ship."

"In a minute," Merrick said. He got to his feet, wincing at the multiple points of pain that seemed to cover his entire back. "I need to get to Anya and Kjoic. Unless whoever's aboard the ship shot them down," he added as that horrible thought belatedly struck him.

"It's okay," Jody assured him, grabbing his right arm and helping him up. "We saw you jump and called Plaine to leave that one alone. He said they've landed on the *Squire*'s portside, and he's keeping an eye on them."

"Good," Merrick said, looking down at her hand. It was unmistakably his sister's hand. Only it was strong. It was *too* strong.

And he'd seen *two* Cobras firing lasers at the Trofts down here. Kemp and...?

He looked up again, to find her gazing back into his eyes. "Yes," she said simply. "But don't talk about it. Not everyone aboard knows, and I'm kind of our secret weapon."

"Got it." Merrick's hand twitched as a figure appeared through the residual smoke from the roller he and Jody had destroyed, relaxed again as he saw the figure was human. "Kemp?" he called.

"Yeah," the man said as he came up to them. "Merrick?"

"Yes," Jody confirmed, tapping a small device on her shoulder. "Rashida, we're on our way. Get the *Squire* ready to go."

"Wait a second," Merrick said as the three of them slipped between the huts and headed toward the Dominion ship, Jody still gripping his right arm. "I told you I need to see Anya and Kjoic first."

"And do what?" Kemp asked, coming up on his left side.

"We either need to get Kjoic aboard our ship or find him one of his own," Merrick said. "Anya comes aboard regardless."

Out of the corners of his eyes he saw Jody and Kemp exchange looks around him. "Kjoic is your pet Troft?" Kemp asked.

"He's an ally, not a pet," Merrick growled. "And I need to talk to him."

"Fine," Jody said. "We'll go with you."

The aircar had indeed landed, and without any damage Merrick could see. Briefly, he wondered if he would have to go up and knock; but even as the three of them crossed the open space the hatch opened and Anya and Kjoic stepped out. Kjoic had a laser belted to his side, his hand resting on the grip. He hesitated a fraction of a second, then strode toward the three Cobras. "Truth, we at last obtain it," he said, his voice harsh, his membranes fully extended. "A *koubrah*-soldier, you are one of them."

"Yes, I am," Merrick said, keeping his voice calm even as he put a target lock on Kjoic's laser. "Is that going to make a difference now?"

For a moment Kjoic stood rigid. Then, slowly, his membranes began to sag. "No," he said. "I have freed you from the Drim'hco'plai. The bargain, your side must be kept."

"I'm ready to do so," Merrick said. "You want to ride with us, or get your own ship?"

"My own ship," Kjoic said. "We do not travel further together. There are five long-range ships nearby. One will suit me."

"You still have the drug sample?"

"I do."

"Good," Merrick said. "Then let's go get you a ship."

"Hold it," Jody said. "First: *what* drug? Second: you're in no shape to go anywhere."

"Kjoic got me out of the Drim prison and stole this aircar to bring me here," Merrick said firmly. "He also helped *me* get a drug sample, which we're not going to go into right now. Bottom line: I'm helping him get a ship."

"No, you're not," Jody said, just as firmly. "If he needs help"— she shot Kjoic a suspicious look—"then Kemp and I will go."

Merrick shook his head. "Out of the question."

"Hold it," a faint voice came from the comm on Jody's shoulder. "Ask him if he's talking about the row of heavy fighters about a hundred meters south."

"Yes," Kjoic confirmed after Merrick relayed the question.

"Good," the other voice came. "New plan: Kemp and I will go get him his ship."

"Plaine—" Jody began.

"No arguments," Plaine cut her off. "Best way out of here is to give Merrick's Troft one of the fighters and disable the rest of them. I know how to do that. You don't. Kemp and I are going."

"Then stop wasting time and get out here," Kemp said. "Jody, take Merrick in and get him to sickbay."

"In a minute," Merrick said, shifting his attention over Kjoic's shoulder.

To find that, during their conversation with Kjoic, Anya had somehow slipped away.

"She went that way," Kemp said, pointing toward the aircar's stern.

"Thanks," Merrick said, and headed off.

"Merrick—" Jody called, making a grab for his arm.

"I'll be right back," Merrick called over his shoulder as he broke into a fast jog. "Get Plaine out here so Kjoic can get his ship and we can all get off this rock."

Anya was moving along a line of cargo carts when Merrick caught up with her. "Wait up," he murmured, his senses alert for Troft activity.

She glanced over her shoulder at him, but kept walking. "You have your exit," she said curtly. "Go."

"Wait," he repeated as he caught up with her. "I'm not just going to leave you here alone."

"I'm not alone," she said. "My father and others are near at hand. I will find them, and we shall win our freedom." Abruptly, she spun to face him. "Do you leave? Or do you help us?"

"I—" Merrick broke off, staring at her in confusion. There was an unexpected impatience in her face and voice, along with an arrogance and self-discipline he'd never seen in her before.

"Decide now," she said tartly. "I am content either way."

"You're—what?"

"Do you truly not understand?" she demanded. "You've learned the masters' secret. You've obtained the drug for us. That was all we needed, and you have done well. Now leave us to fight our war." She stared at him a moment, then turned away.

"Wait a second," Merrick said, grabbing her arm, his mind spinning. "What are you saying? That you used me?"

"You were very useful," she said. "So was Commander Ukuthi." She looked pointedly down at his hand on her arm. "The battle continues. Join us or not, but do not interfere."

Slowly, Merrick opened his hand, the last six weeks of his life twisting like leaves in a windstorm.

Anya, sold into slavery by the Drims in punishment for her

parents' failed revolt ... or had it been deliberate plant and manipulation with the goal of sending her to a rival demesne?

Commander Ukuthi of the Balin'ekha'spmi demesne, suspicious of the Drims' ambitions and their secret work on Muninn ... or had Anya been the one who planted those suspicions and fears in the first place and goaded him into action?

And Merrick Moreau Broom, Ukuthi's Cobra prisoner, persuaded by Ukuthi's concerns and driven by Anya's own fears and vulnerability to accept this mission on the Balins' behalf ... or had Anya ever been vulnerable at all?

Everyone had apparently done exactly what Anya had wanted. But even with the drug driving Ludolf's soldiers there was no way he could win freedom for his people against the vastly superior Troft forces. Could he?

Merrick didn't know. And suddenly, he didn't care.

"Good luck," he said, taking a step back.

Anya turned away again, not even acknowledging his comment. He watched as she reached the end of the line of carts, peered cautiously around the corner, then headed toward the sound of fighting in the distance.

He knew he would never see her again.

Jody was waiting when he returned to the Dominion ship, standing alone by the open hatch. "You okay?" she asked as he came up. "What happened?"

"She's gone," Merrick said. It was all she needed to know, and he didn't feel like talking about it. "Are mom and dad and Lorne all right?"

"They were when I left Aventine."

"That sounds oddly unreassuring," Merrick asked, frowning at her. "What exactly did I miss?"

"Too much to go into now," Jody said, studying his face. The Anya conversation was far from over, Merrick knew, just postponed to a calmer time. "Come on, I need to get you inside."

"Not yet," he said, stepping back as she reached for his arm. "We need to make sure the Trofts don't rush the ship while your friends are helping Kjoic."

He stepped to the other side of the hatch, frowning as he looked around. Even granted that a fair percentage of the Trofts were presumably being pinned down by Ludolf's forces, the Trofts should have made *some* response to the Dominion ship's arrival by now.

"Yeah, they're being pretty quiet, aren't they?" Jody said, agreeing with his unspoken thought. "Aside from the group we hit—thanks for the assist, by the way—and the ones Plaine chased away earlier we really haven't seen many of them. Best guess is that the rebels hit the spaceport barracks while we were coming down, and the Trofts are still catching their breath over that one."

"That could explain why they haven't put any fighters in the air," Merrick agreed doubtfully. "But these can't be everything they've got on the whole planet."

"Oh, I'm sure they're not," Jody said. "But Rashida's keeping an eye out for anything coming in from elsewhere."

"Good," Merrick said. Yet another unfamiliar name. "Just how big an entourage did you bring?"

"It's just the five of us," Jody said. "Kemp and Smitty are Caelian Cobras, Rashida's our pilot—she's Qasaman—and Plaine is a Dominion Marine."

"The Dominion of *Man*?" Merrick echoed. "Are *they* here?"

"Three ships' worth of them are, anyway," Jody said grimly. "We're not sure exactly why, but we think it has something to do with a war they're fighting on the other end of the Troft Assemblage."

"And you?" Merrick asked. "When did Aventine start... you know?"

"You mean with women? They haven't. I was a special case."

"Like Mom?"

"Basically," Jody said. "So what's this drug you and Kjoic were talking about?"

"It seems to be a strength enhancer," Merrick said. A movement to the side caught his eye, and he tensed as he keyed in his infrareds. But it was just a small animal, scavenging in a tuft of weeds. "The one time I saw it tested it also seemed to create loyalty to the Trofts. That was apparently the biggest goal of the research—strength enhancement by itself has been something the humans here on Muninn have been using for a long time."

"Which explains the gents with the rocks," Jody said. "You think the Trofts are trying to create their own version of Cobras?"

"And testing out the drug on humans?" Merrick shook his head. "I doubt human and Troft physiologies are close enough for that to make sense. But I've been thinking. Do you remember how the Cobras were used during the first Troft invasion of the Dominion?"

"They were dropped on occupied worlds to coordinate resistance forces, right?"

"Right," Merrick said. "So what if you drugged a bunch of the people here on Muninn and dropped them on Dominion worlds?"

"Ouch," Jody said, her forehead creased with concentration. "Though it wouldn't be quite the same, since there wouldn't be any resistance groups for them to link up with."

"Are you sure?" Merrick countered. "We have no idea what the political situation is in the Dominion right now. If the war and government are unpopular enough, there could be some unrest."

"Point," Jody conceded. "We can ask Plaine about that. But even if everything is sunshine and flowers, a bunch of violent Troft loyalists could cause a *lot* of chaos on the ground."

"Forcing the Dominion to divert resources from the war to deal with it."

"Yeah." Jody hissed between her teeth. "Terrific. So is that what we're sitting on? A planet-sized test-tube for Troft experiments?"

Merrick gazed across the field, noting the distant flickers of reflected laser light from the various pockets of battle. "No," he said quietly. "The people here have been Drim slaves for a long time. Mostly they've been sold to other demesnes to fight in combat-style games."

A shiver ran up his back. Yes, Anya had used him. But if the situation had been reversed, wouldn't he have grabbed any tool he could to throw off that kind of oppression? Would he have even considered the ethics of manipulating another person to do whatever he considered necessary?

"Terrific," Jody murmured.

Merrick snapped his attention back to the situation at hand. "What's terrific?"

"Rashida just called," Jody said grimly. "She's picked up a flock of fighters coming in from the north—ETA about fifteen minutes."

"So we need to be up and out of here in ten?"

"Something like that," Jody said. "Kemp? Plaine? Anyone listening?"

She paused, frowning. "Trouble?" Merrick asked, stepping closer to her and boosting his audios a bit.

"They're not answering," Jody said. "Kemp? Plaine?"

"Jody, get in here and take over the gunbay," a new voice came faintly from her comm. "I'll go look for them."

"No, you stay put," Jody said, straightening her shoulders. "Rashida's fighters might get here sooner than expected. Merrick, you stay here and guard the hatch."

"Better plan," Merrick said. "Seal up the damn hatch and we'll both go."

"Merrick—"

"Yeah, what is it?" Plaine's voice came through Jody's comm.

"Plaine?" Jody called. "It's Broom."

"Yeah, I got that," Plaine said. "Is there a problem?"

"Rashida's picked up incoming fighters," Jody said. "ETA about fourteen minutes."

"Okay, fine," Plaine said. "We're almost finished. We'll be back in five."

"Is Kemp all right?"

"Sure," Plaine said. "Why wouldn't he be?"

"I just—neither of you were answering," Jody said, foundering a little.

"You get Kjoic his ship?" Merrick asked.

"He's prepping it now," Plaine said. "We're setting the rest of our charges."

"Make it fast," Merrick warned. "I've seen these fighters in action. We don't want to be on the ground when they get here."

"Well, then, stop bothering us and we won't," Plaine said tartly. "Out."

"At least they're okay," Merrick said, stepping back from his sister.

"Yes," she murmured, her expression tense as she gazed across the open ground. "So far."

The minutes ticked by. The flickers of laser light moved across the background, and Merrick could hear occasional sounds of fighting and scuffling, but for the most part the battles played out in eerie silence. Both sides apparently knew their respective goals, and neither side wanted to sacrifice stealth for the emotional boost of war yells.

He was wondering if he should ask Rashida for an update on the fighters when Jody abruptly caught her breath. "They're coming," she murmured.

"Where?"

Jody nodded toward a gap between a shed and a tipped maintenance cart. Merrick turned his gaze that direction, making sure to pay attention to his audios and peripheral vision. If this was a Troft ruse...

It wasn't. Five seconds later Kemp and Plaine came into sight. They checked their perimeter, then sprinted toward the ship. Plaine, Merrick noted, carried a sleek laser rifle and had a handgun belted at his waist. Kemp the Cobra hadn't bothered with either. "They're here, Rashida," Jody murmured as the men approached. "Get us moving the minute I get the hatch closed."

Ten seconds later, all four were inside, the hatch was closed, and Merrick found himself grabbing for a handhold as the ship angled up and to the side and climbed toward space. "You get them?" he called.

"What?" Kemp asked.

"Did you disable the fighters?" Jody clarified.

"Oh," Kemp said. "Yes. At least, I think so. That was all Plaine. I just got your brother's Troft to one of them and cleaned out the other Trofts who were hanging around."

"Plaine?" Jody asked.

"Yeah, yeah, I got the fighters," Plaine said impatiently. "Now shut up and let me get to the gunbay."

"That may not be necessary," Rashida's voice came over a corridor speaker. "I've just received a transmission."

Plaine swore. "If they think we're going to surrender—"

"Attention, world of the Drim'hco'plai demesne," an authoritative voice—an authoritative *human* voice—boomed from the speaker. "This is the Dominion of Man War Cruiser *Dorian*. You appear to have one of our courier ships.

"We want it back."

CHAPTER TWENTY-THREE

"You're frowning, Colonel," Corwin said.

Colonel Reivaro turned from the row of status displays. "Excuse me?"

"I was remarking on the fact that you were frowning," Corwin said. "Bad news from the *Dewdrop*?"

"Not bad, just a bit confusing," Reivaro said. "The shakedown crew is coming aboard, with twelve Cobras among them."

"Really," Corwin said, feeling his throat tighten. Surely Lorne hadn't fallen for the Dominion's trick. "How do you know they're Cobras?"

Reivaro pursed his lips. "Because all twelve are wearing our neckbands."

"Really," Corwin said again. "Interesting. And you didn't kick them off?"

"They're not officially under Dominion control," Reivaro reminded him. "But I'm definitely rethinking the situation. Either they don't think the neckbands can be activated once they're far enough out, or else the satellite attack has been changed from the main mission to a diversion."

"A diversion for what?"

Reivaro smiled tightly. "That *is* the question, isn't it?"

"Lifting off now, Colonel," one of the techs called.

Reivaro did the data stream thing again and nodded. "Yes, that's the question, Governor Moreau. Let's watch together and learn the answer."

✧   ✧   ✧

"Signal from Jeffries," Emile reported from his post by the top-floor window. "*Dewdrop* has lifted off. All Cobras are aboard."

Lorne nodded. He'd expected nothing less. Reivaro had clearly hoped to add a few ghost Cobras to his stable, and the colonel was probably wondering why the only ones aboard were ones he'd already identified and collared.

What he *wouldn't* do was abort the mission just because it wasn't following his expectations. The man was far too unflappable for that.

"Huh."

"Huh what?" Lorne asked, checking the rope on the table one more time for tangles and potential snags.

"Question from Nissa Gendreves," Emile said. "She wants to know if we can detect laser fire coming from inside Reivaro's HQ."

"What laser fire?" Lorne asked, the rope momentarily forgotten. "Where's it coming from?"

"It's not coming from anywhere," Emile said with exaggerated patience as he flipped his white card up and down in Dida code. It was the safest and most secure communication system available to them, but it drove Lorne increasingly crazy. Not just because it was slow, but also because only the city Cobras could use it. Having to rely on men like Emile to pass on all messages made him extremely uncomfortable. "Just a theoretical question, I gather."

"Well, let's try spending our time on practical questions, shall we?" Lorne suggested. "Starting with whether we have confirmation that Reivaro is in there."

"Still working on that," Emile said. "We still don't know who all was in that transport they sent out two hours ago."

Lorne glowered at the rope. And if Reivaro had sneaked out and was monitoring the *Dewdrop* shakedown flight from somewhere else, this whole thing would be for nothing. "Well, *keep* working on it," he said.

"Yes, thank you, we are," Emile growled. "Wait a second...huh."

Lorne took a careful breath. "Emile—"

"No, no, this is weird," Emile said, frowning as he flipped his card back and forth. "Gendreves just said...when we see laser fire from Reivaro's HQ, we'll know he's in there."

"She said *what*?"

"Yeah, I know," Emile said. "Requesting confirmation...yeah, that's what she said. What do you suppose she's planning?"

"No idea," Lorne said. "Has she left yet? Can we still stop her?"

"Sure, we can stop her." Emile raised his eyebrows. "*Should* we stop her?"

Lorne stared out the window at the city. He was the one in charge of this operation. Anything that affected it—especially anything involving Reivaro's HQ—was under his authority. If he gave the order to grab Nissa, the Cobras at the other end of the communication line would obey.

But Emile had a point. Nissa hated Lorne's family, but so far she'd proved herself trustworthy on matters concerning the Dominion's campaign against her people. Furthermore, she knew enough of tonight's plan to know what would interfere with it and what wouldn't.

My goal has always been the same, she'd told him once. *To do everything I can to defend and protect the Cobra Worlds.*

"No," he told Emile. "Let her go. But have someone watch her."

"Yeah," Emile said, manipulating his card again. "Count on it."

"We've finished the initial climb," the pilot's voice came from the speaker at the monitor station in the center of the high-ceilinged, single-room warehouse that Reivaro had converted into his headquarters. "Controls are sluggish, maybe a little more than expected. We're having to boost drive power to compensate, but we're still well within safety margins."

"Very good," Reivaro said. "Any trouble with the crew or observers?"

"None, sir."

"Good. Feed me the readings."

For a moment the warehouse was silent as Reivaro did the data stream thing. Seated off to one side at Reivaro's desk, a pair of watchful Marines towering over him, Corwin took advantage of the moment to look around the room.

It was about as crowded a setup as he'd ever seen for something not aboard a spacecraft. The monitor and communications stations were at the center, encircled by Reivaro's desk and cot and the cots of the three techs. The sergeants' cots and free-standing lockers were in the next circle, with the rest of the thirty Marines' living quarters crushed together further outward. On one side of the room were three doors: two human-sized ones flanking one that could accommodate large vehicles. The other three walls were fully lined with equipment and food-storage lockers, food prep facilities, and washroom/shower cubicles.

Personally, Corwin would have cut back on the number of Marines bivouacked here and given everyone a little more breathing space, especially since he'd never seen more than fifteen people in here at any given time. Reivaro might want the ability to quarter thirty-plus Marines, but so far he seemed to be keeping at least half his personal force out on the streets at any given time. Maybe he was hoping to bring more men in from the outer districts once he'd pacified them.

Corwin smiled to himself. If that was Reivaro's plan, he should seriously rethink it. Capitalia citizens and Cobras might be willing to back down in front of an invader. The rural folk weren't nearly so compliant.

"All right," Reivaro spoke up. Apparently, the data download had finished. "Continue."

He stepped away from the station, eyeing Corwin closely as he walked over to the desk. "So," he said. "If they're going for the satellites, they're being rather coy about it."

"Oh, I don't know," Corwin said, wishing once again he had some idea what Lorne was up to. He was perfectly capable of skewing conversations and slanting other people's expectations, but he needed to know which way to slant them. "They'd want a solid idea of their capabilities and liabilities before they tried anything. That's the whole purpose of a shake-down cruise, isn't it?"

"True," Reivaro said. "We'll see." Abruptly, his eyes went datastream unfocused again. "Interesting. Yes, send her in."

"We have company?" Corwin asked.

"*You* do," Reivaro said, taking a step back and turning toward the door. "Your good friend Nissa Gendreves is asking to see you. Any idea what she wants?"

"None at all."

"Let's find out together." Reivaro raised his voice. "Ah, Ms. Gendreves," he called. "Please, approach."

Corwin swiveled his chair around. Nissa was walking in from one of the smaller doors, a pair of Marines walking close beside her. She glanced once at Reivaro, her eyes seeming to measure him, then shifted her attention to Corwin as the group wove their way through the obstacle course of cots and lockers. "Governor," she said gravely, nodding to Corwin as they finally reached the central section. "I see Colonel Reivaro has been taking good care of you."

"As jailers go, he's been a decent enough host," Corwin said. "Did Governor-General Chintawa send you to check up on me?"

"No, this is all me," she said, walking the last few meters between them. "I wanted to speak with you." She looked at Reivaro again. "In private, if I may."

"Certainly," Reivaro said. He gestured to Nissa's Marines, and to Corwin's. "Give them some air."

Obediently, the Marines all moved back a few paces. Not far enough, of course, if their helmets contained any sort of enhanced audio capabilities, which Corwin assumed they did. Reivaro would hardly let his prisoner have an actual unmonitored conversation, after all. Presumably Nissa also knew that.

Still, everyone seemed willing to play the game. Nissa waited until the Marines had finished their retreat, then looked pointedly at Reivaro until he did likewise. Only then did she turn back to Corwin. "I trust they're genuinely treating you well?" she murmured.

"They genuinely are," Corwin assured her.

"Good." She hesitated, a series of odd expressions flicking across her face. "We've had our differences, Governor, you and your family and I. I wanted—"

"*Differences?*" Corwin interrupted. "You call bringing them up on charges of treason *differences*?"

"I wanted to tell you," Nissa continued doggedly, "that none of it has been personal. Everything I've done—everything I've ever done—has been what I thought was best for the Cobra Worlds. I just wanted you to know that."

"All right," Corwin said, a shiver running up his back. Something dark and eerie was forming in her voice and expression, something that felt poised on the brink of no return. "I appreciate you clarifying that."

"I just wanted you to know." Nissa took a deep, shuddering breath.

And abruptly, she flung herself back as if he'd shoved her away from him, coming within an ace of tripping over one of the cots in the process. "Look out!" she shouted, jabbing a finger at Corwin. "He has a bomb!"

For a fraction of a second, Corwin froze, his mind skidding in disbelief. What was she talking about? He looked down at his shirt, knowing she hadn't gotten close enough to plant anything on him but still wondering if she somehow had.

That small head movement was apparently all it took to snap everyone else from their own stunned paralysis. An instant later the nearest Marines were on the move, all four of them converging on him, their arms stretched to grab, their laser epaulets poised to deliver fiery death. Corwin froze again, wanting to raise his hands but afraid that would be misinterpreted, settling instead for just opening his hands where they'd been gripping the arms of his chair and splaying his fingers.

The Marines reached him. There was a sudden, vicious scream—

And Nissa, all but forgotten in the reflexive rush toward Corwin, spun around and threw herself toward Reivaro.

"Stop!" Reivaro snapped, taking a rapid step back, ducking sideways around the corner of the communications station, his hand dropping to his belted laser. "I said *stop!*"

Nissa ignored the order. She was at full sprint now, weaving between the obstacles as she closed the gap. As Reivaro yanked his weapon clear of its holster, she raised her hand over her head, and Corwin saw a flicker of light from something shiny gripped in her fist.

"*No!*" he shouted, trying to push himself up out of his chair.

But he was too late. Even as Nissa leaped over a downed chair the room lit up with a lightning storm of laser fire as every Marine in the room fired at the crazed woman attacking their commander.

Nissa nearly made it to Reivaro anyway. Even as her legs collapsed beneath her, her momentum slammed her torso into the comm station, folding her across the dull metal cabinet. Reivaro held his ground, his laser leveled but apparently still unfired, as she slid off the cabinet and collapsed to the floor, her blackened clothing smoking from the multiple burns crisscrossing her torso.

A second later, a pair of hands caught Corwin's shoulders and shoved him hard back into his chair. He didn't remember having stood up.

For a long moment Reivaro just gazed down at the dead woman. Then, slowly holstering his laser, he walked over to the knife that had fallen from her hand. He stooped over, picked it up, then held it out toward Corwin.

It wasn't a knife. It was a meal-pack lid with the inner aluminum foil seal turned outward.

Corwin looked at the lid, then up at Reivaro. The colonel was staring back at him, a look of bewilderment on his face. "Why?" he asked quietly.

Corwin shook his head, feeling numb. What in the Worlds had Nissa thought she was doing? He opened his mouth to tell Reivaro that he didn't have a clue—

"Colonel Reivaro, this is the *Dewdrop*," a voice came from the monitor speaker. "Sir, we're experiencing trouble with our starboard main thruster and grav lift. We're going—it looks like we may be going down."

"Laser fire!" Emile snapped. "Repeat, we've got laser fire inside Marine HQ."

Lorne blinked at him. How in the Worlds could Nissa have pulled that one off?

But for the moment that wasn't important. What mattered was that they had confirmation that Reivaro was there.

It was time.

"Signal the *Dewdrop*," he ordered, scooping up the rope and heading for the stairs. "Tell them it's a go."

He was on the roof, the ropes coiled over his shoulder, when the *Dewdrop* appeared, scrabbling its way across the sky toward him. All according to plan, though for the first twenty seconds Lorne wasn't sure whether the pilot was faking engine trouble or actually experiencing it. The ship moved ever closer to him, until with a final sideways crabbing maneuver it slipped directly overhead.

Lorne was ready. Crouching down, he leaped upward, his servo-powered jump taking him to the *Dewdrop*'s portside landing skid. He caught the skid and pulled himself up, lying flat across the top to reduce his visibility from the ground. The ship continued its erratic flight; two minutes later, Werle and de Portola had joined Lorne, the two newcomers balancing on the starboard skid. A quick round of thumbs-ups, and the three Cobras got to work, tying their ropes to widely spaced sections of their skids.

The *Dewdrop* continued to move erratically over the city, the crew presumably firing off reports on the failing thrusters and grav lifts. But through its crabbings and random twitches it moved ever closer to the building where Reivaro was overseeing the operation.

And then, suddenly, they were there.

The *Dewdrop* did one final pitch upward, raising its nose and coming to a sudden stop a hundred meters above the Marine HQ. It rolled sixty degrees to starboard, coming perilously close to the grav lifts' stall angle; and as Werle and de Portola threw their ropes outward, the ship's hatches popped open and six of the Cobras leaped out. They caught the ropes in midfall with gloved hands and began sliding down toward the rooftop below. As the ropes tightened the *Dewdrop* righted itself, then rolled the other direction, again flirting with stall angle. Lorne threw out his ropes, and three more Cobras appeared from the ship. They caught this second set of ropes and started down.

And as they rappelled down, Lorne, Werle, and de Portola each grabbed a rope and headed down after them.

They were committed now. Time to see just what Reivaro was prepared to do to stop them.

"Incoming!" one of the techs at the monitor station snapped. "Incursion from above."

"Interesting," Reivaro said calmly, stepping over to him, Nissa's death apparently already forgotten. "All from the *Dewdrop*?"

"It appears so, sir, yes," the tech said. "There were twelve Cobras in the ship, and twelve are on their way."

"But they're coming down on ropes from the skids," one of the Marines added. "Those ropes weren't there when the *Dewdrop* left, and it would be damn tricky to put them there in-flight."

"So they picked up a couple of hitchhikers along the way," Reivaro concluded. "Certainly Cobras; almost certainly uncollared Cobras. Well, this was always one of the other possibilities. Activate the perimeter, Sergeant." He half turned and raised his eyebrows at Corwin. "At a guess, Governor, I'd say they're coming for you. Let's see how they like having their rescue turned into a trap."

Lorne was halfway down the rope when, on the streets below, Marines suddenly began appearing.

He smiled tightly. Emile had warned that Reivaro's HQ couldn't possibly be as open and undefended as it looked, and in fact he and the other Capitalia Cobras had identified a couple of hidden guard boxes in the blocks around the warehouse.

But it was quickly clear that they'd missed most of the stations. At least fifteen Marines were already moving into the streets, with more streaming out after them, the whole crowd emerging from at least ten different doorways.

It was, in Lorne's opinion, a lot of overkill fuss to go through just to capture a handful of uncollared Cobras.

Below him, the ground lit up as the nine Cobras from the *Dewdrop* began firing their antiarmor lasers at the warehouse roof, each group of three focusing their efforts on a single section of tiling as they carved out three two-meter-diameter holes. The Marines converging on the HQ countered with multiple volleys of laser fire toward the descending Cobras, though they had to lean back awkwardly in order to angle their epaulets high enough.

But the distance was still too great for them to deliver fully effective fire. Worse, from their point of view, the Cobras were rapidly reaching the point where the edge of the roof would block any further counterattacks from the street.

Clearly, someone in charge had also figured that out. In perfect unison the whole Marine contingent started running toward the warehouse, their laser barrage intensifying.

And in less than perfect unison they all stumbled to jerking halts as a triple arc of laser fire from above cut across their paths.

Lorne looked up. The three remaining Cobras from the *Dewdrop* had emerged from the ship and were now balanced on the skids, each one swinging his left leg back and forth, blasting out a third of a defensive circle into the pavement below with his antiarmor laser.

The Marines were just barely able to target the rappelling Cobras. There was no way they could fire at a steep enough angle to reach the Cobras at the *Dewdrop*'s altitude.

But they had clearly planned for such a contingency. Even as half of them continued moving toward the building, more cautiously now as they were forced to dodge the sweeping laser fire from above, the other half stopped and dropped onto their backs on the pavement. With their lasers now able to bear on the *Dewdrop*, they fired a salvo at the Cobras.

One salvo was all they got. An instant later, they jerked as if they'd been stung as a coordinated volley of Cobra arcthrower blasts slammed into the tops of their helmets, frying circuits and knocking them unconscious.

The Marines still standing spun around to this new threat. But before they could open fire on the Cobras themselves, their autotarget systems exploded into action as a flurry of mudballs converged on them.

And with that, battle was joined.

"There," the Marine sergeant said, jabbing a finger at the ceiling. "And *there*, and *there*."

"I see them," Reivaro said. "You see them, Governor?"

For a moment Corwin thought about pretending he couldn't see the spots where the Cobras were burning through the ceiling. But the heat-stress circles were obvious, clustered close together above the center of the room, and there were limits to how convincingly he could play dumb. "Of course," he said. "Twelve Cobras on their way and..." He glanced around the warehouse. "Ten Marines in here. That could be a problem."

"Not for us," Reivaro said calmly. "But it will be for them. I've been trying to keep these confrontations nonlethal—you know that. But an attack on my HQ isn't something I can ignore. We'll do our best to take them alive. But if we can't..." He let the threat hang unfinished in the air.

"I'm sure they'll appreciate that," Corwin said, his mind racing. What *was* Lorne up to here? Did he not realize how obvious the roof-cutting would be? "Just as I'm sure they'll exercise similar restraint. You really think they're going through all this just for me?"

Reivaro frowned at him. "What are you suggesting? That this is about revenge?"

"You were the one in charge in Archway when you *weren't* keeping things so nonlethal," Corwin pointed out. "As far as I know, you've never offered an apology for that. They may be here to ask for one."

Reivaro looked up at the circles again. "I hope they're not being that foolish," he murmured. "Still... Sergeant, deploy to contain. You and I, Governor, will step back here out of harm's way."

He took Corwin's arm and wove him through the maze of

cots to the food-storage wall. As he did so, the Marines formed a circle about halfway out from the center, far enough back for their epaulet lasers to target the Cobras the moment they breached the ceiling.

Corwin watched, his heart racing. He could only hope Lorne knew what he was doing.

Below Lorne, the rest of the Cobras had halted their descents, hanging from their ropes a couple of meters above the warehouse roof as they continued to blast away at the tiling. Another thirty seconds, he estimated, and they would break through.

He reached a spot just above the other Cobra hanging on his rope and pushed off, arcing past the man's head and landing on the roof well to the side of the laser activity. Werle and de Portola were already down, sprinting toward the side of the building where the three doors were situated and where the main part of the street battle was taking place. Lorne put on a burst of speed, caught up with them, and then shot past.

From above, two of the *Dewdrop*'s landing lights flicked on, marking two spots ahead and about two meters back from the roof's edge. Lorne glanced back to see Werle and de Portola adjust their vectors to aim at those spots, then turned forward again, setting his own vector for a point directly between them. He reached the edge of the roof and leaped off, giving himself enough of a sideways spin to achieve a one-eighty as he hit the street.

Which left him on the pavement and facing the two Marines standing guard in front of the two human-sized doors.

He'd half expected that by now the door warders would have left their posts and joined in the melee taking place on the street in front of them. But they had a job to do, and undoubtedly also had the supreme confidence Lorne had seen in every other Dominion Marine, from Reivaro on down.

Lorne's sudden appearance in front of them did seem to startle them, though. Their faces were unreadable behind their helmet visors, but they each gave a small twitch of surprise, probably as they also locked their autotarget systems on him. Keeping his arms at his sides, Lorne straightened up from his landing crouch.

Just as Werle and de Portola, the Marines' positions pinpointed for them by the *Dewdrop*'s lights, landed feet-first on their shoulders.

The four of them went down in a pair of tangles. The Marines didn't get up.

Neither, immediately, did the Cobras. Rolling off the Marines and onto their backs, Werle and de Portola fired their antiarmor lasers at point-blank range into the doors' lock mechanisms and then, for good measure, into the hinges. Leaping back to their feet, they slammed into the doors, sending them crashing in onto the warehouse floor. Charging forward, they disappeared inside.

Lorne was right behind Werle, sparing a quick glance at the two unmoving Marines as he passed. There was no time to pause and see if they were badly injured, and he could only hope any broken bones or internal injuries could be successfully treated once they were back aboard the *Algonquin*. Turning his eyes and thoughts away, he ran through the door and into the warehouse.

Just as three circular sections of roof collapsed and the nine Cobras from above dropped through the openings, sending a diversionary volley of mudballs at the circle of waiting Marines as they fell toward the floor.

From the look of the Marines' circle, they'd been prepared only for the overhead assault. The sudden appearance of Lorne and his friends through the doors had clearly surprised them.

But again, they were prepared for an unexpected change of plans and tactics. The four closest Marines spun around to face this new threat.

Without slowing, Werle and de Portola angled off to their respective sides, still heading for the Marines. Lorne continued a more straight-line path, shifting to a dodging stutter-run as he reached the first line of cots and lockers. Across the room, the mudballs had drawn the other Marines' fire long enough for the main Cobra assault group to hit the floor and take cover behind the electronic equipment, desks, and lockers scattered around the center. The whole area was blazing with laser fire as both sides blasted away.

All except the four Marines facing Lorne, Werle, and de Portola. For the first two crucial seconds they just stood there, watching the Cobras bearing down on them, unmoving, not firing. Then, abruptly, their epaulets opened up, spitting fire at their attackers.

But not the deadly accurate fire Lorne had become accustomed to. These shots were irregular, almost hesitant, often missing completely as the Cobras did their jerky in-out around or over obstacles as they closed the gaps. Even the shots that connected were often grazing rather than solid hits, the heat barely stinging through the layers of ablative material under the Cobras' outer clothing.

A movement off to the side caught Lorne's eye. Reivaro and Great-Uncle Corwin were standing together, well back from both parts of the battle, their backs against a group of storage cabinets lining the wall. To Lorne's mild surprise, Reivaro wasn't standing behind Corwin, using the old man as a shield against the Cobra assault, but was instead actually standing in front of him.

Though that could change at any moment. Even that quick glance showed a taut expression on Reivaro's face as he watched Lorne, Werle, and de Portola moving in against his Marines' totally ineffective fire. The rest of the Marines were doing better, pinning down the main Cobra force hunkered behind their barriers.

But the Marines facing Lorne and the other two were part of that greater containment circle. If those four were overrun, that could have unpredictable consequences for the rest of the group.

Reivaro had so far resisted the temptation to use his ultimate weapon. But Lorne could sense that his restraint was running out. Already Lorne was nearly to arcthrower range—

A brilliant flash lit up the room, brighter even than the crisscrossing laser fire at the center of the warehouse. One of the Marines jerked as de Portola's arcthrower blast took out his left-hand epaulet.

"Stop, Broom—damn it!" Reivaro shouted. "Stop or die!"

At Lorne's other side Werle answered with an arcthrower shot of his own, while de Portola finished off his Marine's other epaulet with a second shot.

"Damn you, Broom!" Reivaro snarled over the chaos. "Damn you to hell for making me do this. *Rache!*"

There was a brief succession of small explosive *pops* from the center of the circle. The Cobra laser fire faltered and died. The Marines likewise halted their attack, and a few of them started to take a step inward.

"Take him!" Reivaro ordered. His voice was black and angry and bitter. "Take him, or kill him."

And then, with the suddenness of an ocean wave breaking over a rock, the nine supposedly dead Cobras leaped from their concealment and charged their attackers.

The Marines were caught completely off-guard. For a pair of

seconds they just stood there as the Cobras jumped over obstacles and raced toward them. The earlier flicker of laser fire was
replaced by the brighter, more ragged flashes of arcthrowers as
the attackers targeted the Marines' epaulets.

Two seconds was all the Cobras got before the undamaged
Marine lasers once again opened fire. But it was too late. The
Cobras dodged the uncoordinated shots with ease, and kept going.

And then Lorne had reached his own target, and he had no
more time for watching anything else. The Marine tried to fight
back, but without his epaulet lasers the fancy defenses of his
combat suit were useless. He threw a gauntleted punch at Lorne's
head; Lorne's programmed reflexes took over, snapping his arms
up to catch the arm and pinion it between them. Some pressure
from his arm servos, and the Marine was forced to bend over at
the waist. Lorne's left arm closed and tightened, locking around
the Marine's wrist at his elbow, while he snaked his right arm
over the other's shoulders and yanked off his helmet. A quick
low-power electrical jolt from his stunner, and the man went limp.
Lorne let the Marine drop to the floor, keeping his grip on the
arm as he fell to keep his head from hitting too hard, and fired
his arcthrower into the next Marine's epaulet—

"Hold!"

Lorne looked over. Reivaro was still standing by Corwin, but
had taken a step forward. He was gripping his laser by the barrel,
holding it high above his head like a flag of truce.

"You talking to us?" one of the Cobras in the main group
demanded.

"I'm talking to all of you," Reivaro said, his voice tight but
controlled.

"We don't take orders from you," the Cobra bit out.

"I think he's trying to surrender," Lorne said.

"Sure," someone else said sarcastically. "Now that he's losing."

"I'm trying to avoid any further bloodshed," Reivaro said,
looking hard at Lorne. "Are you in charge of this force, Broom?"

"More or less," Lorne said, looking across at the head of the
Capitalia Cobra group from the *Dewdrop*. The man's lip was
twisted with scorn, but he gave Lorne a reluctant nod. Lorne
returned the nod and turned back to Reivaro. "Order your men
to take off their helmets and power down their lasers. The ones
outside, too."

Reivaro nodded, his own expression still rigid. "Putting it in the data stream now."

The Marines in the warehouse were already complying, popping their helmets and setting them aside, then starting on the rest of their combat suits. Lorne caught de Portola's eye, gestured behind them. De Portola nodded and headed back to the door they'd entered by.

Reivaro was walking toward Lorne, his laser lowered but still held by the barrel. Corwin was trailing at a respectful distance behind him. "I trust you'll comply with the Dominion Articles of War regarding the treatment of prisoners?" the colonel asked.

"You mean like with dog collars?" one of the other Cobras countered.

"We'll treat your men as prisoners of war," Lorne promised. "Which of course requires you to acknowledge the Cobra Worlds as our own nation, and not part of the Dominion."

Reivaro snorted. "You know I don't have the authority to make that kind of political statement."

"No," Lorne agreed. "But it's a foot in the door. For now, that's enough."

Reivaro's eyes flicked to the main Cobra group. "How did you do it?" he asked quietly.

"These," Lorne said, touching the band around his neck. "We deciphered the IFF microengraving code in the epaulets and were able to duplicate them. Once your autotargeting systems refused to fire at us—" He shrugged. "We're pretty good at evading enemy fire."

"For archaic hundred-year-old technology, anyway," de Portola added as he walked up. "Looks good outside, Lorne. The Marines have surrendered and Emile and the others are disarming them."

"Tell them to snap it up," Lorne said. "There are probably fighters already in the air."

"I wouldn't worry," Reivaro said. "You still have the *Dewdrop* with you as a shield, and its armor is strong enough to fend off anything a fighter can throw against them."

"Yes, thanks for that," de Portola said over his shoulder as he headed again toward the door. "We'll still snap it up."

"My congratulations to you, too, Governor," Reivaro added, turning to face Corwin. "We really did think we'd taken all your collar-defense factories."

"Something we learned from the Qasamans," Corwin said. "Always build your defenses in layers. That way the opposition is never sure they've gotten everything."

"And their—?" Reivaro stopped, nodding in understanding. "Of course. They were wearing their IFFs *underneath* their loyalty collars."

"Of course," Lorne confirmed. "Otherwise the chokers would have been destroyed when you triggered the explosives."

"So if I hadn't triggered the collars...?"

"You'd probably have killed us all."

Reivaro smiled lopsidedly. "Well," he said. "If you know nothing else, you Cobra Worlders *do* at least understand irony."

"Oh, we understand a lot more than *that*." Stepping up to him, Lorne took his laser with one hand and his upper arm with the other. "We also understand the concepts of *hostage* and *prisoner exchange*. Come on, let's get you out of the data stream and inside a Faraday cage, and then give Captain Lij Tulu a call. I'm sure he'll love to hear from us."

CHAPTER TWENTY-FOUR

Jody hadn't expected a parade or twenty-gun salute for her role in rescuing her brother. She would have been satisfied with a pat on the shoulder, a warm handshake, and a sincere *well done.*

She didn't get them.

She also didn't expect to be taken aboard the *Dorian* under full Marine guard and marched to a conference room to face criminal charges.

Those she got.

"...pursuant to the Dominion of Man Unified Military Code, Section Eight, Sub-Section Three," Acting Captain Filho said, "you are hereby charged with sedition, theft, and felony treason. Have you anything to say before you're remanded into custody?"

Jody looked at the others. Kemp and Smitty were standing stolidly at something resembling military attention, their faces hard. Only their eyes moved as they looked around, assessing the situation and no doubt searching for options. Merrick, with no context for any of this, was wisely keeping his mouth shut. Rashida stood beside Smitty, her eyes on the floor, the perfect image of a quiet and submissive Qasaman woman.

Of course, Jody remembered her projecting that same image—along with a hefty dose of feigned terror—just before she and Smitty took down the *Squire*'s other Marine gunner shortly after they left Caelian.

She scowled to herself. Fine. If no one else was willing to take Filho up on his offer, she'd just have to do it herself.

"Yes, I have a couple of points," she spoke up. "Let's start by you telling us where Captain Moreau is."

One of the Marines standing against the briefing room hatch stirred but didn't speak. "Why exactly do you think that's any of your business?" Senior Commander Castenello spoke up before Filho could respond.

"How about Commander Ling Garrett?" Jody persisted. "Or Lieutenant Meekan?"

"I repeat: why do you want to know?" Castenello asked.

Jody nodded to herself. Filho might have taken over as acting captain, but it was clear that Castenello was the man in charge. "Because I submit that this whole thing is ridiculous," she said. "We didn't steal the *Squire*. We were authorized to borrow it to go look for my brother." She raised her eyebrows. "And considering that in the process we uncovered a Troft plot the Dominion didn't have a clue about, I think trumping up a bunch of unfounded charges is going to be more embarrassing than helpful."

"Do you, now," Castenello said, his voice going unexpectedly silky. "So you're saying Commander Garrett and Lieutenant Meekan were part of the plot?"

"They were part of the conversation," Jody said, frowning. "I don't know what you mean by a *plot*. It seems to me that if you call someone *commander* it should follow that he has the authority to command."

"It should, and it does," Filho said, a little stiffly. "But only within the bounds of that commander's mission parameters. In this case—" He shook his head.

"But up until now we've assumed Captain Moreau and Commander Ling Garrett were solely responsible for this breach of orders and mission," Castenello added. "Thank you for adding Lieutenant Meekan's name to the list."

A muscle in Filho's cheek tightened, and Jody felt fresh anger and frustration boiling up inside her. So her attempt to defuse this whole thing had accomplished nothing except to throw another of Captain Moreau's allies under the wheels. "Is this how the Dominion does things?" she demanded, trying to cover up her chagrin. "Rumor and innuendo are all it takes to kick a captain over the cliff and steal his ship?"

"Hardly," Filho said. "You and your friends will be giving your testimony to a full Enquiry Board as soon as we've finished our mapping orbits and return to hyperspace."

"Have you spotted any Troft warships, sir?" Plaine spoke up.

"No warships, no flights of fighters, no ground-based weaponry," Filho said, sounding relieved to be back on purely military ground again. "Nothing has lifted except that single armed transport you mentioned, and that was very definitely going the other direction as fast as it could."

"Yes, sir," Plaine said. "The reason I ask, Commander, is that—"

"Acting Captain," Castenello interjected.

"Acting Captain," Plaine corrected himself. His voice was polite enough, but there was a subtle edge to it. "The reason I ask, sir, is that according to Cobra Broom the project down there is of extreme value to the Drim'hco'plai Trofts. I find it highly unlikely that they would leave it unprotected. The fact that there's been no response strikes me as dangerously suspicious."

Filho and Castenello exchanged looks. "You think they're waiting in ambush?" Filho asked. "Because we've seen no indication of any staging area within easy strike range."

"We certainly haven't seen evidence of an ambush," Castenello added.

"Well, you *wouldn't*, would you?" Jody said scornfully. "That's the whole point of an ambush. What Gunnery Sergeant Plaine is saying is that the Drims are *somewhere* planning *something*. It would be a really good idea for the *Dorian* to be an entirely different *somewhere* when they make their move."

"Fine," Filho said between stiff lips. "Commander Castenello, make this mapping orbit our last and then get us underway. Sergeant Bleys?" He beckoned to one of the Marines by the hatch. "You and your squad will stand guard over the three Cobras here until the full board is ready to convene. Gunnery Sergeant Plaine, you'll report to sickbay for a full physical exam. Corporal Kai—" he nodded to another Marine "—you'll escort Ms. Broom and Ms. Vil to the Women's Section."

The Marine threw a startled look at Jody. "Sir?"

"They're women, Corporal," Filho said stiffly, a sudden odd discomfort in his voice. "The only place for them is the Women's Section." His lip twitched. "I'll inform the matron that they're... special guests."

"Yes, sir." The corporal turned to face Jody and nodded toward the door. "This way Ms. Broom; Ms. Vil."

"And don't get too comfortable in there," Castenello warned as the three of them headed toward the door. "The board will convene within the hour."

A minute later they were walking down the corridor. Corporal Kai stayed about half a step ahead of the two women and a couple of steps to the side, where he could lead the way and still keep an eye on them.

Not that they were likely to lose themselves in any crowds. The corridor was nearly deserted, with only a few other men hurrying about on various errands.

"So we're going to be special guests," Jody commented as they walked. "What exactly does that mean?"

"Corporal Kai?" Plaine's voice came from behind them.

Jody turned. The gunnery sergeant had appeared and was hurrying toward them. "Sir?" Kai said.

"You're dismissed, Corporal," Plaine said, trotting to a halt. "I'll take them from here."

Kai frowned, his eyes flicking to Jody. "Acting Captain Filho told *me* to take them, sir."

"Yes, I know," Plaine said grimly. "But Acting Captain Filho doesn't appreciate just how dangerous those Cobras back there are. I do. You need to head back and bolster Sergeant Bleys's force. I can drop them in the Women's Section before I report to sickbay."

Kai looked at Jody again. "Sir—"

"Dismissed, Corporal," Plaine cut him off. "If the Cobras decide to make trouble, Bleys will need all the help he can get." He raised his eyebrows. "And you do *not* want to have to explain to an Enquiry Board that you were in the Women's Section when your fellow Marines were being slaughtered."

Kai winced. "I suppose not. You've logged your order?"

"Yes," Plaine said. "Log your receipt, then get back to Bleys."

"Yes, sir." Kai's eyes briefly unfocused. Then, with a brisk nod, he headed back down the corridor.

"Come on," Plaine murmured, taking Jody's arm and continuing along the corridor.

"They're not going to make trouble, you know," Jody said.

"It's not them I'm worried about." Plaine glanced over his shoulder.

And suddenly changed direction, pulling Jody back the way they'd come. "Whoa," Jody said, peering at his profile. "What's going on?"

"I don't know, but nothing good," Plaine said. "Anyway, you do *not* want to go to the Women's Section."

"Why not?"

Plaine threw her a sideways look. "You really don't know?"

"No. Tell me."

"The Women's Section is for...look." Plaine took a deep breath. "We revere women in the Dominion of Man. We really do. We revere them, honor them, and protect them. But we're on a long voyage, and men have...needs."

Jody stared at him, a horrified chill running through her. "Are you saying...?"

"They are called comfort women," Rashida said quietly.

Jody spun her head to look at the other woman. "You *knew* about this?"

"I know the pattern," Rashida said. Her face and voice were calm, but Jody could see a tightness in her throat. "Our history of the worlds we left spoke of such things. Usually during wartime. But not always."

"The point is, special guests or not, you don't want to be in there," Plaine said. "More important, whatever's going on here, I need my combat tunic." He looked hard at Jody. "You *did* keep my tunic, right?"

"Kemp had her destroy it," Rashida said. "Can you not obtain one from here?"

"Every ship has its own activation code, and I don't have the *Dorian's*," Plaine said. His eyes were steady on Jody. "Broom?"

Jody sighed. "It's locked away aboard the *Squire*," she said reluctantly. She didn't dare look at Rashida, but she could feel the Qasaman's disbelief and disapproval.

"Good," Plaine said. "Let's go get it."

The officers had left, leaving only the Marine guards, who had wasted no time shackling the Cobras' hands behind them before settling in to wait.

Merrick sat in one of the chairs at the table, eyeing everyone— Smitty, Kemp, and the Marines—trying to get his brain around what was happening.

The Dominion of Man at Aventine. Cobra friends of his sister from Caelian. A Qasaman woman, flying a Dominion courier ship, all of them defying everyone to come all the way to Muninn to find him.

They would be sorry that they had. Very sorry.

But not yet. The Marines were dangerous enough, with their shoulder-mounted epaulet lasers and autotargeting sensors. But they were small fish, minor targets, hardly worth his efforts.

The officers were the big fish. Filho, Castenello, Moreau . . .

He frowned. Moreau. Jody had told him on their short flight up to the *Dorian* that Captain Barrington Moreau was the grandson of Jonny Moreau's brother Jame. A relative, and a reasonably close one. Should that make a difference?

Merrick didn't know if it should. All he knew was that it didn't.

He checked the clock circuit on his nanocomputer. *Within the next hour*, Castenello had said. It had been eighteen minutes since he and Filho left.

Forty-two minutes or less, if the commander had been telling the truth.

Settling himself in his chair, listening with half an ear to the quiet conversation between Kemp and Smitty, he settled in to wait.

Jody had expected to find a guard posted by the *Squire's* hatch. But there was no one there. "Where is it?" Plaine asked as they slipped aboard.

"There's a pump room near CoNCH," she told him, leading the way down the corridor. "I thought you might need it, so I just locked it away so you couldn't get at it on your own."

"How did you do that?" Plaine asked, frowning. "None of the pump rooms have locks."

"I did a quick spot-weld on the—"

"Quiet," he snapped, his head half turning around and up.

"What is it?" Jody asked.

"We've left orbit," Rashida said. "The change of engine sound is distinct. Are you feeling all right, Sergeant Plaine?"

"Sure," Plaine said, his voice oddly distracted. He let go of Jody's arm, slapped the fingers of his left hand against his upper right arm above the biceps. "Sure. Come on, come on—quit stalling."

"I'm not stalling," Jody said, frowning at his arm. What had *that* been about? Some kind of strange itch?

"Because you don't seem well," Rashida pressed. "You seem confused and restless. Are you feverish?"

"You're the one who's confused," Plaine shot back. "Let's go. Let's *go*."

"Yeah, we're going, we're going," Jody said, keying her infrareds. Rashida was right about the fever—Plaine's face was blazing with heat. "You sure you're okay?"

Without warning, Plaine grabbed both of Jody's upper arms, spinning her halfway around and yanking her toward him. "Quit *stalling!*" he snarled, his face bare centimeters from hers, his fingers digging deeply into her skin. "Get me my *damn tunic!*"

Jody gasped with pain.

And abruptly realized where she'd seen that intensity of facial glow before.

It had been on the men she'd seen during Merrick's rescue. The ones Merrick had said had been pumped full of a drug that conferred phenomenal strength and perfect loyalty.

Somehow, during the brief time Plaine had been out of her sight, he'd been given the drug.

He had the strength.

Who had his loyalty?

"It's right here," Jody said, trying to pull away.

But not trying too hard. Plaine was a trained soldier and super strong. The only ace she had was that he didn't know she was a Cobra.

Which gave her a huge advantage. She could drop him where he stood with a stun blast. She could hit him with her sonic, which at this range would probably accomplish the same thing. For that matter, she could pick him up and bounce him off the CoNCH hatchway if she wanted.

But that wouldn't get her any answers. And answers were what she needed most.

"It's right here," she said again, nodding toward the pump room where she'd hidden his tunic. "I'll need a cutting torch to get it open."

"Not you," Plaine bit out. "You—Vil—go get a torch."

"Go ahead, Rashida," Jody said, trying to think against the pain his fingers were still pressing into her arms. Whoever had gotten the drug into him had to have done it when he and Kemp were getting Merrick's Troft friend to his escape ship. They could have injected him, or gassed him, or gotten him to drink something—

Or gotten him to inject himself.

She focused on his right sleeve, keying her infrareds. The spot where he'd tapped himself was just faintly warmer than the surrounding skin. A recent trauma, like something injected under the epidermis, could inflame the tissue that way. She looked further down the sleeve.

And felt her stomach tighten. There wasn't just one warm spot. There were twelve of them, evenly spaced down his arm. "What are those?" she asked, reaching up to touch his right sleeve.

She wasn't prepared for the vehemence of his reaction. Digging his fingers even harder into her arms, he yanked her right up against his chest, putting his face barely ten centimeters from hers. "Don't touch me," he rumbled, his voice barely loud enough to hear even from that close. "Don't ever touch me."

Jody cringed back. And now she couldn't even use her stunner or sonic without risking blowback. Great.

Well, she could fix that. "You mean like this?" she asked. Swinging around her left hand, she jabbed him hard in the ribs.

An instant later she found herself flying backwards across the corridor as he shoved her violently away from him.

With a normal person, that would have been that. Jody would have slammed back-first into the metal wall, getting the wind knocked out of her lungs and probably hitting the back of her head hard enough to knock her unconscious or give her a concussion.

But Plaine hadn't reckoned on Cobra reflexes. He'd barely released his grip when Jody's nanocomputer took over her servo network, twisting her torso around, catlike, to face the wall rushing toward her and snapping up her arms. An instant later she hit, palms flat against the metal, wrist and elbow servos absorbing the impact and decelerating her body, bringing her face and chest almost but not quite into contact with the wall. An instant later, with the skin of her palms tingling, her left arm servos reversed direction, shoving her off the wall and spinning her back around to face her attacker.

Plaine's eyes had widened, and his mouth was starting to fall open in astonishment, when she fired a burst from her sonic.

The sonic wasn't really designed as a stunning weapon. But

the blast was enough to startle him and send him staggering back against the pump room door. Jody gave him a second burst, then charged.

Merrick had said the Drim war drug gave its user extra strength, and after Plaine's grip and shove Jody had assumed she'd already seen its limit. She was wrong. Shrugging off the double sonic tap, Plaine caught her right arm as she grabbed for his shirt, twisting it up and away from him.

The unexpected force of the move threw Jody off balance. As she fought to get her feet back under her Plaine brought up his right hand, placed it against her chest, and again pushed her violently away down the corridor.

But not before she got a servo-locked grip on his sleeve. As she flew backwards down the corridor the force of his shove ripped the sleeve off the rest of his shirt.

Once again, Jody's nanocomputer was up to the challenge. With the torn sleeve still gripped in her hand her servos twisted her half around, bent her at the waist, threw her into a shoulder roll on the floor, and used her remaining momentum to roll her back up onto her feet. She spun around—

To see Plaine sprinting toward her, a look of raw fury on his face.

But he was still two seconds away... and with his sleeve gone Jody finally had a good look at his arm.

There were twelve spots there, all right: red, warm, and slightly swollen, tracing a line from his upper bicep nearly to his wrist. Something had been inserted under his skin at those points, something that a strong tap with his fingertips would activate.

There was no time for further study. Another second and he would be on top of her. She had to subdue him before she could do anything else; and with his enhanced strength, that was going to be a challenge. She braced herself, holding her arms out to hopefully catch his wrists before he could grab her—

And then, from a cross corridor behind Plaine, Rashida stepped into Jody's view. A fraction of a second's assessment; and then, in a single smooth motion, she hurled the cutting torch fuel tank in her hand down the corridor straight at Plaine.

The Marine was reaching for Jody's wrists when the tank slammed into his back, sending him lurching forward. Jody managed to sidestep him, caught his right wrist as he passed her and snapped the arm straight out. Up close, the welts looked even redder and angrier than they had at a distance.

She was staring at them, trying to figure out what they were, when Plaine twisted back around and grabbed her throat with his left hand.

She gasped, or rather tried to gasp, as pain and panic flooded through her. She got a grip on the hand wrapped around her neck and tried to pull it away. His response was to squeeze even harder.

Cobra gear included some protection around her trachea. But it wasn't enough, not with the kind of strength coursing through Plaine's muscles. Spots were starting to dance in front of her eyes, and through the haze she could see the pain in Plaine's own eyes from Rashida's fuel tank attack.

Pain.

Jody had no idea if it would work. But with Plaine about to collapse her windpipe it was all she had. Shifting her eyes from his face to his arm, she glanced target locks onto all twelve of the hot spots. With a supreme effort she let go of the hand choking her, got her thumb on her fingertip laser's lowest setting, and fired.

Plaine gasped as the laser slashed into his skin. Jody kept firing, her nanocomputer running the laser blasts systematically down his arm. The grip on her throat wavered, loosened...

And then, suddenly, Rashida was there, crouching over them and prying Plaine's hand away from Jody's throat.

Jody took a shuddering breath, concentrating on finishing her demolition job. She had no idea whether burning the warm spots would do anything to whatever was in there, but at least it had distracted him enough to give Rashida time to join the party. "Hold him," she croaked to the Qasaman. One last shot—

Without warning, Plaine gave a convulsive jerk, pulling his arms inward and slamming Jody and Rashida into each other. An instant later he reversed the movement, shoving the two women the opposite directions, clearly trying to shake them off.

Good luck with that. Jody was still a little shaky from the choking, but her Cobra gear was completely unaffected. Locking her finger servos around Plaine's wrist, she prepared herself to ride out his latest ploy. Again he swung his arms inward and then outward, tossing the women around like dolls. Jody tightened her grip—

And flinched back as a sudden flash lit up the corridor. Even as she reflexively squeezed her eyes shut, she felt Plaine's arm go limp in her hand.

"I'm sorry," Rashida breathed into her ear. "I know you wished to speak with him, to learn what has happened. I hoped that your burning of the drug patches would work, but there is too much already in his blood."

"Yeah," Jody said, staring at her. That flash of light... "Anything you can do about clearing it out?"

Rashida nodded. "I have a drug designed to clear other drugs from the body."

"How long will it take to work?"

"Not long," Rashida assured her. "I'll get it from my quarters." She started to stand up.

Jody caught her wrist. "Rashida...?"

Rashida's lip twitched. "I'm sorry, Jody Moreau Broom. Shahni Moffren Omnathi ordered me to keep my transformation a secret."

"Yeah," Jody said, feeling the universe tilting around her. The Qasamans, with all their prejudices and old-fashioned cultural feelings about women... and yet, Omnathi had made Rashida a Cobra. A secret weapon—*his* secret weapon—completely unsuspected by anyone. "Don't worry," she added, releasing Rashida's arm. "No one will hear it from me."

Rashida nodded, acknowledgment or thanks, and finished standing up. "I'll be quick," she said. "Yet I find it difficult to believe Gunnery Sergeant Plaine is alone in this plot. Should we alert the men of the *Dorian*?"

Jody felt her lip twitch. Acting Captain Filho, the man who'd ordered them sent to the *Dorian*'s on-board brothel. Commander Castenello, who'd snidely warned them not to get comfortable there. "Let's wait until we know a little more about what's going on."

"Understood," Rashida said. "I'll be as quick as I can."

"Yeah." Jody looked at the line of burn marks on Plaine's arm. "Try to make it even quicker."

CHAPTER TWENTY-FIVE

The abrupt summons came from Captain Lij Tulu, and once again Jin found herself being escorted down the *Algonquin*'s maze of corridors inside a phalanx of guards.

But this time was different. All the other times the Marines had been alert, but at the same time relaxed; watchful, but strangely cocky. Now, the calm and smugness were gone. In their place was a grim darkness, the sense of men no longer playing a game.

Whatever Lorne and the other Cobras had pulled off down there, it had apparently shaken the Dominion forces' confidence.

Good.

The shuttle was waiting when Jin and her escort reached it. To her surprise, so was Lij Tulu himself. "Cobra Broom," he greeted her gravely as he gestured to the seat beside him. "You can remove those," he added to her guards.

Jin frowned as the Marines took off her wrist cuffs. "Treating our hostage better today, are we?" she asked.

"You're not a hostage anymore," Lij Tulu said, again gesturing to her. "We're in a bit of a hurry, though. So if you'd be seated?"

"Of course," Jin said, slipping past him and sitting down. "Thank you for that."

"For what?"

"For acknowledging that I *was* a hostage," Jin said as she strapped in. Lij Tulu was in a hurry, all right; barely had she snapped the last belt when the shuttle broke away from the

327

Algonquin and headed outward. "I don't think you ever openly admitted that before."

"Perhaps," Lij Tulu said. "As I say, that's all over now."

"Ah," Jin said, peering closely at him. "So are you giving up and leaving Aventine? Or am I being exchanged for someone?"

"Do you *want* us to leave?"

"Of course."

Lij Tulu shook his head. "No, you don't. Look out that viewport beside you. I think you'll find this interesting."

Jin turned her head. The shuttle was making a half circle around the *Algonquin*, passing the pie-piece-shaped gap where one of the armed courier ships used to be. "Look inside," Lij Tulu instructed. "Tell me what you see."

"All right." Jin keyed her telescopics and light-amps as the shuttle continued to pull away on its journey to the planetary surface.

And frowned. She'd expected to see mostly smooth metal or ceramic, perhaps with some docking connectors to secure the courier when it was in place. Instead, the walls of the wedge-shaped opening were bristling with small- to medium-sized openings, making the whole thing look rather like a giant ceramic Swiss cheese.

"They're missile tubes and antiship lasers," Lij Tulu identified them. "Short range, of course, since it's assumed that by the time the captain deploys the couriers for combat the ship is already in a close-in fight for its life."

"Having already had all its external weaponry destroyed or disabled?" Jin asked.

"Exactly," Lij Tulu said. "One final surprise for the attackers: undamaged lasers and unspent missiles capable of delivering a devastating blow. Did you see what was tucked in all the way at the back?"

Jin keyed her telescopics to their full magnification. All the way in the back... there it was, a curved canoe-shaped object, about thirty meters long, set between a pair of the laser tubes.

But even though there was plenty of sunlight blazing into the opening, the object was strangely hard to see. It was like the surface of an iridescent butterfly she'd seen once as a child, or some kind of optical illusion puzzle. "Another shuttle?" she tentatively identified it.

"It is," Lij Tulu confirmed. "But one unlike any other shuttle class in the Dominion of Man Navy. It's a highly stealthed, highly protected intruder boat, designed to slip across the gap between ships during a firefight and deliver up to three squads of Marines to a Troft vessel. Each of our ships has three such shuttles."

Jin turned to face him, feeling her eyes widening. "So you can actually *board* Troft warships?"

"That's the plan," Lij Tulu said, smiling faintly at the expression on her face.

The smile faded. "And the theory, and the hope," he added. "In actual fact, the system has never yet been tested in combat."

Jin keyed her infrareds. Lij Tulu's face seemed unusually warm. "What's going on, Captain?" she asked carefully.

"Your son and his friends have pulled off something amazing," Lij Tulu said. "They've managed to capture Colonel Reivaro, alive and unharmed, which I would have sworn was impossible. I'm giving you back to them in the hope that they'll give him back to me."

Jin nodded. From hostage to bargaining chip. She should have guessed. "And if they refuse?"

Lij Tulu gave a small shrug. "Then I'll have to do without him."

"And I'll be on my way back to the ship?"

"No." Lij Tulu nodded toward the viewport. "I would guess you've never gone through an atmo entry like this before."

Jin looked back at the viewport. She'd had plenty of space-to-ground transits over her lifetime, including one trapped inside the hulk of a ship that had been shot down over Qasama. Still, most of her atmospheric travel had been smooth and controlled.

But as she gazed at the cloudy streams of ionized air flowing past she realized the shuttle was careening groundward at a much faster pace than normal Cobra Worlds spacecraft ever took the trip. Much faster, yet with iron stability and apparently under solid control. Lij Tulu was clearly in a hurry to get to Capitalia.

But why? He'd said that Reivaro had already been captured. Was he hoping to turn the tables on the resistance without having to release Jin? If Lorne and the others were moving Reivaro—or worse, if Reivaro had been carrying a tracker that allowed Lij Tulu to pinpoint his exact location—then things could get bloody. *Very* bloody.

But in that case, why remove Jin's wrist cuffs? If they were heading into combat, the last thing Lij Tulu should want near him was an unrestrained Cobra.

She was still puzzling at that when the shuttle came to a breakneck halt and touched down on the landing pad outside the Dome. "Come," Lij Tulu said, popping his restraints and standing up. "Your son warned that if I threatened force over his abduction of Colonel Reivaro I would face an unstoppable response. I'm curious to see what he's come up with."

Two Marines were waiting by the hatch. An unexpectedly small escort, Jin thought, considering all the threats and counterthreats flying around.

Which only meant that the rest of the Dominion forces were in concealment, waiting for their commander's order to attack.

Lij Tulu gestured silently, and the hatch slid open. Taking Jin's arm in a strangely courteous manner, he walked through the opening into the late afternoon sunlight, the Marines falling into step on either side of them.

Lorne was standing alone, facing the shuttle hatch from twenty meters away. "Welcome, Captain Lij Tulu," he called. His eyes flicked to Jin, then back to Lij Tulu. "I'm a bit surprised you came yourself." He nodded toward the two Marines. "And so trustingly."

"Not as trustingly as you might think," Lij Tulu called back, coming to a halt. Jin started to continue on, stopped as Lij Tulu tightened his grip on her arm. Whatever this game was they were playing, she had no intention of making any moves until she at least knew the rules. "But I didn't come here to fight. Did you?"

"No," Lorne said. "But I *did* want to show you what you'd be up against if you did." Raising his fingers to his mouth, he gave a long, piercing whistle.

For a long moment nothing happened. Jin scanned the nearby buildings and rooftops, keying in her infrareds and telescopics, searching for the trap or assault force that Lorne must have put in place somewhere. But she could see nothing.

She was starting a second, slower sweep, when she began to hear footsteps.

Not just a few footsteps, either. There were a *lot* of them. They weren't marching in step like trained soldiers might, but were approaching with a myriad of different paces and speeds.

And then, they began to appear.

Not just Cobras, though she was sure some were present. Not just Governor-General Chintawa and the Dome politicians, though they were also there.

Mostly it was people. Just ordinary, normal people.

They came from every direction, from around every corner,

walking shoulder to shoulder, silent except for some muffled crying from babies in their parents' arms. There were no weapons
Jin could see; no raised fists of anger or defiance; no scowls or
bubbling anger. Just thousands—maybe hundreds of thousands—
of Aventinian citizens, their quiet resolve more unnerving in its
own way than a hundred screaming berserkers would have been.

Lorne let the leading edge of the crowd come to within a hundred
meters of the landing pad. Then, he raised his arm high over his
head, and they all shuffled to a slightly desultory halt. "I know you
think the Dominion of Man can do anything, Captain," he called
into the silence. "I know you think your Marines are superior in
every way to our outmoded Cobras. I know you think we're a bunch
of backwater people who have no idea how the universe operates.

"But we've proved now that the Dominion can indeed lose. We've
proved that we can take your Marines, head to head. And while
we may still be backwater unsophisticates—" he gestured to the
mass of people behind him "—I don't think even you could justify
slaughtering *all* of us."

"Very dramatic, Cobra Broom," Lij Tulu said. "Also completely
unnecessary. I came here today to tell you that our mission is over.
I'm giving you back your mother. In return I expect you to produce
Colonel Reivaro and anyone else you may have taken."

"What do you mean your mission is over?" Lorne asked, frowning.

"I mean," Lij Tulu said, "that at this moment a Troft battle force
is gathering at the edge of the Aventine system. Our mission was
to draw enemy forces here, to divert some of their attention from
the Dominion war front. We've succeeded, though far earlier than
anyone anticipated. No matter. We're here; they're here; and it's
time for us to engage and destroy them."

Lorne's eyes flicked upward, as if by willpower alone he could
see the ships Lij Tulu was talking about. "And if you can't?"

"We will," Lij Tulu said.

But Jin could hear the stiff control in his voice. He wasn't at all
sure his single ship could take on the Trofts by itself.

"Glad to hear it," Lorne said. He half turned and waved toward
someone in the crowd. "So why are you here instead of preparing
for battle?"

"Don't worry—the *Algonquin* is being fully prepped as we speak,"
Lij Tulu said. "But I need my Marines—*all* of them—and this seemed
the best way to persuade you to give me back their commander."

A man had disengaged from the crowd and was heading over to Lorne, and Jin saw that it was his fellow Cobra Badger Werle. "What do you need Marines for in a space battle?" Lorne asked.

Lij Tulu inclined his head toward Jin. "Cobra Broom?" he invited.

"They have three stealthed transports designed to get troops aboard Troft ships," Jin said.

"You've seen them?"

"One of them, yes," Jin confirmed. "Very strange hull. Almost impossible to focus on even with light-amps and IR. I'm guessing normal sensors would have the same trouble picking it up."

"Interesting." Lorne spoke briefly to Werle, who nodded and hurried toward one of the nearby buildings. "Okay, I've sent someone to get Reivaro out of storage. What about the Cobra neckbands?"

"They've been deactivated," Lij Tulu said.

"And the citizens you've detained?"

"Already being released."

Lorne pursed his lips. "Mom? Do you believe him?"

"You're the one with the extra-fancy IR vision," Jin countered. "Is he lying, or isn't he?"

Lorne gave her a tight smile. "Point taken. How much time do we have, Captain?"

"I'd guess they'll start their approach within the hour," Lij Tulu said. "There are three demesnes represented, so they're probably holding back while they set up their command structure." He considered. "Or else they're waiting for reinforcements."

"How many ships are out there?" Jin asked.

Lij Tulu shrugged microscopically. "Four."

Jin stared at him. "*Four* ships? Against your *one*?"

"We're the Dominion of Man," Lij Tulu said evenly. "Four-to-one odds don't bother us." He gestured. "Go to your son. Go."

Jin looked at the two Marines. They had the same grim expressions as the ones aboard ship. Maybe four-to-one odds bothered *them*. "Thank you," she said. "Good luck."

She tensed the whole way over to Lorne, half expecting a last-minute shot in her back. But no attack came. "You okay?" Lorne asked quietly as she reached him.

"I'm fine," Jin said.

"You think he's telling the truth?"

"I do," Jin said. "There's a sense of tension aboard the ship, not like anything I've seen there before. I can't believe he would be that subtle just to get me to help him set a trap."

"Mm," Lorne grunted, his eyes flicking back and forth across the Marines, the shuttle, and Lij Tulu himself. "Well, we'll know soon enough. Reivaro will be here any minute. If Lij Tulu doesn't spring something once he has him back, that'll be a good indicator that he's playing straight with us." He nodded. "There."

Jin looked in that direction. Werle had reappeared, along with Dillon De Portola, Colonel Reivaro, and the Capitalia Cobra Emile Chun-Wei. "You had him that close?"

"Lij Tulu said he'd be bringing you back, no strings attached," Lorne said. "I figured he still planned to do a trade and wanted to get the exchange over before he could pull anything."

Jin looked back at Lij Tulu, her hands automatically curling into laser-firing position. If the Dominion was going to make a move, this was the time.

But the captain just stood there, watching Reivaro and the Cobras approach.

There was a brush of air on Jin's cheek as Chintawa stepped up beside her. "Did he say there were Troft ships in the system?" he asked, his voice tense.

Jin nodded. "Yes."

"And the other Dominion ships are gone?"

"They are."

"Then what in—?" Chintawa broke off. "Damn them," he muttered. "Damn them all."

Jin pursed her lips. It was a hard sentiment to argue with, given everything the Dominion had done since their arrival. But still...

"We should send for help," Lorne said. "The Tlossies might be willing to send a ship or two."

"They'd never get here in time," Jin said.

"Not for the *Algonquin*, no," Lorne said. "But they could be here in time for the occupation."

"Assuming the Dominion loses the fight."

"Four against one?" Lorne shook his head. "They're going to lose, all right. When they do, the Trofts' next stop will be Capitalia."

Chintawa hissed. "I am *so* tired of my planet being occupied," he growled. "By anyone." Abruptly, he started toward Lij Tulu.

Jin and Lorne exchanged looks. Then, without a word, they both set off after him.

They caught up with him just as Reivaro and the three Cobras also reached Lij Tulu. "What can we do?" Chintawa asked without preamble.

Lij Tulu gave a small snort. "You can go to ground and hide," he said. "That appears to be what you do best." He inclined his head to the Cobras. "With certain notable exceptions, of course."

"I'm not joking," Chintawa insisted. "We've got the *Dewdrop* and its damn armor plating. How long would it take to add in some lasers or missiles?"

"Too long," Lij Tulu said, frowning at him. "But it's good to see that you've finally grown a backbone."

"Oh, he's had one all along, sir," Reivaro said sourly. "It's just been stealthed. He's the one who fed me the Cobras' alleged plan to attack our satellites that had us looking the wrong way when they grabbed me. Along with, I dare say, certain other bits of disinformation."

"None of which matters anymore," Chintawa said impatiently. "There must be *something* we can do to help."

"Like maybe taking aboard a few Cobras for your assault teams?" Emile suggested.

They all turned to look at him. "What?" Lorne asked.

"Come on, Broom, think," Emile said with exaggerated patience. "We were *designed* to fight Trofts. We'd be hell on wheels inside a closed ship."

"With no armor?" Reivaro countered. "You'd be cut to scraps."

"You might be surprised," Emile said. "Face it, Colonel—you need all the help you can get." He gave Lorne a lopsided grin. "Besides, we pull this off and it would finally shut up all you outer province hotshots about the great job you did during the invasion."

Lorne glared at him. "You think this is about bragging rights?"

"Of course not," Emile said. "That would just be a bonus."

"Colonel Reivaro is right," Lij Tulu said in a tone that made it clear the conversation was over. "I appreciate your offer, but you're hardly trained for this sort of action. You'd be more hindrance than help." His lips compressed. "Besides, if we lose, you'll be needed here."

"To continue pinning down the Dominion's enemies for you?" Jin asked.

"*And* to defend your world." Lij Tulu gave her a wry smile. "You see? Sometimes our goals and purposes *do* coincide. Actually, there is one thing you can do for me." He pulled a small cylinder from his pocket. "I was planning to leave this in orbit for Commodore Santores to pick up," he said, handing it to Chintawa. "But you can probably find a safer place for it. You were certainly able to hide Qasama's location."

"What is it?" Chintawa asked, holding it gingerly.

"The *Algonquin*'s log and data-stream entries," Lij Tulu said. "Sooner or later the commodore and Captain Moreau will return from Qasama. Possibly even in time to intervene before the Trofts have done too much to your worlds. When they do, I'd appreciate you giving that to him."

"Of course," Chintawa said.

"Thank you," Lij Tulu said. "Then this is good-bye, Governor-General. Whatever happens to the Dominion of Man, I have no doubt you and the Cobra Worlds will continue to hold the torch of humanity high. Colonel Reivaro?"

"I've initiated combat prep, Captain," Reivaro said, his eyes briefly unfocusing. "We'll be ready when you need us."

"Then we'd best be on our way." Lij Tulu nodded to the others in the group. "A shame the battle will probably be too far out for you and your people to watch. It should be quite a show."

Ninety seconds later, with all Dominion personnel back inside, the shuttle lifted into the sky. Again, Jin noted, it was traveling far faster than any normal transport. "Now what?" she murmured.

"Now we do what we can," Chintawa said. "Cobra Broom—*and* Cobra Broom—" he added, looking at Jin. "You two will assemble a Cobra escort for the diplomatic team I'm sending to the Tlossies. Grab your uncle, too—he's had good relations with them. I want you and the *Dewdrop* ready to go in thirty minutes. Can you do that?"

Jin looked at Lorne. "How close is Uncle Corwin?"

"Close enough," Lorne said. "And the *Dewdrop*'s been sitting on needles since the Reivaro pickup, waiting for the Dominion to try something, so it's basically ready."

"Good," Chintawa said. "You'll first go to the Hoibies and ask the demesne-lord for help. After that, you'll take this to Qasama." He handed Jin the cylinder.

"None of this will be in time to help the *Algonquin*," Jin reminded him.

"I don't care about the *Algonquin*," Chintawa retorted. "My job is to care about Aventine." He leveled a finger at Lorne. "Clock's running, Cobras. Move it."

CHAPTER TWENTY-SIX

"There's no chance they're someone else?" Paul asked, feeling the blood pounding in his ears.

"None at all," Santores said grimly. "All four ships have the markings of demesnes who are at war with the Dominion. Those are our attackers, all right."

Paul looked at the main CoNCH display, and the faint pinpricks of reflected light moving slowly toward them. "It's only been five weeks since you arrived at Aventine. How did they get from the other end of the Troft Assemblage this quickly?"

"Good question," Santores said. "The answer has to be that they didn't. These must have been ships that were already traveling through the Assemblage, probably trying to recruit more demesnes to their side."

"And when they heard that you were here, they got together and redefined their mission," Paul concluded. "Terrific."

"I suppose there's *one* silver lining, though," Santores continued. "The fact that they sent out warships to look for allies—even relatively minor warships like these heavy cruisers—suggests more of a strong-arm approach than persuasion or even bribery. That may mean they're getting desperate."

"Maybe," Paul said. "On the other hand, if they can go back to those potential allies with a story of how the Dominion invaded this end of the Assemblage and they destroyed the intruders, they may not need nearly as much persuasion to get the demesne-lords to sign up."

"True," Santores said. "Which makes it that much more impera-tive that we don't let them return."

"Yes," Paul murmured. "I don't suppose the reinforcements you told me about could arrive in time to help?"

"Unfortunately, no," Santores said. "The timing of the second wave assumed our enemies would need to first hear about our arrival at the Cobra Worlds and then assemble a force from the battle front to oppose us. This is all happening far too early." He lifted a finger. "Shahni Omnathi is calling." He touched a key on his board. "This is Commodore Santores, Your Excellency."

"I'm told there are enemy warships approaching," Omnathi's voice came from the speaker. "Do you have the item I requested?"

"Yes," Santores said hesitantly. "But I'm still not sure whether I should give it to you. The Trofts will certainly drop at least two shuttles to your location, more likely three or four. A single short-range missile isn't going to make much difference."

"Nevertheless, my plan requires one," Omnathi said. "Your officer said the ships will be upon us very soon. If you mean to refuse my request, tell me so now. At the very least, I need you to send Cobra Paul Broom to us."

Santores shot a frown at Paul. "Why do you need him?"

"For my plan," Omnathi said. "I told your officer earlier that I would need him."

Santores's eyes defocused briefly. "That request isn't in the data stream."

"That fault is not mine," Omnathi said. "Please send him at once. He must be here before the Trofts attack."

Santores looked at Paul. "Did you know anything about this?"

"No," Paul said.

"You have any idea how you could help?" Santores gestured to Paul's body. "Especially like that?"

Paul felt a lump form in his throat. "You mean with my Cobra gear useless? With *me* useless?"

Santores didn't even flinch. "Yes."

Paul shook his head. "No idea."

Which wasn't entirely true. Very likely this was Omnathi's way of getting him off the *Megalith* and to the relative safety of the planet before the fighting started.

Emphasis, of course, on the *relative*. If the Trofts decided to be satisfied with destroying the sham manufacturing complex the Dominion and Qasamans had put together, then the rest of the planet should be mostly safe. If they decided instead on a full-scale occupation, things would get very bad very quickly.

"Very well," Santores said, turning back to his board. "I'll put Cobra Broom aboard a shuttle and send him down."

"Thank you, Commodore Santores," Omnathi said. "In return, we shall do everything in our power to drain some of the strength from the enemy. I suggest you pull back once Cobra Broom's shuttle has returned to you and allow them to make their landing in peace."

"Not a good idea," Santores warned. "They may not treat you as well as the last batch of invaders."

"Nevertheless, it is a necessary part of my plan."

Santores looked at Paul. "Broom?" he murmured.

Paul shook his head. "Sorry. I have no idea what he's up to."

"But you trust him?"

"It's his world," Paul pointed out. "If he's wrong, he'll pay the consequences."

Santores's lips compressed briefly. But he nodded. "Very well," he said, turning back to the microphone. "The shuttle and Cobra Broom will be there as soon as possible."

He keyed off the radio. "So is that the Qasaman answer for everything? 'It's all part of the plan'?"

Paul shrugged. "It is from Omnathi."

For a moment Santores gazed at the main display. Then, he gave a sharp nod. "I suppose in the end it won't matter where any of us are standing when we die." He gestured to the Marines standing a few paces back. "Take Cobra Broom to the Number Four shuttle and put him on board. Quickly."

"And the missile Omnathi asked for?" Paul asked as one of the Marines stepped forward and unlocked his chair from the deck.

"It's already aboard the shuttle," Santores said. "Might as well make it a package deal. Good-bye, and good luck."

The trip to the surface was short, much shorter than any Paul had ever taken. Clearly, the shuttle's pilot had also gotten the message that the clock was ticking down.

The Qasamans had been busy over the past two weeks, nearly filling the forest clearing with fake factories, barracks, and support buildings. There were only three open spaces where a space-capable shuttle could land: a strip of open ground along the western edge that could handle two or possibly three of them, and two smaller areas to the north and southwest that a good pilot could set down in. The Dominion pilot, presumably acting under orders, headed for the northern spot.

He was a good pilot, and made it down without trouble.

Omnathi and a pair of Djinni were waiting when Paul emerged from the shuttle. "Cobra Paul Broom," the Shahni greeted him gravely. "It is good to see you again. I trust you are well?"

"Quite well, thank you," Paul said, walking carefully toward him. He'd been working his muscles hard since losing his servos, but he was still far from casual in his movements. "Are you ready? The Trofts are attacking sooner than Commodore Santores expected."

"Do not worry." Omnathi raised his eyes to look at something over Paul's shoulder.

Paul turned. A handful of Qasamans were maneuvering a small missile out of the shuttle's cargo bay. "Can I help with that?" he asked, turning back to Omnathi.

"*Can* you help with that?" Omnathi countered.

Paul grimaced. He should have guessed that the Shahni would notice his new physical limitations. "No," he admitted. "My servos don't work anymore. My muscles now have to carry all my own weight, plus the added weight of the bone laminae and the servos themselves. There's also a drag component in the artificial tendon system that makes everything feel even heavier."

"I see," Omnathi said, his voice going ominous. "How did it happen? Who is responsible?"

"It wasn't deliberate, if that's what you're asking," Paul said hastily. At least, he was pretty sure it wasn't. Regardless, marking Santores or Lij Tulu for Qasaman vengeance wasn't something he was prepared to do.

And he *certainly* didn't want Omnathi to think he'd been hurt protecting the Shahni's world and people.

There was a sudden rush of air behind him, and he turned again to see the shuttle disappearing into the sky. On the ground, the Qasamans were moving the missile on its grav lifts into the woods surrounding the complex.

Trees alone probably wouldn't hide its presence from the Trofts. Hopefully, Omnathi had some other means of concealment set up back there. "What now?" he asked.

"You will accompany me to a point of observation," Omnathi said. "Together we shall see if my plan succeeds."

"Your Excellency?" a Qasaman called from beside a pair of heavy-duty off-road vehicles at the edge of the trees. "The Troft ships have reached their positions. Four landing craft have been launched and are approaching."

"Has the Dominion of Man vessel retreated?" Omnathi asked.

"It has pulled back a short distance," the man said. "But it still risks danger."

"A courageous man," Omnathi rumbled. "But perhaps a foolish one. We shall see. Is all prepared?"

"All is prepared, Your Excellency."

"Then let us go," Omnathi said, gesturing Paul toward the vehicles. "The volcano stands ready to protect its world."

A moment later they were headed up the hill, entering the forest through the same gap the missile's handlers had taken. The terrain was extremely bumpy, jolting Paul nearly out of his seat every couple of seconds. But the drivers had clearly already mapped out their routes, and while they came perilously close to many of the trees as they traveled they never actually hit one. "I hope you're right about the volcano," Paul commented as the cars came to a halt under a textured camo canopy beside a rotting log. "I was looking at it on the trip down, and it seemed quieter than usual."

"It is," Omnathi agreed. "We have sealed its cone."

Paul stared at him. "You've *sealed* it? But that's—" He broke off, stifling back his reflexive comment. *Crazy* and *stupid* weren't words you threw lightly at a Qasaman Shahni. "I thought you were going to trigger an eruption to blanket the site with smoke and ash. I thought that was your plan."

"The volcano is too far away for such an attack to be effective," Omnathi said. "But it will serve in other ways."

Paul was still wondering how a blocked volcano could possibly be of service when the Troft landing craft appeared.

They came in fast, faster even than the *Megalith*'s shuttle that had brought him down. They split formation as they approached the ground, disappearing behind the trees before Paul could see where they went.

"Here," Omnathi said, gesturing to a display in the vehicle.

Paul focused on it. The image was a bird's-eye view of the factory complex, with a gentle swaying that suggested the camera was mounted at the top of one of the nearby trees. The Troft pilots had clearly done the same topography analysis Paul had on his trip in, and had put down in the same three open areas he'd tagged. Two were settled at the compound's western edge, one was in the southwestern slot, and the fourth was in the northern one directly below Omnathi's current command post.

Pouring out of all four shuttles were lines of Troft soldiers.

Paul winced. From the size of the vehicles he guessed each could probably hold fifty or more combat-suited soldiers. And given the number of ships up there, this was probably only the first wave of what they had available.

What would they think, he wondered—more importantly, what would they *do*—when they found out the factory they were attacking was nothing but a decoy?

The Qasamans had done exceedingly well against the first Troft invasion of their world. But much of that success had been due to the carefully prepared city infrastructure and their heavily trained fighters. Now, most of that infrastructure was gone, and many of the soldiers dead. All the Qasamans had left were some Cobras, some Djinni—

"Now," Omnathi said quietly.

One of the Djinni opened a protective cover on the car's console and flipped a switch. There was a muffled explosion from the west, and on the display Paul saw a small geyser of dirt and dead leaves burst from beside the two landing craft on the settlement's western edge.

And suddenly, the forest erupted with a violent roar as a roiling white cloud blasted from the ground behind the dirt geyser, knocking over trees and throwing the two nearby spacecraft into the air as if they were toys. Reflexively, Paul flinched back as a wave of foul-smelling gas washed up over them from the clearing, instantly turning the air almost hot enough to singe flesh. He threw up an arm to protect his face, squinting at the display in confusion.

And then, he got it.

The volcano might be too far away to be of any use. But that didn't mean all of the volcano's side vents were.

"A volcanic steam vent, close to the surface," Omnathi confirmed Paul's thought. "Deep enough to escape detection from above, should the enemy search for it, yet close enough for a small shaped charge to bring its fury to the surface."

"And then some," Paul said mechanically. The steam was still blasting from the opening, creating a plume he could see even over the treetops and sending an ongoing flow of heat and stink across the clearing and forest. The initial burst subsided a little, and as the tendrils evaporated he could see the Trofts who'd been scattered by the explosion starting to gather themselves back together.

And as the steam cleared further, the Qasamans appeared.

They came from inside the protection of the barracks and support buildings: Djinni in their combat suits, Cobras in light ablative armor, their lasers slashing out at the invaders. The Trofts by the western shuttles, still dazed or injured by the violence of the volcano's attack, were easy prey; the aliens by the northern and southwestern shuttles, less damaged or shaken, were more quickly able to return fire.

"They have joined battle," Omnathi said. "Our task now begins. Come, Cobra Paul Broom."

The drive down the hill was somewhat slower than the trip up, but no less bumpy, and with the added distraction and discomfort of the foul-smelling steam still billowing from the vent. Paul's light-amps were of no use in the cloud, and the cloud's overall heat made his infrareds only slightly better. If the Trofts were running similar systems, they would be at an equal disadvantage.

Except that the Qasamans knew the territory. Hopefully, that would diminish the Trofts' numerical advantage.

The cars emerged from the forest beside the flank of the northern Troft landing craft, its bulk shielding their view of the main battle as well as giving them partial protection from the billowing steam. Paul's infrareds worked slightly better here, but only slightly.

And of course, being behind the landing craft didn't mean they weren't in danger. Far from it. The whole forest around them was flickering with reflected light from the laser fire, some of the flashes looking extra bright as they were diffused through the billowing clouds of steam and smoke that now filled the whole sky. Around the edges of the landing craft Paul could see more solid flashes as the two forces maneuvered around the buildings of the complex. Some of the nearby roofs were visible, and he could see that some of the Qasamans—and possibly some of the Trofts—had moved to the high ground.

Most dangerous of all were the two flat laser turrets on top of the landing craft itself. At the moment both were silent, but if the Trofts inside the vehicle spotted the humans moving down from the hills the laser could be trained on them at a second's notice.

Or maybe not. Even as the car came to a bouncy stop two Qasamans stepped out of a half-open hatchway near the shuttle's bow. Apparently, in the time it had taken to drive down the hill, the Djinni and Cobras had captured the Troft vessel.

Paul smiled tightly. Of course they had. After all, the vehicle had landed exactly where the Qasamans had planned for it to put down, and its occupants had been distracted by possibly the most unexpected attack weapon in the history of warfare. Why *shouldn't* it have been swarmed and captured by now?

Certainly Omnathi's expression showed no surprise. He got out of the car and motioned for Paul to join him, and together they walked to the waiting men. "The missile?" Omnathi asked.

"Inside," the Qasaman reported, nodding toward a larger hatch near the shuttle's stern. "It is being secured now."

Omnathi nodded and gestured to the closer, forward hatch. With the two Qasaman warriors leading the way, they all went inside, walked through a large staging room filled with ceiling-mounted Troft landing harnesses, and continued forward to the command deck.

To find an extraordinary sight waiting for them. Two Trofts were in the pilot and co-pilot chairs, their eyes glazed, their radiator membranes limp, their hands moving over the control boards in response to half-heard commands from a pair of Qasamans standing over them. Two other Qasamans, their eyes disturbingly shiny, watched closely from the sides of the board. "What's going on?" Paul asked softly.

"The Trofts are teaching our pilots to fly this vessel," Omnathi murmured back.

Paul frowned. They were *teaching*—?

He winced. Of course they were. Not voluntarily, but under the influence of some kind of hypnotic drug.

Just as the pilots themselves were fast-learning the system with another Qasaman drug coursing through them. Quick, efficient, and guaranteed effective.

Also potentially lethal. Paul had seen one young Qasaman permanently crippled by a drug side effect, and had heard of many others who had suffered similar reactions. The pilots were taking a horrible risk with this.

Or were they?

Because those side effects seldom showed up right away. They were more of a long-term hazard, something that would manifest hours or days or even months after the user had achieved whatever goal he or she had been working toward.

A captured Troft shuttle. A short-range missile being secured beside a large hatch.

Four enemy Troft warships orbiting the planet.

A motion caught Paul's eye, and he turned to see Omnathi settle into a seat at a small console at the side of the room. "Are you ill?" he asked quietly, stepping over to the Shahni.

"Ill? Not at all." Omnathi gestured to the console. "This is my seat."

Paul peered at the controls and displays. Some of the cattertalk words were unfamiliar, but he recognized enough of them to establish this was the communications console. "Are you planning to talk to them?" he asked.

"At some point, yes," Omnathi said.

"Such as when the warships ask for the docking security codes?" Paul nodded toward the two Troft pilots. "Codes you're no doubt getting from them as we speak?"

Omnathi studied his face. "You disapprove?"

Paul took a careful breath. "It's a good plan, with the boldness and dedication I've come to expect from you and the Qasaman people. But it's also dangerous. Too dangerous for the planet's most important leader to undertake."

"How do you consider it dangerous?"

"You're planning to fly to one of the Troft ships," Paul said, watching him closely. So far, the old man's expression was unreadable. "You're hoping to get far enough inside the point defenses to fire the missile and destroy or at least disable it."

"Ah," Omnathi said, inclining his head. "You are gifted. Not many would understand my plan so quickly."

"I've had some experience with the way Qasamans think," Paul said. "But there's a problem. Even if you succeed there will still be three enemy ships left . . . and because I also know how Trofts think I know they'll do their very best to take vengeance on you."

"Warfare requires the taking of risks."

"Agreed," Paul said. "But this risk should not be yours."

"Then who else will accept it?" Omnathi countered. "All are engaged with warfare. The pilots do not speak Troft cattertalk. Who else can fill this requirement?"

Paul took a deep breath. "I can."

"You are not of Qasama. This is not your battle."

"You saved my wife from a disease that was killing her," Paul reminded him. "You saved my leg. You protected my family—" *except Merrick* "—to the fullest of your ability," he added with a sudden ache in his heart. "I owe you. I owe Qasama. Permit me to repay some of my debt."

For a long moment there was silence, broken only by the murmuring of the interrogators. "You honor me, Cobra Paul Broom," Omnathi said at last. He stood up. "I accept with gratitude and humility. May God guide your path."

"Thank you," Paul said.

Omnathi looked briefly at the interrogation. Then, with a final nod to Paul, he and his escort walked to the aft hatchway and disappeared into the troop staging area behind it.

Taking another deep breath, Paul sat down at the communications console. It was a good plan, he reminded himself firmly. It was vital.

It was also suicidal.

He had no illusions. Neither, he knew, did Omnathi. Even if they breached the Troft defenses it was unlikely that a single missile would do more than partially disable its target.

But it might be enough. With the *Megalith* waiting to join the attack, damaging even one of the enemy ships might be enough to tip the balance, especially if it threw confusion into the other three.

Paul was a Cobra. Ever since the Troft invasion his job had been to fight, and to be ready and willing to die in the defense of his people.

Qasama wasn't the world he'd taken an oath to protect. But these were still his people, even if only by adoption. It was a gamble he was willing to take.

He hoped Jin would understand. Jin, and Lorne, and Jody. They probably would.

But he wished he'd had the chance to say good-bye. Too late now.

For that matter, one or more of them might already have joined Merrick in death.

The interrogation ended. The questioners helped the Trofts out of their seats and led them off the command deck and through the hatchway as the newly skilled Qasaman pilots took their places. Ninety seconds later, the shuttle lifted smoothly into the sky.

Paul craned his neck, trying to get a look through the forward canopy to see how the battle was going. But the angle was too steep, and the plume of steam quickly hid the ground from sight.

The battle was out of his hands. Time to get to work. "I need the docking security code," he said.

One of the Qasamans half turned to him. "Your pardon, Cobra Broom?"

"The Troft docking security code," Paul repeated. "I need to know it for when they hail us."

The Qasaman shook his head. "We have no code."

Paul felt his eyes widen. "You don't—? Damn it, we *need* that code."

"No," a voice came from the hatchway behind him. "We do not."

Paul twisted his head around, his eyes going even wider. Standing in the hatchway, still flanked by his two guards, was Omnathi. "Your Excellency?" he half breathed, half demanded. "I thought you left. You were *supposed* to leave."

"This is my world," Omnathi said mildly. "I keep my own counsel, and make my own choices. Or did it not occur to you that with two pilots the Trofts might need two different voices to speak the security codes?"

Paul winced. That thought hadn't even occurred to him—

Wait a minute. "You're deflecting my question, Your Excellency," he growled. "One or two voices; but you just said we wouldn't need the code."

"That is correct." Omnathi gestured to Paul's console. "May I?"

"Oh. Of course." Hastily, Paul unstrapped and moved away.

"Thank you." Far too leisurely, in Paul's opinion—especially under the circumstances—Omnathi seated himself. "Our position?"

"We are outside the attack range of the Troft ship, Your Excellency," one of the Qasamans at the main board reported.

Paul frowned. *Outside* the range? But anywhere near the battle should be within attack range. Were they trying to circle around and sneak up on the enemy from behind?

"And the Dominion of Man ship?"

"We are outside its range as well, Your Excellency."

Paul looked at Omnathi, a horrible suspicion suddenly hitting him. Were they *running*? "Your Excellency. I thought..."

"You thought we were attacking the Troft ships?" Omnathi shook his head. "No. That is the mission of the other undamaged vessel, the one that landed to the southwest of the complex. Its hold is filled with explosives, and *its* pilots are equipped with the security codes."

A shiver ran up Paul's back. "A suicide mission."

"A mission for the defense of Qasama," Omnathi said. "As you said, we all have our own tasks and our own risks."

"And you?" Paul asked. "What are *your* risks, Your Excellency?"

"My risks?" To Paul's surprise, the Shahni gave him a tired smile. "The risk that all of this has been for nothing. The risk that my plans will fail. The risk that the Qasaman people will yet die or be enslaved.

"The risk that I have been betrayed."

Paul stared at him. *Betrayed*? "Betrayed by whom?"

"By those I have trusted," Omnathi said. "Or betrayed perhaps by my own confidence and arrogance. Let us learn the truth together." Turning to the comm board, he keyed a switch. "I am Shahni Moffren Omnathi of Qasama, speaking for the Qasaman people," he called toward the microphone. "Are you there?"

"I am Commander Ukuthi of the Balin'ekha'spmi demesne of the Trof'te Assemblage," a Troft voice came promptly. "I speak for my demesne-lord. Your side of the bargain, have you fulfilled it?"

"I have," Omnathi said. "I have brought you an assault vehicle from the attackers, and a missile from the Dominion of Man."

"Excellent," Ukuthi said.

"And you?" Omnathi asked.

"My part of the bargain, it now begins," Ukuthi said. "Behold."

"Rotate us," Omnathi murmured to the shuttle pilots. The vehicle's nose dipped and came around a quarter turn.

Paul caught his breath. Framed against the stars were a pair of ships, smaller than the *Megalith* but at least as big as the four warships currently over Qasama.

"Commodore Santores of the Dominion of Man," Ukuthi continued. "This is Commander Ukuthi of the Balin'ekha'spmi demesne of the Trof'te Assemblage. I am moving to assist the defense of Qasama; prepare to receive my ship profiles, that you may factor them into your attack plans."

There was a long moment of silence. The Balin ships surged forward, Paul's landing craft continuing its turn as they sped past toward the besieged planet. The planet came into view...

Just as a massive explosion rocked the side of one of the enemy ships.

The Qasamans in the second landing craft had fulfilled their mission.

"Commander Ukuthi, this is Commodore Santores," the commodore's voice came hesitantly over the speaker. "Your assistance is unexpected, but appreciated. One of our opponents has been damaged; two others are heading your direction. I'm feeding you my updated plan and suggested coordination pattern. Are you willing to help me take them?"

"Your enemies are our enemies, Commodore," Ukuthi said. "An end to this, let us make one."

Omnathi keyed the switch, and the conversation went silent. "So that's what it was about," Paul said. "You made a deal with this Ukuthi."

"He wished to see what weapons and equipment might one day be turned against his demesne lord," Omnathi said. "I wished his assistance to protect Qasama and the warriors of the Dominion of Man. We have both achieved our goals."

"Yes," Paul murmured. Very logical, and very much Moffren Omnathi. Still, he couldn't shake the feeling that it was all wrong somehow.

Or maybe he just didn't like having been a pawn in the whole thing. "You could have told me," he said. "Explained the plan and then let me leave before we took off."

Omnathi shook his head. "I could not let you leave," he said. "I also set myself the goal of protecting you from Commodore Santores's hand. I could do that only by removing you from Qasama."

Paul looked out the canopy. The battle had been fully joined now, and while it was still in its early stages it looked to him like the *Megalith* and the Balin ships were beating the living daylights out of the attackers. "You still could have told me."

"Indeed," Omnathi agreed. "And for that omission I apologize. But..." He stopped.

"But?" Paul prompted.

"You will think it foolish," Omnathi said with reluctance Paul had never seen in him before. "But I confess that I enjoyed hearing your offer to sacrifice your life for Qasama."

"Really?" Paul asked, frowning. "Why?"

"Because once, a long time ago," Omnathi said, "I came to the conclusion that the Cobra Jasmine Moreau was a dangerous threat to my world and my people."

He smiled. "It is good, Cobra Paul Broom, for a man to occasionally remind himself how very wrong he can be."

CHAPTER TWENTY-SEVEN

Having just seen the incredible physical strength the Drim war drug gave its user, Jody naturally assumed Plaine would shrug off the effects of Rashida's stun blast with relative ease.

She was wrong. Twenty minutes after the jolt he was still lying unconscious on the *Squire's* deck, his breathing steady but slow, his skin not responding to touch, his ears not answering Jody's increasingly frustrated orders to wake up.

Meanwhile, the clock continued to tick, and the time bomb the Drims had planted waited to be triggered.

"Why are they not here?" Rashida murmured.

"What?" Jody asked.

"The rest of the Dominion of Man forces," she said. "We've been here too long with no response from the others in the ship. Should they not be wondering what has happened to us?"

Jody frowned. She'd been so caught up in her own thoughts and concerns that she hadn't even thought about that. "Maybe they're so busy getting the ship out of here that they haven't noticed we're not where we're supposed to be."

"That seems unlikely."

"Extremely unlikely," Jody agreed grimly. "You suppose whatever the Drims set up has already been triggered?"

Before Rashida could answer, without any warning whatsoever, Plaine abruptly woke up.

"What the bloody *hell*—?" He broke off, jerking at the sight

351

of the two women crouching over him. He started to move his arms, twitched again as Jody kept both wrists pinned firmly against the deck. "What in hell are you doing?" he demanded.

"Don't you remember?" Rashida asked.

"I don't know," Plaine muttered. "I—" He broke off, his face abruptly screwing up with pain. He craned his neck to look at the seared sections of skin on his right arm, then snapped his eyes back up to Jody. "*Damn* it all," he breathed. "You're a *Cobra*?"

"I guess he remembers *some* of it, anyway," Jody said to Rashida. "Keep going, Plaine. Let's start with how you got those drug packets in your arm."

"I..." He stopped again, his eyes focusing on something past Jody's shoulder. "They grabbed me. They grabbed me and—" He looked at his arm again. "*Damn* them. What did they put in? What did I do?"

"You attacked Rashida and me," Jody said. "You don't remember that?"

"A little," Plaine said. "I thought it was a dream. And I... asked you for my tunic, right?"

"Right," Jody said. "What did you want it for?"

Plaine frowned past her shoulder again. "We were given instructions," he said slowly. "Orders. Each time we hit a patch...extra strength. Extra...but the first injection came with orders."

"You said *we*," Jody said. "Who else did they do this to?"

He closed his eyes, his forehead furrowed with concentration. "It was...Kemp. Yeah. Kemp was with me. They ambushed both of us..." He snapped his eyes open. "We're supposed to disable the ship," he breathed. "Disable the ship, kill the captain and senior officers—"

"Damn," Jody swore, jumping to her feet. "Come on, Rashida."

"Wait," Rashida said. "To what goal are you to disable the ship? What do the Trofts want?"

"Not sure," Plaine said. "Does it matter? We've got to stop Kemp before he—wait a second. There's a hearing coming up, right?"

"Right," Jody said.

"Well, that's where they'll do it," Plaine said grimly. "Get me my tunic, will you? You're going to need me."

He started to get up, but Rashida held him down with a hand against his chest. "What did you say to keep them away from us in here?" she asked. "Then tell me in which order the officers are to be murdered."

"What?" Plaine demanded, trying to push her hand aside. She didn't budge. "What difference does any of that make? Come on, we're wasting time."

"We need to know where they expect us to be and what they expect us to do before we enter again into the main ship," Rashida said firmly. "We need to know if there is a priority to the assassinations. If so, we may be able to prevent it or slow it by removing the first link of the chain."

"There's no order," Plaine said impatiently. "We're just supposed to kill as many as we can get to. And I put a pair of notes in the data stream before we came in here that I'd arrived in sickbay and you'd made it to the Women's Section."

"And no one followed up on that?" Jody asked.

"Sickbay's big enough that anyone who checked probably thought someone else was working on me," Plaine said. "And no one bothers to check on what happens in the Women's Section. Come on—get me my tunic."

"I'm thinking we'll just lock you up instead," Jody said, glancing around. One of the storage compartments and a spot-welded door should do the trick. "Safer for all of us."

"Don't be stupid," Plaine snapped, finally pushing aside Rashida's hand and getting to his feet. "You think they'll believe you? They won't. *I'm* the Dominion Marine. *I'm* the only one they might listen to."

"You're also the one who might suddenly go rogue on us," Jody pointed out.

"No," Rashida said. "The drug has been driven from his system. His mind and body are clear again."

"Except for this," Plaine said, lifting his injured arm. "I'll thank you for that if it ever stops hurting. Come on, get me my tunic."

Jody looked at Rashida. "Are you sure he's okay?"

"I am," Rashida said. "Perhaps I should get the tunic while you try to raise the alarm."

"Wait a minute," Jody said as a sudden thought occurred to her. "The data stream. You could upload all of this, alert the ship, and we could have Kemp pinned down before he knew what was happening."

"Risky," Plaine said. "If Kemp's figured out a way to tap into the stream, he'd know we were on to him and make his move while everyone was still trying to figure out what the hell I was talking about."

"How could he tap into the data stream?" Rashida asked.

"How should *I* know?" Plaine retorted. "You want to risk it? Besides, if all we do is put it in the data stream all they'll do is start asking questions, which again would tip him off and start the slaughter a little earlier. We need to find a senior officer and talk to him—*quietly*—and get him to issue some direct orders."

Jody hissed between her teeth. It seemed ridiculous that Filho and Castenello wouldn't take a threat like that seriously.

On the other hand, she, Rashida, and Plaine were under just as much suspicion as Merrick and the Caelian Cobras. Maybe Filho *would* start by simply asking questions.

At which point, he would likely be the first to die.

"Fine," she growled, heading for the pump room. "We'll do it your way. Come on, let's get your tunic."

Twenty seconds later she had the welds burned off the door. "Here," she said, handing Plaine the tunic.

"I'll be damned," he muttered, eyeing her as he pulled it on. "I suppose I should have guessed, with your mother and all. Kemp knows?"

"Of course."

"Too bad," Plaine said. "A secret weapon would have been nice to have. Come on—I think I can find us a shortcut back to the conference room."

It had been seventy-three minutes, Merrick noted. The hour Filho had promised them had now come and gone.

Typical lying Dominion humans.

But it looked like things were finally on the move. Castenello had returned in the company of a young man wearing lieutenant's insignia and a name plate that read *Meekan*. Too junior to be one of the major officers; probably someone's aide. The captain's, maybe? That might indicate that the captain was on his way.

Merrick frowned. On the other hand, if the captain had been deposed was he really the captain anymore? If not, did they even need to wait for him?

He looked across the room at Kemp. The other Cobra was

talking to his friend, Smitty, but his eyes kept flicking between the main hatch at the back of the room and the smaller, service-type door by one end of the long table. Merrick wasn't absolutely sure Kemp was an ally, but the fact that he and that Marine, Plaine, had gone off with Kjoic to steal a ship suggested that the Drims had caught them both while they were out of everyone else's sight. That had been the plan, anyway.

Too bad the Drims hadn't had the opportunity to turn everyone. Two more Cobras could have been extremely handy to their mission. And of course, it would have been wonderful for Merrick to have his own sister fighting at his side.

He smiled. Only two female Cobras in a hundred years of Cobra Worlds history, and both of them in his family. Too bad Jody wouldn't also have the distinction of being in the select group that led the way to the ultimate defeat of the Dominion of Man.

Merrick would have to bring that honor to the Moreau and Broom families by himself.

The main hatch again slid open, and Acting Captain Filho and another man wearing commander's insignia walked in, another Marine close by the commander's side. The second man's name plate was out of Merrick's view, but the fact he had a guard tagging along implied that he was First Officer Ling Garrett, who'd been deposed along with the captain.

The man turned slightly, bringing his plate into view, and Merrick keyed his telescopics. Commander Garrett, all right.

Which left only Captain Moreau himself still unaccounted for.

Merrick frowned. Captain Barrington Moreau. Another member of the Moreau/Broom family, distant in terms of light-years, not so distant in terms of blood.

Sad; but there was nothing Merrick could do about it. Family or not, Barrington Moreau had chosen the side of the Dominion. What happened now was on his own head.

Filho walked to the far side of the table and sat down beside Castenello, and the two men began a conversation that pointedly excluded both Lieutenant Meekan and Commander Garrett. Coordinating their plan for the interrogation, no doubt.

Almost time.

Merrick let his eyes drift around the room, noting the Marine guards' parrot-gun epaulets and setting his first group of target locks. His hands were still shackled behind his back, but he already had the edge of the chair back lined up with the next patch on his right arm. A quick twitch of his arm should send the drug into his bloodstream and enable him to do what had to be done.

Turning his gaze back to Filho and Castenello, he prepared his mind for combat.

A *debriefing*, Castenello had labeled the meeting in the *Dorian*'s data stream.

Barrington knew better. It would be a full-bore, flat-out interrogation. An interrogation, moreover, with the unspoken but undeniable goal of making the prisoners look guilty of whatever crimes and misdemeanors Castenello could think of to throw at them.

And, by extension, to throw at Barrington himself.

It would be painful. It might mark the beginning of the end of his career.

Or maybe not. Barrington's decisions and actions had resulted in Merrick Broom being located and rescued. The Marine and armed courier ship he'd gambled had returned safely. Above all, Merrick had gathered vital information on a hitherto unknown Troft plot against the Dominion. Castenello's patron was powerful, but against all that even he might not be able to bring Barrington down.

And if he did, Barrington would still have the satisfaction of knowing that everything he'd done here had worked out for the best.

"Captain Moreau?" a voice came from behind him.

Barrington paused and turned, his Marine guard, Sergeant Oponn, stopping as well. A Marine and a young woman were hurrying toward them. A quick check of the data stream identified them as Gunnery Sergeant Fitzgerald Plaine and the Qasaman woman, Rashida Vil.

He frowned, taking another look at the stream. Plaine had been ordered to sickbay; Vil had been sent to the Women's Section. What were they doing out and about, especially without an escort?

Oponn had obviously checked the stream and arrived at the same question. "Hold it," he ordered, stepping between the newcomers and Barrington. "Who let you two out?"

Plaine ignored the challenge. "You're in danger, Captain," he said as he and Vil continued forward. "One of the Cobras has been programmed by the Trofts back there to attack you, your officers, and your ship."

Barrington felt his throat tighten. Maybe the jury was still out on that *everything working out for the best* thing. "Who told you that?" he asked.

"No one." Plaine held up his bare right arm, revealing a line of burn marks. "They gave me the drug, too, along with the conditioning. But I've been cured."

"Really," Oponn said, holding out his hand, palm outward. "No closer—just stand right there. Captain?"

Barrington studied Plaine and Vil as the two of them came to a reluctant halt a few meters away. They looked completely sincere, which of course meant nothing at all. "Let's assume what you're saying is true," he said. "What do you expect me to do about it?"

"We want you to stop it, sir," Plaine said, sounding surprised that Barrington would even have to ask.

"Jody Broom has gone to the conference room," Vil added. "She'll try to get the other officers out without alerting Cobra Kemp that we're aware of his purpose. But we fear the officers will not obey her request."

"But you could call them out right now, sir," Plaine said. "Log an order for them to meet you out in the corridor, and we can sort through it once they're out of danger."

"I see your point," Barrington murmured. It might indeed get them out of danger.

It might also get them out in the corridor where they would be sitting ducks for Plaine himself. The Marine had freely admitted that he'd been drugged, and Barrington had only his word that he was no longer under that influence.

Certainly there'd been no signs of trouble in the data stream. Nor were there any reports of confrontation or violence.

Unfortunately, what Plaine didn't realize was that there was nothing Barrington could do about it even if he'd wanted to. Once the Enquiry Board had removed him from command position, the ability to upload orders to the data stream had also been taken away. "Your concerns are duly noted," he said. "Let's go take a look."

"Sir, I strongly suggest you reconsider," Plaine said, taking another step forward.

"One more step and I drop you," Oponn warned.

"You have a choice, Gunnery Sergeant Plaine," Barrington said as Plaine again reluctantly stopped. "You can come with us—*quietly*—or you can go back to sickbay where you belong."

He looked at Vil. "And Ms. Vil will be returned to the Women's Section as ordered."

Plaine's jaw clenched, but he nodded. "Thank you, sir. We'll come with you."

"Good," Barrington said. Turning his back on them, he resumed walking. Unwarranted, unproven, and ultimately untruthful rumors were the stuff of legend aboard Dominion warships.

Just the same...

"Sergeant?" Barrington murmured to Oponn as they headed toward the conference room.

"Sir?"

"I think it would be a good idea to raise ship-wide Marine alert status," Barrington said. "Just in case."

"I'll make the recommendation, sir," Oponn said. "Unfortunately, there's no guarantee the colonel will accept it."

"Especially because he'll assume the request is coming from me?"

Out of the corner of his eye he saw Oponn's lip twitch. "Yes, sir. Commander Castenello made it clear...you understand, sir."

"I do," Barrington said. "But if there's a problem, we need to sound the alarm."

"Yes, sir," Oponn said. "Upgrade request is in the stream."

Barrington nodded. "Thank you."

"Yes, sir." Oponn hesitated. "And thank you, sir, for being willing to risk all to bring back one of our own."

Barrington glanced over his shoulder at Plaine and Vil. "You're welcome, Sergeant. Let's hope we don't live to regret it."

Plaine had assured Jody that the service passageway would be deserted, with zero chance of running into anyone along the way. She'd thanked him and headed in, firmly expecting he would be wrong.

Which made her unhindered arrival at the conference room a few minutes later both surprising and anticlimactic. Apparently, data stream maintenance and personnel information was *very* detailed.

Now came the tricky part. Bracing herself, she tapped the hatch release.

The room was filling up nicely, she saw as she stepped inside. Acting Captain Filho and Commander Castenello had returned, and had brought another pair of officers with them. One of them was Lieutenant Meekan, the officer Jody had met briefly back on Qasama; the other's name plate said *Garrett*. Garrett had a Marine standing behind him, apparently a guard, and there were eight other Marines flanking the main hatchway in the back and positioned along the side walls. Across the table from the Dominion officers, their backs to the main entrance, were Merrick, Kemp, and Smitty, sitting right where Jody had left them.

Kemp, Jody noted, was half turned in his chair, either keeping watch on the Marines at the back of the room or watching for Captain Moreau to make his grand entrance, and Jody could see that his wrists were shackled behind his back and the back of his chair. Smitty and Merrick, no doubt, were under similar restraints.

A reasonable precaution. But not nearly as secure as Filho probably thought. With Kemp's hands free, he could curl his fingertip lasers around and cut straight through the metal and plastic binding his wrists. In a couple of seconds, maybe less, he would be free.

Which meant if Captain Moreau came in before Jody could make her move, he was dead. Hopefully, Plaine and Rashida could keep him away long enough.

Not that Jody's own entrance wasn't grand in its own way. All eyes turned to her as she walked in, including Kemp's. "Hello, everyone," she greeted the room casually as the hatch closed behind her. "I hope I'm not late."

"What are you doing here?" Castenello demanded.

"I'm here for the hearings," she said, watching Kemp as she headed toward the table. Throughout the voyage from Qasama, she'd seen a hint of something cross his face every time she came into his presence. She wasn't ready to put any kind of label on the expression, or to speculate as to whether there were any particular emotions behind it, except to mark it as a sign of recognition and appreciation.

Only now, here in the *Dorian*'s conference room, there was nothing. Kemp had clearly noted her arrival, but there was no spark, not of affection, friendship, or anything else.

More ominously, his expression reminded her of the way he'd been when she first met him on Caelian. His face, his eyes, and his body language were those of a man who knew that death was all around him. A man fully prepared to meet that death head-on, and deliver some of his own.

Jody hadn't wanted to believe Plaine's story that Kemp had been turned. Now, down deep, she knew he'd been right.

"What are you doing?" Filho asked, sounding more confused than angry. "Who ordered you here?"

"No one," Jody said. She shifted her eyes to Smitty, got the spark of recognition that she hadn't gotten from Kemp. At least he seemed okay. She looked at Merrick.

And felt her foot suddenly falter.

There was no friendly recognition from her brother. In fact, he had much the same expression as Kemp.

She recovered her pace and continued across the room, keying her infrareds. Plaine had had the drug's telltale heightened facial heat. Kemp also had it.

So did Merrick.

A hard knot twisted into her stomach. Of course Merrick had been drugged. He'd been on the planet for weeks. Of course the Drims would have made sure to drug him before sending him back. How in the Worlds had she not seen that coming?

Because she hadn't wanted to. Because she was so relieved to get her brother back that some core part of her had refused to accept the possibility that the man she'd rescued wasn't the man she'd come here to find.

And with that, suddenly everything had changed. She'd come to the conference room to rescue the Dominion officers, knowing that if she had to hurt Kemp, she would have to brace herself and do it.

Kemp was one of the closest friends she'd ever had. But he was just a close friend.

Merrick was her brother.

Family had always been the most important thing to Jody. Family was why she'd defied the Dominion back on Aventine. Family was why she'd come on this mission, risking trouble with not just the Dominion, but also with the Qasamans and her own people. Family was why she'd become a Cobra. Merrick's life, Merrick's safety, *had* to be her first priority.

Only he couldn't be. For once, he couldn't be. There was more at stake here than one single person. *Any* single person.

She continued on, her feet running on autopilot, trying to think. Filho and Castenello, as the most senior officers present, would probably be the assassins' secondary targets after Captain Moreau. The Marines lined up against the walls seemed alert enough, and Jody had already seen how effective their laser epaulets could be, especially in close quarters. But like the ones she'd encountered on Caelian these seemed a little too confident in their superiority over Cobra technology. Behind the Cobras, between the table and the main entrance—and the bulk of the Marine force—were twelve additional chairs lined up in two rows of six each, apparently there to accommodate visitors or observers. They looked to be the same type as the ones at the table, with a full 360-degree swivel but also set on slender columns bolted to the deck. They were big enough to crouch behind, and a laser burst to the central column should cut them loose, but Jody guessed they would be of only minimal use for either defense or attack.

Which left the table everyone was currently grouped around. It was solid-looking, more so than the chairs surrounding it. Still, the *Dorian* was a warship, and she'd been aboard enough spacecraft to know that weight and mass were important considerations. That suggested the table was probably no stronger or heavier than it had to be to support papers, small electronics, and people's elbows. The fact that it was supported by a single curved pillar anchoring its center to the deck also suggested it was quite light, possibly to the point of being flimsy. Again, no use as a shield against laser fire.

In theory, she could get close enough to use her sonic or her stunner and end this before it even began. But Kemp and Merrick both knew she was a Cobra. Would they let her get in range, even if they didn't know she knew what had happened to them?

Or maybe they *did* know. Maybe they could read it in her face, the same way she could read the treason in theirs.

But she had to try. A few more steps...

At the rear of the room the hatch abruptly opened. Jody got a glimpse of a Marine and a Dominion officer outside—

And suddenly, it all went to hell.

Kemp and Merrick leaped out of their seats, turning their backs to each other and in perfect coordination firing brief bursts of antiarmor laser at each other's shackles. Jody charged toward the table, firing her sonic at them as their hands came free, hoping she could at least slow them down.

But she was either still too far away or the Drim drug gave them extra protection against all sorts of attacks. Both men shrugged off the effects as if nothing had happened and continued their spins, Merrick turning toward the rear hatch, Kemp turning toward the table where Filho and Castenello were trying to slide sideways out of their seats.

But the officers' reaction was too little too late. Kemp raised his fingertip lasers—

Jody braked to a halt between the officers, dropping into a crouch and shoving both of them violently to the sides out of Kemp's sight and line of fire.

And as she grabbed the edge of the table with both hands, the room erupted into chaos.

Laser fire was everywhere: Kemp and Merrick firing at the Marines, both at their epaulets and at the men themselves; the Marines returning fire; the Cobras dodging and ducking and rolling around and through the lines of seats; the Marines crouching or ducking in place; the Cobras systematically dropping the Dominion forces to the deck; the Marines grimly standing their ground, seemingly refusing to accept that two men could be doing this to them.

It was awesome and terrible at the same time. But Jody didn't have time to be either amazed or repulsed. She twisted her left leg up out of her crouch and sent a quick horizontal slash of laser fire across the table's support column. The column splintered, dropping the weight of the table into her hands. Shifting her leg back around into a bracing position behind her, she shoved the table with all her strength toward Kemp and Merrick.

The intensity of the laser fire might have faltered as the Cobras reacted to this new attack. Jody couldn't tell, and she didn't have time for further assessment. Castenello and Filho had scrambled halfway back to their feet; reaching behind her, Jody grabbed Filho by the collar, gave Castenello a shove in his back toward the side hatch she'd come through barely two minutes ago, and got the group moving.

Castenello was still a couple of meters away from the hatch when it unexpectedly slid open.

Jody snapped her hands up into firing position. But it was only Rashida. "Hurry!" the Qasaman called urgently.

"Go!" Jody said, giving Castenello another shove and glancing behind her to confirm that the other officers were following. If Kemp and Merrick finished off the Marines before they could get out of the room . . .

The battle was still raging when the last of the four officers made it through and the hatch slid shut behind them. Meekan, the last in line, did something to it and a *locked* logo lit up.

"This way," Rashida said, starting down the service corridor.

"Like hell," Castenello growled, braking to a halt. "Who the hell do you think—?"

"Move it," Jody snapped, giving him another shove.

"More Marines have been summoned," Rashida added. "Captain Moreau will also meet us."

The route Rashida led them along was longer and more twisty than the path Jody had taken earlier. But when they finally emerged into some kind of workshop they indeed found four Marines waiting for them. Two were standing guard, facing the workshop's main hatch, while the other two were hurriedly climbing into battle suits they'd obviously grabbed along the way. "Where's the captain?" Filho asked as Meekan again sealed the service corridor hatch behind them.

"Captain Moreau decided to shelter in an electrical room thirty meters from the conference room, sir," one of the Marines said. "He was hoping to see what the intruders did if they got out."

"What they'll do is hunt him down and kill him," Jody bit out. "Didn't you try to stop him?"

"We weren't with him, Ma'am."

"Never mind Moreau," Castenello said, pulling a small cylinder from his belt.

"The man with the captain is Sergeant Oponn, sir," the Marine said.

Castenello nodded and clicked a switch. "Senior Commander Castenello for Colonel Mwando."

"Mwando, sir," a voice came back promptly. "Are you and Acting Captain Filho secure?"

"For the moment," Castenello said, throwing a glower at Jody. "Report."

"The two intruders seem to have split up," Mwando said. "They're heading—"

"Hold it," Castenello interrupted. "Splitting *up*? Why haven't they been contained in the conference room?"

"Because they got out before my reinforcements could reach them."

"They stopped *eight* Marines?"

"They stopped nine, sir," Mwando said tartly. "Four are dead, the other five unconscious and on their way to sickbay now. The intruders also left behind the third prisoner, Cobra Smith."

Jody looked at Rashida. Like Jody and Kemp, Rashida and Smitty had become close over the past few weeks. "Is Cobra Smith all right?" she called toward the comm.

"Quiet," Castenello growled, sending her a warning glare.

"Cobra Smith has a severe laser wound in his left lung," Mwando said. "We have him in custody."

Rashida's face had gone rigid. "Why isn't he in sickbay?" Jody asked.

"He's in custody in sickbay," Castenello snapped. "One more word and you'll be with him. Colonel, you said the intruders had split up?"

"Yes, sir. They disabled the security cameras in the conference room, and when they left they went in opposite directions, destroying the personnel sensors as they went."

"You're tracking them?"

"We're trying, sir," Mwando said. "They're moving fast, using a mix of regular passageways and service corridors, and burning the sensors as they go. We have a squad in pursuit of each, but they also appear to be occasionally doubling back to areas that they've blacked out, which throws us off the mark."

"I assume you've locked down CoNCH, engineering, and weapons?"

"Yes, sir," Mwando said. "But..."

"But what?" Castenello demanded. "Are they locked down, or aren't they?"

"They're locked down against any normal threat," Mwando said reluctantly. "But these are Cobras. I don't know if—"

"Cobras are hundred-year-old technology," Castenello snapped. "*Ancient,* Colonel. They might was well be carrying flintlocks."

"It's not quite that easy, Commander," Mwando said. "On their way out of the conference room they stripped two of the unconscious Marines of their tunics."

Castenello shot an unreadable look at Jody. "The *hell?*"

"Yes, sir," Mwando said. "Even if my squads find them, they may not be able to do much."

"Understood," Castenello said between clenched teeth. "All right. Tell me how the rest of your men are deployed."

Jody stepped closer to Rashida as the conversation switched to shipboard numbers and equipment specs. "Any idea what the deal is with the tunics?" she murmured.

Rashida shook her head silently. Her face was still rigid.

"The deal is that it's trouble," a new voice came quietly from over Jody's shoulder.

She turned to see that Meekan had come up behind them. "How bad?"

"Very," Meekan said. "Marine tunics include an IFF system that blocks other Marines' ability to autolock and autofire. They can still lock and fire manually, but it's slower and less precise."

A shiver ran up Jody's back. "And Cobras are very good at dodging."

"Yes, we've noticed," Meekan said. "Even worse is that we only have fifty Marines aboard." He hissed between his teeth. "Correction: forty-one functional Marines."

"*Fifty?*" Jody echoed, frowning. "We had way more than that on Aventine."

"That's because Captain Lij Tulu had most of our contingent as well as the ones from the *Megalith*," Meekan said grimly. "Commodore Santores thought a larger force might be needed if the Cobra Worlds continued being uncooperative."

"Great," Jody muttered. "How did they figure out the trick with the tunics?"

"Most likely from Gunnery Sergeant Plaine," Rashida murmured.

"Or from the Trofts," Meekan said. "They figured it out a long time ago, but since the IFF requires the wearer to be running a human body temperature and to have a carotid pulse that comes from a four-chamber heart there wasn't much they could do with the information."

"Terrific," Jody said. "So how are we going to—"

"Listen," Rashida cut in. Her eyes were focused on infinity, her mouth half open. "The hyperdrive. It just went off."

"Are you sure?" Jody asked.

And suddenly, the room was filled with the harsh blare of an alarm. "What the—?" Castenello broke off as he gazed into space. "Damn. *Damn.*"

"What is it?" Jody asked, her heart thudding suddenly in her ears.

"We've hit a flicker net," Meekan snarled. "The Trofts laid a trap for us.

"And we walked right into it."

CHAPTER TWENTY-EIGHT

The news scrolled past on the data stream, sending a chill through Barrington's blood.

A flicker net. The Trofts had set up a flicker net.

No wonder they hadn't attacked over the planet, or even raised any kind of threat. Why risk local damage from an orbital battle when they had a net waiting to gather in their prey?

And the *Dorian* had flown straight into it.

His thoughts bounced back to his earlier conversation with Garrett, where his first officer had confidently asserted that the Trofts would never suspect a Dominion ship coming from Qasama. But just as someone had anticipated the Aventine-to-Qasama route and set up the net that had earlier snared the courier ship *Hermes*, so to the Drim'hco'plai had clearly expected a Qasama-to-Muninn flight, as well.

Only how had the *Dorian* failed to hit it on the way into the system? Barrington had set his course directly from Qasama to Jody Broom's coordinates, and Filho had presumably simply reversed the course for their departure. Deviating from a known route through unmapped space was always time-consuming and sometimes dangerous, and the acting captain would have wanted to return to Qasama and Commodore Santores as quickly as possible. Had the Drim'hco'plai thrown the net together in the brief window between the *Dorian*'s two passages through this area?

Or had the net been deliberately inactive during the *Dorian*'s approach? Did the Drim'hco'plai not care who came into the Muninn system, but only who left it?

Did they want Merrick Broom back *that* badly?

But there was no time to wonder about that now. Barrington's ship was dead in space, and the only way it was going to survive was if it got undead, and fast.

Updates were flowing across the stream, almost too fast for him to read. There were four major Troft warships out there, arrayed in the standard bent-square formation about eight hundred klicks out. So far they hadn't opened fire, but the *Dorian's* sensors showed their laser capacitors powering up.

And thanks to Castenello's grand inquisition plan, not a single one of the command officers was currently in CoNCH.

That needed to change, and fast. "Sergeant, check the passageway," he ordered Oponn.

"It's clear, sir," Oponn said, his eyes moving as he checked the data stream.

"No; *look* in the passageway," Barrington told him. "I don't trust the data stream on security matters anymore."

Oponn shot a look at Plaine. "Yes, sir." He stepped to the hatchway of the electrical room they'd sheltered in, opened it and glanced both ways down the passageway. "Clear, sir."

"Good," Barrington said, starting toward him. "Let's go."

"Just a minute, Captain," Plaine said, stepping in front of him and holding up a hand. "Where exactly are we going?"

"Where do you think?" Barrington countered. "CoNCH."

"Not a good idea, sir," Plaine said. "If the Cobras are lying in wait along our route you'll be a sitting duck."

"Would you rather I wait here until the Trofts destroy the ship?"

"No, sir," Plaine said. "But you should at least collect a bigger Marine escort than just Oponn and me."

"If you'd checked the stream, you'd know they're being deployed at CoNCH, engineering, and weapons," Barrington said, frowning as a sudden ominous thought struck him. "What makes you think they'd be lying in wait for me?"

"I told you, sir, I was drugged like they were," Plaine said. "Our orders were to decapitate the command structure in preparation for this attack."

"Only you were cured."

"You're still alive, aren't you?" Plaine retorted.

"Yes, about that," Barrington said, eyeing him closely. "It occurs to me that you don't need to kill the senior officers if you can simply neutralize them. By, say, keeping them locked out of CoNCH."

Plaine's eyes narrowed. "I already told you—"

"Someone's coming," Oponn muttered suddenly.

Barrington checked the data stream. No personnel were indicated in their area. "Are you sure?"

"I hear footsteps," Oponn said, tapping the control to close the hatch. "Coming this way."

Barrington felt his stomach tighten. So the *Dorian*'s security system was well and truly fouled. "Stay quiet," he murmured. "If we're lucky, they'll pass us by."

"And if they don't?" Plaine asked.

Barrington stared at the closed hatch. "Then here is where we make our stand."

"You sure you know where you're going?" Jody murmured as she and Rashida hurried down the deserted corridor behind Lieutenant Meekan.

"I'm sure." Meekan glanced over his shoulder. "If you'd rather go with Filho and Castenello, you can probably still catch up with them."

"Thanks, but we'll stay with you," Jody growled. "I was just asking—"

"It's the only one in the area," Meekan interrupted tersely. "They have to be here." Abruptly, he stopped in front of a hatchway. "Stay behind me."

"Right." Jody stepped partially behind Meekan and raised her hands into firing position. Even if Meekan was right, they could still be too late. Meekan tapped the release and the hatch slid open—

Plaine and another Marine were standing shoulder to shoulder in front of them, completely blocking the opening. Behind them, alive and well, was Captain Moreau.

Jody exhaled a relieved *huff.* "Captain," Meekan said briskly. He was trying to be casually courteous, Jody could tell, but the relief in his voice was unmistakable. "Are you all right, sir?"

"So far, Lieutenant," the captain said, also clearly relieved. "Come in. Quickly."

A moment later all six of them were inside. "All right, what have we got?" the captain asked. "Where are Filho and Castenello?"

"They headed to CoNCH, sir," Meekan said. "Along with all the Marines Colonel Mwando could spare for escort duty."

"Which probably isn't a lot," Moreau said. He scowled into space, probably checking the *Dorian's* data stream. "Looks like Colonel Mwando took your suggestion earlier, Sergeant, about raising the Marines' alert status. Good."

"What does that mean?" Jody asked.

"It means they were already gathering at the *Dorian's* critical areas when this thing went down," Plaine said, "with twenty percent of them already in combat armor. In theory, that should keep Broom and Kemp out of CoNCH, weapons, and engineering."

Jody nodded, suppressing a grimace. Every time they talked about her brother that way it was like an extra twist of the knife in her gut.

"But surely Kemp and Merrick know those places will be guarded," Rashida spoke up. "Why then would they go there?"

"The drug programming," Plaine said. "Maybe hubris. Maybe both."

"Plus Broom's never seen Dominion Marines in action," Meekan said. "He has no idea what he'll be up against."

"No, but Kemp has," Jody said, frowning. Plaine had a reasonable point. Still, while the Drim war drug might make them crazy focused, it presumably didn't make them stupid.

Or did it? Would it drive Merrick into a suicidal action simply because he couldn't think for himself anymore?

"Merrick may have, as well," Rashida said. "I assume, Gunnery Sergeant Plaine, that you fought somewhat against the Trofts while you were securing a ship for his Troft ally?"

"Yeah, a little," Plaine conceded. "I forgot about that. So I guess we're back to programming and hubris."

"It still doesn't make sense for them to just throw their lives away," Jody said.

"They may not need to do that," Meekan said. "Just keeping the senior officers out of CoNCH may be enough for their purposes."

"Along with the immediate goal of sowing confusion," Moreau said. "They've managed to knock out half the internal security sensors, which means as long as they stick to that side of the ship we have no idea where they are. Until and unless they launch an attack, we've been forced onto the defensive."

"While meanwhile the Trofts out there blast the *Dorian* to rubble," Meekan said grimly. "Sir?"

"I see it," Captain Moreau growled. "All right, conversation's over. Whatever their game is, we're not playing."

"What's the matter?" Jody asked.

"Two of the Troft ships have moved closer and opened fire," Plaine told her grimly. "Extreme range, no real damage, probably just probing our point defenses. But the battle's definitely started."

Jody curled her hands into fists. And her own brother was the traitor who was making it happen. "How can we help?"

"Talking your brother down would be a good start," Meekan said. "Other than that, just stay out of the way."

"Actually, there is something," Captain Moreau said. "That antiarmor laser of yours. Is it strong enough to cut through a bulkhead this thick?" He tapped the side wall.

"Probably," Jody said, frowning. With the hatch right there in front of them, why would he need her to cut through the side wall?

Meekan was obviously wondering the same thing. "I presume you don't mean *this* particular bulkhead, sir?"

"No," Captain Moreau said. He started to reach a finger in front of him, then paused. "No," he said. "No. If they've—no. All right, here's my thought. There are only two access points to CoNCH, both of which are heavily armored and presumably by now heavily defended."

"There's a double Marine guard at both entrances, sir," Oponn confirmed.

"*If* we can trust the data stream," the captain countered. "I'm not sure I do anymore. The point is there's a back door no one's thought of."

"Just a moment, sir," Meekan interrupted. "Before you say any more—" he turned a suddenly intense look on Plaine "—I think we should figure out how to isolate Plaine from the data stream. Or else isolate him from us."

"What?" Jody asked. "Why?"

"Because as the captain said, the data stream's been compromised," Meekan said. He was standing at Plaine's left side now, almost pressed up against the Marine's shoulder. The exact spot, Jody noticed suddenly, where Plaine's epaulets could bring the least amount of firepower to bear on him. "Half the ship's lost security sensors, and Plaine's the only one of the Muninn group who had access."

There was a heartbeat of brittle silence. "I didn't do anything to the data stream, sir," Plaine said. "I'm not working with Broom and Kemp."

"But you *were*," Meekan said. "You admitted that."

"You also admitted you got into the stream and tweaked your orders," Oponn added.

"He did *that*?" Meekan asked, his eyes narrowing.

"It was while he was still drugged," Jody said firmly. "He's cured now."

"Is he?" Meekan countered. "We only have your word for that." His eyes flicked to Rashida. "Rather, we only have *her* word. She's Qasaman. Who knows what special instructions Omnathi might have given her before you left?"

"What about it, Ms. Vil?" the captain asked. "Any secrets you want to disclose?"

Jody held her breath. But Rashida merely shook her head. "No. But I assure you he *is* cured."

Meekan opened his mouth—"I don't understand the problem," Jody jumped in. "Can't you just lock out his access or something?"

"I don't have the authority to log orders like that anymore," Captain Moreau said. "Neither does anyone else here."

"Then call Filho or Castenello," Jody suggested. "Have one of *them* do it."

"Risky," Plaine said before the captain could answer. "If their escort has them running stealth, a comm signal could give away their position." He looked at Captain Moreau. "If you want me to go away, sir, I will."

"Did you do anything else while you were drugged?" the captain asked.

"Nothing I remember."

"But you said it was all like a dream," Rashida reminded him. "Has anything else come back?"

"No, just...images. One of the Trofts cackling about how this was the perfect...something...double the money for sure. And your brother's Troft friend was cackling right along with him."

"*What* was perfect?" Captain Moreau asked.

"I don't remember, sir," Plaine said through clenched teeth. "*Damn* them all." He took a deep breath. "Fine. You don't trust me. I don't trust me, either. So let's do this."

He took a step away from Meekan and took off his tunic.

"There," he said, handing it to Rashida. "You can all keep an eye on the stream. If something goes funny, and you think I'm doing it, you can shoot me." He waved a hand. "Now can we get this on the road before the Trofts get tired of pinpricks and start unloading the heavy stuff?"

"Lieutenant?" Captain Moreau invited.

Meekan still didn't look happy, but he nodded. "Probably as good as we're going to get, sir."

"So where's this back door?" Plaine asked.

Moreau pursed his lips. "From the flying bridge."

"The *what*?" Plaine asked. He frowned into space, his eyes twitching back and forth. "I'll be damned. And it's got its own *elevator*?"

"Which only runs between there and CoNCH," Meekan said, frowning. "And there's the Three-Twenty-Six water tank behind it. How would anyone get access?"

"Through the water tank," Moreau said. "The containment bulkheads are thick, but not especially armored. All a Cobra would have to do is cut through and let the water drain out. One more bulkhead to cut into the flying bridge, and they'd have full access."

"With no more than a couple of Marines inside CoNCH ready to stop them," Meekan said. "Sergeant, upload an alert to Colonel Mwando."

"Yes, sir." Oponn stared into space ... "Uploaded and red-marked. But if he's focused on escort duty he might not notice it fast enough."

"That's why we're going there ourselves," the captain said. "If the route's been compromised, we can come in right behind them. If it hasn't, it's our way into CoNCH. Lieutenant, can you plot us a good route?"

"Got it now, sir," Meekan said.

"Plaine, you'll take point," the captain ordered. "Ms. Broom, you're with him." He eyed her closely. "If we run into your brother or Cobra Kemp...?"

"I'll do whatever's necessary to stop them," Jody said firmly.

"I'll count on that," he said. "Lieutenant Meekan, behind them to give directions. Ms. Vil and I are behind you; Sergeant Oponn, you're on rearguard. Questions? Let's go."

A minute later they were moving down the corridor. Jody

keyed up her audios, trying to block out the sounds of their own footsteps and breathing. If Kemp or Merrick was moving around out there, she might have a chance of hearing them before they came into view.

"Thanks for standing up for me," Plaine's whisper came to her. "Meekan was ready to bounce me, and we need all the people we can get."

"No problem," she murmured back, trying to adjust her volume so that Plaine could hear and Meekan couldn't. "Just don't prove me wrong."

"I won't," he whispered back. "Just *you* be ready to take down your brother when the time comes."

Jody felt her throat tighten. "It might not come to that," she said.

"It will," Plaine said, and even in his whisper she could hear the dark certainty. "Trust me. It will."

It had been a long, complicated journey, and Merrick's servos had been pushed to the limit as he ran, jumped, crawled, or swung through passageways, service corridors, and ventilation shafts. But finally, he'd arrived.

As anticipated, the Dominion Marines had already reached the engineering strong point. There was a double wall of them, in fact: half of them armored, the other half crouching behind portable laser shields with only their heads and repeater-gun laser epaulets showing. They were facing down the corridor that led to the armored door behind them, no doubt feeling secure in the knowledge that they would have all the time they needed to gun down any intruder who came around that corner.

Unfortunately for them, Merrick had no intention of running that whole gauntlet. He was already halfway toward them, in fact, hanging just inside the cargo elevator in the passageway's side wall.

All the elevators near the *Dorian*'s strong points had been frozen the minute he and Kemp had launched their attack in the conference room, of course, and anyone who wanted to ride one needed a special clearance code. But an open shaft with a few handholds along the side were all a Cobra needed.

Merrick peered through the small gap he'd made by prying the elevator door open a couple of centimeters, feeling a twist of guilt deep in his soul. He and Kemp should have done better in the conference room. They'd eliminated all the Marines just fine, which had of course been the first step. But they should have been able to kill at least one of the senior officers afterward. That was their job, and it should have been easy.

Only it hadn't been. Captain Moreau had been yanked out barely half a meter into the room by his Marine guard, while Merrick's own sister had hustled the others to safety.

He scowled to himself. The masters who'd set this up hadn't known about Jody. How could they have? But that was no excuse. *He'd* known who and what she was. He should have compensated. He'd failed the masters, and the masters would be angry.

Worse, they would be disappointed.

But he could fix it. He *would* fix it. Starting right now.

He peered through the gap again. About five meters in front of the Marines and their door were a pair of wide air-flow gratings, one in the ceiling and one in the deck. From his angle he couldn't see through either, but he'd passed many similar grates along the way and knew they simply led up and down to the next deck in line, instead of into ducts or shafts. Exactly what he needed.

The warmth in his blood was starting to fade. Easing the door closed again, he slapped the next patch down along his right arm. There were only four left, but that should be enough.

The elevator shaft was dark, with only bits of illumination seeping in from above and below him. Keying in his light-amps, he gave the door a quick examination. The panel itself was thick and heavy-duty, with a grillwork of support bars crisscrossing the center. The door ran between a pair of horizontal upper/lower tracks, with the driving mechanism a simple wheel-and-bar system. A short burst from his antiarmor laser to sever the bar, another to soften and deform the lower track, and he should be good to go.

The heat was flowing back into his muscles. Not that a Cobra really needed any extra strength, but the sense of unity that came with the warmth was both comforting and invigorating. He waited until the warmth reached its peak and plateaued out...

Resettling his grip on the door's support frame, he targeted the bar and the track and triggered his antiarmor laser.

His nanocomputer reacted instantly, swinging his leg up and bending him at the waist as the servos brought the laser into firing position. Merrick squeezed his eyes shut—no sense going into battle with a purple afterimage glob in front of him—as the laser blasted through the bar. He triggered the laser again, felt his leg drop and then swing sideways as the servos lined up the weapon with the section of track he'd targeted. Swinging his torso around his handhold, he slammed his shoulder into the door, knocking it off its damaged tracks into the corridor and sending him flying out right behind it. Even as the door wobbled and started to fall, he caught the grillwork, lifted it upright again in front of him, and charged.

From the sudden shouts and flickers of reflected light bouncing around the walls and ceiling, it was clear the Marines had opened fire. But the door was heavy and thick, and the Dominion weapons were clearly mostly designed for use against light body armor. He could feel heat starting to come through the metal, but they surely knew he would be on top of them long before their lasers cut all the way through.

If, that is, he had ever intended to go that far.

He angled the top of the door slightly forward, bringing the ceiling grate into view. Four quick target locks on the corner fasteners...

And then he was in position. Giving the door a massive shove toward the Marines, he fired his fingertip lasers up at the grating and jumped. There were four flashes of light—four sizzlings of vaporized metal—he hit the grating with the palms of his hands—

The now-freed grating sailed off its supports and out of his way. He shot through the opening, completed a short arc that landed him on the deck almost directly above the Marines.

And now, with everyone on the deck below pinned down, and anyone else in his general vicinity presumably rushing down to assist in the strong point's defense, he could get to the real reason he was here.

It took three tries to get the right kind of twitch to access the *Dorian*'s data stream. He still didn't know how the masters had worked this trick, or what they'd had to implant into his eyes or skin, but it had been an incredibly valuable tool. The proper power cable...there it was, tucked in with a dozen other thick conduits. A quick but careful blast from his fingertip lasers to burn off the insulation, followed by a pair of blasts from his arcthrower, and the job was done.

Seconds later he was racing down a side corridor, getting as far away as he could from the Marines and the strong point. The job was done, and by the time they untangled themselves from the elevator door he'd thrown at them, he'd be long gone.

Best of all, they would be shaken by what had just happened. And for possibly the first time in their lives they would be afraid. A single Cobra had outmaneuvered them and delivered a crippling blow to their ship.

And he *might* be back. They had no way of knowing his plan, or of tracking his movements, and that uncertainty alone would keep them close to engineering. Perhaps thinning the numbers by the door as they considered the strong point's other possible vulnerabilities, perhaps drawing off the roving patrols to bolster their defenses.

Merrick smiled tightly to himself. They would stay, or they would shuffle themselves, and he would go. And by the time they learned the truth it would be too late to do anything.

The masters would be pleased.

CHAPTER TWENTY-NINE

And in a single heartbeat, it all went from critical to catastrophic.

"What the *hell*?" Meekan bit out. "Captain?"

"I see it," Barrington said, skimming the sudden flow of data stream reports.

"What is it?" Jody asked.

"The hyperdrive's been scrambled," Barrington told her grimly. "A burst of high-voltage current through one of the control lines. Not the end of the world," he hastened to add as her eyes widened. "The breakers caught the surge before it damaged anything."

"But it set the whole recalibration procedure back to zero," Meekan said. "Which means your brother just bought the Trofts another twelve minutes to tear the *Dorian* apart."

"Or it was Kemp," Barrington added at the sudden pain in Jody's face.

"Thanks, but that doesn't really help," Jody said. She looked uncertainly up at the ceiling. "When do you think they'll start the main attack?"

"Seems to me like they're already giving it a good shot," Meekan said bitterly.

"I mean the Trofts," Jody said. "When are they going to start really hitting us?"

Barrington frowned. Come to think of it, that was a damn good question.

Three of the four Troft ships were still hanging back out of

379

combat range. The fourth continued to ease toward the *Dorian* and blast away from extreme range. But it was being strangely tentative, as if it was afraid that moving closer would open it up to sudden and violent destruction.

Maybe the light probe was a calculated effort to learn the *Dorian*'s capabilities. The Drim'hco'plai demesne was a long way from any of the battle fronts, and they might not trust whatever they'd been told by allies or potential allies.

Or maybe this was simply the overture to a more sophisticated attack. Any damage they could inflict on the starboard sensors would weaken the *Dorian*'s defenses on that side, opening the ship up to a concentrated assault. Even if the sensor destruction cost them one of their ships it might be worth it to—

Barrington's brain froze in mid-thought. The *starboard* side?

Quickly, he skimmed back through the data stream. There it was: the particular half of the ship that the Cobras had knocked out of the internal security sensor system.

The starboard side.

"Sir?" Meekan said urgently.

"Just a minute," Barrington said, distantly aware that he had stopped in the middle of the passageway with the rest of the group now gathered around him. "Lieutenant, remember the net that took the *Hermes*?"

"On our way to Qasama?" Meekan said. "Of course."

"Do you remember how relatively little damage the *Hermes* took?" Barrington asked. "In fact, at the time I argued that point with Commander Castenello. The Trofts didn't want to destroy the *Hermes* then, and they don't seem to want to destroy us now."

"They want the ship," Meekan said with a touch of impatience. "Yes, sir, I already figured that out—"

"Not the ship, Lieutenant," Barrington cut him off. "They want *us*. The officers and crew." He leveled a finger at Plaine. "They want to turn us into him, and send us home."

Meekan's eyes widened. "You mean as—?" he shot a look at Plaine. "But we're months away from the Dominion. Would the drugs and hypnotic programming even last that long?"

"I don't know," Barrington said grimly. "Maybe they don't, either. Maybe we're their field test."

Meekan swore under his breath. "Well, they can't take us from the outside," he said. "Not without a huge amount of damage. So they have to get in somehow."

"On the side of the ship where we're now half blind, inside *and* out," Barrington said. "If you were trying to invade the *Dorian*, where would you come in?"

Meekan's eyes defocused. "The mid-aft cargo bay," he said. "Anywhere else you could only bring in small boats and small boarding parties. I'd want a beachhead of at least a hundred or more, and mid-aft is the only bay where you could bring in that many at once."

"We should alert the Marines, sir," Plaine said. "Get every available man converging on the cargo bay."

Barrington gazed at the data stream. "We can't risk it," he said reluctantly. "Not yet. All we've got is speculation, while Mwando has actual attacks. He can't and shouldn't pull men from their positions for that."

"So let's get him some proof," Jody said. "Let Plaine and Rashida and me go to the cargo bay and see if we've got incoming Trofts."

"Or see if Broom and Kemp are waiting for them," Plaine said grimly.

"Oh," Jody said more soberly. "Well... it's still a good idea."

"Agreed," Barrington said. "But we're all going, not just you three."

Meekan drew himself up. "Sir—"

"No arguments, Lieutenant," Barrington said. "We don't have time; and besides, I'll be safer with two Marines and a Cobra than I will with Sergeant Oponn alone."

Meekan opened his mouth, apparently got a closer look at Barrington's expression—"Yes, sir. Same marching order?"

"Yes," Barrington said, pointing toward the cross-corridor that would take them toward the mid-starboard area. "And double-time it. The Cobras bought the Trofts twelve minutes. That's our window, too."

"You have a plan, sir?" Meekan asked as they headed off.

"I have," Barrington said. "Let's see how fast we can put it together."

Merrick had expected Kemp to be waiting at the rendezvous point when he arrived. But the Caelian Cobra was nowhere to be seen. Merrick checked the *Dorian*'s data stream, but could find no report of sudden trouble at CoNCH or weapons. Maybe Kemp had found another way to generate confusion and distraction.

Or maybe he'd just gotten lost. On a ship this size that was always a possibility, especially since Kemp didn't have access to the data stream and deck plans like Merrick did.

This part of the ship was very quiet. He keyed his audios, just to see if there was anything at all going on. The alarms had long since shut off, and there was nothing but the hum of circulating fans and the occasional clank or rumble or grunt of distant machinery.

And, of course, the not-so-distant crack and sizzle of Troft lasers scouring the sensors off the *Dorian*'s starboard hull.

Merrick half turned to look behind him. Even in the couple of minutes since he'd arrived the sizzling had faded a little. Hopefully, that was an indication that the real attack was about to begin.

He hoped so. The Marine tunic he'd been ordered to wear wasn't particularly heavy, but the sleeves were more confining than he'd expected, and all his upper body movements felt slow and somewhat awkward.

He frowned. Were those footsteps in the distance?

He keyed his audios up another notch. Definitely footsteps. More than one set, too—at least two, possibly more.

And they were definitely coming this way.

He looked around. Behind him was the big cargo hatch; sealed, no chance he was hearing the boarding Trofts through all that metal. To his left and right were wide corridors designed to handle the grav-lift lorries that would normally haul incoming cargo to their designated holds. He could see a good fifty meters along each, but there were a couple of cross corridors into each passageway that the intruders could be approaching along. Directly in front of him, perpendicular to the cargo passageways and heading inward toward the ship's core, was a narrower corridor, about forty meters long, its size scaled for foot and small-cart traffic. All the ceilings here were higher than those he'd seen in the rest of the ship, again with the thought of bulky cargo loads in mind. Three meters in front of him, set into both the ceiling and the deck, were another pair of airflow gratings.

No one was visible in any direction. But the footsteps were getting closer.

He was just wondering if he should move to the partial protection of a corner when one of the sets of footsteps suddenly changed from a stealthy walk to a flat-out run.

Merrick clenched his teeth, trying in vain to sort out where the steps were coming from. But the echoes were confusing his sense of direction. Still, it had to be either one of the corridors crossing the passageway ahead of him or else one of the side corridors leading into the cargo passageways to his right and left.

But why would anyone run toward him down any of them? Extra speed wouldn't help an attacker. In fact, it would be completely counterproductive. No matter where they were coming from, once they emerged into his sight they would have to slow down for a right-angle turn before continuing toward him. The faster they were going when they hit the intersection, the more awkward that turn would be.

He was still trying to figure it out when a figure wearing a Marine tunic shot into view from the nearest cross-corridor ahead of him.

Merrick snapped his hands up into firing position, thumbs on the third-finger triggers, his eyes ready to put a target-lock on the attacker as soon as he made that hard-left turn. But to his surprise, the man simply raced through the intersection with no attempt to turn or even slow down. A fraction of a second later he disappeared into the other side of the corridor.

A fraction of a second after that, Merrick slapped the next patch on his arm and charged full speed down the corridor.

Because he'd seen this trick before. Back on Qasama, after his capture by the Balin Trofts, Commander Ukuthi had thwarted one of his escape attempts by putting three soldiers in different doorways, popping them out at random to shoot at Merrick, the unpredictability of the attack making his target-lock system useless. The Marine who'd just run past, plus the one or more right behind him, were setting up for the same randomized pop-and-shoot gambit.

A cautious Cobra would take cover behind one of the nearby corners and hope he could take the attackers out one at a time. But that would allow the Marines pin him down, and with two more corridors leading to him that kind of single-minded focus could be fatal. A clever Cobra would burn open the ceiling grate and find a way to attack his enemies from behind. But that would mean abandoning the hatch and the masters who were coming to join him, and he had orders not to do that.

When defense and escape weren't possible, all that remained was attack.

He was halfway down the corridor when, just as he'd predicted, the second Marine poked his head around the corner and sent a quick salvo toward him. Merrick dodged to the right, and the laser fire burned harmlessly past his shoulder. He fired a return shot, but the Marine had already pulled back, and the lasers merely scorched the metal of the corner.

Both Marines were in position to start their game. But so was Merrick. He target-locked the ceiling just in front of the cross corridor, took two more steps, and jumped.

This time there was none of the possible ambiguity that had accompanied his leap into the spaceport battle back on Muninn. This was a straightforward ceiling jump, something his nanocomputer was more than capable of executing. His servos took over, doing their programmed magic to flip him over, hit the ceiling with his feet, push off and send him back down toward the corridors' intersection, and turn him back over again in time to slam onto the deck directly between his attackers. He caught a glimpse of two men crouching behind their respective corners—so there were only two, after all—and did a pair of quick target-locks on each. He let one of his legs collapse, giving himself a slight sideways shove as he did so, then rolled over to drop onto his back.

And as the fall and the sideways momentum sent him spinning like an upside-down turtle, he fired his antiarmor laser.

The flickering blasts briefly lit up the corridor as his optics and servos lined up the shots perfectly. Merrick got a glimpse of both Marines collapsing to the deck, fired a stunner blast at each of them just to make sure, then rolled back up to his feet and hurried over to check them out.

The second Marine, the one who'd fired at him earlier, wouldn't be giving him any more trouble. He backtracked across the main corridor to the Marine who'd run past.

And felt his eyes widen. The man lying on the deck was Gunnery Sergeant Plaine.

For a long second Merrick just stared, his mind spinning. Plaine was supposed to be on *his* side. His side, and the masters'. Wasn't he?

Of course he was. Plaine himself had said so when he and Kemp got to the *Dorian*. And he'd had the definitive facial glow...

Frowning, Merrick keyed in his infrareds. The glow was gone.

He was still gazing at Plaine's face, wondering what could have gone wrong, when he suddenly noticed a quiet hiss coming from somewhere in the distance.

He spun around, dropping into a crouch, looking along the corridor behind him. No one. He spun back, looking past Plaine down that side of the corridor. No one that direction, either.

But he could still hear the hissing. He notched up his audios, trying to locate the sound.

And for the second time in ten seconds felt his eyes widening. *The hissing was coming from the cargo hatch.*

Cursing under his breath, he leaped back to his feet. He was supposed to be there to open the hatch when the Trofts arrived. If they'd been forced to cut their way in, they would be very unhappy with him. He tore around the corner—

And froze. A figure was lying on the deck, leg raised, antiarmor laser fire blazing into the edge of the hatch.

The Trofts weren't trying to break in. Someone—a Cobra—was trying to weld the hatch shut.

Well, Merrick could deal with that. The Cobra's head was toward him; Merrick flicked a target lock onto the top as he raced down the corridor. If he got close enough, he could manage this with a stun blast. If not, his antiarmor laser would end things more permanently.

Even with the *Dorian*'s other noises, vibrations, and thumps Merrick's approaching footsteps apparently were able to penetrate the Cobra's concentration. Merrick was halfway there when the other's laser shut off and the figure rolled over and shoved off the deck, springing back to vertical—

Merrick stumbled to a halt. He'd assumed the Cobra was Smitty, recovered somehow from his injuries, or possibly Kemp, if the same drug malfunction that had affected Plaine had also affected him. But it was neither.

It was Jody.

For a long moment they just stood there, staring at each other. Merrick's face was rigid, his eyes looking Jody up and down as if it was the first time he'd ever seen her.

Or maybe as if he meant it to be the *last* time he would ever see her. She was, after all, standing between him and his new allies.

So far he hadn't made any moves against her. But that wouldn't last. If the Drim war drug was as powerful as Plaine had warned, there was no way Merrick could let her bar him from the hatch. He might try to order her away, or stun her, or pick her up bodily and throw her down the corridor.

Or he might skip all the subtleties and simply kill her.

But he wasn't going to do any of it without at least talking. On that point she was determined. "You all right?" she called.

He blinked. "What?"

"I asked if you were all right," Jody repeated. "You've been running around the whole ship stirring up trouble and having people shoot at you. I wondered if you'd been hurt."

"No," Merrick said, sounding confused. Maybe Troft victims weren't supposed to talk to their executioners that way. "No. I'm fine."

"I'm glad," Jody said, feeling a fresh layer of sweat breaking out on the back of her neck. Merrick was talking, but he'd started moving toward her again. Slowly, one step at a time, but still moving. He hadn't shot her out of hand—yet—but he clearly hadn't lost sight of his primary mission. He would stun her, or move her.

And then he would die.

Because death was already waiting for him. Pressed against the wall by the corner to Jody's right, the sound of her approach and Jody's masked by Merrick's earlier running attack at Plaine and Oponn, Rashida was standing ready to act the instant Merrick came around the corner into view.

And with the war drug enhancing his resistance to attack, Captain Moreau's orders had been crystal clear. Here at the cargo hatch was their best chance of stopping or containing the Troft incursion. The man who stood in the way of that containment had to be neutralized.

Rashida wasn't to use her stunner or her sonics, or to try any other nonlethal attack. The second Merrick came into sight, she was to use her arcthrower or her antiarmor laser and kill him.

Jody had until then to somehow talk her brother down.

"I'm glad," she said again. "Mom always told me I was supposed to look after you."

His forehead wrinkled, then cleared. "Mom . . . no," he said slowly. "No. Mom always told *us* to look after *you*."

"Us?" Jody asked. "You mean you and Lorne?"

Again, the wrinkled forehead. "Yes. Lorne and...and me."

"Ah," Jody said. "Really does go both ways, though. You must have had a hard time down there. You must be really tired. I'm so sorry we couldn't get to you sooner. But we *did* come, right? We *are* bringing you home."

He opened his mouth. Closed it again. "Jody..." He stopped, his eyes flicking around him as if he was seeing the *Dorian* for the first time. "I can't betray them, Jody."

"Can't betray whom?"

"The—" He looked around again. "They gave me orders. They told me to help them. I...promised to help them. I can't be a traitor."

"You aren't betraying them," Jody said, feeling her heart speeding up. Plaine had never gotten to the point of even questioning the Trofts' orders before she and Rashida took him down. Was Merrick actually starting to break free of the drug? "You're helping them. You're helping everyone."

His eyes went to the hatch, and the section of spot welding he'd interrupted. "They need to get aboard," he said. "They told me to help them get aboard."

"But if they get aboard they'll all die."

Merrick's eyes jerked back to her. "What? No. They'll get aboard and...and then they'll make me new friends."

Jody shivered. So Captain Moreau had called it correctly. The Trofts were going to come in, take over the ship, and use their drug on everyone. And then send them back to the Dominion to kill. "They'll get aboard and die," she repeated. "The *Dorian* is on to them, Merrick. Captain Moreau will have Marines and heavy weapons here any minute, and they'll kill them as they come through the hatchway. They can't escape."

Merrick looked at the hatch again. "They can," he said. "They must."

"Besides, you don't need any new friends," Jody continued, daring to take a step toward him. "You have us. You have your family." She took a second step. "You have *me*."

Again, he just stared at her. Jody took another step, aware that she was getting dangerously close to Rashida's line of fire. Merrick didn't move. Struck by a sudden thought, Jody keyed in her infrareds.

Merrick's face was a little flushed, whether from exertion or churning emotion she couldn't tell. But it wasn't the heat signature of the drug, the signature she'd seen in Plaine and the men on Muninn. Was it somehow wearing off?

If so, he had surely already noticed, which meant he could hit the next patch any moment. She looked down at his arm, searching for signs of inflammation.

But there was nothing. Probably the implants had been done long enough ago that his skin had recovered.

Carefully, wincing at the thought of what she was preparing to do, she ran a target lock along his whole forearm. At his first move toward the patches, she would have no choice but to burn the whole area and hope she got the rest of the implants. Then a stun blast, hopefully knocking him out. Hopefully before Rashida got in her own killing shot.

Merrick was on the move again, slowly walking forward. A few more steps and he would be at the corner. "Merrick?" Jody said, forcing back her fear and desperation as she took another step of her own toward him. One more step and she would completely block Rashida's line of fire...

And suddenly, Merrick's knees wobbled, and his torso started to shake. He looked at Jody, again as if seeing her for the first time, and stumbled forward. *"Jody?"*

Stumbled past the corner.

Jody had only a split second to act. But she had no choice. She leaped forward one last step, forward and to her right, putting herself directly between Merrick and Rashida. Merrick started to fall; snapping out her arms, Jody caught him, locking her servos around him. If this was a trick, now would be the perfect time for him to spring it.

But he didn't suddenly leap into action, throwing off her grip and blasting them both into eternity. He sagged in her arms, still shaking, muttering incoherently. "It's all right," Jody soothed, turning her grip into a hug. "It's all right—"

Her only warning was a footstep behind her; a footstep, and a small and incautious shuffling of feet. But it was enough. Before the sounds had even consciously registered her nanocomputer took control, throwing her and Merrick forward back into the corridor.

As the blazing fury of an antiarmor blast sizzled across the back of her left shoulder.

She clamped down hard on the yelp of pain that tried to burst out. Dropping Merrick, catching a glimpse of Captain Moreau and Lieutenant Meekan at the corridor's far end kneeling over Sergeant Oponn, she dropped to her stomach and eased an eye back around the corner.

Rashida was lying on her side on the deck, her back to the wall. Her left leg was tucked to her chest and she was gripping her left ankle with both hands.

Beyond her, striding toward them, was Kemp. His eyes were narrowed and grim, his expression impassive.

His face blazing with war drug heat.

That one glimpse was all Jody saw before she was forced to duck back again as Kemp sent a second burst of laser fire at her, this salvo from his fingertips. Jody got up into a crouch, glancing behind her again and measuring the distance with her eyes. If she could get Merrick down there, at least he would be safe.

But there was no way to do that. Not before Kemp could reach her current corner and burn down both of them.

And after that he would take up where Merrick had left off, cutting out her spot-welds and reopening the *Dorian* to Troft attack.

She couldn't let that happen. No matter what it took—her life, or Merrick's or both—she had to stop him.

From around the corner, Rashida gave a gasp. "Kemp—please," she pleaded. "Don't hurt me. Please."

"Get out of the way," Kemp called back, his voice as emotionless as his face. "Get out of the way, or I'll burn you."

"All right—all right," Rashida said, and Jody heard the scrabbling as she got awkwardly to her feet. "Please—don't hurt me. My ankle—God in heaven, it hurts. It *hurts.*"

A sudden cold chill wrapped around Jody's heart. Rashida's ankle...but there was no way anything that had just happened could have damaged a Cobra that way. She was fine and uninjured.

Only Kemp didn't know that.

Cautiously, Jody eased her eye around the corner again. Rashida had made it to her feet, her left hand pressed against the wall for balance, her face turned toward Kemp.

Her body directly between him and Jody.

And with a flash of premonition, Jody knew what was about to happen.

Kemp didn't know Rashida was a Cobra. He also didn't know, or more likely didn't care, what his and Merrick's attack in the conference room had done to Smitty. With the carelessness of someone who knew he had nothing to fear, he would ignore Rashida until he was closer.

And Rashida would kill him.

Kemp was Jody's closest friend, with a trust and loyalty between them that had been forged in combat. Whether she meant anything more to him, or whether he meant more to her, she still didn't know. If Rashida killed him, Jody would never know the truth.

But Merrick was her brother. If Rashida didn't stop Kemp, Merrick would probably die at Kemp's hand for his treason against their new Troft masters.

Where did Jody's allegiance lie? Where did her duty lie?

Where did her heart lie?

Rashida was on the move now, limping toward Kemp, still moaning and pleading like a helpless, beaten woman. With Kemp's face blocked from Jody's view, she couldn't tell whether or not he was buying the act.

But she could see Kemp's feet, and could see that he, too, was still striding forward toward the hatch. Five meters, Jody decided tautly, was the critical distance where even his bone laminae and drug-heightened resistance would be unable to protect him from a killing shot from Rashida's fingertip lasers.

They continued toward each other. They reached the critical distance.

And continued past it. For a frozen second Jody felt her mental wheels spinning...

Then, suddenly, she got it.

She glanced up at the ceiling above Rashida's head, putting a target lock on it. Her timing would have to be perfect. Rashida took one more step—

Rising half out of her crouch, Jody slipped around the corner into the wide corridor and jumped.

She'd done the ceiling flip exactly twice during her training. She'd succeeded both times—or, rather, her nanocomputer had succeeded—but she'd never felt comfortable with it. Now, with every life aboard the *Dorian* hanging in the balance, she was suddenly overwhelmed by the fear that this time she would fail.

But she didn't. Her servos flipped her around as she flew

upward, turning her just enough to bring her feet against the high ceiling. Upside down, facing the deck, she saw Kemp's look of shock and fury as she soared above him. Even as her knees bent to absorb the momentum of her impact she saw him snap his arms up, tracking his fingertip lasers toward her—

And as her knee servos began to reverse themselves to send her back down she saw Rashida bend her right arm at the elbow and send two quick laser shots into Kemp's little fingers, burning away the joints and the weapons hidden within them.

Kemp bellowed with surprise, pain, and rage. His own pro gramed reflexes kicked in, throwing him to the side.

But it was too late. Rashida was within range; and even as he dived toward the bulkhead she leaped forward, wrapping her arms around his torso and her legs around his legs, immobilizing him as they fell to the deck.

They were lying together, Kemp struggling uselessly against her servo-powered grip, when Jody hit the deck behind them and sent a stun blast into the back of his head.

He collapsed in Rashida's arms and lay motionless. Jody and Rashida looked at each other over his shoulder, and for a moment Jody felt the depth of understanding she'd never had before with anyone but her family.

The moment passed. "Thank you," Jody murmured.

"I would not have killed him," Rashida assured her. "Not unless it was truly necessary."

"Even after what he did to Smitty?"

"I do not believe he was the one who hurt Smitty," Rashida said, a wave of heartache sweeping across her face. "But even if he was, I would not have killed him. I know what he means to you."

Jody was still searching for something to say when Captain Moreau came around the corner. His eyes flicked across the three of them, taking it all in. "You all right?"

"Yes," Jody said. Behind the captain, she could see Meekan helping Merrick to his feet. "Did Merrick—?"

"The Marines are alive," Moreau said, jerking his head back along the other corridor. "Plaine and Oponn both. Your brother simply took out their epaulets and then stunned them."

Jody exhaled a sigh. She should have known that, even under the influence of a Troft drug, he wouldn't kill unless absolutely necessary.

Which meant it must have been one of the Marines in the conference room who had shot Smitty.

Whether it was true or not, that was what she would choose to believe.

But the whole thing might still be for nothing. If the Trofts got aboard... "We need to get the Marines here," she said. "The Trofts—"

She broke off as a sudden multiple thud sounded from the hull nearby. The captain, she noted with some confusion, didn't even flinch. "That won't be necessary," he said calmly. "That sound you just heard was pieces of the Troft boarding boat. Or possibly pieces of the Trofts."

Jody looked down at Rashida. "You mean... we won?"

"Hardly," Moreau said, his voice going a little sour. He looked over his shoulder as Merrick and Meekan came slowly toward them, Meekan with his arm around Merrick's waist for support. "I have a message for you, Cobra Broom," he continued to Merrick. "The three Trofts ships that just took out the net and our Troft attackers sent it to us a moment ago."

"A message?" Merrick asked, frowning. He was still trembling, but his face had cleared and he was starting to come back to full function.

"Yes," Moreau said. "They said to tell you that Commander Ukuthi sends his apologies that he can't be here in person, but hopes that these, his other warships, will be sufficient."

"Oh," Merrick said. "I see." He took a deep breath. "Captain, this may sound strange, but Commander Ukuthi is sort of an ally."

"You seem to have a lot of Troft allies, Cobra Broom," Moreau said tersely. "Something we'll have to sort out in the *very* near future." He gave a little snort. "But don't worry about this one. Ukuthi and I have already met."

A tentative smile tugged at the corners of Merrick's lips. "Let me guess. He offered you a deal?"

"That he did." Moreau took a deep breath. "But that, too, is a conversation for later. Let's get you to sickbay—" he looked down at Kemp "—get him into full-body restraints and *then* to sickbay—"

He looked at Meekan. "And then let's get to CoNCH and get the hell out of here."

CHAPTER THIRTY

The group seated together in the hastily assembled conversation ring in the *Megalith*'s main hangar bay was not exactly what Jin would call cheerful. But still, amid the swirling tension, there was a certain level of relief.

The Trofts had been defeated. For now.

But only for now.

"So they have this war drug," Commodore Santores rumbled, his eyes coming back from the data stream and Captain Moreau's final report, which he'd insisted on reading before he would let any of them leave. "May I ask why you didn't go back to Muninn and level every place that could possibly be a lab or storehouse?"

"The *Dorian* wasn't in any shape for that kind of mission," Captain Moreau said. His voice was level, but Jin could hear an underlying edge of frustration, as well. "And if we had, we'd have gone in alone. The Balin'ekha'spmi ships made it clear that they were there only to assist our escape, not to engage the Drim'hco'plai in open combat."

Santores turned his glower onto Ukuthi. "Commander Ukuthi?" he challenged.

"Captain Moreau is correct," Ukuthi said calmly. "My demesne-lord does not seek open war with the Drim'hco'plai. He wished merely to sow doubt and distrust between them and the demesne-lords who currently battle the Dominion of Man, thus diminishing Drim'hco'plai power and prestige in our region of the Trof'te

393

Assemblage. That goal has now been accomplished." He looked at Merrick. "Were I you, Commodore Santores, I would focus my thoughts on the fact that you will be returning with your task force unpoisoned and with knowledge of this new weapon that will soon be unleashed upon you."

Beside Jin, Paul's fingers tentatively touched the side of her leg. Jin reached down in response, entwining her fingers with his. Yes, most of Santores's force would be returning to the Dominion.

But not all of it. A message had arrived at Qasama earlier this morning from Aventine, carried by a Hoibie courier ship, informing Santores that the *Algonquin* had perished in battle against the invading Troft force. That the attackers had also been destroyed was of only limited comfort to the commodore.

For Jin, the fact that Captain Lij Tulu, the man responsible for most of the misery on Aventine and the loss of her husband's Cobra abilities, had died with his ship was of no comfort at all. Revenge, she had long ago learned, was the most hollow of victories.

"Even if Captain Moreau had gone back it wouldn't have accomplished anything," Merrick spoke up. He was sitting between Lorne and Jody, his fingers restlessly stroking the arm of his chair, his eyes never seeming to touch anyone else's face. Kemp, sitting on Jody's other side, looked even more uncomfortable, and had yet to lift his own eyes from the deck.

Or maybe it wasn't the deck he was staring at but his hands, and the bandages where Rashida Vil had burned off his fingertip lasers in order to save Jody's life.

Rashida. A Qasaman woman, now a Qasaman Cobra. Briefly, Jin thought about the Qasama she'd first visited, so many years ago, and wondered if anyone there would ever have dreamed such a thing could happen.

"It might have stopped this thing before it got going," Santores countered harshly.

"No," Merrick said, again not meeting the commodore's glare. "Because Kjoic had already left Muninn with a sample of the drug. The Kriel demesne-lord will pass it on to whoever set up the deal, and collect the payment." He gestured to Ukuthi. "None of which the Drims will get a share of. In case you want to add that to the list of ways the Drims came out badly in all this."

"I do," Ukuthi promised, his radiator membranes fluttering.

"And I will. Perhaps my demesne-lord will use some of his new leverage to free the humans of Muninn from their slavery."

A flicker of emotion crossed Merrick's face. "I'm sure they'd appreciate that," he murmured.

"Are you sure he *had* a sample?" Santores pressed. "I can't see the Drim'hco'plai Trofts being that careless."

"He didn't get it from the Drims." Merrick lifted his arm a few centimeters. "He got it from me."

"From *you*?"

"From the last four doses the Drims implanted," Merrick said. "Either before they were injected or right afterward." He gave Jody a hooded look. "I'm sorry, Jody. I know you thought you were the one who talked me down. I was hoping that, too. At least then the Dominion might have a counter to use against it. But the fact is that it was already draining out of my system when I came after you."

"So there's no counter?" Paul asked.

"Of course there is," Santores said firmly. "Every weapon has a counter. We'll look until we find it." He gestured across the circle. "Which is why Cobra Kemp is coming back with us. He still has two samples in his arm for us to study."

"Wait a minute," Jin said, frowning. "Why do you need him? Can't you just remove a sample here?"

"We have," Santores said. "One sample, anyway. But that's not enough. We need to know how long it lasts inside a human host, how exactly it was implanted, and how they keep it from leaking into the target's bloodstream before it's been activated. We can't know any of that without taking him along for tests."

"And besides," Kemp said quietly, "Acting Captain Filho intends to bring me up on charges of murder."

Jin tightened her fingers around Paul's. "Whatever you did aboard the *Dorian* was warfare, not murder."

"Then he tries me for treason, or aiding and abetting the enemy, or some such," Kemp said. "There are men dead on the *Dorian*, and Filho is determined that someone pay."

"Besides himself?" Jin countered, feeling a stir of anger. First all but mutinying against Captain Moreau, and now looking for a scapegoat to cover up his ineptitude.

"I'm sure it will all work out," Captain Moreau said.

"It will," Santores confirmed. "But Acting Captain Filho and

Commander Castenello have filed the charges, and they have powerful patrons. The best thing—for all of us," he added, looking at Captain Moreau "—will be to take this matter to Asgard and the Dome and hash it out there."

"What about Qasama and the Cobra Worlds?" Paul asked. "What happens to us now?"

"In the short term, we need to call off the follow-up fleet that's on its way and send them back home," Santores said. "The encrypted orders and confirmations I'll send back to Aventine with you should cover that. In the long term—" He shook his head. "That's up to the Dome." He looked at Jody. "And possibly Cobra Broom."

"What do you mean?" Jin asked, frowning.

"It means I'm going to the Dominion with Kemp," Jody said.

Jin stared at her daughter, her heart suddenly pounding. *"What?"*

"I'm going with Kemp," Jody repeated. Her face and voice were tense, but there was a stubbornness in her eyes that Jin remembered far too well. "Someone needs to plead the Cobra Worlds' case. To make sure they never pull this sort of stunt on us again."

"But—" Jin began.

"The agreement has been made, and the arrangements finalized," Santores cut her off. "And I'm sorry, but there's no time for discussion. We need to head back immediately, before the war drug is handed off to our enemies and goes into production. Captain Moreau, return to the *Dorian*—we'll be leaving Qasama in thirty minutes. Commander Ukuthi, you may return to your ship at your convenience. I understand you'll be transporting the rest of the Broom family across to the *Dewdrop*?"

"I will," Ukuthi said. His radiator membranes fluttered. "It will be an honor to serve them in such a fashion. I trust the Dominion of Man will grant them equal honor?"

"I'll do my best to make sure they understand," Santores promised.

"Thank you." Ukuthi's membranes stiffened briefly. "Make certain, too, that they know not to again permit their war to spill into our region of the Assemblage. If it does, I assure you there will be consequences all will regret."

"I'll pass that on to them." Santores rose from his seat. "Cobra Kemp, you'll come with me. Cobra Broom—*Cobras* Broom, I suppose I should say—again, the Dominion of Man thanks you for your service."

"I will await you in my shuttle," Ukuthi added as he stood from his couch. "Captain Moreau, may you find justice."

Five minutes later, Jin's family was alone. Together again.

Maybe for the last time.

"Do you really have to go?" Jin asked, trying to fight back her tears. Jody looked nervous enough without her mother adding to any guilt she might be feeling.

"I don't see any other way," Jody said. She, too, was fighting back tears. "Not just for Kemp, but for all of us."

"Why can't Commodore Santores tell them?" Lorne asked. "Or Merrick. He's the one who found this damn drug."

"Lorne!" Paul admonished.

"I'm just trying to help," Lorne insisted. "The way the Dominion treats women—"

"It's okay, Lorne," Jody said, putting a hand on his arm. "Commodore Santores and I have sorted that out."

"But—"

"Besides, Merrick can't go," Jody said firmly. "He injured or killed several Marines and nearly helped the Drims take the ship. From what Captain Moreau said about Dome and Navy politics, his opponents would tear him apart over that. He'd be under the same charges now as Kemp if Ukuthi hadn't intervened with Santores."

"Whereas you're a hero," Paul said.

Jody gave him a somewhat tight smile. "Crazy, isn't it? But that's how it's shaped up. I was the one who found out where Merrick had been taken, I'm the one who found him, rescued him, and got the drug samples back to Santores. And I'm the one—well, Rashida and me—who finally stopped him and Kemp and kept the Trofts off the *Dorian*."

"You also stole a Dominion courier ship," Paul pointed out.

"Yes, but they've already nailed Barrington with all the blame for letting me do that," Jody pointed out. "Thing is, if they now accuse me of stealing the ship, that leaves them with less of a case against him, and therefore less of an excuse for having kicked him out in the first place. By the time they see how Santores and Barrington are positioning me, it'll be too late for them to backtrack. Or so Barrington thinks."

Lorne snorted. "They've got some strange politics back there."

"Probably no stranger than ours," Paul pointed out.

"Yeah," Lorne said. "Maybe."

"That's also why Kemp and I are traveling with Santores in the *Megalith*, out of reach of Filho and Castenello," Jody said. "Santores doesn't want them to get a hint of Barrington's plan, and Barrington doesn't trust them not to be vindictive."

"Well, damn," Lorne said. "So that's it? We finally get the family back together, and you're just going to leave?"

"Oh, I'll be back," Jody assured him. "Really, I will. Kemp and me both."

"Of course you will," Jin said firmly. "We just...we're going to miss you, Jody."

"I'll miss you, too," Jody said. And now, Jin saw, she was no longer trying to hold back the tears. "But I'll be okay. Really. At least I'm not flying off into the middle of a war on Qasama like you and Merrick did."

"Or heading off to Caelian like you and Dad did," Lorne added.

"Or dodging Trofts on Aventine like you did," Merrick countered. He hesitated. "Speaking of Caelian..."

"Smitty's recovering just fine," Jody assured him. "He's getting the absolute best care possible. If for no other reason than Rashida's sitting beside him and there'll be hell to pay if he doesn't."

"Good." Merrick's face screwed up. "I just wish I remembered..."

"No, you don't," Paul said.

"Dad's right, Merrick," Jody said quietly. "Kemp doesn't remember, either. Whatever happened—and I'm still thinking it was one of the Marines who shot him—it's not your fault."

Merrick sighed. "I wish I could believe that."

"Believe it," Paul said firmly. "Rashida's interest apart, Omnathi needs him alive and well if he's going to position him as the first hero of the new Caelian/Qasama alliance."

"That's still happening?" Jin asked, frowning. "I thought that was just a ploy Uy dreamed up to use against Santores."

Paul shrugged, an oddly stiff movement with his useless servos. "As far as I know it's still on. Actually, it makes a lot of sense, given that the Djinn combat suits may be the key to finally taming the Caelian ecology."

"What about you?" Lorne asked. "They're going to give you a suit, too, aren't they?"

"Omnathi's offered me one," Paul said. "I may take it. Or I may just go on the way I am."

"You mean half-crippled?"

Jin winced. But Paul just smiled. "Yes; half-crippled," he said. "It wouldn't hurt for someone to be a continual reminder to Aventine of the cost of war, and of what the Cobras and others gave up to protect our worlds."

"They'll forget anyway," Lorne muttered. "Or try to ignore you."

"Oh, no, they won't," Paul said firmly. "I'll make sure of that."

"Being a thorn in everyone's side *is* kind of a Moreau family tradition," Jody pointed out.

"Along with fixing other people's messes," Jin said. "I was just remembering your Great-grandfather Jonny's last trip to the Dominion. The last trip anyone in the Cobra Worlds made."

"I hadn't thought about that," Jody said. "He was trying to keep them from stirring up the Trofts against us, too, wasn't he? So really, this is just more of our family history."

Jin looked at Merrick. He was staring at the floor now, the same way Kemp had been earlier, a tightness in his throat. "Something like that," she said to Jody. "Let's hope you come back with the same result: peace for the Cobra Worlds."

"I will, Mom," Jody promised. "I'm a Moreau—" she smiled at her father "—*and* a Broom, *and* a Cobra. There's no way in the Worlds I can fail."

A warning tone sounded, the note echoing across the hangar bay. "Sounds like Santores's getting antsy," Paul said.

"Yeah," Jody agreed. "I guess I'd better get inside. And *you'd* better get to Ukuthi's shuttle."

"So this is goodbye?" Lorne asked, looking pained.

"For now," Jody told him firmly. "Only for now."

The next minute was spent in farewells. Jin felt herself tearing up again as she hugged Jody, and could see her daughter likewise crying silently as she hugged her father and brothers.

And then, it really was time.

"I'll see you all in a few months," Jody said, giving Merrick one final, lingering hug. "I'm so glad we found you, Merrick."

"You be careful," Merrick said, touching her hand gently as Jody pulled away.

"I will," she promised. "You just watch yourself as you help Lorne put the pieces of Aventinian politics back together."

Merrick snorted. "Who says anyone's going to listen to us?"

"You're the heroes." Jody smiled at Jin and Paul. "You all are.

Weird, isn't it?" She took a deep breath, let it out in a sigh. "Now it's my turn. I'll see you soon."

She turned and headed for the hatchway. One of the two Marines standing guard touched the release, and she disappeared inside.

"We'd better go, too," Paul said, his eyes on the hatchway. "Santores and Ukuthi are both going to be annoyed if the *Megalith* has to stop halfway out of the system and let us out."

"Go ahead," Jin said. "I want to talk to Merrick a moment."

Paul's forehead creased briefly, but he nodded. "Not too long," he warned. "Come on, Lorne."

Jin watched until they had disappeared through the Troft shuttle's hatch. "You okay?" she asked, turning to Merrick.

"Sure," he said, the bitterness in his tone belying his words. "Why not?"

"Anya," Jin said. "Jody told me about your . . . what happened."

Merrick sighed. "It's not her, Mom," he said. "Or not just her. It's . . ." He shook his head. "I guess I'm just tired of being a puppet."

"You mean because of the way she manipulated you into helping her family?"

"She manipulated me, she manipulated Ukuthi, and Ukuthi manipulated me," Merrick said. "So did Kjoic. So did the Drims. The Dominion manipulated you and Dad and Uncle Corwin, and now they're manipulating Jody. And don't deny it. She may think she's doing this for the Cobra Worlds, but they're going to twist everything she says and does for their own political ends."

"Of course they will," Jin said.

He flashed her a puzzled look. "And you don't *care*?"

"Whether I care or not doesn't matter," Jin told him gently. "It's the way of the universe. Everyone watches out for their own interests. If those interests run over someone else's, well, for a lot of people that's just the way it goes."

He snorted gently. "I never realized how cynical you were."

"I prefer the term *realistic*," she said. "And being realistic—and old—I've learned two things that you'd do well to remember. First, no matter what kinds of schemes people try to embroil us in, we're usually able to find a way to reach our own goals anyway. Part of that is because we have friends and allies; and a big part of *that* is because we try *not* to bulldoze other people's interests on the way to achieving our own."

She lifted a finger. "And make no mistake. Most of those allies are genuine, not just manipulators like Anya or Ukuthi. For every Kjoic there's a Werle or a de Portola." She swallowed hard. "Sometimes there's even a Nissa Gendreves."

For a moment he was silent. "Maybe," he conceded. "You said there were two things?"

Jin smiled. "Remember that, all the way back to Great-grandfather Jonny—a hundred years now—people have been trying to kill us. And every one of them has failed."

She smiled. "We're the Moreau Broom family, Merrick. Whether the universe likes it or not, we're here. And we're here to stay."

She reached over and took his hand. "Come on. Time to go home."